SITUATION CRITICAL

"Andrew, you're bleeding inside. You've got a shell fragment in your right lung. I've got to go in and get it out."

"Pat, Roum," Andrew whispered.

Pat leaned forward.

"Hold Roum at all cost. I stay there. Don't move me to Suzdal. I stay there."

"Now, Andrew," Emil interjected.

"I stay in Roum. That's where we stand." He reached up, grabbing Emil by the shoulder. "Emil?"

"Here, son."

"Not a cripple, don't leave me a cripple, let me go."

The doctor finally nodded.

He saw the cone of white paper come down.

"Just breathe deep, Andrew."

The sickly sweet smell of ether engulfed him.

Don't miss the other exciting books in
William R. Forstchen's
The Lost Regiment series!

RALLY CRY
UNION FOREVER
TERRIBLE SWIFT SWORD
FATEFUL LIGHTNING
BATTLE HYMN
NEVER SOUND RETREAT

THE LOST REGIMENT #7

A BAND OF BROTHERS

William R. Forstchen

A ROC BOOK

ROC
Published by the Penguin Group
Penguin Putnam Inc., 375 Hudson Street,
New York, New York 10014, U.S.A.
Penguin Books Ltd, 27 Wrights Lane,
London W8 5TZ, England
Penguin Books Australia Ltd, Ringwood,
Victoria, Australia
Penguin Books Canada Ltd, 10 Alcorn Avenue,
Toronto, Ontario, Canada M4V 3B2
Penguin Books (N.Z.) Ltd, 182–190 Wairau Road,
Auckland 10, New Zealand

Penguin Books Ltd, Registered Offices:
Harmondsworth, Middlesex, England

Published by Roc, an imprint of Dutton NAL,
a member of Penguin Putnam Inc.

First Printing, January, 1999
10 9 8 7 6 5 4 3 2 1

Cover art: San Julian

 REGISTERED TRADEMARK—MARCA REGISTRADA

Printed in the United States of America

For Professor Dave Flory, who years ago translated a few paragraphs from *Rally Cry* into Spanish, thereby encouraging me to stick it out in his class. I never thought I could make it through a language course and that the dream of a Ph.D. was attainable. Dave, your simple gesture helped to push me on, so this little dedication is for you.

Chapter One

Cold. It's so damn cold.

Eddies of snow swirled around Lieutenant General Patrick O'Donald, commander of the Army of the East. The world disappeared around him so that for a moment he felt as if he had fallen into a frigid eternity, a blanket of white that would suck the last pulse of warmth from his soul.

"General, over there."

The voice was muffled, hollow, a snatch of sound that swirled off into the white and darkness.

The snow squall passed, rolling northeastward, the horizon pulling back like a ruffling curtain.

Pat raised his field glasses to where his adjutant was pointing. Nothing. He lowered his glasses and looked over at the boy.

"They're there, sir, believe me. You can almost smell 'em."

Pat nodded; the boy was young, better eyes, trust to his judgment.

"We're waiting for your orders, sir."

Pat said nothing, raising his glasses again. For a moment the tree line on the crest of the hill stood out sharply, dark trunks of soaring pines etched against the backdrop of the storm. Was that a puff of smoke on the far side? Hard to tell. Dirty white smudges against the dark trees . . . campfires, maybe the smoke of a land ironclad as well.

Movement. A shifting shadow under the trees, arms flailing, standing up, stamping. Someone as cold as he. Tall, eight, maybe nine feet . . . Bantag!

The figure raised something to his face—field glasses. The Bantag was looking this way. Pat waited, motionless. The Bantag lowered the glasses and said something to someone behind him, invisible below the crest. Their watch had to be numbed by the long night, thinking of relief, a fire, something warm to eat.

What they were eating he didn't want to think about. Yesterday the 6th Rus Mounted Rifles had been ambushed over in that next valley. A massacre, a bloody massacre. The bastards were most likely gorging themselves.

Another eddy of snow swirled around him, decreasing visibility, obscuring the ridge. Taking off the white blanket he had slipped over his shoulders as camouflage, he slipped down from the edge of the ridge. Standing, he staggered through the knee-deep snow to the grove where his staff waited for him.

Through the scattered grove of trees he could see them again, troopers on horses, a guidon fluttering as another gust of wind swirled around them, a golden regimental flag waving, threatening to tangle in the branches of a stunted pine bent over with the weight of snow. The troopers and horses looked like half-formed snowmen, black slouch caps blanketed in white, heavy sky-blue greatcoats white on the shoulders, steam rising from horses, all of it shadowy, surreal.

Even in the frigid cold the familiar smells came through: horse sweat, the rank smell of saddle sores, wet leather and wool, a faint whiff of liquor as several men passed a canteen back and forth. He wondered if the stench was strong enough for the Bantag to sniff it out on the next ridge. No, they would have sent a patrol this way if they suspected trouble. But still, damn incautious of them. The bastards were usually more careful, especially a raiding force moving behind our lines. Simple damn arrogance, that must be it. Wipe out a regiment, then gorge, figure no one else was about. The bastards would soon learn different.

If this is just a raid we'll cut their guts out before breakfast. But if it's more, an umen, or worse yet, a force with ironclads, our Capua Line is lost. They're ten miles behind our left flank. Then what? Fall back on Roum? We were supposed to hold this position right through till spring.

Don't worry about it now, he thought. Don't let the boys see you're worried. Just get this job done, get vengeance for the loss of a regiment, and worry about the rest later.

At his approach, the brigade commander, a young Rus boy, son of an old boyar and a natural on horseback, snapped to attention and saluted. The lad was thirsting for revenge; he had lost a regiment yesterday, nearly a third of his entire command, and he wanted to redeem himself; redemption in the eyes of the army and of family, for his brother had commanded the regiment surprised just after sunset.

Pat motioned for the brigadier, the two regimental commanders from what was left of his command, and their staff to gather round.

"They're up there, lads. Might have an ironclad with them. Not sure on their strength—might be a regiment out here raiding our flank or it might be half their damn army. We go in quick, slaughter the bastards. If there are any of our men still alive, we get them, then get the hell out. Don't blow your horses—we might be in for a long chase."

The youngsters looked at him, heads bobbing excitedly.

"Sir, your place is not in this charge," the brigadier protested.

Pat chuckled. "Son, a slam-bang charge with cavalry—wouldn't miss it for the world."

"Sir, Colonel Keane's standing order regarding you was that you were to stay to the rear. If you don't, we're to report any violations directly to him."

Pat stepped forward and looked down at the young officer.

"Would you do that, son?" he asked coldly.

"Yes sir, I would."

Pat laughed softly and shook his head. "All right, I'll come up with the guns. Will that satisfy you?"

"Not really, sir, but all right."

There was a momentary lightening of the forest, a break in the storm. Pat looked up, cursing softly. Not now, don't break now. . . . A brief glimpse of a pink swirling cloud catching the dawning light far above the storm, a faint patch of blue, then the darkening clouds closed in again, gray racing shadows as the storm closed back in. Looking back to the southwest he caught a glimpse of the next ridge half a mile away, and then it disappeared, another wall of swirling snow racing toward them.

"Go in when the next squall hits!" Pat barked excitedly, the feverish anticipation of battle taking hold. "Remember the rendezvous point if you get cut off. Now move!"

The officers saluted, spurred their horses around, snow kicking up around them. The brigadier leaned over and extended his hand.

"Sir, thank you, sir, for this chance."

"Just don't get caught with your pants down the way your brother did," Pat said harshly. The boy visibly flinched. Good, it'd make him more alert.

Softening, Pat extended his hand. "God go with you, son."

The boy spurred his mount and galloped off.

Pat trotted down the line, passing troopers deploying into attack formation. The excitement was shaking off the numbed lethargy of the long night's watch. Carbines were drawn, men checking loads, pulling hats down tight and securing the chin straps. Most were taking off their gloves, willing to brave the bitter cold for a better grip on bridle and weapon.

The edge of the next snow squall swirled around them, the slope up ahead disappearing. Muffled, distant, a bugle sounded . . . Charge!

Troopers around him spurred their mounts, kicked up snow in high plumes of powder; horses screamed, and men howled with the release of tension.

"Good luck, me hearties!" Pat roared.

The charge swept forward and within seconds disappeared into the storm. Pat spurred his mount, dodging around a line of troopers weaving through the trees. He heard the jingle of chains, the unmistakable clatter of a fully loaded caisson and fieldpiece ahead. Urging his mount forward, he saw the moving shadows, gunners riding three of the six horses pulling the piece, two more clinging for dear life atop the caisson, the rest of the crew riding beside the gun.

God, it's like the old days again, Pat thought with a wild exuberance. In the shadows, the piece almost looked like his beloved bronze Napoleons of the old 44th New York. When he swung in alongside, the illusion faded; a different gun for a different war on a different world, it was a breechloading ten-pounder.

He fell in with the crew as they crested over the ridge. Reaching the top, he caught glimpses of lines going forward, heard the high shrill cries of troopers, the queer rebel-yell-like scream adopted by the cavalry on this world. The bugles picking up the call of the charge, the crack of a carbine, and the low bone-shaking rumble of a narga, the Bantag war horn, sounding the alarm.

"Forward boys, forward!" Pat cried. The fever was upon him now. Ignoring the shouted protests of his staff, he lashed his mount forward, the horse bounding like a gazelle through the snowdrifts. For an instant he caught sight of a regimental flag silhouetted on the crest of the next ridge, the flag-bearer reeling in his saddle, a Bantag reaching up to pull him down. Another rider surged up, horse knocking the Bantag back. They disappeared as the storm closed back in.

Crossing through the shallow ravine, Pat started up the slope into the Bantag position. A splash of pink ahead and a dark form in the snow marked where a trooper had gone down. By his side a Bantag thrashed in the snow, clutching his face, blood pouring out between his fingers, a high keening wail bubbling out of him. Pat ignored him, pushing on. The snow was churned up, more blood, three Bantag sprawled by a still-smoldering fire, one of the bodies in the flames, its leggings smoking. Their uniforms were black, tunics and hats made of heavy furs, roughly made cartridge boxes, bayonet scabbard, haversack and water skin hanging from cross belts. The snow squall was racing ahead, the curtain again pulling back. The crackling of carbines thundered ahead, commingling with wild shouts, screams, hysterical cries of triumph and terror.

He caught glimpses of the left-flanking regiment, the Roum Mounted, sweeping down into the valley ahead, crashing into a dark mass of Bantag who were crawling out from under snow-covered shelter halves, racing to get to their mounts. Letting go of their carbines, which dropped and hung to their sides on leather slings, men were drawing their heavy .45 dragoon revolvers and firing at near-point-blank range.

Directly ahead the 4th Roum was wading into the mass of Bantag, some of them already up into their saddles. Pat reined in hard. Hundreds of Bantag were springing up from the snow, racing in every direction. On the next ridgeline he saw dark shadows shifting through the trees, a flash of light from a rifle erupting, snow on the branches above the Bantag cascading down from the shock of the gun going off.

My God, Pat thought, this isn't a raiding force out here—there must be two or three regiments at least, maybe more. As long as we keep them running we've got the edge, but if they turn we'll get torn to shreds.

Turning, he looked back and saw the two guns of the light battery struggling up the slope. Standing in his stirrups, he waved the guns toward him.

The first weapon reached the crest, skidding around, crews leaping from the caisson and unhitching the trail of the fieldpiece. Pat dismounted and joined them, swinging the gun around, the rest of the crew scrambling to his side to help.

"Case shot, two-second fuse!" Pat shouted. "Put it down on that next ridge!"

Without even waiting for the gun commander to take over, Pat squatted down by the breech of the gun, studied the target, judging the range, spun the elevation screw up and dropped the barrel to aim directly across the valley. Behind him the gunnery sergeant popped the breech open. Loaders came up bearing the shell with its powder bag strapped behind it. The charge was slammed in, and the loader stepped back, raising his hands to show they were clear. The sergeant slammed the breech shut and turned the handle to the interrupted screw breech, locking it in place.

Eyeing the sights one last time, Pat nodded, then held up both hands over his head, signaling that the gun was properly laid, and stepped out of the way.

The gunnery sergeant slipped a primer into the breech vent and, stepping back, uncoiled the lanyard. With a grin he offered the lanyard to Pat. Smiling, Pat took hold of the lanyard.

"Stand clear!" he roared.

The crew stepped away from the gun. With a sharp jerking pull, Pat popped the lanyard. The gun lifted up and back, a ten-foot gout of flame snapping from the muzzle, a swirl of snow kicking up from the concussion, mixing with the dirty-yellow-gray smoke. A dull flash ignited in the trees on the next ridge, the sound of the explosion lost in the wind and the roar of battle. The second gun was already wheeling into place as Pat stepped back, tossing the lanyard to the gunnery sergeant.

"Pour it on 'em!"

"Any land cruisers down there?" the sergeant asked, shouting to be heard above the exuberant whoops of a cavalry troop clearing the crest to their right at a lopping gallop.

"Going down to find out!"

Pat swung back up into the saddle, motioning for his staff to follow. Weaving down the slope, he passed several wounded, two of them on one horse, making for the rear.

"Driving 'em hard, sir!" one of the boys cried as if drunk, blood pouring from a saber slash across his brow.

Pat nodded and pressed on, the battle disappearing for a moment as another squall of snow swept around them. The snow cleared, and looking around he realized he was in the middle of what had been the Bantag encampment area. At the sight of it, he closed his eyes for a moment, wishing that the nightmare would disappear. It didn't.

Wearily he got off his mount and walked up to where the brigade commander knelt in the snow, weeping. One of the brigadier's aides had removed the battered head of his brother from the impaling spike and stood there with it, not sure what to do with the remains. Pat motioned for the boy to lay it in the snow out of sight of the brigadier.

Parts of bodies were scattered in the snow like remnants of broken dolls; heads, half-devoured limbs, charred torsos that had been sliced open, entrails looped and coiled, hideous gray serpents in the pink slushy snow. Men wandered about, crying, weeping, some knelt over, sobbing over the remains of a brother, father, son, or comrade.

Pat knelt by the brigadier's side.

"Andre, you have a battle to fight," Pat whispered.

The boy looked over at him, eyes wide with shock, mad grief, and outrage. He was gone, Pat realized, drifting into the nightmare lands.

Pat stood back up, beckoned for one of the staff.

"I'll take command here. Get him to the rear."

The aide gestured toward the head as Andre started to turn, crawling to pick it up. Pat put a restraining hand out, grabbing him by the shoulder.

"Leave him," Pat whispered. "We don't have time. Leave him."

He didn't want to add that there was really nothing left to bury now.

At that Andre started to scream, reaching out helplessly. Several aides surrounded him, pulling him back. Pat walked away, but the stench of death, charred flesh, spilled entrails was so thick and cloying that he soon leaned forward and vomited, the bile causing him to gag and choke. Spitting, he pulled his canteen around and washed his mouth out with the mixture of vodka and water, then took a deep swallow.

A pile of heads were raised like a pyramid before

him, the skulls cracked open so that the brains could be devoured.

"Jesus wept," he gasped. "This world is hell."

There was a flurry of action in the snow to his right. Turning, he saw a wounded Bantag rising up, having hidden under a collapsed shelter half, only to be flushed out by several troopers. The Bantag tried to run, but his legs were broken. Howling, he crawled through the snow. The troopers circled around him, taunting, using their carbines as clubs. Pat watched, dispassionate, as one of the men finally broke the Bantag's back and then just left him there, howling in pain.

Are we becoming like them? Pat wondered. If we ever finally win, will they have changed us forever, destroying our humanity?

Half a dozen troopers came riding in, leading nearly a score of men, all of them naked, staggering. Pat went up to the group while the troopers dismounted around them, pulling blanket rolls from the backs of saddles, several of the men offering their own greatcoats. Two of the men were missing arms, and with a sickening realization Pat knew the Bantag had been butchering them alive.

One of the men saw Pat and staggered toward him. Shivering, he held a blanket around his shoulders. Fingers black with frostbite, he struggled to raise a hand to salute. Pat motioned for him to be still.

"Captain Petrov Petronovich, B troop, 6th Rus, sir."

"What happened, captain?"

"We were just bedding down when they caught us, sir, came in from both flanks, just as it was getting dark. Almost all the boys died fighting, sir. Some of us got overpowered. They stripped us then and made us watch. . . ." His voice trailed off and a shuttering sob overpowered him.

"Just before dawn they started butchering us who were left, did it while we were alive. Sergeant Kerov there"—he motioned to one of the men missing an arm—"they cut it off and made him watch while they put it in the fire to cook."

Pat nodded and, taking off his canteen, he handed it to the captain.

"You'll be all right, captain. Get to the rear where the ambulances are."

"Sir, they've got ironclads ahead."

Pat, already starting to turn away, looked back, startled. "What?"

"Yes, sir, I seem them."

"How many?"

"Hard to tell. Just over the next ridge. The snow was coming down hard, but I seen them coming up during the night just before the snow started. You could see the sparks, hear them iron devils wheezing away. They hid 'em just below the ridge. I think they were waiting for you, sir."

Without replying, Pat ran back toward his mount. The battle was sweeping up the next ridge. With the coming of dawn the storm was starting to abate, and it was possible now to catch a glimpse of the tree-clad ridge. For a brief instant a shaft of red sunlight bathed the trees. One of them exploded from a shell burst.

"Couriers!" Pat roared.

His staff surrounded him.

"One of you up to the colonel of the 4th, another to the 5th. Tell them there might be ironclads on the reverse slope. If so, break off and let's get the hell out. I'm going forward."

The two repeated the message and, spurring their mounts, galloped off. Weaving through the wreckage of the enemy camp, Pat passed what looked like the tent of a commander. A horsetail standard was planted in front of the pavilion.

An umen standard, Pat realized. He motioned for one of his aides to take the horsetail standard as a trophy.

God, we've struck an umen, a full umen out on our flank and ten miles into our rear. This isn't a raiding party. He started to feel uneasy. The humans had surprise on their side, they'd killed hundreds in the first blow, but if there was an umen out here, it could turn any minute now.

He motioned for two more aides. "Order the retreat. We've bloodied them—now let's get out."

He could see the disappointment. They had a thirst for vengeance that had yet to be satisfied. On the forward slope he could see knots of Bantag still trying to flee, staggering through the snow, many of them armed only with sabers or lances. Troopers circled them, gunning them down. It was a rare moment, humans catching the hated horse warriors by surprise and on foot.

And then he heard it; a high piercing whistle, picked up by others. Lead elements of the charge were just now gaining the ridge ahead. As they did so, several men dropped from their saddles. Others reined in and, turning, started back down the slope. A ragged volley erupted ahead.

Pat spurred his mount forward, spotting a troop guidon, coming back down from the ridge, a captain riding beneath it.

"What's happening?" Pat cried.

"Swarms of them! Mounted, with ironclads! You can see them on the flanks!"

Even as he spoke, a dark snout protruded above the ridgeline, rising higher and higher, than slamming down hard, snow bursting out from under it like foaming surf.

"Bugler, sound retreat!" Pat roared.

Lashing his mount with the ends of his bridle, Pat turned, starting back down the slope. He heard the cry of the bugle picked up and echoed along the line. Troopers were turning, heading back. Mounted Bantag started to appear along the crest, their taunting cries carrying against the wind. Another squall line crossed the narrow valley, and visibility dropped. One of his staff dropped his reins, arms flung high as a spray of blood erupted from his chest. Pat looked over, saw that the boy was already dead, and pushed on.

His mount surged up the slope, breathing heavily, flailing snow out from under him. For a brief instant he saw the pyramid of skulls, wanted to do something to it, but then left it behind. Reaching the guns, he reined in hard and jumped from his mount.

"Get out the ironclad bolts!"

"Where? I don't see any ironclads!" the section commander cried.

"Believe me, they're coming! Get the bolts up!"

The bugles continued to call the retreat. Streams of troopers were coming back up the slope, disappearing and reappearing through the squalls. Wounded who were still mounted were being led, while some were pulling along horses that had lost their riders. One poor beast, its rider gone and right foreleg broken, kicked forward, blindly following its comrades, stumbling, getting up, surging forward again as if as frightened of the Bantag as the men who rode with it.

The snow lifted again and a line of riders was down in the middle of the valley. But these riders were taller, uniforms black, conical leather-and-fur helmets, horsetail-and-human skull standards . . . the Horde.

Pat looked back at the two guns.

"Left gun, canister, try and keep those bastards back. Right gun, load with bolt."

Seconds later the left gun kicked back, geysers of snow spraying up around the Horde riders, and half a dozen of them tumbled into a heap. Several slowed, raised their rifles, and fired, bullets slashing through the trees over Pat's head.

"There's one!" somebody cried.

Pat saw the dark form sliding down the slope, smoke pouring from its stack, and then four more, knots of Bantag on foot moving behind it.

Pat judged the range. Nearly three hundred yards, just barely close enough.

"Open fire!"

The right gun reared back. A high plume of snow erupted a dozen yards forward and half a dozen to the right of the lead ironclad.

"Dammit, do better than that!" Pat shouted.

The cannons on the five ironclads fired back, nearly in salvo. Canister whirled through the trees, bark peeled back from trunks, branches sheered off, cascades of snow tumbling down. One of the gunners went down screaming, clutching his stomach.

A trooper came galloping along the crest and reined in by Pat's side.

"Colonel Sergius's compliments, sir. Bantag ironclads are on the ridgeline, three hundred yards to your right, sir. He's pulling back to the rendezvous."

Pat nodded, still watching as the sergeant laid his gun. The other piece kicked back, more canister going downrange. The sergeant stood, hands up high, then stepped aside.

The gun recoiled. A flash of fire erupted on the front shielding of the ironclad. Some of the men started to cheer, and then cursing erupted. The round had ricocheted off, leaving a bright metallic scar on the forward-sloping armor.

"Should have punched through!" the sergeant cried in disgust. "It was straight in!"

Heavier armor, Pat realized. They've added more armor to their machines. Colonel Keane had warned him there were some reports of an improved ironclad coming up. Damn all!

The gunners started to reload, and then from down the slope a wild piercing scream erupted. Bantag were coming down from the northern flank, sweeping up the side of the ridge, hundreds of them in a swarming mass. The crew of the fieldpiece loaded with canister hurriedly turned their gun and fired, knocking down nearly a dozen, but still the charge pressed forward.

Pat looked at the guns and the deep snow and made his choice.

"Set fuses in the caissons, cut the traces, and leave the guns."

Startled, the crew looked up at him.

"We don't have time to get out. Move it!"

The men raced to the caissons, cut the traces to the teams, and swung up on the backs of the horses. One of the gunners fumbled with a length of slow fuse, sticking the end of it down into a bag of powder, then trailing the other end out of the caisson. Pat looked back and saw the sergeant still by his piece, working the elevation screw.

"Sergeant!"

"Just one more shot, sir!"

The sergeant picked up the lanyard, pulled it taut, stepped back, and jerked. The gun recoiled, and then a second later he was on his back, a hole as big as a fist torn into his chest.

The gunners started to run. Pat followed them, turning to look back. The first of the charging Bantag were already on the crest to the left flank and were pushing down the slope into the next valley.

Pat spurred his mount forward. Seconds later the two caissons erupted, the several hundred pounds of powder in each blowing with a thunderclap roar.

Weaving down the slope, he caught up with the gunners riding the caisson horses and urged them forward. Off to his left he saw where half a dozen more ironclads were attempting to close the flank. Another couple of minutes and they would have had the trap closed.

Settling into the long ride, he passed a thin line of troopers who had reined about for a moment, fired a volley, and then pushed on. The tension in Pat started to ease a bit as he saw that discipline was taking hold after the near panic of minutes before. Fall back, turn, fire a few volleys, push on. We weigh less than Horde riders, so they'll move slower, he thought. If we don't panic we'll get out.

They were past the ironclads; at least the things moved slowly. If we were on foot in this snow, it'd be a massacre.

A trap, he realized. The damn thing had been a trap. Deploy some poor bastards forward, let us come in seeking vengeance, and then encircle us. So they wanted us to see what they did. The screams echoing in the night a call to avenge our blood. We killed hundreds, but still they'd almost gotten us, maybe a hundred, two hundred, more lost, besides the massacre of the 6th.

He thought of the pyramid of skulls . . . of all the pyramids of skulls that marked the nearly five hundred miles of retreat from the Shenandoah River all the way back to the very outskirts of Roum. It was unrelenting, a nightmare, an unstoppable war that had pushed forward through the heart of winter, and soon there would be no place to retreat to. It would come down to a fight for the largest city of the Republic—the city of Roum.

Chapter Two

The throbbing of the drums and the bone-shaking rumble of the nargas filled the early-morning air. The night of the moon feasts was nearly at an end, the first crimson light of dawn seeming to capture and reflect the blood of a hundred thousand cattle which had been spilt that night.

Ha'ark the Redeemer watched dispassionately as his own personal cattle, a colonel taken the month before in the battle to cross the Ebro River, gasped out his last agonized breaths, the shaman listening carefully to each shuddering groan, quick to interpret the auguries.

A ceremonial golden spoon was passed to Ha'ark, and, stepping forward, he took his turn, scooping deep into the open skull, grunts of approval greeting his efforts when the colonel sobbed, his legs beginning to buckle.

"It is good, my Qar Qarth," the shaman cried, "so they will fall beneath your strength."

Ha'ark said nothing. A lone narga sounded, the horn of the Qar Qarth, and the gold-embroidered flaps of the great yurt were pulled back so that the first light of dawn might stream in. A cold rush of air cascaded through the open flaps, wisps of fog swirling up as it clashed with the fetid air that had been trapped inside the yurt throughout the long night of the feast.

Breathing deeply, glad to escape the stench of cattle blood, boiled flesh, and filth, he stepped out into the open. The vast encampment, laid out on the slopes overlooking the Great Sea near where he had first landed with his army four months ago, was alive with activity; twenty thousand warriors greeting the first light of dawn, and with it the first day of the new year, the year of the Golden Horse.

The cries of the shamans counterpointed the nargas, the weird, spine-chilling singsong chant filling him with a strange superstitious fear. It was something from ancient history to him, yet it was real, and he, a former private in a losing war upon another world, was now their Qar Qarth, ruler of the Bantag Horde. Ha'ark the Redeemer, sent to restore a dying race to its pride.

He heard a moan, and looking over his shoulder he saw the shaman pushing the cattle forward, guiding his steps like a puppeteer. The eyes of the cattle were vacant, a blind staring-off into eternity, its mouth gaping, drool running down its chin, the naked legs bright red and swollen from repeated dunkings in the boiling cauldron.

For the briefest of instants he almost felt pity for the dumb beast. Something whispered in his heart that this was a soul as real, as capable, as his own; that on his own world such cruelty would never be practiced upon even an unwitting beast, let alone a warrior of an army which had all but fought his entire race to a standstill.

The shaman uncorked a flask while watching the horizon and still wailing his chant. The sky was as red as an inferno, the brilliant light caught and reflected by the snow-covered fields and the sea beyond so that the world seemed engulfed in frozen fire.

The rim of the sun broke the horizon. A cacophony of noise exploded, wild screams of the warriors, shamans calling their prayers, tens of thousands of rifles firing heavenward, and the whispered moans of the last of the cattle to die that night commingling with the shrieks of fear of those who would be suffered to live a little longer.

"Keane."

He heard the words, a deep shuddering gasp.

Startled, he turned. The shaman had already upended the flask of oil into the open skull and lit it. A tongue of blue flame licked up out of the cranial cavity of the colonel, cooking his brains while he was still alive. The sight was horrific, filling Ha'ark with dread; a burning man, dead yet somehow still alive, whispering again but a single word.

"Keane."

All around him were silent, eyes fixed on the shaman, who seemed as frightened as the most ignorant of guards. The shaman shoved the cattle forward, as if to knock him over, yet he did not fall, rather he staggered and slowly collapsed to his knees, the stench of his cooking brains wafting up into Ha'ark's face.

"It is good," the shaman suddenly cried. "Thus will Keane kneel before you by the coming of spring. Keane shall fall!"

There was a moment of silence, then grunts of approval, as if the feasting party wanted to believe the augury and now struggled to cast aside their fears.

The colonel seemed to dissolve, all muscles going slack as the last of his will, his spirit burned away.

Ha'ark looked down at his feet where the Yankee colonel lay, a trickle of burning oil leaking out from the open skull. Those of his entourage hesitated until the shaman, with a wild cry of lust, drew out his dagger and cut away a long strip of boiled flesh. Then the others fell hungrily upon the body, struggling to taste the ceremonial offering. Ha'ark turned away, afraid that his followers might see him gag. Stepping down from the platform at the front of his yurt, he walked quickly away, wanting to escape the orgy of feeding.

Jurak, one of the survivors of his squad who had fallen through the tunnel of light with him, came up to Ha'ark's side.

"Damn animals."

"Who, the cattle or our own warriors?"

"Both," Jurak snarled.

"Give them twenty years. Look what we've accomplished in less than five. We've transformed this world as surely as Keane's Yankees." He took a deep breath, the nausea passing, control reestablished.

"We still imitate, and the labor is provided by millions of Chin slaves. Even they, however, are not numberless. Ha'ark, you're using them up."

Ha'ark nodded. That was a problem. More than a million had died this year, laboring on the vast rail lines, pouring the iron for guns, carrying the supplies of the army, or simply used as a walking supply of food.

"This winter campaign is destroying us. This is not a modern army, Ha'ark. You can't expect it to campaign right through to spring."

"They did it before we came. You heard the stories of the wars between the Tugars and Merki. One of their epic battles was fought in the dead of winter."

"Nomadic horse warriors. What logistical support did they need? Their horses were food, and they recovered their arrows after a fight. I've looked at the reports, and even those, I might add, are written by Chin scribes using the letters of the Rus. Last month's battle to force the Ebro River consumed twenty thousand rounds of artillery and nearly two million rounds of rifle ammunition. That's a month's production used up in a single day's fight."

"But we crossed the river, didn't we?"

"Yes, and I have no idea what this taking of Capua will cost. And then Roum is still there to be taken. Ha'ark, we've used more than double the ammunition we had planned for. All the stockpiles are just about gone. There's enough here and moved up to sustain us for a couple of weeks of hard fighting, then we'll be down to waiting for the next shipment from Xi'an with no reserves in place.

"Ammunition, weapons—they don't spring out of the ground, Ha'ark. Everything has to be made two hundred miles beyond Xi'an, moved by rail to the harbor, loaded on boats, shipped to here, then moved all the way by rail up to the front."

Jurak sighed and shook his head. "We're using our army up, stretching it beyond its limits while they fall back on their base of supplies. Everything is tied to that one damned rail line, which is falling apart. And the locomotives, Ha'ark, they're ready for the junk pile after three or four runs up to the front and back."

"That is why we have the Chin," and Ha'ark nodded

toward the vast holding pens where tens of thousands of laborers were already up, moving in long lines down to the docks, where they would spend the day breaking ice so that the channel out to the open sea could be kept open.

Jurak wrinkled his nose with disgust as an errant breeze swept up from the prison camps, carrying with it the stench of the cattle. Ha'ark had worked out a fine calculation based upon the harsh realities of the world he had come to. A pound of coarse bread and some green leaves or roots a day would equal so much labor for so many months until the cattle slave finally collapsed and was thrown into the slaughter pits. There were, of course, exceptions who would be given two to three pounds and a handful of rice a day for several months prior to a moon feast. Such calculations had enabled them to wring the last bit of labor from millions and still meet the ceremonial needs of the Horde.

"We can't relent on the pressure," Ha'ark announced. "Don't you think they are feeling it as well? They're about to crack, I can sense it. Their army was never designed for this sustained level of war. Against the Merki it was one intense three-day battle. Against the Tugars it was a siege, but then the numbers were smaller. This is a level of war they can barely comprehend."

A chilled damp wind blew down from the west, swirling around Ha'ark.

"Snowing up at the front," Jurak said. "Should be here later today. Any news on the flanking attack?"

"It appears to be successful. But my concern now is to keep these scum moving. There are three ships locked up in the ice out there, and I need that ammunition. It is moving too slow back here, Jurak. That is why we returned from the front—to sort this out. The bridge over the Ebro is still a choke point. It needs to be finished if our attack on Roum is to be sustained. And as for the track, half of it already needs to be replaced."

"Even slaves reach a breaking point, Ha'ark."

"When they do, feed them into the boiling pots. If it costs the life of a cattle for each bullet delivered, we still win. One less human to worry about once the war is over and one more dead on the other side as well."

"You still need engines, locomotives," Jurak continued. "The few we have are already wearing out."

He nodded, not replying. The Chin were master craftsmen, but even they could not assemble the machines fast enough. He had wanted fifty locomotives. There were only twenty up here now, and five of those were all but worn out. Replacements could not be had for weeks.

"I wish this would end," Jurak sighed. "I'm sick to death of the slaughter."

Ha'ark looked at his old companion closely. Something was breaking inside of him. That was why he had been relieved of command after the escape of Keane back in the fall. If only Jurak had pushed harder; one more umen ten miles closer up and the trap would have been complete. The fact that Keane had outmaneuvered him and that the attack had diverted his attention just long enough for the breakthrough to be achieved on another front had been forgotten, at least to Ha'ark.

If Jurak had been anyone else he would have ordered his death. But he was educated, had a head for figures, for counting and logistics, and he could not be wasted.

"The cattle say this is the worst winter in memory. Our warriors are from a warmer climate, Ha'ark. You must consider that. We're losing more now to frostbite and lung infections than we are to combat."

"And so are the cattle," Ha'ark snarled. "No more complaints from you, dammit!"

"I am doing my job," Jurak replied defiantly. "I must tell you the truth of what is. The others think you are a god and are too terrified to do so."

"The campaign continues. I go back to the front today. I want this tangle of supplies unsnarled, and I don't care if it costs a hundred thousand lives. Get this mess taken care of. Then I will need you back at the front. I will be in their city of Roum within the month. We have to take it now, before the spring thaw arrives. The rail lines are but temporary and will sink into the mud. We must cut them from their supplies of oil to the south of Roum—that will ground their airships. And there is the political side. If we can break Roum, I'll offer survival to them if they leave the Republic. That will isolate Suzdal, and then there are the other blows that have yet to fall."

Ha'ark nodded toward where the delegation awaited him. Jurak hesitated, then finally lowered his head.

"As you wish, Ha'ark."

He was tempted to order Jurak to address him as "my Qar Qarth" or "my Redeemer," but they were alone and so he would suffer the breach of etiquette.

Another gust of wind swirled about them, and he pulled his cloak in tight, trying not to shiver.

"Come, let us meet our allies." And he strode through the snow. As he approached, the human lowered his head, but the other, the Merki, looked straight ahead, as if barely willing to concede that a superior approached.

Ha'ark studied the two carefully. The human was short, stocky, barrel-chested, skin a pale olive color. He looked up at Ha'ark, eyes cautious. The other, the Merki, was thin, drawn, eyes sunken as if he was racked with fever. His left hand was missing, replaced with a silver hook. There was something about him that was troubling. It was obvious he was on the edge of madness, but there was something else as well, a suggestion that perhaps here was the fate awaiting Ha'ark if Keane were not defeated.

Ha'ark ignored the human.

"Tamuka of the Merki Horde, I greet you," Ha'ark announced.

"Qar Qarth of the Merki Horde," Tamuka corrected him, his voice barely a whisper.

Ha'ark wanted to make a sarcastic retort. The Merki Horde was splintered, broken into three bands. The other two had wandered back westward, foraging now a thousand leagues away. Only three umens had stayed loyal to the Qar Qarth Tamuka the Usurper, who had led them to their doom at Hispania. They were a beaten rabble, scavenger raiders on the periphery of what had once been their empire and the empire of the Tugars.

"Yes, of course, Qar Qarth Tamuka," Ha'ark finally said, realizing there was nothing to be gained by insulting him. "You should have joined us for the feast of the moons last night," he offered.

"I was weary from the journey, and I prefer to dine in private."

Ha'ark said nothing. He had already heard the reports from his envoys. Accustomed to cruelty, even they had been awed by the practices Tamuka engaged in with his human captives on the night of the feast. He pushed the thought away, the memory of the dying colonel still troubling him.

Ha'ark motioned for Tamuka to join him, leaving their respective entourages behind.

"I take it you have been properly briefed about our campaign."

"It is interesting to hear of," Tamuka replied coolly. "Keane, I take it, is fighting well."

He said "Keane" as if it were a curse, spat out bitterly. Keane, always it was Keane, Ha'ark thought.

"Yes."

"I heard how they escaped your trap. And tell me, how was it that the present I sent you, Sergeant Schuder, how did he so easily escape?" Tamuka looked over at him, a sarcastic glint in his eyes.

"Such things happen."

"I should have kept him for my own entertainment. I've perfected such things, you know."

"Yes, I've heard. Perhaps too well."

"What do you mean?"

"Letting them observe the funeral of Jubadi Qar Qarth with their airship before launching your offensive. It braced their will rather than terrifying them. It might have made the difference at Hispania, where they fought with desperation." Ha'ark stared straight into Tamuka's eyes.

"Remember, I was not Qar Qarth after Jubadi."

"Oh, yes, one more had to die before you took control," Ha'ark replied smoothly.

Tamuka smiled.

"And your own ascension to power—shall we discuss that, oh Redeemer?"

Ha'ark said nothing for a moment, then finally smiled as well.

"So why have you summoned me across two thousand leagues?" Tamuka asked, breaking the tension.

"To coordinate our effort."

"Our effort?" Tamuka laughed. "Our effort. I have but three umens. Once I had forty. And you, how many is it? Sixty, though I daresay you've lost five or ten since your campaign started."

"You are on their western flank. All their efforts are focused on me. Your three umens could tie down ten, maybe twenty thousand. They have to protect that front. Remember, they are a republic, and the Rus side of it will howl if their soldiers are fighting to defend Roum while your raiders harass the border."

He could sense that the nuances of the political side of the struggle were beyond Tamuka, who stared at him coldly.

"You can have Suzdal for your pleasure," Ha'ark said. "Surely that would please you after the humiliation they gave you."

"Humiliation?" Tamuka growled. "You have no concept of the humiliation, as you put it. I would do it with or without you, leader of the Bantag."

"Then why haven't you?"

Tamuka looked at him, eyes flashing with passion at the insult.

"You had no focus. Their forces held you back, but I tell you now that as this winter campaign continues they will strip their border naked. I am giving you the opportunity for revenge, Tamuka. Now is your chance."

"And Keane?"

"If taken, I give him to you," Ha'ark lied. If Keane was ever taken alive, the privilege of the kill would be his alone, as prophecy demanded. "That human back there, Hamilcar of the Cartha—can he be trusted to keep this alliance?"

Tamuka laughed darkly.

"He has been under my hook for years," and as he spoke, Tamuka patted the silver hook with his good hand. Ha'ark looked down at it and saw that it was stained with blood and bits of flesh.

"Now that they are in the war, we will have this Yankee Republic on three fronts, you to the west, the ocean to the south, and I to the east."

"And what of the sword pointed at your own underbelly, Schuder holding Tyre?"

"He will be blockaded by Hamilcar and left to wither. Madness of them to leave three of their umens down there while the main fight will be before Roum."

"If they break out, though, they could cut your supplies to here."

Ha'ark laughed harshly. "How, three hundred miles, a winter march, limited supplies? If they come out of that city, we'll cut them apart."

Tamuka smiled and said nothing.

Another gust of wind swirled about them, carrying with it the first flakes of snow driving down out of the west. Ha'ark pulled his cloak in tighter and smiled.

"By spring it will be over. Schuder starved down in Tyre, Roum in our hands, and you again on the banks of the Neiper before Suzdal. By spring the Republic will be dead and then together we can transform this world."

The sight of the Forum still filled Colonel Andrew Lawrence Keane with awe, and for a brief wonderful moment he was diverted from the concerns of a commander and was again a historian who could still be captivated by this wondrous world.

The vast square was spread out before him. Straight ahead across the broad open plaza was the palace of Marcus Crassus. The symmetry was perfect, a dozen limestone pillars lining the front of the building. The palace had been heavily damaged when the Cartha had briefly occupied the city, and nearly all the pillars were scored by artillery, but from a distance, the damage was barely noticeable. Flanking the palace to the east was the Senate Chamber, its gilded dome catching the frigid morning light, the flag of the Republic fluttering above it. The sides of the dome were ringed with a wall of sandbags, in part to protect the precious structure, but also to provide cover for the command observation platform, since the dome was the highest point in the city.

Temples to the gods lined the other two sides of the plaza. The fact that the Roum were pagan might have created a problem with the Orthodox Rus. On Earth, Keane remembered, Orthodoxy had a broad streak of xenophobia to it. The saving point, though, was that the Rus here were descendants from nearly a thousand years past, and their brand of Orthodoxy still carried old Slavic paganism in it as well. Long talks with Metropolitan Casmar about the need for unity had defused a potential crisis, with Casmar declaring that the Roum gods were simply saints with other names. As for the Roum, they in turn had displayed the easygoing pragmatism of their ancestors regarding religion; they had simply incorporated Kesus and Perm into their own pantheon, and a small Rus church now shared space on the Forum plaza.

Market stalls filled the center of the plaza, merchants selling food, trinkets, doves for sacrifice in the temples, amulets, amphorae of wine, jewelry. There were even a few fur merchants from Rus and a lone monk selling sacred relics. As Andrew walked by he saw the relics were small icon portraits of Saint Malady, the old artilleryman from the 44th New York who was now the patron saint of all engineers and had become a special favorite of the land ironclad crews. To his surprise, he also saw an icon of Chuck Ferguson, and he slowed to gaze at it.

Merchants and customers were bundled up against the cold wind, heads lowered, and as the crowd swirled about them, few noticed the presence of Andrew, President Kal, and Dr. Weiss making their way through the press with two guards discreetly moving behind them. Everyone was intent upon stocking up; word of the extent of the disaster up at Capua was just now reaching the civilians of the city and there were the first hints of panic in the air. In spite of the warnings to stay within the city a steady stream of refugees had been heading north, hoping to find refuge in the woods beyond Hispania. The food stalls in the forum were swamped, but few were buying, since prices on such staples as hard bread, salted pork, and dried fruit had more than doubled within the last week.

More would buy, he thought, when it was announced later today that official rationing for all civilians within the city would be imposed starting tomorrow. Food had been brought up over the last month from the reserves stored in Suzdal, but the official rations of a pound of hard bread, ten ounces of salted meat, and two ounces of dried fruit a day were barely enough to keep people alive. Fuel was just as much a concern for Andrew. If the city of Roum became the battlefront, wood, charcoal, and coal would run out, except for the hospitals and nurseries, within two to three weeks.

He thought again of Chuck. One of the by-products of the development of coal mining had been coal-cracking kilns in the new city expanding beyond the walls of Suzdal, which converted the black stone to pure coke for the foundries. Chuck had designed piping to feed from the plants into the factories and a small number of homes to provide lighting from the gas by-product. He had talked about developing it for all the cities of the Republic once the war ended, and work had already started for a gas plant in Roum. Well, that peaceful dream, like all the peaceful dreams of progress, was on hold indefinitely.

Chuck, God how we miss you and need you, Andrew thought sadly. The inventor's death from consumption had shattered a confidence that no matter what the Bantag created, humans could trump it with something better. We're on an equal track now, Andrew realized, and the certainty of technological superiority is gone forever.

As he continued across the plaza, greatcoat collar pulled up over his neck to block out the bitter cold, he enjoyed the few minutes of distraction, trying to forget the knot in his stomach over the meeting he was about to face.

He had never been to Rome on Earth. That had always been a dream, to walk the Forum, to stand atop the Capitoline Hill, to walk beneath the Trajan Arch and gaze upon two thousand years of history. Yet here it was, still alive, not a half-exhumed relic of the past. The Arch of Hispania, recently dedicated, was straight ahead, and he slowed in his walk to look up at it. Columns of troops carved in bas-relief marched, struggled, and died on the pillars, with piles of Merki dead at the bases. Atop the column, a rocket battery's salvos arched across the top of the arch, the flame of the rockets carved in stone providing pedestals for the statues of Andrew, O'Donald, Hawthorne, and Marcus in the center. That bit of vanity Andrew smiled at. It was important, of course, to promote local heroes whenever possible. He wondered if historians two thousand years from now would gaze upon the arch in wonder. A darker thought troubled him: would the arch be nothing but ruins, the memory of the Republic dead and buried beneath the hooves of the Horde?

Andrew looked over at Kal, president of the Republic, who was walking beside him. His features were drawn, somber. His beard, which had once been jet-black, was going increasingly to gray. Under his stovepipe hat the hair was thinning, not even gray any longer but white around the temples. His once chubby features had drawn out, thinned, and a deep lacing of wrinkles etched his face. There was a time when Kal's adoption of Lincoln's dress and beard had a certain comic opera quality to it, but now it seemed almost tragically real.

Lincoln. Was President Lincoln still alive? Andrew wondered. The thought had often come to him. More than ten years now since he had come to this world. The war home had been winding down and Lincoln had been approaching his fifty-sixth year, on the day the 35th Maine left forever. It would be pleasant to think of him home in Springfield, retired, maybe still practicing law. Something in Andrew's heart, though, told him that might not be true. Of late, there was a dark foreboding that his hero might be gone. Must be 1876 back home.

The centennial of the Republic, hopefully reunited. Our Republic, less than one-tenth that age—will it ever endure to such a length of time?

A cold gust of wind swept across the Forum, snow swirling up on the breeze, sticking to Andrew's glasses, clouding his sight.

"Give them to me."

Andrew looked over and saw Dr. Emil Weiss by his other side, hand extended.

Both Andrew and Kal chuckled, taking their glasses off. A one-armed man learned to compensate for many things, but the cleaning of glasses was a difficult task. For Andrew it was the left arm at Gettysburg, for Kal the right at the First Battle of Suzdal. Their common joke was that they could shop together for gloves, and the previous winter they had actually engaged in such a foray. Andrew noticed Kal was still wearing his gloves: Andrew had lost his own the week before up at the front.

Turning their backs to the wind, both handed their glasses to the doctor, who pulled out a handkerchief and wiped them clean, then handed them back. Approaching the steps of Marcus's palace they passed through the honor guard, a company of infantry of the 1st Roum. The guard snapped smartly to attention, presenting rifles. Atop the steps, Marcus awaited them, dressed in his strange mixture of the ancient and modern: crested helmet of a consul and golden breastplate, combined with the sky-blue trousers of infantry and black leather belt with eagle plate of the Republic.

As Kal wearily climbed the stairs, Marcus made a show of saluting, then extending his hand. Andrew looked back over his shoulder and saw that the crowd in the Forum had stilled to watch the brief ritual. Marcus had obviously made a point of welcoming Kal on the steps and saluting where everyone could see. Stepping into the foyer, Andrew was grateful when the bronze door behind them closed, blocking out the wind, though the skylight above them was open to the sky. In the large room to one side of the foyer the warmth of the small stove set into one wall was a blessed relief, even though his glasses immediately steamed over.

The rest of their staffs were all ready there, crowded around the table. Present were Pat O'Donald, commander of the Army of the East, thigh-high riding boots still splattered with mud, and Vincent Hawthorne, pale and wasted from the long recovery from his near fatal wound, cane leaning against the wall behind him, and the commanders of the corps at the fronts, all except Schneid of the 1st, who was in nominal command of the front while the others gathered here in Roum. Noticeably absent was Hans Schuder, who was holding the city of Tyre three hundred miles down the eastern coast of the Inland Sea, with three corps of infantry.

Standing among the staff officers were the representatives of the support services: engineering, supply, military railroad, and Colonel Timokin, commander of the ever-expanding regiment of ironclads, and Bullfinch of the navy, and Theodor Vasilovich, who was attempting to replace the irreplaceable Ferguson, and Jack Petracci of the Air Corps, and Metropolitan Casmar, and finally his own wife, Kathleen, who was in charge of the hospital corps.

Andrew looked around the table as Kal circulated like an old-style ward politician, shaking hands, inquiring about wives and children, setting everyone at ease. Andrew settled into a chair at the head of the table, the action a signal for the meeting to begin.

"Pat, why don't you start us off."

Pat stood up, stretching, and walked over to the map spread out on the table.

"We're flanked. It's that simple."

He stopped as if finished with his delivery. Andrew finally stirred and motioned for him to continue.

"It's the age-old balance getting played out again. We have to rely on the railroads for movement. We're tied to two strips of iron, and that makes us vulnerable. Cut our rails behind us and in a week we'll starve and run out of ammunition. In spite of their advances in weapons, the preponderance of Bantag mobility still relies on the horse. However, unlike our previous foes they've also mastered fighting dismounted as infantry, and they have those devilish land ironclads."

Pat leaned over the map and pointed east of Roum, tracing out the line all the way back to their old position at Junction City, which had fallen at the start of the campaign back in the fall.

"After losing Junction City, we thought we could pull back along the rail line. There were six major bridges of more than a hundred yards and dozens of minor ones that we could blow to slow their pursuit."

He shook his head sadly. "Their pursuit was beyond anything we could have ever imagined. Twice, as you know, they cut off a sizable part of our army and we had to turn with everything we had to cut them out. Meanwhile, behind their lines they must have had a hundred thousand or more Chin slaves rebuilding the line. Now we know where the rail production that Hans talked about was going. They weren't laying a line toward Nippon, they were stockpiling the rails so they could rapidly rebuild the line between Junction City and Roum. I estimate their railhead is only fifty miles behind the front and being repaired at three or more miles a day."

"But in the winter?" Emil asked. "We always had to wait till spring to build. I remember something about ballast and such, that the ground shifts with the spring thaw if you don't have a solid foundation under the track."

"Remember, we did lay track and ballast. Most of that track we tore up and took with us or turned into Sherman hairpins. Ties were burned as well. But the roadbed and ballast, that you just can't destroy. They're cutting new ties, bringing them down out of the forests. Granted, though, they are laying track right on top of frozen ground, and remember, we did a rush job on that rail line as well. Come spring it will give in places, and the replacement bridges will most likely give way in the spring floods as well."

"So hold till spring and their supply line becomes a

mess," Stan Bamburg, the new commander of 9th Corps, interjected.

"We can hope so. Last spring, you'll remember, was hard on us; we lost the bridge over the Ebro and tied everything to hell for three weeks. I think their engineers don't have much of a clue how to build a proper bridge the way we've learned. Six major rivers, a good spring thaw with plenty of rain, and they'll grind to a halt."

"That's three months in the future. I'm more concerned about now. How did they break through?" Kal asked. "When I was here a month ago, both you and Andrew said we'd hold them on the Capua Line right through till next spring."

There was the slightest tone of accusation in Kal's voice, something unusual for the president, who was noted for his humor and mildness, even when confronted by his angriest critics. Andrew could see the stress, the worry. It must have been a hard session with the Congressional Committee on the Conduct of the War before Kal came up here, he realized.

"Two factors," Andrew said, coming to his feet and motioning for Pat to cede the floor. "First, none of us dreamed they'd repair the rail line so quickly. Every yard of track must be paved with the bones of a dead slave. I believed, at first, that they'd secure their hold at Junction City. Maybe push us back fifty or a hundred miles, at worst back to the Ebro a hundred and fifty miles east of here, then wait till spring for the big push.

"Their reaching Capua last week before we had fully fortified that line was something I did not expect. No modern army can support a sustained major operation much more than a hundred miles from its supply head—the logistics, the sheer number of wagons needed to keep the army supplied, becomes prohibitive. When we established the line on Capua we had a major river in front of us and a fairly narrow front, somewhat the same as Hispania. I had hoped crossing the Ebro would stall them for weeks before they could marshal the resources to push on."

He sadly shook his head. "But we all saw the reports

from the scouts we infiltrated to within sight of old Fort Hancock. Half a dozen galleys a day were coming in loaded with rails and precut bridging material. I think a hundred thousand is an underestimate for the number of slaves working on the rail line. It might be more on the order of two hundred thousand."

"Poor beggars," Pat sighed.

Andrew nodded and remained silent for a moment. The image of what would happen if they should lose had to be constantly put to the forefront of everyone's thinking. "Never make an enemy desperate" was an age-old maxim, and for the Republic it was one of the key ingredients of survival. The only alternative to victory was death in the slaughter pits of the Horde.

"And then the rivers froze. Winter, rather than playing to our advantage, has played to theirs. Where they've yet to repair the bridges, they've got slave gangs offloading supplies, carrying them across the frozen river and then transferring them to the next train.

"We now know as well that they brought up their land ironclads, at least forty of them, moved them north, made a crossing through the forest under the cover of last week's blizzard, and flanked the position. Their ironclads can't make much more than forty to fifty miles before breaking down. That means they ran the rail line right up to Capua nearly as quickly as we pulled back from the Ebro.

"The screen in front of us was a deception, a light curtain to make us believe they were only shadowing us, when in fact they most likely have twenty or more umens, all with modern arms, less than a day from Capua and fully supplied for a major engagement along with thirty or more batteries of guns and hundreds of those new mortars.

"Mr. President, the position we thought we could hold till spring is untenable. Even if we hold the front at Capua, their mounted umens will swing far outward, maybe even to the suburbs of Roum, and slash in and cut the rail. We can't cover seventy-five miles of track and hold Capua at the same time. The bottom line is that their ironclads have flanked us and are supported by at least an umen of mounted troops with rifles."

"Then throw a corps up against them," Marcus replied heatedly. "We must hold at Capua. The thought of Roum becoming a battlefield is unacceptable. The outer fortifications around the city are barely completed, and the suburbs will be overrun."

"Sir, if I thought we could hold the flank, I would do so. But we need at least four corps to hold the Capua Line, especially with the river frozen over. They can assault us along nearly a thirty-mile front between the forest and the hills to the south. For that matter, they are already flanking around to the south as well. If they've secured a river crossing up in the forest it won't be one umen on our flank, it could be five or six within a matter of days. We get sucked into a fight, the front will keep expanding westward, and finally they'll curl around us, sweep down, and cut the rail. We must pull out now."

"Then you really aren't sure just how much he is putting into the flanks, are you?" Marcus asked.

"Sir, it's sound tactics, and Ha'ark is a damn fine tactician."

"Well, what about air reconnaissance to get a definite answer? We see his machines shadowing us—where are ours?"

Several of the corps commanders nodded in agreement, and Andrew looked over at Jack Petracci, who had come all the way up from Suzdal for the purpose of addressing this one question.

"I wish we were flying, sir," Jack said. "I hate like hell staying back at Suzdal and working on testing the new machines."

"Then test one over the front where we need it," Marcus said. "One flight could lay to rest if indeed we have been flanked or not."

"Well sir, first off it'd take a couple of days just to bring a machine up. But the moment we fly that machine, Ha'ark will know we have a new design, one far better than theirs, and all surprise is lost. Before Chuck Ferguson died he kept saying we had to build a lot of machines first, dozens of them, and only then employ them in mass, sweep the skies of Ha'ark's machines and never let him get back up again. It's the same with the new ironclads we've started to make. Get a lot of them first, then unleash them in one killing blow. I go flying out now in a new machine and that surprise is lost."

"Well, as it stands now, the war might be lost, and Roum might be destroyed."

Andrew held up his hand.

"We are running a race, Marcus. Not just to win this winter campaign, but to win a war. I want fifty of those machines ready, all of them flying at once, before we unleash them on Ha'ark. One or two machines will do nothing but give him warning. I'm sorry, sir, but the Air Corps stays grounded. Besides, we don't need a spy in the air to tell us what we already know. Capua is flanked, the position is untenable. We must evacuate now."

Marcus looked about the room as if seeking support, but Andrew's pronouncement had closed the argument, and he finally nodded in reluctant agreement.

"Even now they're coming out of the woods on the west side of the river, cutting in behind us. We have a mounted division shadowing them, and our ironclads are being positioned to cover the rail line, but the forces in Capua must pull out starting this afternoon and fall back to here."

Andrew did not add that he had already started the movement back of supplies, reserve units, and two corps.

"You are talking about the second-largest city of the State of Roum," Marcus announced coldly. "It is a question of pride. Why can't we flank them in turn and then retake Capua?"

"Even though we're both relying on rail, they still have the greater mobility of horse. We can field but one corps mounted, and they can put the equivalent of ten, twenty mounted corps against us. And as for pride, sir, in this case it would be the death of all of us. The city of Capua is evacuated of all civilians, as was everyone within twenty miles of the front line. The city is dead already."

"You said there were two factors, Andrew," Kal interrupted as if wishing to divert Marcus from Andrew's cold pronouncement condemning a city. "What was it?"

"Winter. This damn winter, the worst in living memory according to what all of you have told me. All the rivers are frozen solid, and even the Great Sea and the Inland Sea are icing along their northern shores. Though the Bantag are a tribe from the far south, they seem to stand the cold better than we do. In the last thirty days I've lost more men to frostbite and lung ailments than to combat."

"What about fodder for their horses?"

"They paw through the snow, and remember the Bantag aren't as dependent on the horse as the Merki and Tugars were. As the horses are used up, they're food, and the warrior still has the weapons and training to fight on foot."

"So where do we fall back to?" Marcus asked.

"Here," Andrew replied, his voice barely a whisper.

His comment was met with stunned silence, all eyes shifting toward Marcus, who sat back in his chair, features pale.

"Before coming out here I assured Congress we'd hold at Capua," Kal announced.

Andrew shook his head. "It won't work."

"At least try, dammit!" Kal snapped.

Startled, Andrew looked over at his commander in chief. Throughout three long wars, Kal had questioned his judgment only once, and even then it was more of a gentle chiding, when he had lost his nerve after the fall of the Potomac Line.

"Though I know you soldiers hate the use of the term, there are political considerations here," Kal announced.

"You were once a soldier," Pat replied sharply. Andrew looked over at Pat, ready to order him to silence if he ventured but one more word.

"Mr. President," Andrew said, emphasizing the use of the formal title, "please go ahead."

Kal stood up, his gaze fixed on Andrew. "You know

this war does not have the same popular support as the last one."

"That's because last time the bloody bastards were at the throats of every civilian, and those of us with guns were all that held them back," Pat interjected.

"General O'Donald, you are out of line," Andrew snapped.

Pat, shaking his head, sat down, features bright red.

"They're at our throats again, Pat," Kal said. "We know that, but there are some who don't see it that way. The war has been, at least for Rus, hundreds upon hundreds of miles away. Before you Yankees came, most peasants never traveled more than ten miles from the place of their birth. The war could almost be on another world for many of them. Since the start of the campaign we've taken nearly sixty thousand casualties, seventeen thousand of them dead. That's nearly what we lost at Hispania, and this campaign has but started. Rus is exhausted."

"I know that, Mr. President, but what alternative is there?"

Kal hesitated, and Andrew sensed he was holding something back.

"Look at this map. If you abandon the defensive line at Capua, which thousands labored upon for months, what then? If the army falls back into Roum, they'll have a straight path to Hispania and the open steppe beyond. They can bypass you here and ride all the way to Suzdal if they desire."

"I've considered that. I half hope they will."

"What?" Kal asked, incredulous.

"We'll be sitting on their flank and will cut them off. Remember, from Hispania all the way to Kev is open steppe. There is nothing there."

"You just said they can eat their horses if need be."

"And fight then with what? They might send mounted archers and lancers, but even the Home Guard militias, deployed at the old defensive lines along the White Mountains, could stop them. They'll be six hundred miles from their railhead. No, if they do that they'll be defeated. Sir, the entire nature of war has changed in the last ten years. The Hordes have been forced to match our weapons, and with the weapons come certain advantages, but also disadvantages. Now there is consideration of logistics. The Hordes can no longer just fight and live off the land—they need an industrial base and a means of drawing supplies from that industrial base, the same way we do."

"Are you suggesting abandoning Roum itself, Kal?" Marcus asked.

Andrew looked at the two sitting across from each other at the table. Though one was president of the Republic and the other the vice president, he could sense both were now thinking not as leaders of a republic, but rather as leaders of individual states in alliance with each other. A cold chill ran through Andrew. Was this the beginning of the destruction of the dream?

"I am not in favor of abandoning Capua either," Marcus announced. "Nearly half the population of Roum lives between here and the eastern frontier. Granted, many have been evacuated, but to leave my land open for pillaging is intolerable."

"We did in the last war," Kal replied. "All our land was occupied."

"There was no alternative then," Marcus snapped. "I still believe there is now."

"I sense something else here," Andrew said. "Could it be the Chin envoys that you allowed through the lines?"

Both of the politicians stirred uncomfortably. Andrew said nothing. This was the main reason for the meeting, and he wanted it out in the open with both Kal and Marcus present.

"They offered terms and you are considering them."

"No, we at least know the folly of surrender to the Bantag," Kal said quickly.

"But there was some consideration."

Kal shifted uncomfortably. "With some senators, yes."

"Who?" Pat snarled. "The old boyars and patricians?"

"It's more complex than that," Kal replied.

"Go on, sir."

"Ha'ark offered a cease-fire if we agree to the abandonment of driving a rail line eastward. That was the only term. Cede eastward to his control and the rest is ours. If we wish to build west, we may do so."

"He's stalling, that's all," Pat replied sharply. "He'll move up more ironclads, guns, ammunition till he is ready to overwhelm us."

"There are some who are willing to listen," Kal replied.

"And you, sir?" Andrew asked.

Kal was silent for a moment, and Andrew felt a sickening knot in his stomach. What would he do if Kal announced that he would indeed agree to the cease-fire? Andrew had helped to write the Constitution—in fact, most of it had come from his hand and mind. Yet if the civilian government agreed to end this fight it would be national suicide. Would I then overthrow the very government I helped to create? The question was so frightful that he pushed it away.

"Personally I am against it," Kal finally announced, and there were audible sighs of relief from the soldiers assembled in the room.

"There's something more here, though," Andrew interjected. "Ha'ark is far too skillful to make such a simple offer which men and women of wisdom could so easily see through. What is it?"

Kal looked over nervously at Marcus, who lowered his gaze, and in that instant all became clear to Andrew.

"You've both been offered separate deals, haven't you?" Andrew asked.

"What do you mean?" Marcus replied defensively.

"The envoys," Andrew snapped. "Mr. President, what was it? That if Roum wishes to continue the fight all you have to do is pull the Rus units out? Is that it? And Marcus, what for you if you should stop fighting and Rus doesn't? If you allow passage they'll bypass Roum and march on Suzdal instead?"

Both were silent. There was a terrible silence in the room.

"Well?"

Kal lowered his gaze and then nodded his head. Marcus started to stand up, as if to offer an angry protest, but a sharp gaze from Andrew stilled him.

"The damage is already done," Andrew announced coldly. "The mere fact that it was allowed to be said means that rumors of it have gone out. A senator talks to a friend, an aide hears it, and in a couple of days the lowest private is talking about it. Damn all, can't you see that?"

His temper slipping, Andrew slammed the table with a balled fist. The rare display of anger startled everyone in the room.

Andrew stood up, all eyes upon him.

"I am requesting the following," Andrew said coldly, holding back the word "demand" by force of will. "Both of you release the story of these secret negotiations to Mr. Gates here," and he nodded toward the newspaper publisher. "I want a full disclosure of all negotiations that might have occurred since this war started."

"Those are issues of state," Marcus protested.

"They are issues regarding a free republic whose officials are elected representatives."

"There could be embarrassment for some in this," Marcus replied.

"I don't care who is embarrassed. I want a full disclosure along with firmly worded statements that you have told the representatives from the Chin to go to hell and are deporting them immediately."

"I thought the military was to answer to the civilian government? And yet you are now ordering us," Kal replied.

Andrew nodded, knowing he was stepping beyond his bounds. Perhaps he had tried to drag these people too far, too fast, but there was no alternative. The sugar-coated promises of Ha'ark would be observed only until he was firmly in position to deliver a killing blow.

"Don't you remember what Sergeant Schuder reported before Congress?" Andrew asked, trying a different tack. "Ha'ark is not from this world. His thinking is advanced. Unlike most of the other Hordes he sees diplomacy as but one more approach to war. He is trying to divide us, because divided we will surely be defeated.''

"Perhaps we already are," Marcus replied. "Nearly half the population of Suzdal has died since your arrival. Roum was nearly occupied once, and now you are casually talking about surrendering half of my territory yet again and turning this city into a battlefield. How much more can our people bear of this nightmare? If you had not come, the Horde would be half a dozen years' ride east of us now."

"And you would be slaves," Pat snapped angrily. "Any man worth his salt would rather grasp freedom in his dying hands than have the chains of slavery about him.

"Damn all of you," Pat continued, coming to his feet. "I've led your boys now in three wars and I've seen them fight like men! There's pride in their eyes. I remember this fellow back on Earth, a black man, a former slave, who said that once you gave a slave a uniform, put a musket in his hand and forty rounds of ammunition in a cartridge box on his hip, there was no power on Earth that could take the right of citizenship and freedom away from him."

Surprised by Pat's memory of Frederick Douglass's famous statement, Andrew said nothing for a moment.

"The army's with us," Pat continued. "They'll die fighting. They know what it is we face, unlike too many fat senators and congressmen who stay behind the lines. I should bring in that lad who commands a brigade of cavalry, or what's left of it. He found his brother's head on an impaling stake, his guts boiling in some Bantag pot. Tell him to quit fighting and he'll cut your heart out. I'm willing to bet any of them that were in the army and have seen a battlefield after the Hordes butchered our wounded and dead would burn in hell before voting for this."

"Andrew, you all but demanded that we print a statement," Kal said. "What if we don't?"

Andrew took a deep breath. "I'll resign my commission."

Gasps of astonishment echoed in the room. He looked over at Kathleen, not sure how she'd react, but she nodded her head gravely in agreement.

"Disastrous!" Kal cried. "You can't do that!"

"I'm a volunteer, have been and always will be. I can resign when I damn well want to. And I will resign if I believe the government is not fully supporting the army and how I propose to fight this next campaign."

"I'm out too," Pat said and then from around the table came a chorus of assertions, even from the Rus and Roum officers.

Andrew found he was holding his breath, waiting for an answer.

"My friends."

Surprised, Andrew saw Metropolitan Casmar stand up. The Rus soldiers in the room immediately lowered their eyes in respect, and even the Roum looked at him respectfully

"Fight to the death. The Horde is the incarnation of the Dark One. We must fight to save ourselves from them. There is no sense now in debating the hows and the whys of the start of this rebellion against them. Have you so quickly forgotten the sight of our daughters and sons being led off in chains as slaves, or worse yet to be the victims of their fiendish rituals? More than that I hereby declare, in the name of the Church, that this war is a holy crusade, not just to save ourselves, but to liberate all those who now suffer under the yoke of slavery."

Kal, who had stood in respectful silence, finally nodded his head.

"I cannot go against my church, nor can I go against you, Andrew Keane, who befriended me when I was but a peasant in the court of Boyar Ivor. I will write the statement and give it to Gates."

He looked over at Marcus, who finally nodded in agreement as well.

Andrew breathed a sigh of relief. The crisis had, at least for the moment, been weathered.

"Perhaps we need a break," Andrew said. "Let's reconvene in half an hour."

Without another comment he left the room and walked out onto the front steps of Marcus's palace.

"Andrew?"

He turned and smiled as Kathleen came up and slipped an arm around his waist.

"I had no idea that was coming," she said.

"Rumors have been kicking around for the last couple of weeks. I felt it had to be out in the open before we got into this next fight."

"Do you think that cleared it?"

He shook his head, breathing deeply, the cold icy air reminding him of home, of the peace of Maine.

"Could you light a cigar for me?" he asked.

She reached into his breast pocket, pulled one out. Turning her back to the wind, she struck a match and puffed the cigar to life, then handed it to him. The sight of her lighting a cigar always made him smile; it had a certain comical touch to it which he found appealing. Looking into her green eyes, he wished more than anything that the two of them could simply be alone today, to walk through the streets, enjoy the snow, and then retire to a quiet room with a crackling fire to greet them.

"You set me up, Andrew Keane."

Andrew braced himself and turned to see Kal closing the door and coming up to join him.

"Sir?"

"You knew all along. That was an embarrassment in front of Marcus I didn't need."

"You angry about it?"

"Yes, damn you, I am."

"Mr. President. First, why didn't you share the negotiations with me?"

"Do I detect a fear that you are losing control? That we Rus are growing up and don't always need our Yankee advisers anymore?"

The tone of Kal's comment was startling.

"Mr. President, that's not it at all. I thought maybe as a friend you could have shared it and not as a president to his commander of the army."

Kal seemed to relent a bit. "I'm sorry, Andrew, but

the pressure from certain members of Congress to find a settlement to end this war is getting worse. It's not out in the public yet, but it's building. I suspect there might even be some bribes involved."

"Any proof of that?" Andrew asked. "Because if so, if Gates publishes that information, there'll be some veterans who will tear their congressmen apart for accepting Bantag blood money."

"No, no proof, but I had to hear them out. That is what this representative government is all about."

"Yes, I know. But Kal, if the army gets wind of this, just before this fight, it could break morale. Rus and Roum are fighting together superbly. The policy of mixing commanders, combining units within corps—it's integrating our countries as I hoped it would."

"Some don't like that either."

"I know, but if we're to survive we have to fight as one. We have to be a United States and not just a group of states in alliance."

"But why didn't you talk to me first? Why in there in front of Marcus?"

"Because he's of the Republic too. If I went to you alone it would be favoritism, a slighting of Roum. I wanted to embarrass both of you equally."

Kal should his head and sighed. "Well, you accomplished that."

"And I think now, sir, that you and Marcus should get together in private, have it out, share a drink, and shake hands. If we don't fight this war united, we're doomed."

"And your plans?"

"As I asked and as I want you and Marcus to support. Evacuate Capua. Fall back here to Roum. Ha'ark will have to besiege us. He can't bypass us. We'll be in the city, fighting house by house if need be. But the houses and the rubble will offer shelter from the winter storms while we shatter everything they try to take. Then hold on till spring and hope our new weapons are ready ahead of theirs."

"Without Ferguson, the dream of new weapons seems distant now."

"Chuck taught his people well, Kal. They're Rus, remember? Chuck came here without much formal training and worked wonders. I daresay young Theodor, even Chuck's widow, will have some surprises up their sleeves. As it is we have the new ironclads coming off the lines, and the new flying machines."

"Then commit them now."

Andrew shook his head. "We wait till spring."

"What about all that Roum territory along the east shore of the Inland Sea? Or suppose he just sends several mounted umens westward toward Kev?"

"I'm detaching 10th Corps to fall back southward to cover the Roum territory along the sea. They can offer some resistance along with most of our mounted units. Ha'ark will concentrate on Roum first, with the thought that after defeating us here he can detach several umens down along the eastern shore to mop up. As for Suzdal, 5th Corps has been battered a lot. They're to detach, cover Hispania, and then if need be fight a delaying withdrawal across the Steppe using the rail line. All other units will fall back into Roum. Supply will come by sea."

"And Hans, what about the three corps with Hans? If you withdrew them up to here, maybe we could hold a line from Roum up to Hispania, Andrew. I think that would be the better path."

Andrew smiled and shook his head.

"Mr. President. Please support me in this. Hans stays where he is. He's tying down at least ten of their umens. That I pray will be our ace up our sleeve. Where Hans is will not change things much here and now, but a year from now, it could be the path to winning this war."

"My God, Andrew," Kal sighed. "I thought it'd be over in another couple of months. And you say a year from now?"

Andrew looked at Kal and said nothing. If we make it that far, he thought, if we make it a year, chances are it will only be the beginning.

Chapter Three

"Damn, how do you stand this?" Admiral Bullfinch cried, crouching against the sandbag wall as a mortar round detonated on the rim of the trench.

Chuckling, Hans Schuder brushed the clods of frozen dirt off Bullfinch's uniform.

"Sorry to have my staff drag you up here, admiral, but I thought it'd be good for morale," Hans replied with a smile.

Bullfinch looked at him wide-eyed.

"My men, not yours, admiral," Hans laughed. Fishing in his pocket, he pulled out a plug, bit off a chew, and offered the plug to Bullfinch, who shook his head.

"Makes me sick," Bullfinch muttered. "Filthy habit."

"Makes you sick. Hell, being cooped up in one of your damn ships rocking back and forth, that'll make any normal man sick. This here is good for you, son."

"Morale? What do you mean, morale?" Bullfinch asked while still shaking his head, then ducking low as another mortar round whispered overhead to plunge into the city.

"My men, of course. Always saying how the navy has the soft life, how you're warm on board, three good meals a day. You know, the usual."

Bullfinch angrily started to draw himself up, but Hans grabbed him by the shoulder, slamming him against the side of the trench.

"Damn, keep down!" Even as he pulled Bullfinch back the crack of a bullet whispered overhead.

"Death Watcher keeps an eye on this part of the trench," Hans announced.

"Death Watcher?"

"Bantag sniper. We think they got a Whitworth, most likely captured up at Junction City. He's pretty good with it—got five men here in the last week."

Hans nodded to an alcove cut into the trench wall. A soldier, a heavy white canvas sheet over his head, was standing on a firing step.

"See him, Daniel?"

Hans was shushed by several men standing behind Daniel.

"Have the admiral stick his head up again," someone whispered. "He thinks he's spotted the smoke."

Hans watched, arms crossed, chewing. A whispered conversation went on between Daniel and the spotter lying on the parapet by his side.

Daniel shifted slightly, and Hans heard the click of the first trigger on the Whitworth rifle. The slightest brush of pressure on the second trigger would set the gun off.

Everyone held his breath. The gun kicked back with such an explosive roar that Bullfinch jumped. Daniel and the spotter remained frozen in place for several seconds. Then the spotter let out a yelp of joy, but Daniel, cursing, slid back down into the trench, pulling his spotter after him. Seconds later clumps of dirt shot up where they had just been.

"You got him," the spotter cried.

"No, dammit, I told you it was his spotter. I got the spotter."

Daniel's spotter looked over at Hans with a grin.

"Head shot at seven hundred yards it was. You could see it burst."

"Still only the damn spotter," Daniel grumbled.

"Well, I bet old Death Watcher's gone home to change his breeches, though," Hans announced with a grin and slapped Daniel on the back.

"Should have waited. Been stalking the bastard all week. Should have waited. Now I'm going to have to find me another spot and freeze my tail off for another day before I get another shot in."

"Just be careful," Hans replied. Taking the plug of

tobacco that was still in his hand, he tossed it to Daniel and moved on.

Hans looked back at Bullfinch, who was nearly crawling on all fours, and laughed softly. Do good for the young admiral to get a taste of the front. He never doubted for a second the lad's courage. Running an ironclad up nearly to Xi'an was an act bordering on madness, and for that alone he owed Bullfinch his life. But three months in the filthy trenches around Tyre were taking their toll. Supplies were never enough, the food, standard-issue hardtack, salt pork, dried cabbage, and beans, was starting to wear thin. If this operation was to amount to anything, he needed everything Bullfinch had.

Reaching a bombproof shelter, Hans drew back the ragged blanket that served as a door and motioned for Bullfinch to head into the gloom.

A dozen feet down, the sharp dry air of above was replaced by a dank fetid warmth provided by a smoky woodstove. Hans pulled an earthenware jug out from a cubbyhole scooped into the wall, uncorked it, and passed it over to Bullfinch, who gratefully took a long pull on the vodka and sighed as he settled down on a stool.

"There's plenty of better houses back in the city," Bullfinch said. "Why set up headquarters out here?"

" 'Cause this is where the boys live two weeks out of every three. Does them good to see me crawling around with them."

"Aren't you getting a bit old for this?"

Hans chuckled and rubbed the gray stubble on his cheeks. Funny, it was sort of a reminder of the past. The siege lines at Petersburg—long time ago, that. He sat down across from Bullfinch, and a groan escaped him. The rheumatism was flaring. Bullfinch was right; this place was taking its toll.

Hans motioned for the jug and took a drink, delighting in the warmth that coursed through him.

"Hans, you've made your point—it's hell up here. Wouldn't trade my ironclad for all the tea in China."

"All the tea in China," Hans said with a soft laugh.

"Haven't heard that in years. Used to think it was as far as anyone could ever go."

Bullfinch laughed softly. "Almost got out there, right after I enlisted. I was on a steam frigate detailed off for the Pacific Fleet, and word was we were going to China and that place that Perry opened up, Japan. Then I got typhoid and was left in the hospital on shore. The frigate sailed without me and I sailed on *Ogunquit* and came here instead."

"Tough luck."

Bullfinch shook his head. "Me an admiral and not yet twenty-nine. Never have that back home. No, glad I came along."

"Even now?"

Bullfinch smiled. "Even now."

Hans shook his head. "Don't know sometimes. I'm a soldier. Funny, never thought that's where I'd go with my life. Political troubles damn near a rebellion in a couple of places back in '48 in Prussia. I was called back to the army but couldn't see fighting for a government I didn't believe in, so I came to America. Then what do I do? Join the army."

He laughed and shook his head.

"Close to thirty years of it now. The fighting's got to stop sometime. Never thought it'd last this long. Never."

He fell silent, gaze fixed on the single candle, set into the wall on the socket of a bayonet, as a chilled breeze swept down into the bunker, almost snuffing the flickering light.

Sighing, he took the jug, downed another drink, and then passed it back to Bullfinch.

"So what's the news up north?"

"We're abandoning Capua."

"What?"

Bullfinch briefly explained the council of war and the plan to fall back into Roum. Hans shook his head.

"What about us? Was there talk of pulling out my boys?"

"Oh, that was a hot and heavy one. Andrew kept control, though, and as of right now you stay."

Hans smiled. He knew Andrew did not fully agree with the strategic implications of holding this outpost three hundred miles away from the main theater of operations. Hans could see his side of it. Three corps tied into what on the surface was a useless defense of a minor port on the shadowy border between Roum and Cartha. The mere taking of it had already triggered a de facto war between the two.

But he could argue that his three corps were tying down at least eight, possibly ten umens. It was diverting, as well, resources from the main front. But it was far more. By the land route, Tyre was seven hundred miles closer to Xi'an than the overland route of Roum to Junction City, then south. And as such, it was a thorn in the side of Ha'ark, a lingering threat. A threat he obviously was concerned enough about it to put in the forces he had. On the reverse side, concede this city and if Ha'ark should ever run a rail line across from the Great Sea to this port, he'd have a base to build a navy from and threaten Roum and Suzdal from the south. Tyre was the hinge, Hans suspected, upon which the campaign might very well turn . . . as long as Andrew was able to hold in the north. If that line should fail, then the defense here was moot.

"I need the support here," Hans announced. "Tell Andrew that. If we're to win this war I need the support here."

Bullfinch was silent for a moment.

"What's the problem?" Hans asked.

"Well, it's this way. When we lose Capua and fall back on Roum, the rail line into the city will be flanked and cut. That means having to support the army in Roum along with half a million civilians by sea."

"And?"

"I'm not sure if the navy can both support you and support Roum. It's going to stretch our transport capability to the limit. And remember, we have to keep an eye on Cartha as well."

"Blockade the bastards."

"We are, and that's yet another operation to be supported. Hans, we never got the appropriations needed to build our fleet up, and what we were getting was going to the second fleet for the Great Sea."

"Are you saying you want me to pull out?"

Hans struggled to control his building rage. Three months here in this damn town, the slow but steady wastage from disease, sniping and the occasional assault . . .

"You want me to pull out?" he asked again.

Bullfinch finally nodded. "Andrew said it would have to be up to the two of us. My vote is to abandon this front, Hans. I can't promise that I can supply you through the winter. Remember, that's a freshwater ocean behind you. It's already starting to freeze up along the northern shore. A couple more weeks of cold and Lord knows what I'll do. Roum must receive the higher priority for supplies. Lose Roum and we lose the war. You claim that this is the jump-off point for victory, but you're talking a year, two years from now. I'm concerned about feeding you two weeks from now."

Hans grimly shook his head.

"Damn all to hell, we stay. Do you understand me, Bullfinch? We stay."

Bullfinch said nothing.

"We stay," Hans repeated quietly. "If we abandon it they'll fortify it and we'll never get it back. We stay."

"Andrew told me you'd sort of feel this way. All right. But if things get nasty in Roum, the final decision has been placed in my hands. If I can't support you, I'll have to pull out."

Hans finally nodded.

"If I make that decision, Hans, will you go along with it?"

Hans smiled and then shook his head. "If it comes to that, Bullfinch, there won't be anybody here to pull out. I'm convinced this is the pressure point. Ha'ark doesn't know that yet, but I do, and so will you and Andrew."

"Andrew, you need some sleep."

Andrew looked up from his desk as Kathleen came into the room.

"Me need sleep?" he chuckled sadly, and motioned for her to sit down on the chair by the side of his desk. Reaching out, he took her hand and squeezed it as she settled down and signed wearily.

Taking off her white linen cap, she shook her head, red curls cascading down. Andrew smiled, released her hand and reached up to brush an errant wisp of hair from her eyes. The faint scent of ether and antiseptics clung to her.

Sighing at his touch, she closed her eyes and leaned into his hand.

"Miss you," she whispered. "How long has it been since we've slept together?"

He laughed softly. Raised in a proper household, living and teaching in very proper Bowdoin College, he had developed a very straightlaced view of such matters. Kathleen, to his occasional shock and hidden delight, was far more blunt.

"Weeks?"

"Three weeks and four days, Andrew Lawrence Keane, and I tell you, me darlin', it is getting troublesome."

Andrew laughed softly, not quite sure how to react. The papers mounded on his desk were all urgent, all had to be dealt with immediately, and though it was past midnight he had braced himself for working through to dawn before heading up to the front to observe the final evacuation of Capua.

"How are things at the hospital?" he asked, thinking to divert her, but also sensing that she needed to talk.

"Nightmare as always," she sighed. "Mostly frostbite and consumption." She shook her head wearily, the spell of enchantment broken. "I miss the children," she whispered.

They were back in Suzdal, in the care of Hawthorne's wife, something Andrew was eternally grateful for. Madison was old enough to remember the retreat from Suzdal, the scent of panic in the air, and it still troubled her nightmares. Roum was no place for them, especially now.

It was a terrible thing to realize, but Andrew could barely remember how the children felt in his arms, their scent when they were fresh from the washtub, the simple pleasure of tucking them in and turning down the night light. It's what I'm fighting for in the ultimate sense, he thought, to protect my family from the Pit, but if somehow we survive all this, what will their memories be of me? There might be a day when they were pointed out as the children of Andrew Lawrence Keane, but would they remember him as well as others would claim to?

"I'm still worried about Vincent," Kathleen said, as if in some way Vincent was almost a child of theirs after all his years of service under Andrew.

"How so? The wound is healed, isn't it?"

"Not really. He'll always have an open sore on his hip. Bits of bone are still working their way out, and that is agony, though he doesn't show it. It's just that he is turning into a shadow, Andrew. That look in his eyes, as if he already has one foot into the next world, or worst yet, perhaps a foot into the world of the Hordes."

"I can't relieve him. We've lost too many good men. I need Vincent as chief of staff and to keep a handle on the research and manufacturing. At least he's out of the fight back in Suzdal."

"Don't let him get a field command again, Andrew."

"Why?"

She shook her head. "I can't really say. This war is beginning to blur the edges of what we are. I've heard the boys talking in the hospital about some of the things done when they capture live Bantag."

Andrew nodded. It had troubled him as well. Though it was a war of no prisoners, still he expected his army to fight cleanly. If there were wounded Bantag, dispatch them and get it over with. He had placed strict orders against anything beyond that, but as for enforcing those orders. . . .

"I'll look into it. We have to keep discipline, and no, Vincent will not take the field again, especially in this weather."

"And what is happening with you?" she asked softly.

Andrew nodded to the papers. "Tens of thousands of refugees, especially children and nursing mothers, had to be evacuated on the last trains out to Suzdal and relocated for the winter. Transport of supplies shifted from rail to boat in order to keep Roum alive. Production problems on the new flyers, Kal fighting with Congress, Marcus still upset about the withdraw from Capua, worried about how we'll keep Hans's front in operation. The usual."

She smiled and reached out to touch his cheek. It made him feel self-conscious. In the previous year his hair had gone to gray, and now a great shock of it was streaked from his forehead back. When he looked in the mirror to shave, he saw wrinkles about the corner of his eyes, his cheeks sinking in. Something seemed to happen, he thought, as you roll past forty. The aging speeds up. Funny, in a way he still felt in his early thirties, the age when he had first taken to the field, but his body was telling him different. How many more campaigns are still inside me? Pray God this is the last one, at least for this generation.

And when it does end, if we win, then what? Back on Earth, when the dream had drifted of a life after the war, it had been to return to Bowdoin. Even that, however, was a dream that had paled. He had sensed that no matter what came afterward, the pivotal events of his life were unfolding on the field of battle and everything afterward would be anticlimatic.

Never did I dream of ten more years of war, especially this kind of war, he thought. He looked at her, wondering what it would be like to live with her in a time of peace. Good, it would be good. At least the fear would be gone, and the children could grow unafraid.

But then what? Teach, most likely. Gates, the eternal optimist, was already talking about Andrew writing his memoirs and an official history of the campaigns of the 35th Maine.

The 35th. Even that was becoming a ghost of things past. Maybe half a dozen of the original men who served in that unit back in 1862 were still in action. The regiment was now the West Point of this world, the training unit for young men destined to higher rank in the army. The 35th was coming forward, pulled from its barracks at Suzdal to serve at the front. It would be good to see the precious colors again, a last link with Maine.

Maine. Just thinking of it conjured again the fine scent of a summer day, rich with pine and salt air. Or up on the lake in the autumn, the haunting cries of the loons in the moonlight, the call of Canadian geese at dawn as they took wing on their southward journey. He sighed with the memory.

Tomorrow the front again. How many times have I played chance with death and beaten it? How many more times? He sensed, of late, an exhaustion with the game, a deadening of the senses, a feeling that it would simply go on and on until finally the darkness won. Pray if that's the case, let it be swift, not lingering under the knife, or worse, crippled, an object of pity, consigned to some chair by a window and then forgotten.

Maine. If only that was still real. To retreat to that precious land, a land that was once his entire life . . .

"Andrew?"

Surprised, he looked up and saw her staring at him.

"You haven't said a word in five minutes, Andrew. Are you all right?"

He smiled. "Just tired."

She leaned over and kissed him lightly on the forehead.

"Not too tired I hope, dear," she whispered. Extending her hand, she led him out from behind the desk.

For a brief instant he looked back at all that still had to be done. Pat was back at the front, he was to go up tomorrow to observe, all this had to be cleared out first.

"Tomorrow, Andrew me darlin'," she whispered, deliberately slipping into a lilting brogue which she knew could always work its spell.

"Tomorrow," he whispered, glad that she would at least block out, for a few minutes, all the fears and all the memories.

Chapter Four

"A good day for a fight it is," Pat announced cheerily, coming to attention and saluting as Andrew stepped down from the armored train, which was coasting to a stop. Pat, having come back up to the front immediately after the meeting, was obviously exhausted; most likely he had been up all night directing the evacuation of the line.

Even above the sound of the venting steam Andrew could hear the sharp reports of artillery. On a low ridge, a mile to the north, he saw a battery dug in around the rubble of an abandoned villa firing at an unseen target.

"Probing on the flank, ironclads, at least twenty of them coming down."

Pat pulled a burned-out cigar from his mouth and motioned toward a wooded grove to the left and rear of the villa. Half a dozen ironclads were in reserve waiting for the enemy, while a thin line of calvary were mounting up and deploying farther back to the west.

"Been coming out in echelon since dawn."

"How wide a front?"

"Five miles or so, but it looks like the main blow is shaping up here, trying to cut this rail depot before the last of the troops get out of the town."

Andrew said nothing. Pat was a master of the fighting withdrawal. His final sting would be the ironclads, though that tactic did worry Andrew. If the enemy came on too fast, the precious machines might have to be abandoned, since it took time to load them onto the trains.

Straight ahead, the scene had an apocalyptic aura to

it. The city of Capua was on fire, the pillar of coiling smoke rising straight up on the still morning air, mushrooming out, the image dark and sinister. The dark column blocked the morning sun, so that the landscape seemed dim, shadowy, illuminated more by the soaring flames than by the cold winter sun.

Trains lined the sidings which had been hastily constructed in anticipation that here would be the front line. Regiments pulled out from the front under cover of darkness were wearily loading into the boxcars, men moving slowly, stiffly, gratefully holding out their tin cups and canteens as they shuffled past a commissary unit that had been boiling up hundreds of gallons of tea. Once past the tea they opened their haversacks for commissary department women who dumped in handfuls of hardtack, salted pork, and dried beans. The endless column shuffled by, oblivious to the bombardment raging along the ridgeline.

Another train, fully loaded with three regiments of troops, started up, pulling out of the siding and onto the main track heading west. Five more trains were lined up, waiting for the last of the troops, the last division of infantry to leave the flaming city of Capua behind. The withdrawal had gone without a hitch. Two corps had disengaged and pulled out by foot two days ago. Two more corps had evacuated yesterday and were now fifteen miles to the west, while the last two corps had been pulled out during the night. After years of experience his railroaders were masters at the game, and he felt they would have beaten the old United States Military Railroad hands down when it came to operations in support of an army totally dependent on the railroad for survival.

Even his own train was a masterpiece of design. Heavily armored, the cab in front of the engine carried two gatling guns, powered by a steam line hooked back to the engine. Two cabs behind carried six breechloading fieldpieces and two more gatlings, and a car was loaded with extra rails and tools in case they came across a break in the line.

Andrew filtered into the group of weary infantrymen shuffling past, motioning for the men to stand at ease.

"Which unit you boys with?"

"16th Suzdal sir," a hollow-eyed boy replied.

Andrew did a quick mental check; 3rd Division, 6th Corps, three weeks on the front line.

"You'll get a couple days' relief back at Roum, son—warm food, beds, a roof over your head."

The boy nodded, and for a second Andrew thought the lad was about to break down in tears.

"Tough time up there?"

"Lost near to half the regiment," a sergeant interjected. "Sir, did you just say a couple of days? Rumor was we were pulling back to Hispania, maybe to Kev, and wait till spring before we fought again."

Andrew shook his head.

"Sorry, sergeant. We're building defenses around Roum. We hold there."

"Let Roum defend itself," someone behind Andrew said.

Andrew turned around and saw an angry captain, frozen bandage around his forehead, glaring defiance.

"Captain, they're our comrades, part of the Republic. We can't abandon the city without a flight."

"Hell, we abandoned all of Rus against the Merki. The boys here figure let's do the same again but this time let Roum carry the cost. Some folks said the Bantag won't come any farther if they get Roum."

"That's what the Bantag want us to believe."

"Well sir, my boys here, they've been out in the middle of nowhere for three months now. Every day retreating. We thought we had 'em stopped all the way up on the Shenandoah. Then it was to Port Lincoln. Then we fought at the Rocky Hill. Then on the retreat all the way back to here at Capua. Now it's Roum. Sir, we'll get surrounded in there, our backs to the sea. They could move on to our homes, and then where will we be?"

"In Roum, son. They try to move on Suzdal and we cut them off from behind."

"Let Roum fight for Roum, sir."

Andrew tensed, and the captain, suddenly sensing he'd gone too far, lowered his head, waiting for the blow.

Andrew stared at the captain, not sure for a moment how to react. It had been a long time since someone in the ranks had so openly questioned his strategy. He looked sidelong at Pat, who stood at the back of the group, arms folded, a bit of a mischievous grin lighting his features.

Andrew took a deep breath and blew out, mist coiling around him.

"This how most of you boys feel?" he asked.

Some of the men, embarrassed, averted their eyes or lowered their heads, but more than one nodded.

"Boys, I don't have the time right now to explain it all. Some of you might not like the folks from Roum all that much. I've heard some mutter about them being heathens, or that they haven't carried their share of the fight. Believe me, when it comes to fighting I count on their regiments just as much as the ones from Suzdal, from Rus. You boys were inside the pocket with me and fought at the Rocky Hill. Remember it was two corps of Roum troops that fought their way in to us and got us out of that trap."

Several of the men grudgingly nodded agreement.

"Well, there was not talk then about who was Rus and who was Roum. We can't evacuate all of Roum the way we did Suzdal back in the Merki war. It was early spring then, not the dead of winter. Besides, by holding Roum we'll have shelter to fight from. Every house will be a fortress. If we can hold till spring, the rail lines they've laid will disappear into the mud and they'll be cut off.

"I'm going to have to ask you men to trust me. Now, I'll be back in Roum tonight. If some of you want to come see me tomorrow to talk it over, that's fine with me. Pick out some men from the other regiments—enlisted men only, captain, if you don't mind. Come see me and we'll talk."

Andrew's tone indicated that the meeting was at an end. The men, caught off guard, nodded their thanks, some saluting. The captain looked as though he wanted to say something more but lowered his head.

Andrew turned, Pat falling in by his side and chuckling.

"What's so damn funny?"

"Could you imagine Little Mac or old snapping turtle Meade allowing us boys to talk to him like that?"

"I've got a warm bed most nights, they don't. Besides, this is a republic. There are times a general's gotta listen to a private. I don't have to agree, but I've got to listen."

"Retreat's hard on these boys," Pat said. "He was right on that. We've been running for three months now. It starts to get to be habit. Damn difficult to finally turn an army around to make a stand."

Andrew nodded, distracted because his glasses had fogged over and frozen. Pat reached over, took the glasses, wiped them, and passed them back to Andrew.

"Fabian tactics, Pat."

"Who's that?"

"Roman general who faced Hannibal. Scorched earth, fall back, delay and delay, then fall back. We've got to stretch Ha'ark out to the breaking point and then when we do we cut his head off."

"How, Andrew? We're at the breaking point, too. Fabian or not, retreat's hard on an army, hard on the soul."

Andrew nodded. Hard on the soul. Yes, but could he ever admit that about himself? The strain was almost beyond bearing. The waiting for the day when the Bantag fell behind, gave up, stopped to give Andrew's forces the breathing room to rebuild their strength. Yet Ha'ark kept coming in, day after day. God, to be able to rest, to have a day, a week, a precious season without him always there, always pressing in. Just to rest, to escape all this.

Yet again he realized he had drifted off into silence, staring blankly at the horizon. He stirred, seeing Pat watching him.

"Casualties today?"

"Not bad. Under a hundred pulling out. A few of the pickets out forward were taken—they started to probe in around three in the morning. Buggers are not as afraid of the dark as they were, but we put a real twist on them . . . caltrops, land torpedoes, barrels of benzene with slow fuses buried in the snow. You could hear the devils howling."

"Can you see their front?"

"They're crossing the river now."

"Their land ironclads?"

"Swarms of them up on the flank. The real battle is brewing up there." Pat nodded toward the ridgeline, where the battery dug in around the ruined villa was increasing its tempo of fire.

Andrew took a deep breath. He was up at the front, he had to see, that was expected. He felt a prickle of fear but pushed it aside.

"I want to see."

Pat nodded and motioned for his orderlies to bring two horses over. Mounting, Andrew grimaced as the cold of the saddle seeped through his pants, chilling him. Following Pat's lead, he trotted through the snow, eyes watering in the chilled air. Stopping just below the villa, Pat dismounted.

"Can't ride up there. They're getting pretty good at spotting groups of riders and dropping a mortar round right in on them."

He pointed to his greatcoat, torn open by a shell fragment, a frozen streak of blood soaked into the frayed fabric.

Andrew started to voice a concern, but Pat laughed.

"Far worse than that in my life. Just a nick."

"Don't let Emil hear you say that. He's hollering like mad about the men staying clean. Says that infections from wounds are climbing."

"Everyone and me included is lousy, Andrew. Just how the hell are we suppose to wash in this blasted cold?"

There was a flash of anger in his voice, and then he forced a smile.

"Please keep your head down, Andrew darlin'. Like I

said, they're getting good at spotting us. Ain't like the old days when you could just go galloping around."

Andrew, keeping low, stepped into the narrow trench that zigzagged up the reverse slope and led into the ruined villa. Following Pat's lead, he scrambled through the rubble, motioning for the observation team in the ruins to stay with their tasks. He looked around at the ruins and felt, yet again, as if he had stepped back in time, though this time the wreckage fit more to his image of how the ancient world now looked.

The roof of the villa had collapsed, charred beams overhead standing out darkly against the icy blue crystal sky straight overhead. Flame-scorched frescos covered the walls of the room, the scenes from ancient mythology, or current religion, Andrew mused.

Pat saw him examining the wall, a scene of nymphs being chased by satyrs, and chuckled. "Look in what's left of the next room," he suggested, pointing to a broken doorway, the overhead lintel smashed down.

Andrew stepped to the door and looked into the room, and retreated a second later, a bit embarrassed with the realization he was blushing.

"Better than them French cards we had back with the Army of the Potomac," Pat chuckled. "Never knew people could do some of the things painted in there. The boys here are really miffed—there was a beautiful portrait, never seen a lady with such ample charms, and a shell blew it apart an hour ago." He pointed sadly to the opposite wall, which was now just a pile of shattered bricks and plaster.

Andrew shook his head and followed Pat through ruins and up to what was left of the north wall, where a firing position for a ten-pound breechloader had been hacked out of the ruins. Broken timbers piled up to either side and above provided some protection from the mortars of the Bantag.

A shell whispered down, Andrew ducking for cover as it detonated on the far side of the wall.

"Just about have us zeroed in," Pat announced as he handed over his field glasses to Andrew.

Andrew stepped up to a hole cut in the wall and peered out. The view was panoramic. The long open slope sweeping down from the prominence they were on had been planted in grapes, the trellises covered with dark vines currently covered with snow. The passage of a Republic ironclad directly in front of their position had cut an ugly swath through the orderly landscape. He could imagine a time before the Republic when this land was cultivated by slaves. To damage even one of the vines would have earned the harshest of punishments; now they were tearing them to shreds in order to save them.

The vineyard swept across the open field and up to a low series of hills nearly two miles away. In the glasses he could see another ruined villa up there, a small cluster of outbuildings around it, several of them burning, the villa pouring out dark gouts of smoke. There was barely a glimpse of a village on the next ridge several miles beyond, all of it consumed in fire, a black column of smoke rising from it in feeble mimicry of the conflagration consuming Capua.

Off to his right at the lower end of the valley that emptied out into the flood plains around Capua he saw a ragged line of Bantag skirmishers advancing on foot. A quarter mile in front of them a unit of mounted infantry was pulling back slowly, some of the men dismounting for a moment to fire a few shots, then mounting again to pull back.

"Not much pressure over there," Andrew said.

"The marshy ground north of the city is tough going. Even though it's frozen, those big bastards still break through the crust. The main column's going to have to come through the city, and the way that's burning it'll be sundown before they can advance. The only worry now is the units that flanked us and the ironclads that came with them."

He pointed back to the next ridge to the north, where distant figures moved through the snow.

"And the flanking cavalry?"

"All our mounted infantry, supported by artillery, is

screening the rail line. Timokin's armored regiment is engaging along that ridge ahead, holding their ironclads back. Had one breakthrough to the track but closed it off before they could do any damage."

Andrew nodded, having seen the piles of Bantag bodies ten miles back. Damn all, he thought again. Because a couple of damn umens get behind us we lose this position. Stringing the army out to protect seventy-five miles of track was simply impossible. But his attention was fixed farther forward where a line of a dozen ironclads of the Republic, the center one flying the yellow triangle pennant of the 1st Ironclad Regiment, were drawing back over the top of the ridge, moving in reverse.

A geyser of dirty snow erupted beside the lead ironclad, long seconds later the thunderclap boom echoing over Andrew.

"At least they must be warm in there," Pat announced with a grin.

Cursing the boiling heat, Lieutenant Colonel Gregory Timokin leaned back and reached up, popping open the top hatch of his ironclad, *St. Malady*, breathing deeply as frigid air cascaded down into the turret.

Cursing erupted below as his crew, stripped to the waist in the steaming heat inside the steam-powered ironclad, shouted to him to shut the hatch.

Ignoring their complaints, he stood up, bracing his elbows on the outside of the turret, and quickly scanned the landscape. Another mortar round detonated nearby, fragments whirring past, striking the side of his ironclad with ringing metallic pings. Looking to left and right he saw his first company arrayed in good order, slightly aft of the ridge, hulls down, waiting. Two ironclads burned fiercely over on the next ridge, one Bantag and one of his. He whispered a silent prayer for the crew. It had been their first action . . . and it was a damned waste of a good machine.

Resting his elbows on the top of the open hatch, he raised his field glasses and scanned the opposite ridge. Bantag mounted units were moving just beyond the reverse slope, their deployment revealed by the fine plumes of powdery snow kicked up. Damn, they were learning. Now if only the bastards would charge, the gatling would cut them to ribbons.

Darker swirls of smoke were rising up as well on the still morning air. Waiting, he counted them off. Nearly thirty . . . a full brigade of machines. He grinned in anticipation.

Looking to either side he saw his ironclad commanders, heads out of hatches, waiting for orders. He raised his hand, pointed to the smoke, then extended both arms out, fists clenched, and dropped his arms down, signaling that they were to wait for the enemy to close.

The first enemy ironclad cleared the ridge, followed within seconds by two dozen more, dismounted infantry fanning out around them.

Sliding back down into the turret, he locked the hatch. "Load case shot, five-second fuse. Aim for their mortar batteries if they deploy out!"

Gregory grinned. This was going to be a slaughter.

Another mortar detonated just in front of the villa, Andrew ducking down as fragments sliced the air overhead.

"There must be thirty machines over there. More than I figured," Pat announced. "He's trying for a breakthrough."

Andrew looked back behind him to where the long columns of infantry were still loading onto the trains. If the ironclads should break through, he thought, it will be chaos. They'll shoot up the locomotives and strand the better part of two divisions. He felt impotent; this was a new type of war, and increasingly it was a war that he was forced to be detached from. If that had been a Bantag cavalry or infantry charge coming in, he would have been mounted, deploying his troops out, riding the length of his line. Instead he was crouched down in a dugout, forced to sit and watch, to do nothing.

Pat reached into his pocket, pulled out two cigars,

puffed both of them to life, and offered one to Andrew, who gladly took it and settled back to watch.

The Bantag machines, cloaked in clouds of coiling black smoke, slid down the slope, snow plowing out like waves curling back from the bow of a ship.

Half a dozen mortar batteries, dismounting on the ridge behind them, were opening up, shells raining down around the Republic's ironclads so that it sounded to Gregory like hail rattling against a window pane.

The enemy ironclads lurched to a stop, still two hundred yards short of extreme range for the anti-ironclad bolts, and opened up with a sustained barrage of shrapnel, drenching the slope around Gregory. Bantag infantry by the hundreds charged forward, wading through the snow straight toward him. Sighting in his gatling, he opened the steam cock, lowered the barrel, and squeezed a quick burst, signaling for the other ironclads armed with gatlings to open fire as well.

The long morning's fight had depleted more than half his cartridge rounds, so he limited himself to short bursts, aiming where groups of the Horde were bunching up, dropping one or two, sending the rest scattering.

Still the enemy ironclads did not advance. A thunderclap boom snapped through his machine, the impact of the shell on the forward armor hurling him against the hot barrel of the gatling. Cursing, he pulled his hands back.

"All right below?" he shouted, leaning forward to look down between his legs to where his crew labored. Gunnery Sergeant Basil Vasilovich was cursing loudly, holding his arm, which was torn open just below the elbow.

Basil looked up and nodded. "Damned bolt sheered off. I'll be all right. Let's go for the bastards, sir."

Gregory turned his turret to the left with his hand crank, looking left, then right. One of his machines was backing down from the firing line, the barrel of its ten-pound gun cocked at a strange angle. Damn, a lucky hit on the gun port must have dismounted the piece, he thought.

He looked back forward. Up on the far ridge he could see swirling crystalline clouds of snow powder. They must be moving more mounted units around to the flank. They'd extend our line out, then try to cut the rail.

Uncorking the speaking tube that snaked aft to his engineer, he blew on it.

"Yuri, full steam. We're charging!"

"Full steam it is, sir."

Gregory braced himself as Yuri opened the steam valves into the drive pistons. He could feel the rear drive wheels spin over in the snow until the heavy cleats on the iron wheels finally caught and gripped the ground underneath. *St. Malady* lurched forward. Yuri held down on the steam whistle with three long blasts, signaling to the other ironclads to charge.

"Their orders are to hold, then pull back once the trains are out," Andrew snapped.

"Flanking force, Andrew," Pat replied, pointing to his left. Andrew's glasses were steaming up again and it was hard to see.

"Timokin knows what he's doing; their ironclads are slower—he'll tear 'em up, then cut into the cavalry beyond the next ridge."

"Wish he'd hold."

"Well, it's too late now," Pat chuckled.

Trusting to Basil's judgment, Gregory stayed up in the turret, leaving the aiming of the ten-pounder to his gunner. The Bantag machines had switched over to solid bolts. Another one impacted on their forward shield, sparks flaring up in front of his view port.

One of the Bantag machines erupted, fire and smoke pouring out of its stack, followed less than a second later by a roaring blowtorch explosion bursting out its forward gunport.

He felt his own machine lurch as Basil fired. A second later the brass cartridge ejected, clanking with a bell-like ring. A pillar of snow kicked up just forward of the enemy machine now less than two hundred yards straight ahead.

The Bantag ironclads were holding their position, and he grinned. If they want a stand-up, knock-down fight, well here it comes.

Explosions rippled up and down the line as the two units slowed, lurching to a stop, guns blazing.

From around the enemy machines hundreds of Bantag emerged, charging on foot. In the swirling confusion it was hard to make them out; they were covered in white blankets, and as they went down, they disappeared, then they would lurch back up and rush forward again half a dozen strides, then go down again.

Conserving ammunition, he let off short bursts, aiming at the infantry, then shifting to the ironclads for a moment, hoping to put a shot in through the open gunports.

An explosion rocked him. Unbolting his hatch, he stuck his head out and saw one of his machines, the third one down on his right, cooking off. But straight ahead half a dozen Bantag machines were now ablaze. The enemy machines started to lurch backward, retreating.

Sliding back down into the turret, he called for full speed forward. The Bantag infantry now moving in the middle between the two battling lines went to ground, burrowing into the snow. Well, if they wanted to get run over, let them. Lowering his aim with the gatling, he fired random sprays of shots, kicking up the snow. Occasionally a Bantag would rear up, his white camouflaged poncho streaked bright red, then collapse.

Another Bantag ironclad flamed up. "Good shot, Basil!" he roared.

Turning his turret to either side, he saw that his line of ironclads were advancing, spreading out, the two on the left angling off to advance up the slope to catch their flanking column.

As he started to turn his turret to the right, he caught a glimpse of a signal flare rising up from the enemy-held ridge . . . most likely ordering the infantry to pull back. Good, they're sitting ducks.

Hundreds of Bantag now rose up, but rather than retreat, they broke into a loping charge, leaping through the knee-high snow.

Well, if they want to die, let them, he thought grimly, and held down with a long burst on his gatling, bowling over dozens. The three other ironclads armed with gatlings joined in, so that long stitching lines of machine gun fire laced back and forth across the field.

More Bantag rose out the snow, and he noticed that many of them were grouped in teams of three, carrying long pipes that were painted white.

"What the hell?" he whispered, turning his gun to wipe one of the teams out.

But before he could swing his gun around, the team stopped, two of them hoisting the long pipe onto their shoulders and aiming it straight at him. The third Bantag appeared to strike a spark and hold it to the back end of the pipe, then ducked to one side.

An instant later a flash of light erupted. He barely saw the rocket as it streaked out, coming straight at him, roaring past his turret.

Startled, he held fire for a second, not sure what had just happened. The third warrior reached around to his back, pulled a mushroom-shaped projectile off a harness on his back, and slapped it into the front of the pipe, the mushroom head of the rocket on the outside of the launching tube. Gregory aimed and squeezed off a long burst, riddling the team.

Fighting down a growing sense of panic, he pivoted his turret and saw dozens of teams armed with the rocket launchers running toward his ironclads, fanning out, moving into firing positions on the flanks.

Frantically he opened fire, holding the trigger down while screaming for Basil to switch to canister and to aim for the rocket teams.

A fireball erupted, and swinging his turret, he saw one of his machines blow apart, and then another.

"Yuri! Full reverse! Signal retreat!"

A long sustained blast of the whistle nearly deafened him as *St. Malady* lurched to a stop and then started to crawl backward. He saw a wide swath of snow swirling upward by his flank, the battery on the hill behind him firing canister straight into the melee.

"They're on our left!" Basil screamed.

Gregory swung his turret and saw, less than twenty yards away, a rocket team already in position, raising their rocket launcher. He sprayed them, the close fire tearing the three Bantag to shreds. He saw another team kneeling down in the snow, aiming on *St. Katrina*, the machine to his left. He bowled them over, and then there was an ominous click . . . the ammunition hopper was empty.

Another Bantag team, as if sensing his dilemma, stood up from their concealed position in the snow and charged forward, racing toward his left flank.

"Back us around to the right!" Gregory roared. "Basil, get them, dammit, get them!"

St. Malady slowly started to pivot. The Bantag continued to run, dodging around the side of *St. Katrina*. They wanted the command machine—they could have turned around and hit *St. Katrina* from twenty feet away, but they wanted him. Raging, he fumbled at the holster on his hip, trying to pull out his revolver. The rocket launcher was lowered, aimed straight at him. He felt as if the universe were going down. He saw the loader slide a friction primer into the back of the tube, duck down, and then jerk the lanyard.

At almost the same instant an explosion of steam erupted below him, swirling up into the turret. As if from an eternity away he heard Yuri shrieking hysterically. Panic-stricken, he clawed at the turret hatch, heaved it open, and pulled himself out, expecting the ammunition lockers below to detonate at any second. A humming roar snapped around him, canister going downrange, and the team that had destroyed his machine went down in the blast. Rolling out of the open hatch, he slammed down onto the top deck of the ironclad and fell off into the snow. Gasping, terrified, he got up, staggering, falling, then getting up to run. Looking back, he saw the side hatch opening, Basil, screaming, clutching his face, falling out.

For a terror-filled instant he struggled with the desire to run away, then turned to go back. Billowing clouds of steam poured out the open hatch. Grabbing Basil under the shoulder, he hoisted him up.

"The others?"

"Dead," Basil gasped. "All dead."

Gregory looked around wildly. Half a dozen of his machines were on fire, the others pulling slowly back up the hill, pursued by the rocket launcher teams. Across the valley the enemy ironclads had stopped their feigned retreat and were lurching forward again.

Staggering through the snow, he saw one of the Bantags who had destroyed his machine, sitting in the snow, which was going slushy pink beneath him. The Bantag stared at him blankly and then to his surprise lowered his head, as if awaiting the killing blow.

More Bantag infantry were moving up, and looking back up to the ridgeline he saw a solid wall of mounted warriors deploying out. The bastards weren't flanking, they were coming straight in.

It was a good kill, he thought grimly, a damn good kill, you bastards. Ignoring the warrior, he started up the slope, dragging Basil along with him. *St. Katrina* slowed for a moment, its turret swinging back and forth, spraying out a long sustained burst, and then came to a stop, its side hatch opening up.

"Keep going, keep going!" Gregory roared, but the engineer was already out the door, staggering through the snow, helping to grab Basil. Together they raced to the machine and piled inside while *St. Katrina*'s gunner held the rocket teams at bay. A round streaked past with a loud shriek, corkscrewing through the air in a wild erratic flight.

Close range, Gregory realized, like the one that got us, real close range. How does it work? The mushroom-shaped shell must be all explosive, steel plate wrapped around it to focus the blast against the armor. Damn.

Collapsing against an ammunition locker, he looked up numbly as the engineer threw his machine into reverse and they continued to lurch up the hill. A loud tearing shriek ran through the ironclad, and, terrified, Gregory looked up and saw the bulge in the side armor, flakes of paint and sheared-off metal clanking about inside the machine so that he ducked low, covering his head.

"The bastards are charging!" he heard the forward gunner scream. "By Kesus, there's thousands of 'em!"

The battery was pouring out shot in thundering salvos, Pat roaring encouragement, moving from piece to piece to make sure the aim was low. Andrew looked back down at the trains.

The last of the troop trains were pulling out, men standing on the open flatcars, looking anxiously up toward the hill. All that was left was the train waiting for the ironclads and batteries. But given what was happening below, he doubted if they could get equipment out.

The first of the retreating ironclads clattered by to his right, a hole neatly drilled into its port side. The six ironclads held in reserve crested up to the top of the ridge to provide cover for the retreat, their blasts of gatling fire momentarily holding back the onrush of the triumphal Bantags. Miraculously the boiler and ammunition aboard the damaged ironclad had not detonated and someone inside was still driving it.

"Those rockets," Pat said, "they shouldn't have the power to punch armor like that."

Andrew nodded. Damn all. Again Ha'ark must know something that we don't.

"We better get out of here," Pat said.

Dammit, mobile rocket launchers, shoulder-mounted. We should have thought of that, we should have thought of that, Andrew muttered to himself. With Chuck Ferguson gone, they seemed to have lost the edge on such things.

"Spike the guns!" Pat shouted. "Let's go!"

Andrew followed Pat out through the back of the villa, where their nervous staff waited with the horses. Mortar rounds fluttered down, columns of snow erupted. Looking off to the west, he saw where one wing of the Bantag advance was already over the crest. The gatlings on the rear car of the armored train were arcing long blasts of fire, the tracer rounds soaring high in the still morning air, then arcing over and plummeting down, keeping the advance back.

Andrew's mount shied nervously as a mortar detonated nearby. He swayed precariously, sawing on the reins. He heard another mortar round fluttering in. It was close, too close, barely an instant to realize it, to feel his heart seize up with fear . . . and then there was nothing but blue sky overhead.

It was strange, everything was silent. He could see his guidon bearer, slumped over in his saddle, horse going over, the distant shrieking of the dying animal finally penetrating. He tried to sit up. He knew he was hit. The question, the all-consuming question now, was where? Pat was by his side, mouth open, shouting, looking up, furiously waving his arm.

As if his body were somehow detached he realized he should breathe, he had to tell his body to breathe. He drew air in, and then the pain hit, an exploding wave of red-hot fire in his chest. He started to cough, and the agony doubled. It was worse, far worse than the arm; he had never imagined such pain was possible. Curling into a ball, he rolled on his side, another cough seizing him. Somehow the air wasn't going in, and he struggled with the panic of suffocation. He felt a heavy arm embracing him, someone shouting to him.

"Don't die on me, Andrew! Don't die!" The voice was terrified. It was Pat.

Another spasm of coughing, and something salty filled his mouth, and he spat it out onto snow that instantly turned pink.

Pat was still shouting, something about Emil, and an orderly viciously kicked his mount to a gallop and started down the hill.

He felt arms around him, lifting him up, two orderlies both wide-eyed with fear.

Breathe, I have to breathe! I'm drowning in my own blood. With a shuddering gasp he drew the air in, an obscenity escaping him as he exhaled.

Pat was up on a horse reaching out to him.

"God no," he gasped. "I can't, I can't."

"Goddammit, Andrew, you have to!"

The orderlies, as if cradling a baby, lifted him up, and Pat reached out, sweeping him into his arms. He could hear another shell whistling in, and he felt terror at the sound of it, burying his face into Pat's chest as the round detonated, spraying them with snow.

Pat spurred his mount into a gallop, an orderly riding alongside reaching over to take the reins and guide him. Every step sent a searing wave of agony shooting through his chest. He anticipated each jarring blow, each step of the horse, bracing for the knifelike stab, struggling to breathe, coughing, half vomiting out the blood clogging his lungs.

He opened his eyes again. Everything was blurry. He felt naked and even more afraid now that he couldn't see.

"My glasses," he groaned. "Lost my glasses."

"It's all right, Andrew darlin', you'll make it, you'll make it."

Pat kept repeating the same words over and over, as if reassuring a child. Andrew felt the horse sliding, almost losing its footing. There was a warm blast of heat, steam from the train. Suddenly he realized just how cold he was, and he started to shiver. More hands were reaching up, and there was a stretcher.

He looked up. Someone was swearing, the sea of frightened faces withdrawing. Andrew felt as if he would break down in tears at the sight of Emil Weiss, looking like a guardian angel gazing down at him.

There was a memory of before . . . Gettysburg, that same fatherly look as they carried him into the field hospital behind Cemetery Hill.

Emil disappeared from view, and Andrew called his name.

He felt a hand slip into his. "Right here, son, right here."

They lifted him up into the car. The inside was dark, sulfurous, the roar of gatlings filling the iron-cased chamber.

The stretcher was down on the floor, Emil kneeling by his side. Pat came in, standing behind Emil, looking down while the doctor unbuttoned his greatcoat, folding it back.

"This will hurt, Andrew. I've got to get your jacket off.

Andrew nodded as Emil braced him from behind, leaning him up. Another spasm of coughing hit, more pink foam bubbling up.

He felt the greatcoat come off, then his uniform jacket, a hospital orderly slicing the uniform and shirt with heavy scissors, then Emil laid him back down. He felt the train lurch, and wild-eyed, he looked up at Pat.

"Everyone out?"

Pat nodded.

"The ironclads?"

"The crews are out."

Andrew closed his eyes. They'd lost their ironclads, all of them, and then another wave of pain washed over him, and struggle as he would, it was impossible to focus.

"Andrew, stay with me! Don't close your eyes. Don't go to sleep!"

The voice was insistent, edged with panic.

He opened his eyes. Emil was leaning close, face only inches away.

"Andrew, you're bleeding inside. You've got a shell fragment in your right lung. I've got to go in and get it out."

"Pat, Roum," Andrew whispered.

Pat leaned forward.

"Hold Roum at all cost. I stay there. Don't move me to Suzdal. I stay there."

"Now, Andrew," Emil interjected.

"I stay in Roum. That's where we stand."
He reached up, grabbing Emil by the shoulder.
"Emil?"
"Here, son."
"Not a cripple, don't leave me a cripple, let me go."
The doctor finally nodded.
He saw the cone of white paper come down.
"Just breathe deep, Andrew."
The sickly sweet smell of ether engulfed him.

Chapter Five

General Patrick O'Donald, shoulders slumped with weariness, walked into the office and paused. Somehow it seemed like a sacrilege to go behind the desk and sit down. He hesitated, looking over at Kal, who had been sitting in the room waiting for him.

"How is he?"

Pat shook his head. "Lost a lot of blood. Emil stopped the bleeding, but chest wounds, they're tricky. Seen some you thought would die pull through, but most, well, the infection gets in their lungs . . ." His voice trailed off.

"Kesus save us," Kal whispered. "Of all of us I never thought he'd get hit. First Ferguson, Hawthorne's barely able to walk, now Andrew."

"He always seemed to have that light about him," Pat sighed. "You know? There's some that you just know will never get hit. That was Andrew. It's like a charm has broken for our army."

He was afraid to even say the words. He had seen it in the eyes of the men as word spread that Andrew had been wounded, perhaps fatally. Somehow it seemed to leap ahead of the train. At the station a mob, and there was no better word for it, of troops swarmed about the train, some of them openly crying. At that moment Pat could sense that the very fiber of the army was beginning to disintegrate.

Pat nodded in reluctant agreement when Kal motioned for him to sit down in Andrew's chair. As he settled in behind the desk all the weight of Andrew's responsibility bore down upon him.

"I think this changes things," Kal finally ventured after a long moment of silence.

Pat looked up.

"How so?"

"This defense of Roum. It was Andrew's idea. Maybe with his skill we could have held it." Kal fell silent, embarrassed. "No offense, Pat, I didn't mean it to sound like that."

Pat shook his head. "I'm not Andrew. Point to where you want me to fight and I'll do it. I'm not Andrew."

"That's why I think we should pull out now."

Pat jerked his head up in surprise.

"Sir?"

"You heard me, Pat. Andrew's wounded. Kesus willing, he'll be back, good as new in a month. But Pat, Kesus forbid, suppose he doesn't," and as he uttered the dreaded words the president lowered his head.

"If Andrew dies, by God we still fight. That's what he wanted. Sir, just before Emil put him under, his last words were to hold Roum."

"You know I was against our making our stand here," Kal replied as if not hearing what Pat had just said.

"That decision was made more than a week ago."

"Pat, Andrew is no longer in command."

Pat sighed and closed his eyes. Of all the things he wanted most right now, foremost was a good drink of vodka. He knew where the bottle was in Andrew's desk, but he fought the temptation down. Not now. After this, after the next battle, after the war, or good God willing after Andrew came back to sit behind this desk.

"No, sir, but I am."

"Are you? You were in command of First Army, Hans the Second, and Vincent the reserves and western front. I would think Hans would be senior, and he is not here."

"Sir, Hans is two hundred and fifty miles away. Vincent can barely walk. Andrew said in front of Emil that I was in command, and by all that's holy, I'll follow his orders, even if it's his last one."

"Pat, listen to me, please. Roum is a trap. They could

sweep right past us here, cutting off our army and taking the rail line, then move straight on to Suzdal. All we have there are Home Guard units and what's left of 5th Corps. Nearly seven corps are bottled up here. Get them out while we still can."

"How? In three days' time the Bantag will be north of us and will cut the rail. You're talking about moving nearly a hundred thousand men."

"Then by sea."

"And what about the civilians here? We're hoping they won't move any major forces down the east coast of the sea, and there are nearly a million civilians down there and one corps to cover them. There'll be nearly half a million more in this city and the rest of them moving westward to get out of the way. If we pull out, sir, the pressure will be off Ha'ark. He could take his time, fan out, and slaughter everyone, then in the spring come for us."

"I think they will be slaughtered anyhow."

"Let me get this straight, Kal. You're talking about abandoning not just this city but all the people of this state, aren't you?"

"Pat, I think they're doomed anyhow."

"Not if we stay, dammit. Ha'ark is stretched. He'll have to come straight to us, afraid that if we even break out temporarily and cut his rail line he's finished. By God, sir, you are talking about citizens of the Republic, and this army is sworn to defend them."

"By defending them we might all die."

Pat leaned forward, staring straight at Kal. "This is the Senate talking, isn't it? Some of those same damn old boyars we should have shot years ago. They want to sell out Roum, strike a separate peace with Ha'ark."

Embarrassed, Kal lowered his head.

"He made you another offer, didn't he?"

Kal nodded.

"Out with it. What was it?"

"The army withdraws back to Rus. Any Roum who want to go with us can. We tear up the rail line between

Roum and Rus and he'll acknowledge the rights of the Republic."

"And you believe that horseshit?" Pat snarled.

"It could buy time at worst. Or at best he'll turn about and continue eastward come spring. We've defeated two Hordes. The others, let the others go as they once did, forever riding eastward, and we'll finally have peace."

"First off, they'll be back in twenty years."

"That's twenty years, Pat. Twenty years of peace. We can build, fortify. They would not dare to touch us then." His voice softened. "And the killing will stop."

"And leave the job for the next generation. Some legacy."

"Our generation is fought out, Pat. There isn't a family in Rus that hasn't lost a father, husband, or son. We lost two, three times as many as we would have if we had just submitted to the Tugars."

"As slaves, worse than slaves, as cattle," Pat snarled. "By God, Andrew might be dying, the man who freed you from slavery, and this is your thanks."

"We need to survive now, Pat. Since this war started we've been losing. We've retreated over five hundred miles. Three corps have been smashed. When in hell will this end? When Suzdal is in flames?"

"Well, if it does burn we'll go down fighting. At least the men of the 35th Maine and 44th New York will. This is the second war we've fought to end slavery, and we'll be damned if in the end we crawl on our knees and hold our hands up for the chains. You people did it long enough, but we sure as hell won't."

Kal visibly winced at Pat's bitter words. Pat wanted to apologize, sensing he had gone too far, but his anger was up and he remained silent, glaring defiantly at the president.

"As president I can order a withdrawal."

Pat looked down at his uniform jacket. Flecks of blood—Andrew's blood was on it. And what would Andrew do, the one who wrote the Constitution, who had breathed life into the concept of a republic on this alien world? What would Andrew say?

"Andrew always said the military must ultimately take orders from the civilian branch," Kal pressed, as if having read his thoughts.

"And Vice President Marcus, the Roum, what of them?"

"They can have sanctuary in Rus. Ha'ark said we'd be allowed to withdraw."

Pat laughed sadly and shook his head. "Once we're strung out, halfway through the move, a million and a half civilians with us, he'll strike. I tell you, he'll strike."

"You and Andrew said he's strung out as well. Tied to his rail line as we are. He doesn't want a fight any more than we do at this moment."

"Then why is he here?" Pat snapped. "If he doesn't want a fight, tell the son of a bitch he can leave at any time."

"You haven't answered my question, Pat."

Pat nodded, staring straight at Kal.

"I'm not Andrew, sir."

"What does that mean?"

"Just that."

"You mean you'll refuse."

The shadow of a grin creased Pat's features. "Sir, I think Andrew had some high-sounding words for it, something called a constitutional crisis or something like that."

"You can't."

Pat stood up and came around from behind the desk.

"Kal, you and I go way back. I remember the first time you took me to a tavern, and a fine brawl it was. We've raised many a glass together, and I hope, the saints preserve us both, we'll raise many more. But this, old friend, is a parting of the ways if you press it.

"Roum won't stand for it. The Republic will split. I don't want to act like a boyar of your old times, but I will. I'll tell the army it's ordered to stay, and by God many of them will stay. The army's been their life for half a year or more. I'll tell them that's what Andrew wanted, and they'll listen.

"So I'm telling you that plain and simple, Kal. I'm

also begging you, don't make me do this. If the wound doesn't kill poor Andrew, if this happens between us, it will kill him inside. I remember him telling me a long time ago that once an army disobeys its commander in chief, and that's you, it sets something called a precedent, whatever that is. Even if we win this war, even if we set this whole planet free the way Andrew dreams, that shadow will always be there. If our friend wanted a legacy, it was not the army, not the victories, it was the Republic."

Pat sighed, and going back behind the desk he reached into the drawer, pulled out a bottle and two glasses. Filling them, he offered one to Kal.

The president slowly stood up, and for a brief instant Pat felt a cold chill. Kal had modeled his looks after Lincoln, the black suit, the stovepipe hat, the beard, and in that moment he did look like Lincoln, bowed down with the weighty responsibilities of keeping his country alive.

As he put his hat on, Kal shook his head.

"I can't drink with you now," he whispered and started for the door.

"Mr. President."

Kal paused and looked back.

"Please don't. If for no other reason than Andrew's sake, please don't."

"What purpose is there in my being president?" Kal asked. "You Yanks gave it to me, you gave all of this to us, the Republic, and also this damn war."

"We gave ourselves freedom," Pat snapped back angrily. "Damn it all, Kal, there aren't two hundred boys left of the six hundred who came here. There are the graves of well over a hundred thousand soldiers who fought with them. We did it together, and nobody gave anything to anybody else. Freedom isn't a gift, it's a right paid for in blood."

"And how much more blood do we need?"

"Maybe all of us. You, me, all of us, but I'll be damned to hell if I ever bow to anyone. I'm Patrick O'Donald, and I damn all who think themselves better than me, boyar, some lordship back in Ireland, and especially some damn Bantag."

"I pray that you're right."

"Then we hold?"

Kal hesitated. "For now, yes."

Donning his hat, he walked out the door.

Exhaling noisily, Pat leaned back in his chair. Without bothering to argue with himself about his promise he took both glasses in turn and downed them.

"Pat O'Donald, you're permanently off the bottle, you are."

Pat looked up and saw Emil in the doorway.

Pat sadly shook his head and poured two more drinks, motioning for the doctor to sit down.

Sighing, Emil joined him, and after a false show of reluctance he picked up the glass.

"How is he, Emil?"

"I don't know yet. Cutting into him like that, on the floor of the train, it was impossible to keep the air clean. I think I stopped the bleeding. I'm afraid I'll have to go back in again. Two of the ribs were broken, and bone fragments might be lodged in the lung, but another operation would kill him. He's lost too much blood."

Emil sighed.

"Damn all, he needs blood. I've thought about the idea of taking blood from someone and putting it into him."

"Didn't you try that before?"

Emil nodded. "Five times with boys who would have died if I hadn't tried it. Three times it worked, but the other two times something went wrong. It's like the blood was wrong. Though I don't know why, they both died. I don't want to take that chance."

"And if you don't?"

"I think I'll lose him."

"Then do it," Pat snarled.

Emil lowered his head. "It's one thing to lose him by what happened. It's another to try some damnfool experiment on him and kill him that way."

"How's Kathleen?"

"She's with him now. I relieved her of her other duties—she's no use to anyone else right now."

Pat nodded in agreement.

"What was going on in here between you and Kal? I was standing outside the door and heard some godawful hollering.

"Just that he wants to throw in the towel."

Emil sighed.

"Can we still win this? It seems like nothing but defeat's been dogging us for months now."

"It's not defeat, not yet," Pat announced. Saying the words felt strange. Ever since they had been flanked at Capua the dark thoughts of defeat had seeped into his heart. All he needed to do was voice them, to even whisper them to one other person, and he knew they would spread, take on a life of their own, and perhaps destroy what will was left.

"We hold Roum and we win. That's what Andrew wanted."

"I'd like to believe that."

"You have to."

"Emil?"

Startled, Pat looked up. Kathleen was at the doorway, eye's wide with fear.

"He's bleeding again."

Emil was on his feet, Pat following him. Emil raced past Kathleen, Pat falling in by her side. She looked at him, and reaching over he put his arm around her shoulder, as if to brace her up, and pulled her along as they ran through the old forum which had been converted into the headquarters for the upcoming battle for the city and down a flight of stairs to a secluded room where Andrew lay. As they stepped into the room, Pat instantly felt sweat beading his brow. A woodstove had been moved in, a pipe run up and punched through the ceiling.

Pat had not seen his friend since Emil had started to operate on him aboard the train, and the sight of his waxy features frightened him.

He seemed doll-like, shrunken, head moving back and

forth listlessly, lips moving, a thin trickle of blood at the corner of his mouth. Pat glanced at the floor and saw a rubber tube connected to a bottle. Dark blood was dripping into it.

Emil and Kathleen knelt down by his side. Pat nervously drew closer.

"Tell O'Donald to come up, come up," Andrew whispered. "They're on the wall."

Frightened, Pat realized Andrew had drifted back to some battle of long ago.

Emil glanced at the drain bottle and the trickle of blood at the corner of Andrew's mouth. Gently putting his head down, he listened to Andrew's chest, then straightened.

"I've got to operate," Emil whispered.

"It'll kill him," Kathleen cried.

"It'll kill him if I don't."

Emil walked over to a table by the side of the bed and started to open his medical bag while motioning for an orderly to start preparing for surgery.

Kathleen stood up, tears in her eyes.

"For God's sake let him go in peace."

"I'm not going to lose him," Emil cried. "I can't let him go."

Kathleen looked over to Pat, as if begging for support. Pat swallowed nervously.

"My blood, use my blood."

"That's too risky," Kathleen replied.

Emil looked over appraisingly at Pat.

"I should use someone else. It'll leave you weak."

"Then use mine," Kathleen said. "I'm his wife."

"I don't understand why certain bloods mix and other's won't," Emil replied. "Maybe there's a difference due to the sexes as well, so you're out, Kathleen."

"Dammit, Emil, use me," Pat interjected forcefully. "I can't just stand here and do nothing."

Emil looked back at Kathleen and then stepped to her side, putting his hands on her shoulders.

"You're his wife. You decide, Kathleen dear. Remember, though, its not just Andrew, its the army, the Republic. But if I don't go in there and finish the job,

Andrew will certainly die. At least this way he'll have a chance."

She looked down at Andrew, then finally nodded her head.

Emil called for orderlies to bring in a stretcher. Andrew was gently shifted out of the bed onto the stretcher and up onto a makeshift operating table, which was nothing more than two sawhorses with the stretcher resting atop them. Two more sawhorses were brought in and a stretcher laid across them, and Emil motioned for Pat to take his uniform jacket off and roll up his sleeve.

Suddenly Pat felt nervous, shivering slightly in spite of the heat of the room as he lay down on the stretcher by Andrew's side. Looking over at Andrew, he saw the ugly wound slicing into his side, just below the armpit. As Emil gingerly lifted the bandage off, Emil felt as if he could look clear into Andrew, and he was glad he was lying down as the doctor slipped the drain tube out and a stream of liquid dripped out with it. Strange, he had seen thousands of wounds, but this was different, this was his friend, his comrade, his commander.

Andrew's eyes fluttered open and Pat realized Andrew was looking at him.

"You hit too?" Andrew whispered, his voice full of concern.

"No, Andrew darlin', just Emil here's goin' to put a little of me precious blood into you."

He forced a laugh.

"Make you a regular Irishman it will."

Andrew smiled weekly. "Hope it gets me drunk."

He closed his eyes and then seemed to drift off into his dreams again.

Kathleen held up what looked like an oversized perfume bottle, and walking around Andrew she started to spray the air with a mixture of carbolic acid. Droplets landed in Pat's eyes and stung.

Suddenly there was the cloying fruity smell of ether as Emil opened a vial.

"Not too much," Kathleen whispered.

"I know, I can't."

The cone was over Andrew's face. Emil let several drops of ether splash onto the cone, and Andrew's drawn features relaxed as if he were already dead.

Emil now turned to Pat and held up a needle. A tube snaked from the needle to a rubber bulb, and from the bulb another tube was connected to yet another needle. Emil hurriedly explained what he was going to do, and Pat nodded, feeling quivering in his stomach.

Kathleen came over, poured a splash of Vodka on his arm, rubbed it clean, tightened a strap around his upper arm. He felt the prick of the needle as it slipped in. Pat closed his eyes, then opened them, again to look over.

Emil, down on his knees, was already at work cutting into the wound. As he watched, Pat felt as if Emil were at the distant end of a tunnel, then everything slipped away.

Riding past the burned-out hulk of a Yankee ironclad, Ha'ark reined in his horse and dismounted. In the bitter night cold the ironclad glistened with frost, catching the starlight of the Great Wheel filling the sky directly overhead.

He looked up in wonder. Which star was home? Was it even this galaxy? No, home is here, this is my place of empire. He paused for a moment. It was never proper to show curiosity, or wonder—let them wait a moment. He walked up to the ironclad, examining the hole punched into the side of the machine. Bits of flame-scorched uniform lay by the side of the machine. Some of his warriors had found a convenient dinner within. He chuckled at the thought. Already cooked.

The knot of warriors kneeling in the snow farther down the slope awaited his approach, and he finally deemed to notice them. Approaching, he gave an imperious wave for them to rise.

"Who saw this?" he asked. One of the warriors, an ironclad commander, stepped forward and bowed.

"I did, my Qar Qarth."

"Tell me."

"We were pursuing the beaten machines. The pilot of

my machine"—he paused and nodded toward another warrior, whose arm was in a sling—"shouted that he saw the one-armed cattle. I saw him too. I ordered our machine to turn to fire upon him. Mortar rounds were exploding, and then I saw him fall from his horse."

"There are other one-armed cattle—how do you know it was him?"

"There was a blue-and-golden flag beside him. I saw also the red-haired devil with him. When the one-armed cattle fell there was panic, and many gathered around. The red devil took him up on his horse and they galloped down to the iron rail steam engine and put him aboard it."

"Did you not try to stop this?" Ha'ark asked.

The warrior lowered his head. "My lord, I drove us straight at their iron rail engine. It was the one with great plates of armor all along its sides, with many guns on it. That is where we were hit and my machine destroyed."

His voice trailed off, as if expecting punishment. One of the other warriors stepped forward, carrying a Yankee flag, the one of blue and gold, and in that instant he knew for certain, this was the flag of Keane, he had seen it following him at the Battle of the Rocky Hill.

The flag was offered, and Ha'ark took it, holding it, seeing the flecks of cattle blood which stained it.

"It is as I saw it in my dreams," he announced. "You have confirmed the vision."

There were excited nods, looks of awe, a shaman at the back of the group loudly exclaiming that Ha'ark was indeed the Redeemer.

Ha'ark grinned.

"Their spells are broken," he announced. "Let all know that now. The invincible one-armed Yankee has fallen. All the cattle will now be ours."

Still holding the flag, he turned and walked away, heading down to where the rail line was. The city to his left still burned, casting a lurid light across the land. Warriors by the thousands were marching past, moving along the sides of the rail line, and he stood in the shadows, watching them. Chin cattle, staggering in the bitter night cold, were at work, salvaging rails, working along the line, running track back toward the burning city, and as they died they would help to feed his army.

A long column of horses passed behind him, pulling sleds loaded down with rations and ammunition, all of them heading west.

"Like the armies of ancient times." The words were in the tongue of his old world.

He looked over his shoulder and saw Jurak approaching, wrapped in a heavy cloak, his staff trailing behind him. His second in command dismounted and went through the ceremony of bowing.

"I see things like this and I think we are again living in the times of legends."

"We are making legends," Ha'ark replied. "All of this," and he gestured toward the columns weaving through the night, "this is legend come to life."

"You should call a halt. They've had a hard day. We're losing hundreds to the frost. This damn cold."

"You heard about Keane?"

Jurak motioned toward the flag Ha'ark was still holding.

"Then it's true?"

"Apparently."

"Is he dead or just wounded?"

"We'll know soon enough. Either way it weakens them further."

"Any response to the envoy?"

"They refused him entry through the lines, but the message was handed over. I sense the message will fester. If Keane dies, what holds the army together will die. They'll turn on each other. He is the one link that is neither of them, not Rus nor Roum. That is why we must press the attack. I want our army, not just patrols, our entire army, at the gates of Roum in three days."

"Ha'ark, we have time on our side. Our railhead is thirty miles back. It'll take ten days or more to link it just to this city," and he motioned toward Capua. "I understand we captured most of the rail ahead intact.

Once we connect through Capua and repair the bridge, we'll have an open track nearly to Roum. Give us time to bring up supplies, let the warriors rest, then move forward. We're overstretched as is."

"We press it," Ha'ark snapped. "They're off balance. Press it now and we will win."

"I take it you heard the news."

Offering a chair, Olivia Varinna Ferguson helped Vincent as he slowly walked over and sat down, groaning with relief.

"Cold gets into the wound, and it's hard to walk sometimes."

"You shouldn't be out in weather like this," she chided him while fetching a cup of tea.

Vincent gratefully took it, wrapping his hands around the cup to soak in the warmth.

Vincent saw the latest edition of *Gate's Illustrated* on her workbench, the headlines filling up the top half of the page: KEANE WOUNDED.

That had been a long argument with Gates the evening before, with the editor insisting that the people of Suzdal had a right to know, with Vincent's threats to shut down the printing shop if word was leaked. Unfortunately a telegram from the president, ordering that the truth be told, had arrived and the argument was lost.

"Nothing new," Vincent sighed.

She lowered her head as if offering a silent prayer. Vincent looked around the workshop. It was not yet dawn, and already the crews were coming in, heading to their desks, most holding copies of the paper and whispering among themselves. Several looked over at Vincent, as if wanting to approach him for information, but thought better of it.

Since Chuck's death she had thrown herself into managing the research and ordnance office. At first he had thought the idea to be a sentimental indulgence on Andrew's part, but Chuck had apparently thought things out well. Years ago he had taught Varinna to read and in the last year of his life had spent hours each day sharing with her every detail of his work. After his death, notebooks brimming with plans, detailed drawings, his random musings, and farfetched schemes had been brought out. Chuck looked over at the desk which had been Chuck's and the cot beside it. It was as if his old friend had simply stepped out for a moment for a morning walk and would return shortly, eyes shining, ready with a new idea.

"It seems like we're all going," Vincent sighed. "Mina, Malady, so many boys of the regiment, your Chuck. I'm half crippled, and Andrew. . . ." His voice trailed off.

She reached out, taking his hand, and squeezed it.

"Chuck's still here, Vincent."

He looked up into her eyes. Strange, her face was so horribly scarred from the explosion in the powder mill so many years ago, but still there was a radiant beauty, a beauty Chuck had worshipped to his dying day.

"He was lucky to have you," Vincent said, and he felt a momentary wave of embarrassment. When they had first met, she a servant in Marcus's household, she had attempted to seduce him one evening while he had soaked in the bath.

He lowered his eyes. That was something he had never told Chuck, and he prayed to God she hadn't either.

"Your wife?" she asked, and by her tone he sensed she was remembering as well.

"Fine," he said softly.

"I should go visit her and the children. Speaking of children, do Andrew's know?"

"She told them last night. It was hard, very hard."

"Poor dears. That's one thing I'll always regret. Chuck and I, we never had any."

She had displayed remarkable strength in the months since his death, but he could sense the thinness of it, the brittle edge that could crack if she let her guard down.

Patting his hand, she stood up.

"I received the information about their rocket launchers."

"We lost seven ironclads to them."

"And I assume the rest were abandoned in the retreat."

Vincent nodded. That was information that had not been made public yet. The people of Suzdal had latched on to the machines as a talisman that could counter the dreaded mass formations of the Hordes. The news of the total loss of the ironclad regiment's machines was too much, and even Gates had relented on that part.

"I don't think we'll have time to change the tools," she said, "to redesign our new ironclads with more armor on the flanks. The factory is turning out the new model at one a day now. If we stop to refit, we'll lose several weeks or more."

The new ironclads. The design was risky. It was one of the last things Chuck had seriously worked on. The engine had nearly twice the power of the old one and burned kerosene mixed with the residue of oil it had been refined from rather than coal. Fortunately, thousands of gallons of the fuel for both the ironclads and the flyers had been moved west over the last several months from the oil wells two hundred miles southeast of the city. Now that the Bantag were cutting off the southern flank of Roum, that reserve would have to last.

"One of the men here thinks he knows the secret of how their rockets punched through our armor, though I wish we had captured one intact," Varinna said.

"What's his idea?"

"Something about how the warhead of the rocket is a hollow cone made of high-grade steel. They must have some newer kind of explosive, more powerful than black powder. The hollow cone is packed with the powder, and when it explodes the jet of flame slices into the ironclad."

"Can we make something like it?"

"I've put a dozen people on it, but send word to the front that it'd help if we could capture a rocket intact. For right now we're converting some of our rocket battery rounds for individual use. That at least was a good idea, even if we can't use it against ironclads."

"What about gatling production?"

"It's not a question of making the guns—we can do

that. It's the ammunition. Brass is scarce. Losing the ironclads was bad enough, but there were thousands of empty shells in them, for both the gatlings and the cannons."

She led Chuck over to her desk, and under the glare of the lantern he saw a rough sketch of a man holding a pipe, a second one of a pipe resting on a tripod, a man lying beside it.

"I found some old sketches in Chuck's books. Right after the battle of Hispania he toyed with the idea of taking his rockets and issuing them out to small units as artillery. The rocket would be loaded with a canister round. The rockets weren't reliable enough for accurate aim, but for up close, the way the Bantag used them, I think these will work. We just take a rocket launch tube like the ones we already have. Weld a bracket on it so it can be mounted to a tripod for better aim, though a man could balance it on his shoulder. We could have some of them at the front in a couple of weeks."

"Tactics will have to change," Vincent said. "We can't let ironclads go in alone like that again. I should have guessed that Ha'ark would come up with a counter. They'll need these rocket teams advancing with them, along with riflemen, maybe even tow a gatling on a gun carriage to keep their rocket units back. Also mortars— what about them?"

She motioned to one of the workers, who came over and stiffly saluted.

"Petrov Basilovich, sir. I was with you in the old 5th Suzdal," he announced.

Vincent looked down and saw that Petrov had a wooden leg.

"Ah, lost that in one of the first battles, sir, at the Ford."

"A long time ago."

"That it was. So they sent me here. Didn't like it at first, but the work's important, it is."

"Petrov's our best tool and die maker," Varinna announced proudly.

"We took that Bantag mortar captured at the Rocky

Hill apart and used it as a pattern. The first unit's training with it now. Changed the caliber so it'll fire our standard three-inch shell. Really very simple. Percussion cap at the back end, small powder charge—once you get the hang of it, you can drop it down a chimney at five hundred yards."

The way they got Andrew, he thought. All of this was changing far too fast, and he found himself longing for a time, not so long ago, when volley lines still stood shoulder to shoulder. Artillery, cavalry on the flanks, and masses of infantry in the center. Now there were land ironclads, rocket batteries, mortar batteries, engineering units, flying machines. All of them with their own demands, the need for logistical support, all of it flowing out of the factories here at Suzdal and the new production centers at Murom, Kev, and even in the heart of Roum.

"With the strong engines on the ironclads, could we make a trailing wagon, lightly armored, or a sled even?" Vincent mused. "A mortar crew could ride on it, or infantry support. It could even carry extra fuel."

"The fuel would be dangerous," Petrov interjected. "That's one of the reasons I didn't like the new engine design anyhow. In the old ones the coal bunkers acted like additional armor, same as aboard our steamships. Now, if they get hit, a couple hundred gallons of kerosene will splash around the inside. No one will get out. Hauling a sled with more fuel on board is just asking for trouble."

"Like all things, it was a trade-off to increase range and engine power. The same with this," Vincent said absently. "I want you to work something up. Have a couple of wagons with detachable wheels so they can be converted to sleds made up for each ironclad."

"All right then," Petrov said reluctantly.

"What do you have in mind?" Varinna asked.

"I'm not sure yet. The problem with the ironclads is they break down so damn easy. We've lost more to that than battle. Their range is so limited right now they almost have to be transported right to the very edge of the battlefield before deploying out. With the newer engines, and kerosene, they might range farther out."

"How far are you actually thinking about, Vincent? The longest run we've gotten out of the newer design so far is fifty miles before it needed an overhaul."

"I'll need longer, a lot longer, than that."

"Just how far?"

Vincent said nothing, and she smiled.

"You always were one for secrets."

"Habit."

"A good one to have," and he felt himself flushing, wondering if she was alluding to their near affair.

"So, you're up and about early."

Vincent smiled as Jack Petracci came into the office, moving quickly to the woodstove, pulling off his mittens and rubbing his hands. Behind him was his copilot Feyodor, the twin brother of Varinna's assistant Theodor.

Theodor, coming out of the adjoining workshop, slapped his brother on the back, and the two immediately fell into a heated conversation about flying, Feyodor waving his hands about.

"You ready to inspect the new machines?" Feyodor asked.

"One of the reasons I came here."

"Let's go then."

Putting his greatcoat back on, Vincent gripped his cane and followed Jack out the back door. Varinna pulled on a heavy wool poncho and followed them. Plumes of dark smoke wreathed the factory town along the Vina River, the ancient city of Suzdal looking like a fairy-tale dream rising upon the hills beyond.

The New City, as it was now called, was almost as big as the ancient capital of the Rus. The biggest factory, the one dwarfing all the others, was the foundry. Rail lines snaked out from it, bringing in iron ore, coal, limestone flux. Iron and steel came out the other end, to be loaded on yet more cars, which were pushed by small switcher engines. Rails, crossplates, and spikes were all manufactured right in the foundry, as were the barrels of cannons, artillery projectiles, wheels for rail cars, and armor plating for ocean and land ironclads.

Carloads of iron and the precious steel seemed to pour out of the smoke-clad foundry in endless procession, pushed by small shuttle engines, the sinew of war then shifting into the locomotive and rail car works, the rifle works, the gun carriage works, the new land ironclad foundry, and even the foundry that turned out mechanical reapers and horse-drawn cultivators and plows, for without the mechanization of farming it would be impossible to take so many young men and put them in uniform.

The powder factory, safely located to the north of town, was barely visible out in a vast open field, connected by a single rail line which hauled in the barrels of sulfur from the hot springs north of the ford, saltpeter refined from every barn and privy throughout Rus and Suzdal and from a fortunate discovery in caves near Kev, and charcoal cooked down from stands of ash trees on the western banks of the Neiper. Yet other factories scattered throughout Rus turned lead into bullets, smelted zinc copper, and tin, drew wire for the telegraphs. The slaughter yards built downriver near old Fort Lincoln processed the cattle and pigs brought in each day, salting the meat down with the precious salt produced from mines nearly two hundred miles away near the old Tugar Road to the west. The hides went straight to the tannery, where they were turned into leather for shoes, cartridge boxes, saddles, harnesses, and belts for the army.

Water-powered looms, up near the ancient city of Vazima, turned out the thousands of yards of fabric, heavy wool for greatcoats, trousers, and uniform jackets, canvas for tents, and fine tight-weave canvas, shrunk after weaving and then coated with glue, for the airships.

Every time he took pause to gaze upon it, the sight of all they had wrought filled Vincent with wonder. Ten years ago this land had been pasture for the horses of Boyar Ivor. The dam they had built to power the first foundry and gun works was dwarfed now by the sprawling complex and rough-built row homes of the workers.

The dam, the memory of the slaughter he had created the night he had blown it up—how it had filled him with horror. But now, after all that had happened since, there was nothing but numbness.

Much of this had sprung from Ferguson's mind, though it came in different ways from all of them. Jack came up with the idea of the balloon from his childhood days traveling with a circus. Gates had designed the first printing press, having worked at the newspaper in Augusta as an apprentice. A dozen railroad workers had trained the Rus in how to lay a line, and two engineers with the regiment helped design and build the first engines. Iron forge workers from O'Donald's battery of New Yorkers had designed the first foundry, and the few precious tool and die makers, lathe operators, telegraphers, men from all the different crafts back in Maine and New York, had pooled their knowledge, taught the Rus and the Roum, and spawned the defensive works that had defied the Hordes.

None of them had ever dreamed that it would go this far, that such wonders could be created, some, like the flying machines and land ironclads, not yet built on earth.

He remembered visiting with Ferguson in the winter before his death. His friend had talked of a dream he had for after the wars were finished. The diagrams were a mass of interlocking gears, wheels, and drive belts. At first he had thought it was an elaborate clock, something that appealed to Vincent, since tinkering with clocks had been a boyhood hobby, but Ferguson had told him it was a steam-powered machine that could do calculations. Use of so much mechanical effort to do what any ten-year-old child could do with pencil and paper had seemed an impractical eccentricity, but Ferguson had promised that someday he'd build the machine so that it could work the most complex of calculations. The diagrams were now a cherished heirloom. Perhaps, if we survive, it might come to pass, Vincent mused.

That dream, along with machines that would make electricity that could travel through wires to power arc lights, strange-looking gun carriages with steam pistons to absorb the recoil, even flying machines so powerful they wouldn't need the dangerous hydrogen bags to keep them aloft were now but random sketches and pages of notes from a dead hand.

The whistle of the foundry shrieked, its cry picked up by all the other works signaling the end of the night shift. From out of the crowded hovels thousands of workers were emerging into the early-morning light, wending their way in long streaming columns to yet another twelve hours of backbreaking drudgery.

Emil had told him that lung diseases were on the rise with them . . . galloping consumption, asthma, the blackened air and fumes they breathed slowly killing them as certainly as a Bantag arrow. Emil was expressing special concern for the women who worked in the factory that made percussion caps out of fulminate of mercury, wondering if the air was causing a strange wasting disease. For a lingering moment Vincent could understand their confusion, frustration. Ten years ago, he thought, they were peasants, ignorant, living under the dread of the boyars and the Tugars. We offered them freedom, and now they labor in stygian darkness with no end in sight.

Up on the front, they could see what the Bantag were, the terror of their onslaught, and though he would never admit it, the joy of the charge, the exaltation of the kill. Fifty thousand of them labored thus, to keep the armies equipped and in the field, and when their boys turned seventeen they disappeared into the ranks to fight a war hundreds of miles away.

A swirling eddy of wind came down from the northwest, carrying with it a few flakes of snow. The smoke from the factories coiled, shifted, floating low across the open plain and up the slopes of the riverbank, cloaking the factories from view.

"We'd better hurry. I don't want to fly if the wind starts to pick up," Jack announced.

Passing down a snow-covered street past a long row

of clapboard-sided houses where the men and women who worked in Ferguson's labs lived, they reached a field on the bluffs above the mill lake. A row of huge hangars, each over forty feet high and a hundred feet long, lined the south side of the field. As they passed the first hangar Vincent opened a door and looked inside. A blast of hot air greeted him. An airship that had been nothing but a wicker frame two weeks before was now three-quarters covered with canvas. The building was kept warm by three massive wood-burning stoves that heated water-filled iron pipes ringing the walls. The glue used to fix the canvas was highly volatile, so the openings to the stove fireboxes were on the outside of the building where two boys slowly shuffled back and forth, opening each box, throwing in wood, closing it, and moving to the next one.

The glue brushed onto the canvas was curing in the hot air, and the stench of it made Vincent's eyes water.

"She'll be ready in another week."

Vincent nodded approvingly as they continued to the third hangar. As they approached, a crew started to nurse a ship out of its hangar, half a hundred men struggling with the lines to steady the ship against the light breeze. As the tail cleared the hangar some of the crew let it go, the ship windmilling around to rest its nose into the breeze.

"Here's the beautiful part. Watch how quickly we can get it ready," Jack announced as some of the ground crew raced to either side of the ship, scrambling up rope ladders dangling from the sides. Within a couple of minutes, the bilevel wings were unfolded from the side of the ship and locked into place. Guylines running from the wings back to the sausage-shaped body of the ship were locked in place and tightened.

"The engines are mounted between the wings for support," Jack continued. "Once the wings are unfolded we can fuel up and be ready to fly in ten minutes."

"Wish we could just keep it assembled, though," Vincent replied.

Jack shook his head. "We tried to figure that out. The

building would have to be over a hundred feet wide at the base and forty feet high, with no internal support beams. If we used some iron we could do it, but that's a lot of metal needed elsewhere. With the wings folded back the ship just barely fits—twenty feet wide, eighty-three feet long. Anyhow, at thirty miles an hour it has enough lift from the wings and hydrogen to carry a crew of four, fuel for twelve hundred miles, and a thousand pounds of munitions mixed between aerial bombs and shells for the guns."

Vincent nodded approvingly. It still wasn't the biggest one Chuck had dreamed up, a monster of a ship two hundred feet long and capable of carrying five thousand pounds of bombs, but that was coming.

"And the small one."

"The Hornet?" Jack said with a grin, and he pointed to where a ground crew was moving a diminutive airship out of another hangar. Vincent walked up to the smaller airship, which needed only half a dozen ground crew.

The gas bag was less than a dozen feet across and thirty feet long, the wings to either side adding maybe thirty more feet to the machine's width. The curious arrangement was that the engine was mounted aft at the tail and high so that its propeller was unobstructed by the bulk of the airframe.

The pilot's cab was forward, a wicker basket arrangement closed in with glass.

"Feyodor, take the Eagle—I'm flying the Hornet today."

Feyodor started to grumble that it was his turn, but a look from Vincent sent him on his way.

The ground crews were already warming the engines up and after several minute the propellers on both aerosteamers started to windmill over. Jack, strapping on his air umbrella so that he looked like a hunched-over clown, needed help up the narrow ladder. When he swung into the seat the ship sagged down, coming to rest on its wheels.

Vincent stepped back, Jack waving for the crew to release their grips on the side of the ship. Ahead of him

Feyodor was powering up the Eagle. The four engines revved up, propellers turning to a blur. The ship lumbered forward across the field, which had been laboriously cleared of snow by hundreds of workers the night before. The ship slowly gained speed, caught a light breeze, and soared up. The nose dipped, Feyodor dropping down slightly to gain airspeed, then pulled back, the ship gaining altitude as it crossed out over the mill pond.

Seconds later Jack followed, his Hornet taking less than a third the distance of the Eagle to get airborne. Pushing the nose up high, he clawed into the sky. The Eagle, now more than a hundred feet up, pivoted over the frozen pond and started back toward the field. Vincent studied it closely. The turn radius was tighter, wing dipping down low, the purr of the engines coming back on the morning breeze. The ship leveled out and came straight on.

"Must be making over fifty miles an hour," Vincent announced excitedly.

"Chuck figured sixty," Varinna replied proudly. As the four-engine aerosteamer approached the edge of the field, white bags detached and soared down, two of the six striking a bull's-eye of coal dust scattered in the center of the field. And at nearly the same instant Vincent saw Jack diving, engine howling, The Hornet swept across the tail of the Eagle, leveling out for a second, and then broke off in a tight circle. The Eagle continued to lumber on across the field and then moved upward in a shallow climb. Jack, however, swung his ship back around and nosed over, as if aiming straight at the bulls-eye. Puffs of smoke erupted from under the nose, and for a second Vincent thought that somehow the ship had caught fire. Then he saw clouds of snow kicking up around the bull's-eye, and then finally there was the stuttering staccato of a gatling firing.

"Steam line from the engine feeds it," Varinna announced proudly. "Lose most of your power, but you can get off a good five-second burst. It's deadly."

Grinning, Vincent waved his cane in salute as Jack winged back over and cruised low over the field.

"How many can we have in another month?"

"Five of the Eagles, twenty Hornets."

"Damn all. We need fifty, a hundred."

"We're working as fast as we can, Vincent. We're out of silk. The looms are turning out the new tight-weave canvas as fast as we can put it on the ships, but we need more looms and trained riggers, and that takes time. Another two looms are supposed to be in operation in another six weeks, and that will just about double production. But it's training the riggers, mechanics, framers, and engine makers that takes more time. We've got one ship that will never fly—it's a model for them to learn their skills. We can't just have this new system running overnight.

"Then there's all the other things needed—ground crews, vats for mixing the hydrogen gas, tons of raw zinc and sulfuric acid, temporary hangars that can be set up where needed. We're talking over five thousand men and women that need to be trained.

"Though I know he'd shoot me if he knew I was saying this, I think Jack should be grounded."

"Why? He's our best pilot."

"Exactly why. You know the life expectancy of pilots. Jack should be kicked up to General of the Air Corps. We're going to need that rank to run this program. It's not simply a few machines anymore—we're talking about a whole new branch of service."

Vincent slashed at the snow with his cane. We need the machines now, he thought, not three, six months from now. A hundred machines and a hundred ironclads and there wouldn't be a siege of Roum. Again it was time, dammit, always time, and it seemed to be on Ha'ark's side now.

"General, sir."

Vincent looked up. An orderly had approached silently in the snow. Though his attention was focused on his general, Vincent could see a curious eye flickering up toward the airships, which had been built in secret over the last three months.

"Yes?"

"From headquarters telegraph office, sir."

Vincent swallowed hard, suddenly afraid. He took the telegram and opened it, Varinna coming up to read by his side.

"Telegraph lines are reported cut above Roum. They must have raiders farther out ahead of the army. We're in the dark now."

"And Andrew?"

"We don't know."

Vincent watched as Jack circled once again, strafing the bull's-eye target. The siege of Roum had begun. They were cut off, and he would be damned if he simply sat here and did nothing.

Chapter Six

"My Qar Qarth, the cattle city of Roum."

Leaning forward and resting his arms on the pommel of his saddle, Ha'ark gave a grunt of approval. Nearly four moons of campaigning through the autumn rains and bitter winter . . . at last the goal was within reach.

Dismounting, he pulled his telescope from its carrying case. One of his guards came forward so that Ha'ark could rest the tube on his shoulder. The city was still half a dozen leagues distant, but in the cold winter air it seemed far closer, as if he could reach out and grasp it in the palm of his hand.

He had half expected to see it burning, as the damnable cattle had been burning every dwelling, barn, anything that could offer shelter in their retreat. Though his warriors were of the Horde, they were used to far warmer climes, and the cold had indeed been taking its toll. He had started this northern wing of his campaign with forty-one umens, nearly the same number that the Merki had thrown against the cattle. But unlike the Merki, more than half his warriors were armed with modern rifles, and he had more than two hundred pieces of artillery, nearly as many mortars, and fifty of the precious land ironclads.

The problem was that close to half his force was strung out along the five hundred miles of track all the way back to the rail junction seized at the start of the campaign, needed there to move supplies along, and to drive the hundreds of thousands of Chin and Nippon slaves brought north by land and across the Great Sea. They were needed as well to herd along the hundreds of thousands of horses and four-legged cattle, over a thousand a day to feed his army, along with the thousands of two-legged cattle who died each day and went into the boiling pot as well. But the two-legged cattle had been worked to death first and offered little sustenance.

He had hoped that the cattle would abandon Roum, take his offer, and fall back to their precious Rus. That would have eased the supply problem, for the Cartha would then be able to ship food across this smaller sea and he would no longer be dependent on the single rail line laid atop the frozen ground.

"Still no sign of troops moving back up their rail line toward Rus?"

The head of his reconnaissance force lowered his head and shook it.

"None, my Qar Qarth. Just before cutting their rail line and telegraph we observed two trains loaded with crates coming into the city. The three trains going the other way were carrying wounded, old cattle, and their young."

"They're going to hold the city," Jurak ventured. "Damn all, let's just wall them in and let them starve. The rest of the army can move on into Rus."

"My Qarth, there was this as well."

The reconnaissance officer stepped up to Ha'ark, unfolded a sheet of paper, and handed it to him.

"Your orders were to bring these sheets to you. This was found in the hands of a dead soldier earlier today."

Ha'ark unfolded the bloodstained sheet. It was one of their newspapers. He had learned a little of their scribblings. Many of the captives back in the factories were of Rus, and their writing had become the standard, since the strange picture-writing of the Chin was simply too difficult for technical use. Strange how we have to adapt so much from them, he thought. The idea was troubling.

He scanned the sheet and the bold print at the top. A grin slowly creased his features as the realization finally formed. His gaze went to his staff. The game had to be played.

"Yes, I saw this as well," he announced. "The spirits of my ancestors spoke to me in my dreams. This paper confirms it."

"What is it?" Jurak asked.

"Keane is dead."

Wild triumphal shouts erupted from the group, and Ha'ark looked from one to the other, nodding solemnly as if he had been the instrument of this destruction.

"Then let us drive on into Rus," Jurak replied. "With Keane dead their army will be demoralized and will not strike our rear."

The prospect was indeed tempting. Turning to look back at the city, he weighed his options, then finally shook his head.

"No, can't you see it?" Ha'ark snapped. "Keane is dead—that is the first blow. The army is all that stands between us and final victory. If we smash it here, take this city, Rus will collapse and beg to surrender. If Keane were alive, the defense might be more spirited, but they will cave in now."

Ha'ark raised his glasses again, studying the ground. The rolling steppe around him sloped gently downward toward the city, which was laid out on a series of low hills on either side of the river.

The hills, linked together by an inner city wall, offered clear fields of fire in every direction. The city was far bigger than he had expected, almost as big as the sprawling ramshackle cities of the Chin before his Horde had settled in to stay. In some sections the city extended half a league or more out from the inner wall on either side of the river. A rough line of earthen forts, connected by trenches, ringed this outer part of the city. Though it was hard to judge at this distance, he could see that this outer line would keep his own position beyond mortar range of the port. The port was the key to everything—it had to be held, kept open for the precious shiploads of ammunition and food.

"It's a tough position," Jurak offered. "They've destroyed everything outside the perimeter and its open

Once that was gone the city would be dependent on water from the Tiber, the same river which also served as the sewer. Emil was demanding that the precious supply of coal be used to boil water for drinking, yet another demand Pat knew would most likely not be met when the siege started in earnest.

Raising his own field glasses, Pat swept the outer perimeter of earthworks ringing the city. Fortunately Andrew had ordered their construction before winter had set in, but the work had been halfhearted, no one expecting that before the winter was half out the enemy would be at the gates. In a final desperate effort over the last week, tens of thousands had labored to pile up snow, pack it down, and cover it with water to add some additional protection. The ice walls covering the raw earthworks gave them a crystalline fairy-tale look, the fortresses of children who were about to fight with snowballs rather than rifles, artillery, and the point of a bayonet.

His seven corps were deployed around the city; the 1st, 3rd, 9th, and 11th, the units that had served with him on the Shenandoah Front, now occupied the outer perimeter. Their paper strength of sixty thousand had been cut by more than a third, and the line was stretched thin, forty thousand men to cover an arc from the southwest anchoring on the bank of the Tiber around to the north, then across the Tiber, and finally back to the bank on the southeast side of the city, a circumference of nearly twelve miles.

His main strength, what was left of the 4th, 6th, and 12th, was the reaction forces in reserve, well concealed behind the inner wall of the city proper, a force of forty thousand men well rested and ready, while 10th Corps had been deployed out to cover the eastern shore and the south of Roum. Additional men with artillery, engineering, and auxiliary units took the number up to near a hundred thousand. In a pinch he could arm the civilians with older weapons from the Home Guards, muzzleloading Springfields and even a few flintlocks from the early days of the Republic.

It was odds of roughly three to one, nowhere near as

bad as when the Tugars laid siege to Suzdal or even at Hispania, where the Merki had outnumbered them nearly five to one. The difference, though, was that this foe was equally armed, and beyond that their leader thought in terms of modern war.

Ha'ark would use his artillery to advantage, concentrating fire for a breakthrough. The mortars would make life in the trenches hell, and chances were he'd bring up airships to spot troop deployments.

"He'll come straight in," Pat announced. "No fooling around, no drawn-out siege. He'll want the shelter of the city, and besides, he wants to crush our will now. Two days and the storm will hit."

Marcus nodded, pointing to the northeast sector on the map.

"Where I figure as well."

"And you want to keep to this plan of yours?"

"The one chance we have."

"You know what morale is like."

"I have ears," Pat replied. "That's part of the reason I hope he attacks with everything he has. Put our backs to the wall now and scare the shit out of everyone. Make us desperate and we'll fight like we always have. I want this fight to explode."

"And what about Kal?" Marcus asked.

"What do you mean?" Pat replied innocently.

"I know what the offers were," the vice president replied coldly.

"And they are?"

"Rus pulls out of the fight, they go free while Roum is occupied."

"Tell me, what was your offer?" Pat asked sharply.

Marcus hesitated.

"Ha'ark isn't so stupid as not to play both sides against each other. What is it?"

"Surrender Roum and we avoid pillage and the traditional taking of one out of ten for the moon feasts."

Pat uttered a sharp curse, slamming a balled fist against the masonry wall of the watchtower.

"Do any of the men in the army know this?"

Marcus shook his head.

"Do you believe his offer?"

"I believe that," Marcus announced, pointing to the distant group that was still surveying their lines. "In two days they will assault my city. This won't be like the last time, when the Cartha occupied Roum. This will be the full fury of the Horde. Roum, the city of my fathers, of my ancestors for two thousand years, will be consumed as a burnt offering."

His words were sharp, bitter. "And if we win, what do we have left but smoking ruins?" he added.

"You'll have your freedom. The city can always be rebuilt. Freedom cannot."

Marcus nodded, but his features were clouded, torn with pain.

"Can't you see this will be the end of it?" Pat said. "We win here and we win for keeps."

"Oh, really? Even if we smash that army, Ha'ark can withdraw. Fall back five hundred miles. Or fifteen hundred, all the way back to where his factories are. Then what? Do we go after them?"

"Yes. We have to."

"You're talking eternal war."

"Eternal vigilance, Andrew once said, is the price of freedom."

"Andrew," Marcus sighed. "Perhaps if he was in command now we would feel differently."

Pat did not react to the insult. He felt the same.

"I'm sorry, but you're stuck with me."

Marcus smiled and extended his hand, patting O'Donald on the shoulder in an almost fatherly gesture.

"You do fine. I'll never forget you at Hispania. Andrew always said you were his master of defense."

Pat leaned against the battlement, slapping his bare hands together to drive out the chill. He looked up at the sky. The sun had dimmed since dawn, a high thin sheet of clouds making it look as if it were hidden behind a pane of ground glass.

"Snow later today. I was hoping it'd stay clear."

"Damn weather."

"Think how those bastards out there feel. We might not have much fuel for heat, but at least we've got roofs over our heads."

"Until he burns them down."

"Ah, it will be a grand fight, it will," Pat replied. He looked over at Marcus and regretted his words. The grand fight would be the destruction of the old consul's beloved city.

"Emil wanted to see me," Pat said. "I'll meet with you again later in the day."

Leaving Marcus on the battlement, Pat went down the narrow circular stairs, coming out into the old Senate Room, which now served as his headquarters. Staff officers looked up from the plotting board which filled the center of the room. Spotters up on the dome had already called down the information that Ha'ark had been sighted. A wooden block, painted gold, was positioned up at the northeast corner of the table. Blue oblong blocks marked where each brigade was positioned, and soon red blocks would be encircling them.

Telegraphers, connected to each division and corps headquarters, sat idle, but he could sense that soon this room would be in chaos.

Not a word was said as he stalked through the room, heading for a door guarded by two sergeants armed with Sharps carbines. Out of everyone in this city he was the only one they would allow to pass.

Going through the door, he went down another staircase and then turned down a narrow corridor where two more guards were posted. As he reached the door he saw Emil stepping out, eyes dark with fatigue.

Emil pointed to a basin set by the door. Pat obligingly washed his face and hands with the caustic carbolic acid, and feeling somewhat foolish, he donned a heavy canvas smock and cotton face mask.

Emil opened the door and led him in.

"Are they here?" the voice whispered.

Pat drew up a chair and sat down by Kathleen's side and then looked at the patient.

"How are you, Andrew?" Pat whispered.

"Been better, Pat. Good to see you."

"Good to see you," Pat sighed. He looked over quickly at Kathleen, wanting to ask, but a quick glance back told him that the fever still held. Beads of perspiration dotted Andrew's forehead. His features were still deathly pale, his eyes were like two sunken coals.

"I think your blood did get me drunk," Andrew sighed, and then his features contorted.

"Damn, I need to sneeze."

Kathleen leaned over anxiously.

"Don't. Fight it back. Don't think about it."

"Can't help it."

She pressed her finger against his upper lip, leaning over him, whispering to him as if he were a sick child. He nodded, struggling, then his face contorted.

The sneeze was followed by a gasp of pain, Emil and Kathleen both hovering over him.

"Morphine," Andrew whispered pleadingly. "The pain."

Emil hesitated, looking at Kathleen, who finally nodded. Emil drew out a needle, Andrew watching him anxiously as he filled it with the soothing potion and slipped it into his arm. Andrew sighed and laid his head back.

Pat looked down at Andrew's side. In the struggle the sheet had pulled back. The incision from the surgery was red, puckered, the black thread of the stitches standing out sharply. A rubber tube came out of the wound, leading down to a bottle. Pat didn't want to look, gazed down quickly at the fluid still draining from his lung and then wished he hadn't.

"Terrible-looking stuff, isn't it?" Andrew said. "Thought I'd faint when I saw Emil empty it."

"Do you think they found the untimely announcement of my death?" Andrew asked.

"Ha'ark was nearby where the papers were planted. He has it."

"Rather a morbid idea of yours," Pat said.

A faint smile creased his features.

"Think like they do, Pat. If there was any temptation for him to bypass us, that ended it. He figures we're three-quarters beat."

Pat didn't want to reply that perhaps they were. When the battle finally let go, the last thing he wanted was overall command. It was the type of moment Andrew was a genius at, he realized. Just give me a battery and a place to kill the bastards! Getting stuck back here was worse than hell.

"And there's something else, though," Andrew continued after pausing to struggle for breath. "He'll claim he saw my death."

"How's that?"

"Remember Tamuka? Remember how I said he could sense my thoughts? I've not felt that power with this one, though. He's more like us than those he leads. But he has to play that he has the power. Now he'll boast. His army will believe. That can make a difference."

Even getting that one statement out exhausted him, and he lay gasping for breath.

"Enough now," Emil interjected. "All right, you big mick, out of here."

Pat reached out and gently touched Andrew's hand. Andrew stirred, looked at him, and forced a weak smile.

"Guess we're blood brothers now," Andrew whispered.

"Always have been, Andrew."

Pat squeezed his hand and started to stand up, but Andrew didn't let go.

"If I don't make it," Andrew whispered, "don't let Kal and Marcus fall out. No separate peace. Fight to the end."

"What I always planned to do. They haven't beaten us yet."

Andrew finally let go, and again there was that fearful look in his eyes, something Pat found unnerving. Even with the morphine dulling the senses, the look of pain was in his eyes. He seemed to drift out, whispering something unintelligible, head tossing back and forth, Kathleen dampening a cloth and wiping his face.

Clearing his throat, Pat nodded and went for the door, Emil following. Stepping out into the corridor, Pat gratefully removed the mask and robe, looking over at Emil as he did the same.

"How is it looking?"

"A long way before we're out of the woods," Emil replied. "The lung's draining. That was a piece of work right there—have to keep the wound airtight but still have a drain. Took some doing."

Pat thought about a drink, and the look on his face caused Emil to open a cabinet and pull out a bottle.

"Medicinal use only. One sip. Your blood's thin and you're light-headed."

Pat gratefully took the drink, then reluctantly handed the bottle back.

"But will he make it?"

"Live? Even chance right now, but that's better odds than what I figured on yesterday. Using your blood scared me to death, but they seem to have mixed together. If this damn war ever ends I want to retire as I had planned to when we beat the Merki. Maybe research this blood thing. It'd be a lifesaver for thousands, but I've got to figure out why some mix and others don't.

"But will he live? If the wound continues to drain, if infection doesn't get any worse, if he doesn't get galloping consumption. There have been some cases of typhus and typhoid among the army and the civilians. This damn cold and lack of fuel—people can't stay clean. That touches him and he's dead. I know you've got to see him, but even then it makes me nervous. Kathleen is locked up there with him, and I'm the only other person."

Pat nodded. Orders had been passed to all units as they came back from the front to strip off their uniforms and have them boiled, and to bathe. Fortunately the Roum had massive public baths. Whoever was stuck with the job of cleaning them after the tens of thousands of men had passed through had his pity. The stench of the boiling wool uniforms had carried halfway across the city.

"Wish we could treat all the boys as well," Emil whispered. "Two doctors for one patient while we've got more than a thousand wounded and nearly ten times as many sick from the cold."

"Andrew's worth a corps, an entire army, to our cause."

"Tell that to the mothers of the seventeen-year-old boys who are dying in the hospitals," Emil said wearily.

"He scares me in a way," Pat finally said.

"How?"

"I don't know. Seen it before, you know. Fine officers or a good tough sergeant. In a dozen fights and never scratched, and they can fight like the demons, they can. Then they get hit, lose an arm, a leg. They come back, but they're never the same.

"Always wondered where the soul lived in us. Figured it was the heart, it was. But seen fellows like that, something of the soul is gone later, maybe it got cut off by one of you sawbones and didn't heal back. Seen that with Winfield Hancock. Damn near died at Gettysburg. They said when he came back a year later he weren't the same. Heard some rebs say how old Baldy Dick Ewell and John Hood were devils themselves when they commanded divisions. Lord knows that's true, since my battery faced both of them at Antietam and Second Manassas. Well, they got tore up, Ewell at Manassas, Hood at Gettysburg. They came back and something was gone from them."

His voice trailed off, and he looked longingly at the bottle. Emil took it and put it back in the cabinet.

"Time will tell," Emil replied. "Remember, I took his arm off at Gettysburg. He was a hell of a fighter then and was afterward."

"He was not much over thirty then—that was ten years ago. Something in the eyes," Pat sighed. "He's afraid now. And if he's afraid when he comes back, then God help us all."

Andrew smiled as the gentle spring breeze drifted across the lake, stirring the thick green stalks of winter wheat so that they wavered and shimmered.

The warmth was delicious, and unbuttoning his uniform jacket, he lay back, plucking a stalk, chewing on the rich taste a delight.

Funny, I unbuttoned my uniform with my left hand. He looked down. The ghost hand was real, and for a brief instant the realization was so startling that consciousness of its all being a dream almost shattered the illusion.

But the image held. No, of course it's my hand. He sat back up, looking down on the lake. Someone was out in the rowboat, laughing, rod raised high as a bass leaped on the end of the line. God, so long since I've been fishing. Standing, he walked down the hill toward the shoreline, the scent of the water rich, heavy, the surface of the lake mirror-smooth, reflecting the scattering of cumulus clouds that were slowly dissolving as the sun went down.

"Andrew?"

She came through the high wheat, the rich green stalks parting as if by magic. Her dress was simple, long, white, a dog bounding by her side, barking joyfully.

Strange, it was all blending together. Was it Kathleen? Was it Mary from so long ago? The dog—was it his old Border collie? He wasn't sure, it was hard to see . . . he was crying.

She drifted, floated up to his side, hand slipping into his, face upturned for a chaste loving kiss, almost childlike in its innocence.

They walked hand in hand, saying nothing, the foolish dog leaping ahead, disappearing, wanting to play their old game of hide and seek, then jumping back out, barking, tail wagging so furiously that his whole body was shaking. And the tears continued to flow. He was a boy again, a young man, this was eternal in his heart. And he was whole, body young, left hand feeling the warmth of hers clinging tightly.

"I love you, I'll always love you," she whispered.

His own voice was choked, he couldn't speak, for in the woods he saw something else. They were standing there, smiling, beckoning. All of them so young, his brother John, and Mina, and so many others, so many he couldn't remember their names.

He felt a shiver of fear. Was this the edge of their domain? Am I dying?

Strange, the thought was comforting. I could be whole again, I could be young.

She had stopped, her hand slipping from his. He looked back, and somehow he sensed all that he had once been was back here . . . Maine, springtime at the lake fishing, long lazy summer evenings and the calling of loons. How I miss that.

"Stay here with me," she whispered.

He sat down, leaning back against a pine tree that swayed and whispered with the breeze.

"I'm so tired," he sighed. "I want to go home."

"Stay here."

How peaceful, dreamlike. The lake was golden and red, each ripple a band of light. Loons, their haunting call, and geese, coming down in perfect formation, wings flapping, flaring, water splashing, their happy cries echoing.

Precious. There had been moments like this. How fleeting they were, how I thought they were eternal and wasted them the way a child spins out summer days of play not realizing all that will come.

He didn't look at her, not sure, afraid that if he did she would disappear.

Maine . . . I wish I had stayed here forever. No war. Yes, there had been a war. Dreams of glory at first, then the all-consuming passion of it. Maine, his Maine, started to fade, but he willed it to stay and the nightmare was held at bay, though he could sense them still watching, beckoning.

"I'm home," he whispered. He wanted her to lie with him in the high grass, to nestle by his side, listening to the night whispers, to watch the fireflies dancing through the trees. And then the moon would rise and there would be stillness and peace.

Another loon called. Strange . . . distant, quavering, louder . . . louder. I want to go home.

The world shook a flash of brilliant light, and oh God the pain, the unbearable pain . . . drowning, drowning in my own blood . . .

Screaming, he sat up. Arms were around him, hushing his cry.

The explosion rumbled through the building. Another shell streaking in. He tensed, waiting for the explosion.

"The Bantag?" he whispered.

"They've started shelling," Kathleen said, still trying to ease him back down onto his cot.

Blinking, he looked around. All was darkness.

"Light, please. I want light. It's too dark."

She stirred, slipped away. A match flared. She touched the flame to a candle, then returned to sit by his side, rinsing a cloth out in a basin and wiping his brow.

"You were dreaming."

"I know."

"Go back to sleep."

"How long have they been shelling?"

"It started an hour ago."

"I saw Johnnie."

She stiffened. The first time they had met, aboard the *Ogunquit*, it had been the dream, the one that used to torment him, of his baby brother, dying at Gettysburg. He had been asleep in the ship's wardroom and she had come in, gently talking to him as he awoke screaming. By the candlelight he could see her, eyes wide.

"He wanted me to go with him."

She shook her head, her voice quavering. "Don't listen to him, Andrew. Stay with me."

"That's what you said. Stay with me, stay with me at home. Home . . . where is it?"

"Here, Andrew."

He said nothing, laying his head back, closing his eyes, listening as she talked softly, as if he were a child, the lilt of her Irish brogue returning, sounding so gentle and warm . . . and he wanted the warmth, the gentleness, to stay forever.

Chapter Seven

The bombardment grew in intensity across two days and nights. It was impossible to see a target to fire back at, for with the shelling had come the snow, not heavy, but constant, dimming vision, cloaking the men waiting in the trenches with a soft white mantle that muffled all sound except the insistent thumping of the guns. Fires erupted in the city, and bucket brigades laboring in the cold struggled to keep the flames in check. Companies of soldiers moved through the confusion, shoulders bent under the weight of their greatcoats, weapons, and packs, moving like ghostly shadows, shuffling soundlessly through the night.

Field batteries which had once stood in open array were now deployed on narrow streets, cobblestones pulled up to form barricades, gunners huddled inside adjoining buildings, gathered around flaming hearths, burning their precious rations of firewood and coal to keep warm.

Down at the harbor occasional supply ships from Suzdal still came in. Five hundred tons of food a day was the barest requirement to keep the army and the civilians alive, off-loaded by work gangs and moved under guard to warehouses.

Heading into the headquarters office the hour before dawn, Pat went up to the map board and turned to the officer on duty.

"Anything since midnight?"

The office walked over to the northeast corner of the map and pointed.

"Sir, forward pickets report noise, sound of equipment

moving. There's been flare-ups of skirmishing, driving the pickets back, since two. The snow's been falling steady. Visibility isn't twenty yards at the moment."

Pat nodded.

"Everyone awake."

"As you ordered, sir."

Pat nodded as he flared a cigar to life and sat down by the table. He could feel it in his bones . . . they were coming.

"All is ready, my Qar Qarth."

Grinning, Ha'ark nodded to Jurak, who would directly command the attack. Spurring his mount, he cantered through the snow, passing the heavy columns of assault troops deployed in massive block formations.

Looking up, he saw that the snow was still holding, a blessing from the ancestors the shamans had called it. If it was a blessing, it was twofold. First, it had allowed him since the afternoon before to move ten umens of troops down from behind the Apennine Hills and to within half a league of the city without being detected. The second blessing was that with the storm the temperature had risen almost to freezing. After the long weeks of frigid cold it almost seemed warm in comparison.

He could hear the rumble of guns to the north. Good—the diversion a mile away was heating up. In the dim light he could sense more than see the vast power at his command. Each umen of ten thousand was drawn up into regimental blocks of a thousand, twenty warriors across and fifty deep. Marker pennants had been set in the snow just after dusk pointing the way toward the city.

As he rode along the lines he could see his warriors were ready. The bitter months of struggle through the cold had thinned the ranks of weaklings; what was left was the hard inner strength of an army thirsting for blood. And that thirst had been fed by the sacrifice of five thousand Chin brought up and parceled out one to each twenty warriors. The slaughter had been cruel; since fires were forbidden the flesh was eaten raw and the snow was splattered thick with blood, offal, and bones gnawed clean. His master of cattle had protested the slaughter, arguing that it was the waste of five thousand trained slaves when the looting of the city would offer the same and more, but Ha'ark had insisted, knowing that the scent of blood aroused the lust for more.

He could see now that it had worked. Here and there along the line his warriors had decided that entertainment was better than eating and had spent the night devising ingenious torment which was still being drawn out, but as word now passed that the assault was about to go in, the last surviving cattle were slaughtered, their throats cut, limbs torn off, brain, heart, liver, and lungs drawn out and devoured.

Turning to look back to the east he could sense the rising of the light. Individual snowflakes swirling past could be seen now at arm's length.

He looked over at Jurak.

"Remember, just get over the wall. You'll lose control once that happens—all will be confusion. The regiment commanders know to drive for the harbor. That's enough. Now begin!"

Jurak saluted, spurring his mount forward. Guidon bearers stood tall in their stirrups, waving red standards that still looked black in the dim light, and raced off down the length of the half-mile-wide column. Discipline held; there was no cheering, no chants. That would not begin until they hit the wall.

Ha'ark reined his mount in, letting the swaying columns pass, and standing tall he raised a clenched fist in salute to the victory about to come.

Colonel William Shippey walked the battlement, collar of his greatcoat pulled up over the back of his neck to keep the heavy wet flakes out. The night had dragged out for an eternity, but now, looking over at his sergeant major, an old Rus veteran, he could distinguish the dark craggy features, the beard flecked with ice. Dawn was approaching.

"Still think they'll come, sergeant?"

"I can smell 'em," the sergeant announced, sniffing the air.

Shippey laughed.

"Serious, sir, I can. Smell like wet bears they do. Wind's been backing around to the east and you can smell 'em. They're out there, thousands of them."

Shippey tensed at the suggestion. Strange how it's worked out now. Saw battle in the Tugar war, then missed the entire Merki war with the typhoid. Then this one always seemed to be somewhere else, first out on the western frontier watching for raiding Merki, then to reserve here in Roum, finally replacement commander for this regiment.

Now was the chance to prove the worth of getting a brigade. Hell, Hawthorne was only six months older, and him in command of an entire army. Luck, nothing but luck.

The sergeant tensed, leaning up against the ice wall.

"What is it, sergeant?"

"Here they come! Here they come!"

The sergeant, not even waiting to reply to his colonel's question, started to run along the battlement wall, tearing back the blanket curtains of dugouts cut into the ice wall, shouting the alert.

Shippey looked out over the field, wondering for an instant what had overcome the sergeant. There was nothing . . . and then he saw it, a darkness deeper than the dull gray world, a solid wall of black coming forward through the knee-deep snow at the double.

Sentries posted along the wall already had rifles up. Shippey wanted to shout for them to hold fire, because pickets from the regiment were still out and forward, but rifle fire was already erupting, and he realized that whoever was out there was in fact already dead.

The charge came on, not wavering, no one slowing to fire, the dark wall advancing, bounding through the snow with great leaping strides, crashing into the entanglements of sharpened stakes, chevaux-de-frize, and traps of telegraph wire strung out on stakes buried under the snow.

Raising their rifles, they smashed at the barriers. Bantag began to drop from the rifle fire atop the battlements, others pressing forward out of the crush, tearing into the barricades. A few snaked their way through, sliding down into the ditch, which was nothing more than a shallow depression drifted over with snow. Floundering through the waist-deep snow, they kicked and struggled to reach the ice wall barricade.

A bugle sounded to his left, and another picked up the alert. A cannon cracked to his right, and startled, he looked and saw a tongue of flame piercing the gloom, files of Bantag going down from the canister blast.

Looking over the wall, he saw a Bantag directly below him, smashing with the butt of his rifle against the ice wall, caving a section in to gain a foothold. Drawing his revolver, he leaned over, fired three times, and the Bantag soundlessly collapsed, but another one was up in an instant, using the foothold to vault up higher, then in turn he raised his rifle and started to smash another hole. To the left half a dozen came forward carrying a ladder and slammed it down against the battlement wall.

Shippey stepped back. I'm the colonel, damm it, he realized. Not my job to shoot the buggers. He ran to his left, dodging around an artillery crew scrambling up from their bunker, one of the men pulling on his greatcoat. He wanted to swear at them—they should have been at their guns, not malingering down in a hole—but he pressed on, racing to his headquarters dugout.

Tearing the curtain aside, he stepped inside, momentarily blinded by the glare of the kerosene lamp suspended from the ceiling.

"Does brigade know?" he shouted to his telegrapher.

"Already told them," the boy replied, obviously frightened. The key in front of him started to chatter, and Shippey stared at it.

"What the hell is it saying?"

"Attack all along the line, sir. There's millions of 'em."

"Sir!"

Shippey saw Alexandrovich, commander of Company B,

come sliding down the steps into the dugout, nearly losing his footing.

"Should I bring up our reserve companies, sir? Company C is giving way."

"Where?" And Shippey scrambled back out of the dugout and started back to the right of his line. In the shadows he saw a lone Bantag gain the battlement wall and instantly collapse as half a dozen rifle shots tore into his chest, but even as he fell he managed to kill, flinging his rifle down like a spear, pinning a screaming corporal.

Shippey raced past the melee and then froze. Dark forms were scrambling over the wall, a knot of them spilling into the street below.

"Damm it, get up the reserves!" Shippey roared, but Alexandrovich was gone, his cry unanswered. Rifle fire stuttered behind him. Looking back, he saw men lining the wall, oblivious to the breakthrough on their right less than twenty yards away. The line was peeling back as more and yet more Bantag swarmed up into the breech.

Grabbing a private, Shippey turned him and shoved the boy toward the melee. The private hesitated, then, levering his breech open, he slammed in a round and started forward, bayonet poised low. Shippey grabbed yet more men, pushing them toward the fight.

Rifle fire from the Bantag line was coming in now, bullets smacking the top of the wall, shards of ice slashing out, cutting his face. He could hear a solid volley, and looking down to the street below he saw a ragged line, Company B, supported by Company A, racing up, crashing into the swarm of Bantag. A vicious hand-to-hand fight erupted below.

An explosion behind him slammed Shippey facedown. Stunned, he rolled over.

"Damn all to hell," he gasped, cursing even louder when a soldier running along the battlement stepped on his legs, bounded over him, and kept on going. There was another flash a dozen feet farther down the line, bowling several men over.

Staggering to his feet, he looked over the battlement

wall. Down in the barrier ditch dozens of Bantag moved about, several of them holding sputtering torches. Several of them held their clenched fists up to the fire, fuses flickered, and they lobbed ball-like objects up and over the wall.

One of them came down at Shippey's feet. He stared at it uncomprehending, remembering at last something about grenades. He scooped the grenade up with his left hand to throw it back and in the next instant he was back down again. Someone was screaming, and it was long seconds before he realized it was his own voice.

Coming to his knees, he tried to brace himself with his hands and collapsed. Something was wrong. Terrified, he looked and saw that his arm from the elbow down was nothing but shreds, blood pulsing out.

More explosions rocked the battlement, grenades showering down. Men screamed, cursed, some rolling down into the shelter of the dugouts. Sitting up, Shippey huddled against the battlement wall, tucking the shattered arm in tight against his chest.

Luck, damnable luck. Bleed to death out here if I don't get help.

In the smoking confusion he looked along the battlement, wanting to call for help, but men were down all around him. A darkness was above him, and looking up he saw an impossibly tall form, a Bantag warrior, leaping down into the line roaring a wild battle cry.

Raising his revolver, Shippey pressed the barrel into the Bantag's stomach and squeezed the trigger. Shrieking, the Bantag fell backward.

Another one slid down beside the gasping struggling warrior. Shippey aimed, fired, missed. The Bantag turned. He cocked, fired again, this time catching the Bantag in the arm so that he staggered backward.

Cocking his revolver, Shippey squeezed again . . . and the hammer fell on an empty chamber. The Bantag, who had been recoiling in anticipation of the killing blow, stopped, staring at Shippey over the sight.

There was a long moment, the Bantag staring at him

with rifle half raised. Cursing, Shippey cocked the revolver again, and again the dead click, a sound that was as shattering as a cannon's roar.

A grin creased the sharp ugly features of the Bantag. He said something dark and guttural while reaching down to his belt and drawing his dagger. He stepped forward, leaning down, and in his final minutes Colonel Shippey learned the mistake of not saving the last round when facing a warrior of the Horde. Fortunately the blood pouring from the lost arm ended the agony at last.

Pat leaned on the table, watching as the headquarters staff moved wooden blocks on the table.

"Damm it, isn't there any word from 9th Corps?" he asked, looking back at the telegraph.

"Sir, the line's still dead."

"All right then, the division headquarters of the 9th. Give me a damn brigade commander if you can!"

"Sir, all the lines are dead. Something must have cut them."

He turned and looked to the next telegrapher.

"First Division, 4th Corps—they moving up to block the center?"

"Last report indicated that, sir."

A messenger came into the room, and there was the faint scent of burnt powder clinging to him. Wet snow puddled off his rubber poncho onto the floor. A staff officer opened the message, Pat watching as the officer nodded, then handed the message over to Pat.

It was from Schneid of 1st Corps reporting that he was preparing to bend back his left flank because of a breakthrough between his corps and the 11th. All of 9th Corps apparently had given way on his right.

Pat looked back at the map. The wooden blocks indicated that only one division of the 9th had lost the wall; the two divisions to the right of the breakthrough supposedly still held.

Damn, if Rick's report was true, 1st Corps was holding in the middle of the eastern wall, but most of the wall curving back to the river, except for the large bastion anchored to the river, was gone, and Schneid was being flanked on the left as well. If it was true, Schneid had to be pulled out and the entire eastern side of the outer wall conceded.

"Get that boy over here," Pat snapped, motioning for the messenger, who came up and nervously saluted.

"You know what this message says, son?"

"Yes sir."

"Did you see any of this?"

"Sir, the general sir, he said we was getting cut off and I was to get back here fast."

"What did you see on the way, son?"

"It's all burning out there, these Roum cities sir, thought they wouldn't burn like ours did, them being made of brick and all, but they're burning."

"Did you see any Bantag?"

The boy nodded, wide-eyed.

"Where?"

"Halfway back to the inner wall. Seen three of them dead in the street, a battery cut 'em up."

"Which battery?"

The boy shrugged and shook his head.

"One of ours, you know, Rus."

He wasn't sure if the boy was making a comment on the Roum.

"Where was this?" Pat looked back at the map. There was no indication that Bantag units had already cut halfway to the inner wall.

"I don't know, sir."

Pat walked over to the opposite wall and snatched his greatcoat from a peg.

"Sir, shouldn't you stay here to direct things?" one of the staff asked.

"Shit, son, you direct it from here. I'm going up to see for myself what the hell is going on."

Pulling on his slouch cap and grabbing a cigar out of his pocket, he stormed to the door, striking a light on the wall and puffing the cigar to life as he headed down the stairs and then out the door and down the steps into the open Forum.

The snow was still coming down hard enough that the opposite side of the square was nothing but a faint shadow. The Forum was packed with civilians, panic in the air, and he was glad for the cloaking of the snow so they wouldn't see him and swarm about asking questions.

A continual thunder filled the air, and looking eastward he could sense the spread of the battle by the sound. It stretched now all the way from the Tiber farther upstream, back around, and down to the bank where the river widened out into the bay.

Staff and orderlies came clattering down the stairs behind him and mounted. With a vicious jerk of the reins, Pat spurred his mount around, the horse nearly losing its footing on the icy pavement. He started to urge it up to a gallop, but then was forced to rein back in as he reached the corner of the Senate. The street leading up from the bridge across the Tiber was packed with refugees fleeing the fighting. Several wagons from the ordnance department were attempting to breast the flow in the opposite direction, and he fell in behind them, cursing the waste of precious minutes as they inched along.

He tried to not look at the refugees. No matter where he had seen them before, in Virginia, the retreat from Rus, now here, it was always the same, the old staggering under the burden of their few precious possessions, young women clutching screaming infants, terrified children lost in the confusion wailing hysterically. Reaching the arched stone bridge, he looked down the river. A wooden side-wheeled steamer was tied up at the dock, crews unloading crates of artillery ammunition and bags of grain and barrels of hardtack and salt pork.

A geyser from a Bantag shell erupted in the river. The labor gangs ducked down for a moment, then went back to work. There was a flash farther down the river; hard to see, but it must be the ironclad that had escorted the ship up the river. Hysterical screaming came from the middle of the bridge, as a woman pressed up to the side in the crush lost her footing and went over the railing into the freezing river, disappearing under the ice floes. For a brief instant there was a stunned silence. An orderly riding ahead of Pat stepped up onto his saddle, leaped over the railing, and crashed into the river.

The boy came up to the surface, floundered, went under. Everyone had stopped, even the wagon drivers, and for an instant the insanity of the battle was forgotten. The boy came back up again, clinging to the woman. All held their breath as he kicked against the current, struggling for the shore. Twenty yards out from the shore he went under, and a groan went up from the bridge. He reappeared, trying to clutch to an ice floe, but lost his grip. Dock workers snaked out lines to him, but he was already so far gone that he couldn't grasp the line. Finally two more men went into the river, clinging to a rope, splashing out to the two, grabbing hold and pulling them to shore.

A happy shout and applause broke out, all united together in that instant. People around Pat reached up, slapping his leg, shouting their thanks, and for one brief moment he felt that they were all united again. Surprised at his own reaction, he wiped tears from his eyes and looked over at a staff officer.

"I want the name of that boy. By God, have him at headquarters tonight."

Grinning, an officer fell out of the procession and turned back, falling in with the flow of refugees back to the western bank.

Reaching the east shore, Pat pushed his way out of the crowd, riding down along the warehouses lining the eastern bank of the river and the canal. A building was on fire. A bucket brigade of the Home Guard, old Springfield muzzleloaders stacked, were pulling water from a hole cut in the canal and working to stop the spread of the conflagration. Horrified, Pat realized that hundreds of barrels of salt pork were stored inside, and he shouted for the men to concentrate on saving the food first before riding on.

Reaching a side street heading east, he started riding

up toward the front. Roum cities still amazed him. Unlike the rabbit warren of crooked lanes in Suzdal, or the haunts of the west side of Manhattan and the Five Points district, this city was laid out with remarkable precision, each block a hundred paces square, every fifth road a thoroughfare twice as wide as the other roads, all of them paved with stone. Shopfronts lined the curb at street level, capped by several stories of apartments. Though the high apartments blocked out most light, still it was better than many another city. Emil had marveled at the sanitary arrangements of underground pipes and sewers.

But sanitation was the least of his concerns as he pressed forward, riding under one of the gates of the old inner wall. Refugees were pouring through, the gate a bottleneck, and it took several minutes to pass. He saw a regiment from the 1st Division, 4th Corps trapped in the press, and pushing his way through the crowd he caught the eye of the regimental commander, to his delight one of his old gunners from the 44th.

"O'Leary, a hell of a mess it is!" Pat shouted.

Grinning, O'Leary asked for a cigar, and Pat passed one over. Not bothering to light it, the gunner simply bit off the end and started to chew, tucking the rest in his breast pocket.

"When did you get orders to move up?" Pat asked.

"A half hour ago at least. There's panic in the air, there is. We've been trying to push our way through."

Pat nodded, disturbed to see more than one infantryman moving back with the crowds. At the sight of the general they ducked low, filtering to the far side of the street. It wasn't his job to chase skulkers and the provost would stop them at the gate, but it was a hard sight to bear and a grim warning of the panic up at the front.

Inching forward, they finally cleared the mob, and O'Leary bawled for his unit to form up and move at the double. Picking up the pace, the long serpentine column of blue surged down the street, Pat keeping to O'Leary's side.

They passed another burning house, then an entire

row, a woman kneeling in front of one of them screaming. A green flag, dimly visible in the snow, marked a hospital clearing area set up in a wealthy patrician's villa. As Pat rode by he could see red Orthodox crosses, white crosses, and even some red circles on the hats of the wounded, designating them as casualties from the 1st and 2nd Divisions of 9th Corps and 1st Division of 1st Corps. What were they doing over in this sector a half mile or more from their assigned position? The entire line ahead must be confusion.

A brilliant flash of light erupted straight ahead, followed a couple of seconds later by a thunderclap roar. The flash disappeared and then long seconds later debris started to rain down. A shell ignited on the roof of the hospital, and another one in the street ahead, cutting down several refugees.

Pat left O'Leary, urging his mount forward, staff trailing behind him. Coming to an intersection with a main thoroughfare he reined in as two fieldpieces, positioned in the middle of the street and pointing south, fired in salvo, the guns leaping back. The gunners tore the breeches open, rammed sponges in, withdrew, reloaded with canister and powder bags, then fired again. Pat rode up to the commander, who was standing between the pieces, looking down the street. It was impossible to see anything except the snow.

"What the hell are you firing at?" Pat roared.

"They're out there!" the section commander roared.

"Damm it, man, cease fire! There are refugees moving back, troops moving up," and he pointed to where O'Leary's column was appearing ghostlike out of the snow.

"Sir, there's Bantag out there!"

"They're not this far in! Cease fire!"

The gunners paused, looking up at Pat and then to their commander, who continued to point down the road.

A bullet snicked past Pat, and suddenly a volley swept the position, the commander wordlessly collapsing in the snow. A piercing ululating scream erupted as a dark wall of Bantag came sweeping up the street and within seconds were into the guns. Pat reined around, drawing his revolver, dropping a Bantag who was swinging at him with a clubbed rifle. Something grabbed him from behind, heavy arms wrapping around his waist, pulling him back off his mount. Swinging his revolver under his left armpit, Pat fired backward, the arms releasing him. Shrieking, his horse started to go down, and pulling his feet from the stirrups, he leaped clear, avoiding the horse as it rolled onto its back, hooves flaying, splitting open the skull of a Bantag trying to scramble over the dying mount to get at Pat.

Two more Bantag came rushing up, Pat emptying his revolver, then rolling out of the way as they collapsed in the snow. The distinctive rattle of Springfield rifles ignited around him, O'Leary's men crashing into the Bantag column from the flank, wading into the press. Pat dropped his revolver, picked up a heavy Bantag rifle, leveled it like a spear, and parried another Bantag trying to close with his own bayonet for the kill. The standoff lasted for several seconds, the two poised, facing each other, making short jabs, recoiling, jabbing again. The Bantag lunged in, Pat ducking under the blow aimed at his head, a common mistake of Horde warriors with their two to three feet height advantage over humans. Pat went down low, driving the bayonet into his opponent's groin, then let go of the rifle, jumping to one side.

Blue-clad infantry swarmed past him, putting the surviving Bantag to flight and setting off in pursuit. Pat saw O'Leary coming through the press, still mounted.

"O'Leary, don't lose control of your men! Call 'em back!"

Orders were shouted, but several dozen men of the regiment had already disappeared into the snow.

The battery was a shambles, half the men dead or wounded in the brief melee. Pat looked around, overwhelmed with guilt. The commander had been right and his own brief intervention had caused an interruption in the firing, giving the Bantag the chance to mount a charge.

"O'Leary, form your regiment here, and give me your horse."

"Now Pattie."

"General O'Donald to you, O'Leary. Give me the damn horse."

O'Leary, shaking his head ruefully, dismounted, handing over the reins. Pat looked around. Half his staff and messengers were gone, some dead, several on the ground wounded, and the others just missing in the confusion. Pat mounted, but O'Leary stepped forward, grabbing the reins.

"Captain Jovonovich, take Company B and escort our good general here."

A young fuzzy-cheeked officer came forward at the double, bawling in a high voice for his company to follow.

Pat nodded his thanks, grateful as well when O'Leary unholstered his revolver and handed it up.

"Now don't go getting killed, Pattie. Not many of us Irish left here to save this godforsaken world. Hell, if I'd known that getting on the boat in Dublin would finally bring me here I'd've stayed in Ireland, famine or no."

Pat laughed, reached into his pocket, pulled out a couple of cigars, and handed them down.

"See you in hell, Sean."

"See you in hell, Pat."

The horse, nervous after the melee and with a new rider, balked as Pat tried to urge him forward and then reluctantly accepted Pat's urgings. Heading on eastward, Pat agreed to the young captain's insistence that his men move ahead, checking each street intersection before proceeding. No sense getting ambushed, or worse, shot by your own men. Mounted men were undoubtedly rare in this city now, and in the confusion and snow there was a fair prospect of turning into another Stonewall Jackson if he wasn't careful.

Within half a block the scene of the melee was lost to view. As he crossed the next street he could hear rifle fire to both sides. Damn all, they were more than halfway into the city, less than six hundred yards from the inner wall, and if they could find a high prominence the riverfront was within easy mortar range.

The way ahead grew darker, coils of oily smoke eddying toward him. The street was carpeted with burning rubble, torn bodies. There was movement ahead, and he paused, then urged his mount on, the horse nearly unseating him when it stepped on a pile of smoldering embers.

Half the street was blocked, flames licking up from the gutted ruin of a temple, the marble columns blown out and resting against the side of a building across the street. Pat shouted for one of the men helping a badly burned comrade to come over.

"What the hell happened here?"

"Ammunition depot for 3rd Battalion artillery reserve," the corporal shouted, trying to be heard above the roaring conflagration. "We had a dozen caissons parked here, more rounds stacked up inside. Got hit by a mortar round. Kesus-damned hell it was!"

Even as the corporal shouted his explanation a dozen men came running down the street from the east, most of them wounded, all terrified, screaming that they were being chased. Two lone Bantag materialized out of the swirling snow and came to a stop. They turned and started to run, but rifle fire from Pat's escort cut them down in the middle of the street.

Pat continued on, having to zigzag his way through side streets to avoid fires, terrified civilians, and demoralized clumps of soldiers running past. At one corner they stumbled straight into a knot of Bantag who were bent over, back turned, and after they were gunned down Pat saw they had been busy butchering some wounded they had cornered, bloodied limbs already dangling from their belts. One of the victims, still alive but with an arm hacked off, staggered to his comrades, sobbing hysterically. Two men grabbed him, and one tore off his belt and tightened it around the stump. They looked up at Pat, who nodded for them to take the man back.

A solid column of troops, several hundred strong,

came down the street, heading back from the front line, this group at least disciplined, the men's hats adorned with white circles, 2nd Division, 1st Corps.

"Why are you pulling back?" Pat shouted, edging his mount over to the commander at the head of the column, an old Rus major.

"Sir, what the hell is going on?" the major shouted back. "We were in reserve, and suddenly they were on our left, behind us."

"Were you ordered back?"

"By who, sir? My colonel's dead, the lieutenant colonel's dead. We haven't heard a damn word from brigade, division, anybody. I figured it was time to get the hell back to the inner wall."

"Where's Schneid's headquarters?"

The major paused, looking around in confusion.

"I guess it's back up toward the fighting, sir."

"Well then, dammit, major, turn your men about. I need to get there now!"

The major looked up at him, obviously reluctant to head back into the confusion.

"Major, post two companies here to hold this intersection, and we'll detail two more off at each street. Get them making barricades, put snipers up in the upper levels of these damn buildings, start digging in, and stop this damn running!"

The major hesitated, then saluted.

Pat remembered Andrew once saying that there was nothing more frightening than coming into a battle from the rear of the lines. No matter how good it was going up front, go back a quarter mile and it will always look like defeat. Even as he mused on the thought, a knot of soldiers came running past, making a show of the fact that they were escorting some civilians but nevertheless running.

All control was breaking down, Pat realized. They had built an army, trained it to fight horse-mounted warriors in the field, or from behind entrenchments. When the enemy shifted to modern weapons, they trained to face that, always adapting tactics to open fighting. He now realized their one glaring mistake: the regiments were trained to fight as cohesive regiments, a colonel capable of seeing his line from one end to the other. This was different. They had thought they could hold the Bantag at the outer wall, or at worst the breakthroughs would be limited. In the confusion of streets, burning buildings, terrified refugees, all of it made worse by the storm, regimental commanders could not find their brigadiers for orders. Company commanders could not hope to see their colonels, let alone receive timely orders, and individual soldiers could get lost within seconds. And in all the confusion, Bantag appeared like ghostly demons, pouring out of the snowstorm, slashing in, spreading terror, then melting away.

He had to force himself to realize that for the Bantag it must be equally confusing, but that was small comfort as he sensed that the battle had gone completely beyond his control. Again he felt the aching loss of Andrew. He wished for a drink, wished he could just dismount, find a battery to command, and let others worry about whether the battle would be won or lost by their decisions.

Taking a deep breath, he tried to clear his thoughts, edging his horse to the side of the road as two fieldpieces clattered past, wounded clutching to the caissons. Pat shouted for them to dismount at the next intersection and train their guns north and south. The commander saluted, then disappeared into the snow. Pat wondered if the man would just keep on going.

"Let's move it!" Pat shouted, and spurring his mount, he continued up the street. The next two intersections were surprisingly quiet, but the next one was the scene of a fierce struggle, Bantag having occupied buildings half a block down. Leaning out of windows, they were firing on anything attempting to move. Pat detailed off a company of infantry to storm the buildings and the men went in.

Sensing that he was presenting too much of a target, he finally dismounted and on foot sprinted across, his staff following. Finally he recognized where he was again, a large public bath occupying half the next block.

It was Schneid's headquarters. Cannons were deployed in front, gunners at the ready, infantry deployed into the upper stories of buildings, leaning out. A firefight was flaring on the rooftops, men firing at unseen targets.

Pat rushed up to the door, ducking low as a rocket streaked straight down the middle of the street and disappeared. Going through the doors, he stepped over wounded who were sprawled in the corridor and went into the vast open room of the baths. Regimental surgeons were at work, a pile of limbs lying out in the open for all to see, and Pat turned to one of the few orderlies who had managed to keep up, shouting for the man to find a nurse and get the limbs hidden.

Seeing a knot of officers gathered in what had once been a steam room, Pat strode in, barely acknowledging the salutes. Schneid looked up from a map, breaking off an angry burst of curses directed at one of his officers.

"O'Donald, what the hell are you doing here?" Schneid asked. "Goddammit, they said you were back at headquarters. I've sent six runners back to you so far."

"Well, I'm here," Pat replied. Stay calm, he told himself, they're on the edge of panic. Andrew could be as cool as ice no matter what—never raised his voice, never cursed.

Pat took a deep breath and walked up, putting his hand on Rick's shoulder, his look conveying that their staff officers were to withdraw.

Pat waited for a long moment, saying nothing, gazing down at the map detailing Schneid's sector of the front. It looked as if a child had been playing with blocks and thrown a temper tantrum; the red and blue markers were all in a jumble. Rick had thirty regiments under his command, and nowhere on the map was there any alignment of those regiments. They were scattered about, red blocks representing reported Bantag regiments of a thousand spread out in every direction, one of them already over the inner wall. He felt a stab of fear. My God, if they're through the inner wall it's over.

He struggled to reassure himself. How the hell would Schneid, without a telegraph, know what was going on a mile away? Even as he wondered, a terrified lieutenant came running in, shouting that his regiment had been overrun and annihilated. A staff officer grabbed the boy, who started to sob, and pulled him from the room.

Schneid looked at Pat, taking a deep breath.

"It's out of control," Rick finally said.

"I know, that's why I came up here. Had to see it."

"The damn telegraphs are useless. We ran those damn lines through the sewers, figuring they'd be safe from shellfire. People must be down there running, knocking into the lines and tearing them loose. We should have thought of that."

"I know."

"And then 9th Corps, they broke, Pat, just broke."

"I think they might be saying the same thing about you," Pat replied.

Rick started to bluster, then lowered his head.

"I'm sorry."

Pat said nothing for a moment, wanting the pain to sink in. Let him go down a bit further, let him realize what was happening to everyone and how it had to be stopped.

Rick clenched his fist and slammed the table, the blocks bouncing, scattering.

"I don't know what the hell is going on," he said slowly, dragging out each word. "Pat, they came out of the snow, tens of thousands of them. And did you hear about the grenades?"

Pat shook his head.

"They had thousands of 'em. Rained them into the battlements, just lobbed them up over the wall, then came scrambling up. Some of our artillery only fired off a couple of rounds before they were wiped out. You couldn't see thirty yards up there. Everywhere, Pat, they were everywhere."

The edge started on his voice. Pat said nothing, staring at him, and he calmed down.

"Tried to reestablish a line with 9th Corps a couple of blocks back. Sent in my entire reserve. We were holding the street corners, but those bastards were smashing their way through buildings, coming out in the middle of the street. Boys started to panic, firing in every direction. Men were dropping from each other's fire. Somehow word broke that they were already over the inner wall, and units just started to melt away."

"What do you know you're holding, Rick?"

Rick laughed, again the struggle for control. "Here, this bath. One more block up toward the wall, five, maybe six blocks to the north, one or two to the south, and maybe three deep back. I had a report a half hour ago that we still held about two blocks along the wall itself and a bastion with four guns."

"11th Corps, or 9th—any contact?"

"Just the units from them that got jumbled in with mine when they cracked us on both flanks."

A burst of cannon fire caused Pat to look up and out toward the street. The gun facing to the east was firing. Crews raced to reload, several men going down from unseen fire. Again they fired. Pat looked back at Rick.

"So what are we going to do, Pat?"

He had been so busy trying to brace up the best corps commander in the army that the question caught him off guard. He was as in the dark as anyone else in this army, he realized. For all he knew, at this moment 9th and 11th Corps could be thrashing the enemy, though he doubted that. They might already be into the old city, but he doubted that as well. 4th Corps had been in relatively good order when he passed through the inner wall.

Chancellorsville. Strange how that suddenly came to mind. He remembered the breaking of the right by Stonewall Jackson's flanking march. It had been a mad night of confusion, so confusing, he later learned, that old Stonewall had been gunned down by his own men.

One corps had broken, but what was infinitely worse was that in the confusion Joe Hooker, the commander of the Army of the Potomac, had broken as well. The morning after the flanking attack, he had looked at the map, seen Stonewall's corps on his right and believed another corps was on his left, and ordered a retreat. He never walked to the other side of the map, never seen it from the other side. His opponent's army was numerically weaker, and only later was it learned that the left wing had less than ten thousand men and that Hooker was firmly entrenched between their two wings. Though all his corps commanders had begged to go over to the offensive, to smash Jackson while his men were isolated, Hooker panicked and retreated . . . just as Lee had expected him to.

They outnumber us, that is certain, but what then? Their supplies are strung out across five hundred miles of frozen prairie; we fell back on to ours. The bombardment of the last two days must have burned up several trainloads of shells and powder. The big difference, though, is that we live in cities, they don't. We know the ins and outs of Roum, even the difference in buildings. We have the maps of this city, they don't. All they know is a general direction.

If we're confused, then dammit they have to be even more confused at this moment. Though our own formations are cumbersome for this type of fighting, theirs is far worse, ten regiments of a thousand to an umen or division. Ha'ark has to be as in the dark as we are, with no idea of what he's taken, what is still holding. They won't run, their precious souls would be laughed at, but they must be damn confused.

He continued to look at the map, and then his gaze finally came back to Schneid.

"Look at the map," Pat said, his voice soft, barely above a whisper.

Rick reluctantly gazed down at the jumble of blocks made worse by his angrily slamming his fist on the table.

"What do you see?"

"Chaos. Defeat, Pat, defeat."

"Now come over here," and he pointed to the other side. Rick, giving Pat a look as if he didn't have time for some ridiculous game, did as he was ordered.

"Now, what do you see?"

"The same damn thing. Why?"

Pat smiled, pulling out his last two cigars and tossing one to Rick.

"Think, man, think. This isn't some game I'm playing."

Rick finally nodded and looked back up. "So he's as confused as we are. We're still falling apart."

"Does he know that? They're lost in this damn city. This isn't the open range, them bastards mounted on horses they were damn near born on. We're afraid of gettin' caught out in the open by them, and we should be—that's where they were born to fight, and we weren't. Now it's our field. We're forgetting that—this is our field, not his. Damn all, we should have come straight back here the day after we got out from the Rocky Hill. Let 'em get in here, let 'em get a taste of fighting in the streets with modern weapons."

Pat started to pace back and forth, lighting his cigar and stopping for a moment to light Rick's.

"Let him get in here, let him get his whole damn army in here. Forget lines. Dig in wherever we still stand right here in the outer city. We'll form a blocking line with 4th Corps and 12th to keep 'em back from the riverfront, but the rest of us, you, the 9th, the 11th, and I'll bring up what I can from 3rd from the other wall, will dig in right where you stand."

"I still think we should pull out while we can."

"To where? The river? You fight right here. This is your headquarters. Hold it."

"Pat, how the hell am I to coordinate this? Hell, I can't even find any of my division commanders and only two of my brigade commanders."

"You got a bunch of damn staff officers out there thicker than fleas. Get them out. This damn city is laid out like a grid of blocks. Number the blocks, give each one a map, get them the hell out, and find who's at each block. I want the order passed: no one to move, get into the buildings. Once inside, smash holes between each of them, link the whole block together like a fortress, dig in, and hold on."

"Fine. And ammunition, food? What about that?"

Pat felt his plan starting to disintegrate even before it formed. If the Bantag could isolate a block, a couple of hours of fighting would deplete the ammunition, and in a hand-to-hand fight a human stood little chance against an eight-foot giant weighing three hundred pounds. But then again, he thought, most of these damn buildings didn't have ceilings much over six foot. They'll be damn near on their hands and knees inside. It will be like us fighting in a city made for leprechauns or dwarfs.

But the ammunition.

"The sewers," Rick said. "The damn stinking sewers. The big ones under the main thoroughfares, you can almost walk upright in them. That's where we ran the telegraph wires. There must be thousands of people down there in them now."

"And they empty into the river, below the waterline," Pat replied, and then realized that the telegraph crews had come up through the cellars of buildings along the riverbank. Smash in the cellars, get gangs of men moving ammunition, and a couple of regiments spaced out in the sewers could move hundreds of boxes an hour.

"The sewer coming up into this bath is huge," Rick said. "They used to flush them pools out every day, hundreds of thousands of gallons of water," and he motioned toward a doorway that led out to the cold-water baths, which were already half empty.

"This is your anchor point, then. I want you to pass the word out now—everyone stand and hold, and for now the hell with trying to make sense of it, just dig in and kill the bastards! I'm heading back to headquarters. I'll detail off a couple of regiments to get underground, try and make connection that way. Get your people out, and send a map back to me of what you know you're holding. Not what you think you've got, but what you know you've got, and no mistakes."

"Why?"

" 'Cause once we know where our people are, I'm ordering the artillery on the inner wall to start smashing down everything else."

He started to button his greatcoat, ready to leave and

head over to try and find 9th Corps, and then he stopped. What would Andrew do?

I'm in command, he realized yet again. Andrew hasn't sent me out here to find out what's happened, I came here myself, and back at headquarters it must be chaos. I have to go back and calm headquarters down, stop the panic before it destroys us. I've done all I can do up here.

He called for their staffs, gathered them around, shared the plan, and quickly detailed runners to find the other headquarters and pass the word.

"And make it damn clear this is a direct order. Not one more step of retreat. Cut off, threatened to be cut off, or holding intact, everyone digs in where they are. Do you understand me?"

There were nods, and to his delight the terror was beginning to subside.

"Now that they're here, it's not them that's got us, it's us that's got them. Now hop to it. I want grid maps made up. Take them, decide among yourselves who heads where. Once you get through to your assignments, make your way back to headquarters. For those of you lads that make it back before sunset, a bottle of vodka and a warm bed await."

"Any lasses?" a freckle-faced boy asked hopefully, and the others grinned.

Good, they can joke again, Pat realized.

"Hop to it, boys. I'm heading back."

Turning to Rick, he wanted to say something else, one final word of encouragement, and saw that his old friend was already back at the map, sweeping the blocks off.

Pat headed for the door. Again the artillery fired, guns recoiling. Huddled in an anteroom adjacent to the foyer he saw his escort from O'Leary's regiment still waiting. He wanted to compliment the young officer but then realized that the boy would have been a fool to wander off—they had a safe hole for the moment, the reassurance of being inside a corps headquarters building defended by artillery.

"All right, lads, out we go," Pat announced. "There's a battle to fight."

With the coming of late afternoon the storm abated, and Ha'ark the Redeemer rejoiced, for it seemed as if the gods of the winds had finally decided to cooperate. When the cloak of the storm was needed it was there, and now that he needed clear weather that was coming. Occasional squalls of near white-out intensity came boiling up from the south but then as quickly lifted, and for brief moments the entire city was again in view.

Vast sections of it were burning, and dark roiling clouds hanging low to the ground tumbled across the skyline. Flashes of light rippled from one end to the other as hundreds of shells burst every minute.

He gazed down at the map and then over at Jurak.

"The inner wall?" he asked.

"We got over it at one point, but they were ready. We lost the position, though I had a report that two regiments were still fighting in there."

"And the rest?"

Juraka pointed down at the map, tracing out the positions. "We have the entire outer wall from the bastion guarding the river to the south up to the bastion guarding the river on the north side, except for one small section held by soldiers with the circles on their hats.

"Within this half," and his hand swept across the northeast quadrant, "it is hard to say what we have. Some of the main streets nearly to the inner wall are firmly in our control, the rest is confusion. In this quarter of the city, they have one large pocket of resistance, maybe ten blocks on a side, but in the rest it is hard to tell."

Ha'ark nodded.

"Fine. Then we bring up fresh troops during the night, consolidate what we have, and crush what's left."

"What about attacking the other side of the city, as you planned?"

Ha'ark gazed at the map and shook his head. "They will expect it, and besides, we will not have the cover of the weather tonight or tomorrow. We've yet to get a bridge across the river farther up to move our supplies. Let us draw the battle in here, force them to fight, bleed them out."

"They're bleeding us out too," Jurak replied. "I think we lost well over thirty thousand today."

"And he undoubtedly lost the same."

"That I cannot say. We gained the wall with fewer losses than I expected. In fact, I saw them panicking. But now we have to dig them out, and it will cost."

"The rise of ground in the outer city—did you take it?"

"Part of it."

"Fine. I want every available mortar up there tonight. Start shelling their riverfront come dawn. I want our artillery that was positioned to support this attack moved to smash down the bastion guarding the approach to the river. We cut their ships off and they starve and run out of ammunition."

Jurak nodded in agreement.

"At least there's food waiting inside the city for us," Ha'ark announced. "That is motivation enough to dig them out."

Jurak's features wrinkled with disdain.

"Still think it's barbaric?"

"Worst than barbaric," Jurak snapped. "These are the enemy, not animals."

"Tell that to my loyal barbaric subjects. They believe the humans to be soulless cattle. Worse, they are cattle driven mad by demons who must be rooted out and annihilated. Drive the demon mad with pain, then devour the heart and kill the demon. That is why they fight."

"And not for your empire?" Jurak asked quietly.

Ha'ark said nothing. Again his companion from the old world had taken a liberty he was no longer willing to allow. The Bantag had not acknowledged the others who came through the tunnel of light as the Redeemer. They had selected him because he had acted first, understanding first where they were. That was fate, that was the will of the ancestor gods, and Jurak would have to learn that if he was to survive once this war was finished.

"No matter what they do, we will bleed them out. We'll have the city in ten days, before the next moon feast. And then what a feast it will be!" Ha'ark announced with a grin.

Chapter Eight

"You saw the latest dispatches?" Admiral Bullfinch asked, coming into Vincent Hawthorne's office and collapsing in the chair before his desk.

Vincent wearily nodded. Standing, Vincent reached up to the kerosene lamp and turned it down. Pulling back the curtains, he rubbed the frost-covered windowpane and looked outside. Dawn was breaking across the old city of Suzdal. Down in the square below, the faithful, almost all of them older women, walked hunched over against the bitter wind, making their way to the cathedral, where Metropolitan Casmar was offering morning mass.

Vincent watched them, remembering the first time he had seen this place, serving on the escort to Colonel Keane when he had come up to the city to meet with Boyar Ivor. How fairy-tale it had all looked then, the onion-domed cupolas, the log walls, the elaborate wood carvings, the exotic women of the court wearing long flowing gowns embroidered with golden thread, and not one whisper yet of the existence of the Hordes.

"They've effectively blockaded Roum," Vincent said. "Isn't there some way we can run the blockade?"

Bullfinch sighed. "That steamer going down in the middle of the channel's what did it, Vincent. We have to hug in close to the eastern shore to get in, right under their damn guns. Two days ago they had a fifty-pound Parrott, one of our guns captured at Fort Lincoln, dug in on the bluffs. For the old transports that's it. Even for our ironclads it makes a bit of a rattling."

"Then use the monitors to take supplies up."

"What I'm planning on. But Vincent, the monitors are designed to fight, not to haul supplies. I got six ironclads left here. We can maybe cram a hundred tons of munitions on board. It takes three days up, a day to off-load, and three days back. So we're getting a hundred tons up a day, less than half of what they need, and all the time we're pounding the engines on our monitors to hell running at top speed. In a month the fleet will all be in dock for refit."

"Why not anchor out in the bay and just have one monitor offloading from a supply ship?"

"Actually, that's what I'm thinking of doing, but we've got two small access hatches, we're out in a rolling sea, the loads will have to be transferred by hand from one ship to the other, so it comes out about the same as loading a monitor up here."

"You wanted that marine division of yours," Vincent said, increasingly exasperated. "You got a brigade almost trained. Move them up, land them, and assault the gun, take it out."

Bullfinch shook his head. "He must have a full umen dug in around that one gun. I tried to shell it out, but I tell you, unless I put a shot right through the gunport—when it's open, mind you—it's useless."

Vincent sighed, and sitting back down, he looked at the report sent back by Pat.

They were continuing to hold eight days after the breakthrough, but casualties were mounting, and ammunition was being used up at a horrendous rate, twice what they had expected. The burning of several key warehouses had put the city on half rations. Pat was still claiming they could win, but it was at least two more months to the mud season of spring thaw and the bogging down of the Bantag's supply system. The numbers simply didn't add up to victory.

"And remember, I still have to supply Hans as well."

"Hans," Vincent sighed. He had just had another bout with the president over that the night before. Try as he could, he simply couldn't get it through that Hans staying where he was had tied up at least ten umens and that to move him north in an attempt to relive the city was worse than useless, it was suicidal in the middle of the winter, and beyond that, even if he did land Hans smack in the middle of the city, how were an additional fifty thousand men to be armed and fed?

"Anything new beyond Kev?" Bullfinch asked.

"Some raids, not much. 5th Corps is dug in along the White Hills. The lines are thin but bolstered with old men, disabled veterans, and boys from the Home Guard. Two of the newer land ironclads and two flyers have been sent up there as well. The flyers are great for keeping an eye on the bastards. We won't have much trouble on that front."

Committing two of the flyers and the new ironclads had been a move he had dreaded. His only hope was that since it was a raiding force there were no trained observers who could accurately report to Ha'ark about the newer technology. If it hadn't been for the absolute demand of Kal and several senators to do this he might have held off anyhow.

"Speaking of flyers," Bullfinch said, "the report really doesn't mention it. I saw them when I was up there. They're getting damn bold. Dropping bombs on the harbor, the palace, the old forum. They've got four airships up there now bombing. Terrible things, firepots and sulfur matches, caused a lot of fires. Pat's screaming for airships."

Vincent shook his head.

"I released them to Kev because they were desperately needed there as eyes for our army. We know where they are around Roum, and wasting our air strength over the city is useless. Besides, where will they land in all that confusion?"

"Well, what about the new ironclads? You've got at least twenty-five now."

"For what? Fighting in the city? They've got them damn rocket tubes all over that city, you told me that yourself. The few ironclads Ha'ark put into the town were burning within the hour. No, not yet."

"Well, damn it all, Vincent, if things don't change

damn quick the city will be lost and it won't matter if you got a hundred of the damn things, they ain't going to stop the Horde when it comes rolling over the White Mountains come spring."

Vincent wanted to reply that if the city did fall there wouldn't even be a fight at the White Mountains. The mood of the Senate was worsening. Shouting matches, even the threat of duels and brandishing of pistols on the floor during a session, were becoming near daily occurrences as the body split between those seeking a truce and the group, made up almost entirely of old veterans, who demanded a fight to the finish. If Roum fell or Pat was forced to evacuate, he knew that surrender would be offered, the honeyed promises of Ha'ark believed.

And then what? We won't surrender, he thought, not those of us who came here with Andrew, not many from the army. Head west—no, Tamuka and what was left of the Merki still lingered out there. Into the forests of the north then, hide with the exiles, the wanderers and outcasts, and be hunted like beasts. The thought was beyond his ability to accept or to contemplate. No, there had to be a victory, some victory, before spring or it would be lost.

"Andrew—how is he?"

Bullfinch shook his head.

"About the same," he whispered, leaning forward as if afraid someone would hear. "The fever was dropping the morning I left there. But he drifts in and out. He's, how can I say it . . ."

"He's fragile," Vincent said. And merely saying the word was frightening to him. It was the brittleness he felt within himself as well. The terror of being hurt again, hurt with a pain no one could ever imagine unless he had been there and survived. It made him realize just how much of a fraud he felt himself to be. Since that final moment on the field he had not heard a shot fired in anger. He had been sent back here to Suzdal to recover, to coordinate the home defense, to oversee ordnance and the industrial complex needed to support the armies. All looked at him as a hero, and in his heart he knew he was a fraud.

Bullfinch said nothing more. Somehow they all felt rudderless. The hand of the young colonel who had gone to middle age building an army, a republic from a race raised up from slavery, was gone, and he felt like a child suddenly forced to be the head of a fatherless family.

"We've got to do something, Vincent. We can't just sit here, let it drag out."

"I know."

"And?"

Vincent finally nodded. "We'll try the plan we've been cooking up."

"Hans will have a fit. Kal will never allow it, and Andrew never even heard of it."

Vincent smiled. "Regarding Kal, well, what he doesn't know he can't stop. As for Hans, since I'm senior to him as chief of staff of the army it'll be an order. And besides, I think he'll like it. As for Andrew, let's just pray that he doesn't fire us all if it fails."

"If it fails, we've lost," Bullfinch said coldly.

"What a damn stink," Pat muttered as he climbed down the steps into the basement, following a line of replacement infantry for the 1st Corps. The far wall of the dank basement was knocked in, revealing the dark cavern of a subterranean sewer. The damp air drifting out was thick with cloying smells, and Pat quickly lit a cigar to block them out.

A staff officer from 1st Corps who was waiting for him saluted and announced that he would be the general's guide. Pat nodded and pointed for him to lead the way. Half sliding down a wooden plank, he stepped gingerly into the ankle-deep muck and set out, the only illumination coming from the occasional drain slits set into the roadway above. Muffled sounds drifted down, the thumping of artillery, the occasional crump of a mortar round detonating, the tramping of feet.

Reaching an intersection with a pipe heading off to

the south, the guide halted for a moment. Rifle shots boomed with rolling echoes.

"Down in the fourth sector they pulled back the paving, dug down. You can smell the fumes from the burning oil they poured in. It's been a tough fight."

Two men came crawling back down the pipe, covered in muck, dragging along a third comrade who was dead, pushing him out into the main sewer. They looked at Pat blankly, then turned and crawled back.

Pat stepped around the body, then pressed himself against the wall as a casualty clearing party came past, bearing half a dozen stretchers. Emil was having a fit about moving men with open wounds through the sewers, but for the surrounded units of 1st and 9th Corps it was the only way out.

Pressing along behind his guide, he stopped again for a moment, a sergeant blocking the way, hand up for them to halt.

The sergeant was intently peering at a grating in the ceiling.

"You can hear them light the fuse for a grenade," he whispered. "If I say run, you got four or five seconds, then get down."

Pat nodded, and the sergeant silently waved them forward. Blast marks scorched the walls from previous explosions.

Pat had barely cleared the grate when the sergeant screamed, "Run!"

Looking back over his shoulder, Pat saw the sergeant scooping up a grenade that had dropped through the overhead grate and pinching off the fuse. Looking up at the grate, the sergeant let loose with a stream of invective, answered in turn by growling roars. Strange, a game almost, and Pat sensed that both sides were actually enjoying themselves. A dim flare ignited ahead, flames balling up, a dull whoosh thumping down the corridor.

"Benzene," the guide announced. "They pour it through the vents. Sometimes they get somebody. Crouch low—the air is better."

Looking down at the muck under his feet, he decided

to endure the fumes. Crossing the next intersection with a tunnel almost as big as the one they were in, he saw a knot of soldiers, rifles poised, aiming at a clear patch of light where an explosion had caved in part of the line.

The sense of hellish confusion was increasing, wounded coming past, a carrying party shouting for the way to be cleared, rifle fire booming with cacophonous roars, another whooshing burst of igniting benzene followed an instant later by animal-like shrieks of agony, all of it combined with the stench, filth, and sick clammy feel of the enclosing walls.

Creeping forward, Pat's guide finally relaxed. "We're inside our lines now—at least inside the section we were holding an hour ago. You missed the coal gas."

"Coal gas?"

"Last night, fumes from a coal fire started to fill up the next sewer line over, which connects to the 9th Corps. The bastards built a big fire, made some sort of pipe with bellows, and were pumping in the fumes to gas us out. The old 7th Suzdal attacked the temple where they'd set this contraption up and smashed it."

Ingenious. Chances were they'd try it elsewhere; to them it was smoking out rats.

Pat saw a stream of light ahead and gratefully accepted a hand that pulled him up into what had once been the cavernous cold-water bath. In the dim glare of a torch he caught a final glimpse of the sewer line ahead, blocked off with piles of rubble, with Bantag holding the other side less than a dozen feet away. Only the day before they had blasted it with several hundred pounds of powder, collapsing a large section and killing a score of men.

Climbing into the baths, he looked up, squinting his eyes against the bright light. The roof was gone, and thousands of shattered tiles and flame-scorched beams half filled the bath. A stretcher party carrying a dozen men stood to one side, waiting for the order to go down, while a line of filth-encrusted men struggled to clear crates of small-arms ammunition and boxes of hardtack.

Scrambling up a ladder out of the pool, Pat quickly

surveyed the ruins. Ten days of nonstop fighting had reduced the headquarters to a smoldering pile of rubble. But rather than rendering the building useless it had in some ways made it even more defensible. Collapsed ceiling beams had been piled up and covered over with tons of bricks to form bombproof shelters. Infantry were dug in along the smashed walls, the men having burrowed down into the ruins, creating dozens of small rifle pits. Following his guide, Pat bent down low, passing under what had once been the bronze doors of the main entryway and into a deep burrow that now served as Schneid's headquarters.

The telegrapher was busy, a small pile of copied dispatches by his side, the key chattering away. The bombproof was rich with the smell of freshly brewed tea, and Pat gratefully accepted a cup, pulling off his mittens and wrapping his hands around the mug for warmth.

A roughly sketched map hung from one wall, pinned against two upended benches.

"Losing block twenty-two," Schneid announced, pointing at the map. "They broke into the villa in the center of the block a couple of hours ago."

Pat nodded. "And the Temple to Venus?"

"Oh, that regiment from 12th Corps you sent up, they're fighting like demons for it. Say they'll be damned if they let Bantag defile it."

"Pagans," Pat muttered with a grin. Making sure that Roum regiments were assigned to hold religious sites had been a shrewd suggestion from Rick, and it seemed to be working.

"Care for a look around?"

"That's what I'm here for," Pat said.

Grinning, Schneid beckoned for him to follow. They crawled up out of the bombproof, and a detachment of filthy-looking infantry, many of the men wrapped in layers of dirt-encrusted blankets, fell in around them.

"Sergeant Zhadovich here can guide us," Schneid announced. Pat turned, expecting to see the typical Rus sergeant, in his late thirties or early forties, graybearded, tough but with a fatherly edge. Instead he was surprised to see a boy not much more than nineteen or at best twenty years old. But the eyes instantly gave him away—they were cold, remorseless, those of a natural-born killer. Pat sensed a strange aura about this young sergeant, that somehow, no matter what happened, he would get through it alive, and thus other soldiers would gravitate to him and follow his orders.

"All right, sirs, one thing we gotta understand. Once over the wall, I'm in command. I say stop, you stop. Get down, you get down. Keep an eye on me. Not a sound out of you, and if I start running like hell, you better keep up. Understand?"

Pat grinned and nodded. "Fine with me, soldier."

"I'll tell you, sirs, I don't like this assignment. Getting one, maybe two generals killed on my watch is not my idea of fun. General, you sure you want to see this?"

Pat nodded.

The boy turned his head and spit. "With his excellency the colonel still down, sir, shouldn't you think twice about it?"

"Sergeant, a hell of a general I'd be if I didn't see what my men were facing."

"Fine then, sir, but if you get killed, that's your responsibility, sir, not mine and my men's."

Pat smiled inwardly. Zhadovich was damn good. Not just covering his ass but making sure his unit was covered as well. It was the type of move that would win him respect with his company long after Pat was gone and would be talked about around the campfire—how their sergeant put a general in his place.

Pat stared at Zhadovich for a moment, the look conveying that he understood the game the two of them were playing. Zhadovich seemed to ease up a bit but still held eye contact. Finally, offering a shrug of resignation, the sergeant started for the south wall of the bathhouse, a quick hand gesture giving the order for his men to move out.

Gaining the wall, Zhadovich bent over to talk softly with a soldier dug in between two broken marble pillars. The soldier nodded, whispered back, pointing to his left.

Zhadovich slipped up to just below the top of the rubble, raised his head for an instant, slid down, then waved his arm for the group to move quickly. As Pat slipped past him, Zhadovich hissed, "Through the broken green door, then wait."

Pat scrambled up over the rubble, sparing a quick glance to his left toward what had once been the outer battlements. They were invisible in the lightly falling snow. Sliding down the rubble, he slammed into the swollen corpse of a Bantag. He leaped over it, nearly twisting an ankle as broken roof tiles skidded on the icy pavement under his feet. Ducking low, he ran for the door and went through it. The interior of the building, which looked to have been a pottery shop, was a shambles. In the middle of the room a knot of soldiers were squatting about a fire, heating cups of tea. They barely acknowledged Pat and Rick as they slipped past, weaving through the building, passing a cluster of men curled up in blankets and asleep in an alcove. Reaching the rear wall of the shop, Pat scrambled through a hole cut in the wall, out across what had once been a garden, and into the ground floor of yet another potter's shop.

The same was repeated through the next two blocks, darting across rubble-choked streets, weaving through the ruins of buildings, at one point diving under a heavy stone workbench when two mortar rounds whistled in. The roar of battle was incessant, and as they drew closer to what was the front line of the pocket it became deafening. Coming into the courtyard of a villa on the third block, Pat paused for a moment to kneel down and chat with half a dozen wounded who were laboriously being moved back to the corps headquarters and the entryway to the main sewer. All the men were exhausted, holloweyed, the wounds the results of up-close fighting.

Next to them a group of men were fashioning crude grenades out of canteens, funneling a mixture of powder, nails, and rock fragments in through the spout, sticking a fuse in, then sealing the spout with hot wax. Zhadovich picked up two of them, their manufacturers stifling their protests at the sight of two generals with the group.

Zhadovich edged up to the shattered outer wall of what had been a wheelwright's shop, spoke with a lieutenant commanding the section, and slipped back to Pat and Rick.

"Think this is the end of the road," he hissed. "All hell's breaking loose in the next block."

Pat didn't need to be told. The way ahead was obscured not just by the light snow but by billowing clouds of dirty smoke. Small-arms fire was snapping overhead, mortar rounds crumping on the street.

Pat looked over at Rick, who was hunched by his side.

"Like Spotsylvania."

"Cold Harbor, but worse," Rick replied.

"Look, no sense two of us getting killed. Let's make it easy on the old sergeant there. You've seen this, I haven't."

"No problem, general. I was in the infantry back home, while you had it easy in the artillery. Be my guest—I'll wait here."

Pat grinned, then looked over at Zhadovich, who shook his head.

"Your funeral, sir."

Sliding back from the edge of the wall, Zhadovich and his men crawled to a side chamber. Pat followed and saw that the room was a privy, the seats torn off. A narrow opening dropped down into the sewer. A lieutenant with three men, spotting Zhadovich, prevailed on him to carry over a box of hardtack, a box of a thousand rounds of ammunition, and some canteens of fresh water.

Burdened down with the extra equipment, Pat slinging half a dozen canteens over his shoulder, they dropped down to the bottom of the privy. It had once been a pipe weaving its way through the block, water flushing out the waste. The pipe itself had been far too small to crawl through. Over the last week a team of men had used the pipe as a guide and cut their way down to the sewer under the street, and another tunnel had been carved up into the next block. Crawling on hands and knees, Pat followed his guides under the street, their exit yet another privy. He saw a rifle, tipped with a bayonet, point down at Zhadovich, who was leading the party. Hands then reached down, grabbing hold of the ammunition box and hardtack. Pat crawled up through the hole. Men started to come to attention in the dusty room until he motioned for them to stand at ease.

He looked around. The ceiling was gone in the barrel-vaulted room, which apparently had been a warehouse for amphorae of wine. Whatever had been stored here, however, had long ago been consumed; hundreds of shattered amphorae were strewn about. To provide overhead protection, broken ceiling beams had been laid out across the racks used to hold the amphorae. Broken tiles, bricks, doors, anything to stop a mortar round were piled on top.

The cavelike room they had crawled into was a regimental headquarters and casualty clearing area. Spotting a captain who was obviously in command by the way he passed orders to men crawling in, Pat scurried over to him.

The captain, squatting on the floor, looked up hollow-eyed at Pat and without rising offered a weary salute.

"Captain Petrov Petronovich, sir, 8th Murom, in command of the regiment."

"Relax, captain." Pat unslung one of the canteens he had hung on to and offered it over. He was pleased when the captain nodded his thanks but then passed the canteen over to a sergeant major and a couple of lieutenants gathered around him. Only after they had drunk did the captain accept it back and take a short gulp.

"Tell me what's going on here, captain. How's your regiment?"

"We've been up here since the breakthrough, sir. Can't we get any relief? My boys have been fighting nonstop for ten days."

"How's the regiment?"

"Had three hundred twenty-eight the morning they broke through, down to ninety-one."

Pat nodded, saying nothing while pulling a handful of cigars from his pocket and passing them around to the captain and his makeshift staff.

"We hold half this block, sir," and even as they spoke a mortar round crumpled on the roof of the bombproof. "They want to take the east wall. We can look down on the battlements, the field beyond, and into the next block. That's where most of the fighting was. This morning they hit from the west side, overran what was left of the 2nd Kev, broke across the street. Got them damn rockets and artillery firing on us from the battlement—can't pick the gunners off, can't see 'em."

"How are the men?"

"Finished," the captain whispered.

"And if I tell you you have to stay?"

The captain exchanged looks with his staff. "Dammit, that's what I figured."

"I'll see what I can do when I get back."

"What about them damn bastards with the 12th Corps sir?" one of the sergeants asked. "They ain't seen no fighting except for a couple of lousy regiments."

Pat nodded. How could he explain the need for a fresh reserve, either to hold if the Bantag launched another full-scale assault somewhere else, or as replacements when all of 1st Corps was pulled out? Sending them in piecemeal would drain off what strength he had left.

"I can't promise, sergeant. It's not just here, it's all around the city. I'm trying the best I can to see no one carries too much. What I'm asking you is, can you still kill Bantag?"

"Kill 'em, sir? Shit, all the livelong day. Just want my friends with the 12th to share the fun, that's all."

Pat reached over and clapped the man on the shoulder.

"Captain, take me around the perimeter."

The captain sighed, and looked over at Sergeant Zhadovich, who finally nodded. "He wants to see it—let him see it."

The captain crawled out of the bombproof, motioning for Zhadovich to come next. "Don't need the others," the captain announced. "Might draw attention."

The men gratefully remained, instantly sprawling out to catch a little rest.

Heading east along a narrow trench cut into the floor of the building and piled high on either side with rubble, they went under a hole in a wall. Looking up, Pat could see the stark ruins of a burned-out temple, its exterior walls made of limestone. All that was left was the shell, the interior having burned and collapsed. A flame-scorched rag doll lay against the wall of the trench, obviously placed there by a sentimental soldier.

Even as he looked up at the wall a rocket shrieked overhead, from the west and crashed into the wall, rubble and shards of stone raining down.

Pat pressed on, crawling along the trench, which sliced into the interior of the temple, and worming his way up through the rubble to the center of the building. It was difficult to spot any men. Rubble had been piled up around window slits on all four sides of the building.

Zhadovich pointed up, and tucked into an overhanging eave Pat spotted a lone soldier swaddled in white blankets. All that was visible was a rifle barrel, poised at a crack in the wall. The gun recoiled, the man ducked back and away, and a second later stone fragments kicked up from return fire through the slit.

"Good sniper," the captain announced proudly. "Eight kills for certain."

The interior of the building rocked as half a dozen artillery rounds slammed into the outside wall on the east side, a section of stone raining down into the inside. Rifle fire erupted along the south wall, return fire cracking through breaks in the wall. Piercing taunts echoed from across the street. The men remained silent, one of them sliding down to a box of ammunition placed under a broken statue, then crawling back up, passing out handfuls to his comrades.

"Grenade!"

Pat barely saw the sputtering fuse as a grenade arced up over the wall and banged down into the center of the temple. The explosion snapped, and he was surprised—it didn't seem to have much punch.

"Only dangerous if it lands in a hole with you," Zhadovich announced. Motioning for Pat to follow, the captain crawled up to the east wall.

"You see a flash from where the battlement is, you duck," the captain announced.

Pat nodded. The captain taped a rifleman on the shoulder, and the man rolled back and away, giving his spot to O'Donald, who slithered into the hollow depression and cautiously raised his head to peek out.

The next block over was smashed to ruins, not a single wall more than a couple of feet high. He thought he saw something move, and a rifleman several feet away fired, the shot nicking a brick, shattering it just inches from the dark form, which ducked down.

Instinct told him to duck down, and he did. A second later a rifle ball hummed overhead. Peeking back out, he was surprised to actually see the outline of the battlement walls, less than seventy yards away. As the storm briefly abated and visibility lifted, rifle fire exploded all around him, puffs of smoke billowing all along the battlement wall. Sharp flashes of light ignited, and he ducked back down when at nearly the same instant solid shot slammed into the temple. One ball passed straight through an opening and slammed into the opposite wall.

A narga sounded, and rockets fired from the battlement, some slamming into the temple, others shrieking overhead. Pat looked back out again. A ragged line of Bantag were up, charging through the rubble of the adjoining block.

There was no need to shout a warning. Everyone inside the temple opened up with a fusillade. Rather than give up his spot, Pat yanked the rifle from the infantryman by his side, took aim, fired, and had the satisfaction of seeing a Bantag clutch his leg and go down into the debris.

Still they came on, now screaming, shouting their battle cries. When the first wave reached the edge of the street, less than ten yards away, they went to ground, seeking what cover they could, continuing to fire. More artillery cut loose, and then a second wave of attackers seemed to emerge out of nowhere, charging forward.

Half dropped within seconds, but the survivors surged on, coming up to the wall of the temple and disappearing from view, directly under Pat. He was tempted to stand up, lean out the window, and see what he could hit with his revolver but knew he'd get cut to ribbons by the supporting fire. Another grenade arced up, slammed against the side of his rifle pit, and fell back down.

Zhadovich shouldered Pat aside and tore the cigar from the general's mouth. Taking one of the canteen grenades, he lit the fuse, then calmly watched as it sputtered down until it had nearly disappeared into the spout. Pat watched him, wide-eyed, admiring his nerve. Zhadovich simply extended his hand and dropped it out the firing slit. A second later there was a concussive roar, followed instantly by screams.

An explosion tore through the temple, stunning Pat. Looking over his shoulder, he saw the debris piled up around the temple doors on the north side of the building soaring skyward, the massive explosion shaking the building.

"Mine! The bastards have part of the sewer here!" the captain gasped.

Rubble rained down, and out of the boiling cloud a swarm of Bantag emerged, charging from across the street. Another narga sounded, and from out of the rubble field directly in front of Pat more Bantag swarmed forward.

"You wanted to see a fight," Zhadovich snarled. "You got it, sir!"

The sergeant lit a second canteen, and using the carrying strap he whirled it over his head, then let go, the canteen sailing through the temple doors and exploding.

Within seconds the interior of the temple was a bedlam of noise, men screaming, Bantag roaring their battle chants, rifles firing, while another rocket slammed straight through the melee, fired by three Bantag standing in the doorway.

Drawing his revolver, Pat took careful aim, dropping one of the rocket crew as they struggled to reload, the rocket igniting and soared straight up into the air.

There were no lines, all was confusion inside the ruined temple, individual Bantag and men fighting out their own bitter war of hatred with rifles, bayonets, knives, rocks, and bare fists. Half a dozen Bantag came scrambling up through the rubble at Pat, Zhadovich, the captain, and the rifleman who was with them. The rifleman stood, dropping the first, then went down, shot in the face at near-point-blank range. Zhadovich, drawing a revolver from his belt, set to with a passion, screaming for Pat to guard the firing slit. Crouching low, he weaved through the Bantag like a ferret, dodging, falling, rolling, each shot slamming into an opponent, the captain followed him, emptying his revolver, then sweeping up a dropped Bantag rifle and using it as a club.

Pat, tempted to join the melee, started to turn, then from the corner of his eye saw a giant dark form appear in the window slit, hand grabbing for a hold. He smashed the butt of his pistol down on the Bantag's knuckles, laughing as the warrior screamed and fell back. Another appeared, and he pressed his gun into the warrior's face and fired. No more came through his slit, but to his right, at the next slit, a Bantag appeared, shooting the infantryman who had been guarding it in the back when the man turned to face the attack from the inside. Pat dropped him. Figuring no one would try his slot for a moment, he crawled over the rubble, arriving just as another warrior started to crawl through. Saving his last couple of shots, Pat picked up a brick and flung it, and the Bantag fell backward. Seconds later a grenade bounced in. Snatching it up the way he had seen the sergeant in the tunnel do it, Pat dropped it back outside, where it exploded.

"General, behind you!"

Pat emptied the last two rounds in his revolver at a Bantag scrambling up with bayonet poised.

More forms swirled into the fight, emerging from the tunnel he had used to enter the temple—Sergeant Zhadovich's men. They attacked with a wild fury, firing at point-blank range, grappling hand to hand with their foes.

Gasping for breath, Pat fumbled with his revolver, unlatching the pin, the barrel levering forward, letting the chamber fall out onto the ground. He plucked a loaded chamber out of his jacket pocket and tried to slide it down on the cylinder shaft. As he struggled to lever the barrel back up and lock it in place, two more Bantag broke through the melee, coming toward him. Other Bantag were pointing at him and trying to break through as well.

Pat locked the barrel in place, cocked the revolver, and emptied it in seconds, one of the dead Bantag falling on top of him. Crawling out from under, he saw two more. Both of them spun around and fell atop him as well.

The thick stench of warm blood and entrails engulfed him, and at the thought of what the bastards might have eaten for breakfast he gagged, cursing, trying to move.

The roar of battle continued. Another explosion rocked the temple, and someone screamed that an airship was overhead. Clawing at the bodies, he tried to squirm out from under the hundreds of pounds of dead flesh.

He felt a hand grab him by the shoulder, and for a second there was a shiver of terror—was it a Bantag?

"He's still alive."

It was the captain.

One of the Bantag bodies lifted slightly, and another hand grabbed him. Kicking and cursing, he was dragged out from under the pile.

The battle still raged. Swirling streamers of thick yellow-gray smoke clung inside the temple, and the snow had picked up again so that everything seemed like ghostly shadows.

"Where are they?" Pat roared.

"Back outside." It was Zhadovich, his voice calm, wiping a cut on his right cheek with the back of his hand. His face was bruised, bloodied. Reaching into his mouth, he wiggled a broken tooth and plucked it out.

Stunned, Pat looked around. More troops were coming up through the access tunnel, crawling, fanning out, several of them using knives to slice the throats of wounded Bantag. The battle was an inferno, the wall above him shaking from repeated artillery hits.

"Christ, this is madness," Pat gasped.

For the first time he saw Zhadovich grin.

"Care to see anything else, general, sir?"

Pat shook his head. The captain was already gone, down by the shattered barricade of the temple door, directing men to pile up pieces of limestone. Scanning the ruins, he could see that at least a dozen men were dead, another dozen wounded. The ratio of so few wounded to dead attested to the ferocity of the close-in fighting.

Reaching the tunnel, Pat stopped and motioned toward a man who had taken a bayonet in the shoulder. Zhadovich hesitated, then grabbed hold and helped Pat drag the cursing soldier down into the narrow tunnel and into the adjoining courtyard. The headquarters area was empty except for several seriously wounded. Pat left the soldier he was dragging when the boy insisted on staying with one of his friends. A carrying party came up out of the tunnel under the street, dragging cans of kerosene. Following them was a company of fifteen men moving up to reinforce the line. Just as the last man cleared the tunnel down into the sewer, a thunderous whoosh echoed, followed instantly by a boiling cloud of smoke.

Zhadovich stopped.

"On your own back, sir. My boys are up in the temple—won't leave them."

"Thanks, sergeant. I think I can manage." He extended his hand.

"This can't go on forever," the sergeant said. "We're becomin' like them. Some of the boys are saying we should eat their dead to get even."

Pat, horrified, said nothing.

"Ain't there yet, sir, but it's how we feel. Reserves or not, sir, you better get the 12th up here on the line. Feelings are getting kind of bad that it seems like Rus is carrying the fight. 9th Corps was Roum, and they pretty well broke—it was the old 1st that saved the day."

Pat nodded.

Zhadovich finally took his hand, then, crouching low, returned up the trench.

Getting down on all fours, Pat slipped down the tunnel leading into the sewer and instantly started to choke. The air was thick with the stench of burning kerosene. As he slipped into the main sewer line he landed on a flame-scorched body, the uniform still smoldering. Another man, lying in the slime, hearing Pat, looked back, his face barely visible in the gloom.

"Get down!"

Pat sprawled down next to him. There was a flash, the crack of a rifle, ahead, and the man fired back. Flames still flickered in the muck around them, and the air was choking.

"Dammit, get out of here, sir!"

Pat, surprised at how grateful he felt to be ordered out by a private, scrambled up the tunnel into the next block. Schneid was peering down at him, reaching out a hand to pull him up. Rifle fire erupted from behind. Seconds later there was a dark guttural roar. Bantag had just cut the line.

Rick looked back at a team of men and nodded. They cut open five-gallon tin cans of kerosene and upended them, letting the fluid pour down into the sewer. He could hear shouted roars. One of the men then lit the fuse to a canteen grenade and lobbed it down the opening. A whooshing roar erupted, a blowtorch of flame snapping out of the tunnel. Wild screaming echoed, and the men roared with delight, shouting curses down into the inferno.

Pat collapsed by Rick's side.

"So you seen it?"

Pat, grateful for the half-filled canteen offered by Rick, took a swallow, then gasped when the shock of the vodka hit him. He nodded his thanks.

"Jesus Christ, Schneid, it's like what that Dante fellow wrote about."

"Thought you were a goner up there—could see the airship bombing the temple. Hell of a mess if you'd gotten killed. Nothing against Marcus, but you don't know if he's lost his nerve or not, might want to throw in the towel. You took a hell of risk coming up here."

"Had to see what the boys were enduring. Can't lead from a chair. Have to let them see me up here with them."

"Well, do me a favor, get the hell back."

Pat nodded, motioning for the canteen, and took another swallow.

"They're starting to go crazy, you know. Days of this crawling around, fighting underground, Bantag five feet away in the next room. The corps is used up."

Looking at Rick, he made his decision, though he feared he might regret it.

"I know. I'm rotating you out. We'll start tonight. The 12th will come up to replace you."

"The 12th? Hell, they ain't seen much action. Might lose this whole sector."

"It's their homes—let 'em fight for it."

A lieutenant came crawling up to the two.

"General O'Donald here?"

"Right here, son."

"Sir, you're needed back at headquarters. Marcus wants you now."

Pat felt a stab of pain. "It's not Colonel Keane, is it?"

"I don't know, sir."

Pat looked over at Schneid. "Come on, let's get back."

"Vincent Hawthorne, what in God's name are you doing here?" Hans Schuder cried, rising from the chair behind the map table and coming forward with hand extended.

Vincent gladly took the hand, surprised when Hans suddenly patted him on the shoulder, a rare display of emotion.

Next came a torrent of questions about Andrew, his wife and child, Vincent's family, the situation around Roum, and the political situation at home.

Finally settling down, Hans poured a steaming cup of

tea, spiked it with a nip of vodka, and offered it Vincent, who smiled gratefully.

"Hate those damn ships," Vincent said. "Didn't keep a thing down the whole way out."

"That'll settle your guts."

"Ship's loaded with half a million rounds of small-arms ammunition, two thousand ten-pound shells, a thousand twenty-pound shells, five hundred rockets, two hundred thousand rations."

"Need it all."

Vincent leaned back in his chair, gaze lingering on the map.

"How tough is it here?"

"Hate to admit it, but as long as you keep me supplied, it's damn easy. They're strung out here—everything has to be hauled all the way across from the Great Sea, near two hundred miles. Mainly facing arrows again—they only have five batteries of artillery. I guess nine, maybe ten or eleven umens ringing us."

Vincent smiled.

"With breechloaders and artillery, if they charge you'll rip them to ribbons."

"They learned better, just dug in. Problem is, for now, if I try and break out, I'll get a hundred miles out into that steppe, then the shoe's on the other foot—it'll be us getting surrounded by them on horse. Now, if you could give me fifty of them land ironclads, the new ones you claim will go a couple of hundred miles without breaking down, I'll be on the Great Sea inside of two weeks."

Vincent shook his head.

"Good God, don't tell me you're sending them up to Roum! They'll get cut up in the streets. I heard about them rocket launchers in the report Pat sent down."

Again Vincent shook his head.

"All right, young Mr. Hawthorne, what the hell do you have in mind? You didn't come out here just to pass the time of day and drink my vodka."

Reaching into his haversack, Vincent pulled out a map. He unrolled it and began to talk.

Chapter Nine

Exhausted and moving slowly, Pat came back into his headquarters, glad to finally be rid of his greatcoat, which was still covered with the gore of the dead Bantag and the filth of the sewers.

One of his staff came up.

"Sir, dispatches just came in on one of the monitors."

"Where are they?"

"Sir, Dr. Keane was up here, and she insisted on taking them to the colonel. Word came back up to find you at once."

Pat whispered a quiet prayer. Andrew was nowhere near out of the woods yet. Emil had briefed him on how the wound inside the lung would take time to scab over and heal. There was no telling if it might suddenly hemorrhage. He was pleased to hear that Kathleen had finally come out of her confinement with Andrew.

Pat headed down the long flight of stairs to Andrew's room. At his approach the door opened, Kathleen barring the way. She took one look and held up her hand, beckoning for him to halt where he was.

"Pat O'Donald, you're as filthy as a pig. Now damn you, we've got a bath down in the basement. You're to get your dirty hide down there and wash. I'll have new clothes sent, then you come up here."

A half hour later, feeling strangely refreshed though he would never admit it, he finally stepped into the sickroom. Andrew was propped half up in the bed. His eyes darted over to Pat, and he forced a weak smile.

"Tell me about what it was like."

Pat briefly talked about the fight at the temple, the

confusion in the sewers, and his decision to pull 1st Corps out and bring 12th up to the line.

"That's the last fresh reserves," Andrew whispered.

"I know, Andrew. But 1st is used up. Besides, there are two other things. One, they're bitter, feel that the Roum troops aren't bearing their share of the fight. After all, it was the 9th that broke."

"That wasn't their fault. The attack was aimed straight at them."

"You can't explain that to a boy who's been eyeball to eyeball with them furry bastards now for near on to two weeks."

Andrew finally nodded.

"Second, something's scaring me a bit. It's the boys, Andrew. They're hardening. I don't mean becoming tough veterans—they were already that on the Shenandoah, at Rocky Hill. It's something more. They've been too close for too long, and they're getting as vicious as the Bantag. Maybe that's what we need to win, but if so, we've also lost something."

Andrew sighed. "Become like your enemy in order to defeat him. Years of war are doing that to us. We saw it a bit at Hispania, but that was only three days of constant battle."

He fell silent and looked away for a moment.

"What is it we're fighting for, Pat?" Andrew whispered.

"Andrew?"

"I don't mean the Rus, Roum, that's obvious. I mean us."

"Because we're here, Andrew, we're here."

"Why? I've wondered that of late. Why us? If it hadn't been for that damn boat, the *Ogunquit,* we'd be home now, you in New York, me in Maine. Home, the war long over for us."

"No sense in wondering on that, Andrew. Hell, me go back to New York, the stink of the Five Points, after being a general and all? And you, a professor type after running an army bigger than the old Army of the Potomac?" Pat chuckled.

His gaze darted to Kathleen, who sat silent, intently

watching Andrew. There had been no mention of her by Andrew, no statement that if it hadn't been for her chance assignment to the Sanitation Commission nurses going down to Fort Fisher, and her missing her assigned boat and scrambling aboard the *Ogunquit* at the last minute, they never would have met.

"How many left of use who came over, Pat? More than four hundred of us dead from your battery, my regiment, the crew of the *Ogunquit*. I saw the casualty reports—five more killed in the last week. Since we've come here to this damn place, twenty more of them insane and locked away, half a dozen just wandering off into the woods or out into the steppe and disappearing. You look up at the stars at night, wondering which world was ours, which one we belonged to. The Lost Regiment, lost never to return."

He hesitated for a moment.

"And thirteen of us suicides. At least the ones who put guns to their heads or hung themselves out of grief, loneliness, or fear. God knows how many others, like poor John Mina, who simply took a gun and ran straight at their lines and disappeared."

"Andrew, what the hell are you talking about?" Pat snapped.

Andrew forced a weak smile.

"I'm used up," he whispered. "I'm resigning my commission."

Pat started to speak, but Andrew held up his hand.

"Hans is a bit too old, and I worry about his heart. Plus, something got taken out of him when he was a prisoner. You'll take over, young Hawthorne will be chief of staff, Hans will be second in command."

"Andrew, darlin', you're tired. You get some of that strength back and you'll be up in the saddle again. This is your army, and you're the only one that could ever lead it."

"And suppose that shell fragment had driven another inch into me? Who'd be running the army now?"

Pat said nothing.

"There comes a time, Pat, when you know you've

been used up. At Hispania I felt that way. But we had a couple of years, I had time to rest, to not think about what it was like. Now I know."

"You could never stay away from a fight, Andrew."

"Now I can," he whispered.

He looked over listlessly at Kathleen, but she shook her head.

"Say it in front of me, Andrew. Say it," and her voice was harsh.

Andrew lowered his head, and to Pat's stunned disbelief tears were in Andrew's eyes.

"I couldn't stay away from a fight," he whispered. "You were right. God help me, I remember Gettysburg, Wilderness, even Cold Harbor. I'd hear the guns, smell the black powder, hear the huzzahs of a charge, and I was one with it. In those moments never did I feel so alive. The joy of battle. Back in Maine, back when I taught history, I'd read of it, tales of Napoleon, of Mad Anthony Wayne at Stony Point, of Alexander and of Homer. I dreamed like a boy of it then and tasted it as a man, and God forgive me, I did love it."

The tears fell silently onto his bandaged chest as he continued.

"Even here, at the start of it all. Against the rebs there was still the restraint of their being men. Even of they're being Christians, fellow Americans. The Tugars, the Merki, you could hate them without guilt, without shame, without fear that God was somehow watching, looking into your heart even though we are millions, maybe billions of miles from home."

Pat nodded, understanding the pure unrestrained passion of battle.

"Yet each time it took its toll from my heart," Andrew whispered, and he pointed to his chest, and Pat felt that if the bandages were removed he could indeed see that heart beating, so fragile had Andrew become.

"And finally I learned to be afraid," Andrew said. "One too many close calls. Too many times had I gone to the edge, and yet still we seemed to win in spite of my mistakes. We lost the Potomac Line, lost Suzdal. Except for poor Ferguson's passion for making rockets we would have lost Hispania. But something happened at Port Lincoln. Ha'ark outgeneraled me."

"Like hell he did," Pat sputtered.

"The truth, Pat, the truth. I should have seen the weakness at Fort Hancock. If I had kept a division stationed there rather than one exhausted regiment of old men and disabled veterans, we could have slaughtered them at the water's edge and held the line. You'd still be on the Shenandoah rather than fighting here in Roum. We got out by dumb blind luck."

"We got out because you had trained the best army on this entire damn world."

Andrew shook his head. "I watched you at Rocky Hill. You still had the passion. I was afraid we had lost, you kept on fighting. Hans got out because he's a soldier's soldier. Vincent got us out by sacrificing his flesh, and Ferguson's dying act was to give us the weapon to shatter their ironclads. All that to atone for my mistakes."

Pat said nothing, feeling a knot of fear, watching his old friend.

"So it kept whispering at me, nagging my soul, in the pull back to Capua. Ha'ark had outgeneraled me. He could do it again. But besides that, Pat, there was the fear. Once too many times under the guns and a voice whispered that my number was about to come up. That it would be me carried back from the line, screaming, the agony of fire tearing into my heart, blinding my soul, my mind."

He closed his eyes, head turning away as if the memory of the agony was again consuming him.

Pat reached out and touched his arm. The memory was there for him as well, the gut shot when they had stormed Suzdal after its capture by the Cartha. Yet it had never struck him like this. He fearfully remembered boys from the old 2nd Corps of the Army of the Potomac whispering how after Hancock was wounded in the groin at Gettysburg he was never the same. But Andrew breaking—it was impossible to imagine.

"Every time I hear a shell burst, I tremble," Andrew

continued, "even down here in the basement knowing nothing could get me.

"Pat, I'm used up. The well is dry. All I want is to go away now, to hide."

"But the army, the Republic?"

"The Republic will survive without me. It was going to have to someday anyhow."

"It's on the edge of collapse," Pat announced. "Kal and even Marcus are thinking about a separate peace with that devil Ha'ark."

Andrew shook his head wearily.

"I'm tired, Pat. I want to sleep now."

"Andrew?"

The eyes looked up at him, dim, unfocused. Andrew stirred listlessly.

"Kathleen, it hurts," he moaned. "Some morphine, I need morphine."

"You had some two hours ago," Kathleen replied sharply.

"I need to sleep, and I can't," and his voice was filled with self-pity.

Kathleen sat still, watching him closely. His gaze locked on her, and finally she lowered her head, nodded, went over to the medical bag, and drew out a needle.

"God knows I love you, Andrew," Pat said, gently reaching out to touch his hand. "You'll come back. Till then I'll just keep the chair warm."

"It's your chair now, your star. My last act in this army is to promote you to General of the Armies effective as of today."

Pat stood up as Kathleen came to the side of the bed and knelt down to scrub his arm before inserting the needle.

"We'll talk more later, Andrew. Get some sleep," Pat said nervously.

"It's yours now. Do better than I did."

Andrew turned his head away as the needle slipped in. He sighed and closed his eyes.

Shaken, Pat backed away from the bed. His gaze caught Kathleen's, and he nodded for her to follow. She withdrew the needle, brushed the hair back from Andrew's brow. He moaned softly, then seemed to drift off.

Leaving the room, she motioned for Pat to go down the corridor, and they stepped into a small room and closed the door. She dissolved into tears, leaning against his chest, and gently he put his hand on her back, holding her close.

"Now, lass, stop that, lass."

He struggled with his own tears but held them back. Finally she stepped back, as if a door into her grief had been opened but for a moment and then firmly locked shut again, her emotions back under control.

"Something's dead. Emil said it's normal—not a man alive it doesn't happen to sooner or later if he's under the stress Andrew has been under for too long. But Pat," and again the tears formed, "he's dead to me too. Something gone. All he dreams of, whispers of, is going away."

"That damn morphine," Pat said. "It needs to stop."

"Without it he can't sleep now. Emil said he needs sleep to heal. And the way he looks at me, like an animal caught in a trap, I just can't refuse it. At least when he sleeps there's no pain."

"Life is pain, Kathleen," Pat replied sharply. "I saw many a good man in the army come back from the hospital with a needle hidden in his pack. You've got to start breaking him of it now. It's poisoning his thoughts."

"Let him heal just a bit more, Pat, just a bit more, then we'll ease him off it."

"He feels unmanned," Pat replied. "Him weak as a baby, you tending to his every need, he can't even lift a spoon."

She said nothing, lowering her head. "At least he's alive. A week ago I didn't even think I'd have that. Emil talks to him, hours a day. Frightful to hear, the dreams, the dead men calling him. The guilt."

"For what?" Pat snapped. "He's saved all of us."

"Not anymore. That doesn't count. It's the price inside of him."

Pat sighed, unable to respond. That was something

he could understand. At Second Manassas he had been ordered to pull his battery out but stayed too long and was overrun. An infantry regiment had charged back up to extract them, but two of his guns were gone, half his crews lost. He had wept bitterly that night and for long nights afterward, and it still haunted him. Lads from the same streets he had lived on, fought alongside against other Irish and German gangs in the street, they were all dead.

Something was broken inside for the longest time, and even now it had never fully returned. But the disintegration of Andrew in one flashing moment of fire and steel, a blow that had nearly killed his body and seemed to have killed his soul, was too much of a burden to bear.

"Maybe as he feels better," Pat offered. "Emil said his strength will come back quick now he's on the mend."

She shook her head.

"I don't think so. He says once he's well enough to move he wants to go back to Suzdal to our home to recover there." She hesitated. "To hide there."

The last three words were spoken softly, her voice hollow.

"Don't lose respect for all that he is, Kathleen."

"No," she whispered, "it's just that though I'll always love him I feel now as if the Andrew I knew is dead and there's but a shadow left of all that he once was. God knows I didn't love him for being the colonel, the leader, the hero. I loved him for what he was. The gentle soul, but the lion beneath, the strength covered with gentleness. Now it's but a hollow core, as if he's already turned to dust."

"I think only you can bring him back," Pat whispered.

Her features darkened.

"Don't do that to me," she snapped angrily. "Emil said the same damn thing. Don't do that to me."

"I'm sorry, Kathleen, but it's true."

She lowered her head and turned away, then reached into her apron and pulled out a bundle of dispatches.

"Emil told me a supply monitor had come in, and I went upstairs and took your dispatches, to wave them under Andrew's nose and get his interest. He ignored them and told me to give them to you. I read a couple of them, Pat, hope you don't mind, and that's why I sent a messenger up to you."

Pat did not want to admit that the arrival of the messenger had been a relief, a reason to return back. That thought made him realize that he too was strung to the edge. He had never liked dark confined places. A glorious fight was one for a spring day's afternoon, rolling fields, a clear range ahead, shining cannons lined hub to hub and battery guidons fluttering in the breeze. Ah now, that was lovely, pretty as a picture, the way war should always be, not the filth, the crawling through sewers that were like the guts of a dark coiling beast crammed with offal. The fires, the darkness, the stench . . . he blocked the thought out.

There was a knock on the door, and without waiting for a reply Emil came in.

"So you've talked to him?" Emil asked him, looking over at Kathleen, who was drying her tears.

Pat nodded.

"Give it time," Emil announced. "He still might come around."

"And do you believe that?"

Emil hesitated, Kathleen looking straight at him, and he finally shrugged his shoulders.

"I'm a doctor of bodies," Emil said, "not minds. We always knew the mind could control how a body heals. We knew as well that hurts to the body could hurt the mind. I've seen wounds worse than Andrew's and a month later the boy was eager for another brawl, I've seen mere scratches and a veteran of a dozen battles would curl up on his cot and cry like an infant or threaten to kill himself if he got sent back to the front. Strange to kill oneself rather than face at least the chance of still living."

"So you don't know, is that it?"

"That's about it, Pat. Andrew was made of stern stuff. Good Maine Yankee stock. Same kind of stock made men like Ames, Chamberlain, even old Howard—though some boys didn't like him, he still had courage. Maybe something will change, rekindle the fire that's burned out."

He lowered his head. "Then again . . ." His voice trailed off.

"Kathleen, I'll need you in a few minutes, and it's time to change the bandages. Why don't you go and start in."

She forced a smile, kissed Pat on the cheek, then hurried out.

"She's on the edge too," Emil sighed.

"We all are."

"How was it up there this morning?"

"Bloody nightmare. Never seen fighting like it. Emil, it's a whole different kind of war from anything we've fought before. These new grenades, fire in the sewers, hand-to-hand fighting through the ruins. Something's changing."

"The machines are changing us, Pat. It's always been that way before, but now it happens faster and faster."

"Well, I wish to God we could go back to what we were. It was cleaner then."

"Oh really?" Emil asked sarcastically. "The wounds still look the same, except maybe for the burns. It was hell then, it's hell now."

Pat collapsed onto a chair, opened up the package of dispatches, and started to thumb through them.

He stopped, holding the first few sheets up to the light so he could see them more clearly.

"What is it?" Emil asked.

"That boy, that damned boy."

"Who, Hawthorne?"

Pat, mumbling a steady stream of curses, held the papers up to Emil, who adjusted his glasses and slowly thumbed through the report.

"He's going off half cocked. This was never talked about," Pat said coldly. "And besides, that equipment was to be kept in reserve or committed to this front."

"Well, you are in a fix here," Emil replied. "We're using everything faster than it can be resupplied. Civilians already on half rations. Unless there's a miracle and the spring thaw comes a month early, we'll run out of supplies before Ha'ark."

"He never talked to me about this, or to Andrew, to anyone. Besides, Hans will undoubtedly tell him to go to hell. The boy's crazy, and he has no business doing this."

Emil chuckled. "Well, if I understand my organization correctly, you command what is now First Army, Hans Second Army, and Andrew is overall command, and Vincent is chief of staff."

"Andrew just resigned," Pat snapped. "He said I was in command now."

"And will you accept that?"

Pat wearily shook his head.

"Not until he's had more time to think about it. Not one word of that is to be public, Emil."

Emil smiled. "Well now, this is a dilemma. If the commander is not present or is temporarily incapacitated, the chief of staff runs the show, following the orders given him by his commander. If that's the case, I think Vincent's within his rights to act. Now if you do accept command, then you can stop this, but I daresay that will be one hell of a public showdown between you and our young Mr. Hawthorne."

"I remember when that Quaker boy was a frightened private."

"He isn't now."

"It violates Andrew's intent to build up a strategic reserve with our new weapons, and besides that, it's suicide. Hans will never do it."

"Well, according to this, he's with Hans right now, and the equipment is being moved even as you and I sit here and fume. So what are you going to do about it? Go back in and tell Andrew? Hell, he'll roll over, face the wall, and tell you to decide."

"One hell of a mess," Pat growled. "If I can get my hands on Vincent I'll skin him alive, I'll bust him back down to the ranks. There's no way in hell they can pull this one off. I remember Andrew and me talking about something like this earlier, even using the same road, but we figured no ironclads could make it that far and infantry out in the open would get cut to pieces."

"Let's look at it this way," Emil grinned. "By the time you get hold of him, either we'll have won and the point will be meaningless, or we'll all be roasting in some damn Bantag pit, or better yet in hell."

"Then I'll hire on as a demon and chase the mad son of a bitch forever."

Peering through a narrow firing slit dug into the earthworks once held by the humans, Ha'ark raised his captured field glasses and carefully scanned the ruins of the city. Jurak was right, it was like the wars of the False Pretender back on the old world, the Battles of Pakana and the siege of Kalinarak. The battle before him seethed and writhed all across the entire east bank of the city right up to the old walls, which still held firm. In the cauldron between the old walls and where he now had his forward command post, over ten umens were now engaged, fighting what he estimated to be four of the seven umens of the humans.

They were grinding them down, but his army was wearing down as well. His warriors, only short years before, dreamed of battle in open array, pennants flying, sword, lance, and bow, the kill an act of glory for all his comrades to witness. Now it was war almost as he knew it from before, street by street, take a block only to lose it an hour later when hidden enemies crawled back up out of the rubble from behind, and then we do the same to them.

His warriors could no longer understand this. They had been driven by the lust of the kill, and the killing had indeed been good in the first two days when tens of thousands had been rounded up and butchered, but now all that was left was the human warriors, and they hid their dead, dragging them away or deliberately burning them.

He knew now it was a question of who would be exhausted first, whose will would crumble under the strain. He could withdraw out of this madness. The enemy would still be pinned here. Pull back thirty miles, rest his army for half a score of days, then send them in two wings, one south into the vast areas of the Roum territory not yet occupied and another wing westward. The two umens he had sent across the vast open wastelands were worse than useless along the fringes of the Rus lands. Ten umens would slice through and devastate their lands. That would break the will of the defenders of this city and serve his plan of dividing them against each other.

But always it was logistics as well. If I send ten umens west, he thought, one pitched battle will exhaust their ammunition, with no hope of bringing up more. Split my army into two wings, and the scum inside this city could move against my blocking force, push it back, and cut off the umens sent to Rus.

And as for supplies, nearly all the stockpiles so laboriously moved up were exhausted. Without the daily arrival of the trains the battle would be finished. Even now he was carefully rationing the ammunition, using enough to keep up the pressure but setting a bit aside each day for the one final strike.

Yet there were ten more umens pinned down against the three of Hans Schuder. Call them back? By the time they arrived here, the issue would be decided.

Cursing under his breath, he realized that he was as stuck in this battle as his human opponents. Neither side now wanted it, neither side could withdraw, one had to prevail.

Walking down the gangplank, Hans took a deep breath, glad to be out of the choking stench of the monitor. The morning was crisp, clear, the promise of another cold day. Turning, he watched as the side-wheeled steamer gingerly edged up to the shore, ice floes cracking and parting underneath it.

A heavy landing plank was laid down, there was the roar of a steam whistle, and with studded wheels digging into the decking the first of the ironclads skidded down the planking and rolled onto the dock.

The small port of Padua, tucked into a long bay of the Inland Sea that jutted into the mountains, was nothing more than a rude village, the terminus of a partially completed narrow-gauge rail line that snaked up into the hills and to the marble and granite quarries a hundred miles away. The quarries had been the main source of stone for the vast Roum building projects, and stone had been cut there a thousand years before the arrival of the regiment. The rock had then been laboriously dragged down the road to this port, loaded, and then shipped up to Roum. Marcus, to the disgust of the army, had managed to vote in an allocation to build the narrow-gauge line to speed up the hauling of stone, claiming it was a strategic necessity, but the line had only been half completed before the resurgence of the war. If only the material wasted here had been used for the running of the rails eastward, Hans thought, things might have been different. But now, who knew, it might make a difference after all.

A second steamship, edging in by the first, started to offload as well. The dock, designed to hold heavy slabs of stone, barely moved under the weight of the ironclads that slowly paraded past.

Hans walked to the end of the dock, watching as one of the ironclads turned and edged up onto a loading platform. The narrow-gauge train had four diminutive flatcars behind it. It would take eight runs to haul the thirty ironclads fifty miles up the line, where they would be off-loaded and then have to move the rest of the distance under their own steam. Fifty miles saved on wear and tear might be crucial, but still, it would take several days to get the job done before they could actually start the advance, and every minute now was precious.

Along a second dock another ship was unloading two regiments of infantry. Hans watched as the men formed up, burdened down with a heavy load of ten days' rations and a hundred rounds of ammunition, and started up the road that led into the forest.

The echo of axes thundered in a glen, and Hans turned, climbing up the gentle slope, stopping as a tree came crashing down, men shouting. A team of horses plodded by, dragging a log, already notched for placement in the makeshift fortress being constructed on the heights overlooking the narrow bay and the landing strip being laid out on a sandy spit of land.

"Hans!"

He looked back down at the trail and saw Vincent, mounted, reining in.

"We're already five miles up the trail. It's like that Roum officer said—a fairly good road. Now if he's on his mark, there should be bridges most of the way. I've already got a mounted unit forging ahead. Once we move the ironclads up, I should be up there within four days, six at the most."

"You?" Hans asked quietly. Without even having to make a gesture his headquarters company, led by his loyal friend Ketswana, came walking over.

Vincent paused, looking around.

"Now Hans, there was never any talk of this."

"Now Vincent Hawthorne, I think it is time to talk of it."

Vincent drew up stiffly.

"Hans Schuder, as chief of staff I thought this idea up. I am senior to you according to how the army is organized, and I should lead it."

Hans, with almost a gentle look, reached out and took the reins of Vincent's horse and turned it about, leading him off the road while an ironclad chugged past. Colonel Timokin was up in the turret, grinning.

"Hell of a machine, a hell of a machine!" he laughed, saluting.

The two returned the salute, then looked at each other.

"Son, I've had twenty years more experience than you," Hans said softly, lowering his voice so no one else would hear. "I was commanding before you were even thought of."

"The hell with that, Hans."

"Next point then," Hans said, obviously having planned his argument. "You know what the political situation is back in Rus. You might be the only person your father-in-law will listen to now. You are needed back there to keep an eye on things. Suppose the Bantag decide to throw an extra five umens westward? If you're not there, I think Kal might quit."

"My staff can handle that."

"All right, Hawthorne, let's try this. I'm getting old, Pat isn't much behind. With Andrew down, we might lead things for a while, but then it's you, son. Andrew had you picked long ago, I think even back as far as when we fought the Tugars. You're him, son. I could see that in you—the next Andrew Keane for this world."

"Thank you," Vincent whispered, but his expression was still grim.

"You need, though, to learn an edge of softness, that's all. Unfortunately you remind me of Sheridan as well, right down to that ridiculous little tuft of chin whiskers and mustache. Good officer, Sheridan, but a bit too much of the hard killer edge to him. I know what they did to you, the wounds, the pain. Hell, I spent years as a slave to the bastards. It's just this—if you get killed, then who leads?"

"I won't get killed."

"It won't be easy up there. You're barely recovered, you can hardly sit a horse, and every step must be agony. You need time to heal, boy. Suppose you get halfway up then you give out? Then what?"

"I can manage," Vincent replied softly.

"Fine then," Hans said, and he looked back at Ketswana, commander of his headquarters company. "You pulled a division from my line down in Tyre for this. We could spare it, and the Bantag don't know we did it. But Vincent, this is my division. They've fought under me for three months now, they retreated with me from our defensive line all the way to Tyre. The boys will fight for me, but if you try and force the issue of who is in command I'll tell them to halt."

"Hans, that's mutiny!"

Hans smiled. "Call it what you want. Nothing will happen in Tyre for a while—they can spare me. Suzdal can't spare you. And one other thing. Bullfinch back there in his monitor, he's got orders to take you back and not me, so that settles it. The admiral's with me, the men are with me."

Vincent started to sputter, and Hans smiled in a fatherly way.

"Mr. Hawthorne, a bit of advice to a general."

"What the hell is it?"

"Fight only the battles you can win. If you can't, withdraw quickly and with grace."

Vincent seemed to slump in the saddle.

"Now there's no shame, boy. My suggestion would be that the official report read that after serious consultation between you and me it was realized that your presence in securing the defense of Rus and the management of our factories was far more important to the war effort. Also, that since the front at Tyre was serving its purpose of diverting enemy troops but offensive operations could not yet be mounted, it was felt safe to briefly release one division and myself to lead this expedition."

"Sounds like you wrote it out already."

"I did," Hans said with a grin, handing up a penciled note.

Vincent seemed to collapse, and Hans, offering his hand, helped him down from his mount.

"I have to admit," Vincent whispered, "I didn't know if I could stand this march, but I had to try."

"It would have killed you for certain, I could see that, and the men would see it too, son. Go home, heal. There will be more than enough fighting come spring."

Vincent reluctantly nodded. Taking off the map case that was hung over his shoulder, he opened it up and pulled out a detailed sketch of the region.

"This bay is a hundred and fifty miles southeast of Roum," Vincent explained, tracing out the details. "This was an old road to the quarries the Roum cut years ago. It'll take you northeastward for just over eighty miles. I'll tell my guide Tigranius to report to you. He grew up here and worked as a teamster on this road."

"Now, you're certain the road can handle ironclads once we reach the end of the narrow-gauge track?"

"At the end of the track it's only thirty-five miles to the quarry. They were hauling wagons with ten-, twenty-ton blocks of marble and limestone on it, so I think it'll manage the ironclads. Tigranius swears that most of the bridges are made of stone, and you know how good these Roum are at building roads and bridges. You'll be right at the crest of what we called the Green Mountains when you reach the quarry."

"And you don't think the Bantag have occupied it?"

"There might be patrols, but no, I doubt it. Small units of Roum mounted infantry were pulling back up into the hills to harass the Bantag supply line and block the passes so refugees might find some safe havens. Last report coming down this road was the Bantag were holding at the pass ten miles beyond the quarry, where the Ebro River cuts through the mountains. Chances are they don't even know that the quarry exists. They're nervous about pushing too far away from the railroad."

Vincent traced out a line on the map.

"This will be the hard part. You leave the quarry and follow the road that continues northeast down to the pass where the road drops out of the mountains and into the Ebro River Valley. The road is a couple miles up from the river, and there it turns north. Chances are that's where you'll first run into the Bantag.

"Once you push them aside, the alert will be out. It's twenty-five miles from there to the railroad bridge over the Ebro, all of it open ground. There are some good roads there, old Roum roads, so you should be able to move fast."

Hans nodded, studying the map.

"You want the main bridge here over the Ebro. It's a span of nearly two hundred yards. Most likely a lot of slaves there. I suspect it's a major turnaround depot as well. A fairly large town went up there when we built the railroad. There's a scattering of villages in the area as well—it was rich farmland."

"This bridge over the Ebro, near the mountains—was it blown in the retreat?" Hans pointed to a bridge marked on the map halfway between the pass out of the mountains and the railroad line which, running east-west, bisected the open valley.

Vincent shook his head. "Didn't see any sense to it. It wasn't the railroad, and we didn't seriously try to hold the Ebro—too many fords. My reports state the bridge was left intact."

"If I could cross there, throw a pincer out, swing in from either side, and sweep everything up . . ."

"Two columns out of touch, in cavalry country?"

"Your whole idea is they don't expect a raid on their line a hundred and fifty miles to the rear. Let's go all the way, pincer in either side. Might sweep up a couple of their trains, and I suspect they don't have that many of them."

Hans traced the route out, fingers sweeping to either side of the river. "We sweep out wide, then close in following the railroad, reuniting where the track crosses the river."

Vincent shrugged. "Well, you stole the operation from me. You decide."

"Now don't go angry on me, lad. If this scheme works, it's your credit. No one else thought it up. Son, that's what a good staff's supposed to do. A bit of a weakness of Andrew's. Build up a stronger staff, train the lads, give them a loose rein once you trust them, and let them do all the planning."

Vincent smiled at the lecture.

"Like you to teach me if we get out of this one, Hans."

"Once this is all over, son."

"I chose this route since it's far enough back from Ha'ark that it will take him a day or more to react once he gets the warning. Would have preferred your cutting across to Junction City, but that would have been three hundred miles, and the new ironclads, they might be an improvement, but I don't think they could do that. Besides, this is supposed to be a good road. So you have just over a hundred and fifty miles to cover. I've assigned two Hornets and one Eagle to this operation. I know it tips our hand on the new designs, but you need air cover.

They're undoubtedly patrolling their flanks by air. If you get spotted before you get to the quarry, you have to come back. Do you understand me?"

"Who's giving the orders here, Vincent? I thought we settled this issue. I know what I'm doing, son."

"As chief of staff I am giving the orders, Sergeant Major Schuder, even if I'm not going up there with you," Vincent snapped. "If he gets a day to react before you hit the rail line, he'll have five or more umens on you and you'll never break through."

"And getting out?"

"You got two choices. Once you know he's closing in, if you can, hightail it back up to the mountains. Bullfinch will be landing a brigade of marines here in seven days as support. They'll have additional supplies and another two ironclads and will move up to secure your line of retreat. The other alternative is head north into the forest. There's some small units up there—hook up and wait till spring."

"That means losing thirty ironclads. Like hell."

"Hans, chances are only ten will even make it to the railroad. Getting them back over the mountains, no chance."

"You're blowing two months of production here. We'll need those ironclads come spring."

"If we don't cut Ha'ark's supply line and break off the battle around Roum, there won't be anything left come spring. We can't throw the ironclads from Kev all the way over to Hispania. Committing them to Roum would be a waste. They'd get torn apart in the city, and Ha'ark most likely has his ironclads in reserve to meet ours if we should commit them there. It's two hundred miles of open ground from Tyre to the Great Sea, and until we can put enough corps in to match those besieging umens, that would be a waste. This is the one place they can fight and do some good, so here it is."

Hans finally nodded in agreement. "Always kind of figured those damn smoke belchers were best for the surprise slash into the rear, that and breaking through an infantry line. All right, this is the place for them, if they can stand the climb over the mountain on icy roads."

"That's why I figured a week. You got five thousand infantry for support, three hundred mounted, and the flyers. Good luck, Hans."

The old sergeant smiled.

Chapter Ten

"God have mercy, Schneid, what the hell happened?"

Barely able to walk, needing the help of a burly sergeant, Rick Schneid staggered into the headquarters and was eased into a chair. His features were pinched, drawn; every breath seemed to be an agony.

"Think I broke some ribs," he whispered, and Pat turned around and snapped for a staff orderly to fetch Dr. Weiss.

"Sewer caved in on us," the sergeant gasped. "Half the headquarters staff are cut off behind us."

Pat nodded. Going to his desk, he pulled out a bottle of vodka and passed it to the sergeant, who gratefully took a long drink before passing it on to the half-dozen other survivors of Rick's headquarters who had staggered in behind him.

Having watched the attempted relief of 1st Corps from the observation tower, Pat was still stunned by the fiasco. The operation had started out smoothly enough, the survivors of 1st Corps moving west, back into the old city, via the sewer under one of the main thoroughfares, men of 12th Corps moving up under an adjoining line to take their place.

It seemed, though, as if the Bantag had figured out what was going on. Just before dawn they had launched another offensive. Pincering in on the road over the access sewer being used by 12th Corps, they had poured hundreds of gallons of kerosene into the line and ignited it with heavy powder charges. Pat had tried to pass orders up for the remnants of 1st Corps to hold their position, but panic had set in, men abandoning the underground passages, sprinting through the rubble, getting cut off by heavy formations of Bantag infantry who relentlessly advanced without consideration of loss. A twenty-block section, held tenaciously for three weeks, had been lost in two hours. What was left of 9th Corps and half of 4th Corps was now completely cut off, while the disorganized 12th Corps fell back to the inner wall.

Emil came into the room, took one look at Rick, and motioned for two of his assistants to help Schneid to his feet and then tried to get his uniform off. The greatcoat was slipped off, but when they tried to remove his tightly fitted twelve-button jacket he gasped with pain. One of the men produced a heavy pair of scissors and started cutting at the back of the uniform.

"Dammit," Schneid gasped, "that jacket cost me half a month's pay."

Slicing the jacket up the back and then unbuttoning it down the front, they peeled the two halves off, and in seconds had his shirt off as well. Schneid started to shiver in the cold.

Pat saw that the whole right front side of Schneid's chest was black-and-blue. As Emil gently touched and pushed, Rick grimaced.

"Four ribs broke, maybe five, Rick. Don't think they punctured anything, but you, young man, are out of the war for now."

"Goddammit," Schneid muttered.

"Get him down to the hospital, wrap him up, and give him a little morphine for the pain."

"Save it for the men who need it," Rick snapped.

Pat smiled at the young corps commander's grit and the string of curses as he was led away.

"Didn't think we'd get him out," Rick's sergeant major said. "The whole thing just collapsed right on top of us."

Pat sighed and looked back at the battle map. It was impossible to tell anymore which sections were still held. The Bantag had finally caught on to the use of the sewers as the main conduit for moving men and supplies back and forth to the various beleaguered sections. Now it looked like they were going to fight every inch of the way for that as well. What was most troubling, though, was the report that the line under the old Capua Way had been seized for its entire length, the Bantag using fire, coal gas, and assault troops advancing behind make-shift iron shields. They had even fired rockets down the length of the pipe.

The scheme of the last three weeks was disintegrating. Again Ha'ark had learned to adapt and to improve upon an idea. If only Ferguson were here, he most likely would have thought up some new ideas.

But Ferguson's dead, Pat thought grimly. Andrew is out, Hawthorne half crippled, Schneid is out, Jacobson in command of the 4th Corps has been missing for three days, over three-quarters of the regimental and brigade commanders are down, three out of the seven corps committed to the defense of the city have been smashed to pieces. They're using us up, he thought as he gazed at the map.

He watched as a staff officer took a sheet of paper from a telegrapher, studied it, and walked back up to the plot board. The marker showing just how far the Bantag had advanced under the Capua Way was moved up another two blocks. Since dawn half a dozen other blocks marking positions still held in the outer city had been removed as well. The bastards were within two blocks of the inner wall in some places.

Break through that and they're on the harbor, and we're finished, he thought.

Pat sighed and sat down, staring at the table, the rumble of a renewed bombardment thundering through the doorway leading up to the watchtower.

He looked up at the staff officer who had moved the marker.

"Pass the order up to Horatius—he's still commanding engineering for the 11th Corps, isn't he?"

"Yes sir."

"Order him to flood the Capua tunnel as planned, empty the Livonian Baths, then pour in what benzene we have left and fire it."

"Sir, remember that tunnel interconnects to the sewer under the Aneius Way. That's the access for units moving up to the 9th Corps."

Pat sighed.

"Can we cut off the Capua tunnel above ground, come in behind them?"

The staff officer looked down at the map and shook his head. "Remember, sir, we talked about that a couple of hours ago. The Bantag must have half an umen or more along that road."

"All right," Pat replied wearily. It was all starting to blend together into one mad confusing swirl.

Should he leave what was left of the 9th out there? No, they were fought out. But how could he get them out? The pullback and rotation of the 1st had turned into a rout. They were simply too closely engaged, the men not trained for what was expected.

Ha'ark must be expecting me to pull them back out, must be ready to pounce. No, it would be a slaughter. It will be a slaughter anyhow, he realized, but at least they'll take the bastards down with them. Maybe when things settle down, maybe tonight, we can start trying to get them out, a regiment at a time.

"Change it," Pat finally said. "All positions hold until relieved. Get that engineering regiment down into the sewers again. I want barricades forward of the inner wall wherever possible."

"And the relief?" one of the staff asked.

"We do it one regiment at a time from now on. The fresh regiment moves up and secures the position, and only then does the old unit get relieved. And no diversion of units on the way up by commanders in the field. That has to stop unless there's a clear breakthrough."

He knew that was going to make it tougher to get the exhausted troops out. The problem was made worse by division and even corps commanders grabbing units not of their command which were passing through their sectors. Even though strict orders had been issued to stop the practice, it still went on; what officer could resist grabbing a fresh unit to plug into his own line and the hell with where it was supposed to be going?

He looked again at the map. He could sense they were starting to crumble under the pressure. Again it was that mind of Ha'ark, modern, far too modern. He had grasped what Pat wanted as soon as the breakthrough had been achieved, to turn it into a battle to grind the enemy down. Ha'ark had accepted the embrace, and now it seemed he was winning.

"I tell you we're finished," Jurak snapped, his voice near to breaking.

Ha'ark looked up, glad that none of his staff were present in the bunker dug into the outer slope of the city wall.

"You press too close," Ha'ark hissed.

"I'm telling you what I saw."

"And I'm telling you that you press too close. I am not some officer of the old world. Here I am the Redeemer, and to dare to speak to me as you just have is death."

"So you want to kill me?"

"The thought has crossed my mind."

Jurak undid the filth-encrusted belt to his revolver, took it off, and flung it on the table.

"Before you shoot, though, remember I am the only commander in the field who understands this fight. To the others it's just the slaughter of cattle gone mad."

"I know that, Jurak, and I remember what else it is I still owe."

There was the unspoken acknowledgment that in the war on the old world Jurak had taken Ha'ark under his wing, breaking him in to the rigors of combat and saving his life more than once. The memory of it rankled. To be indebted as Ha'ark the Qar Qarth was an uneasy balance.

"You remember the siege of Uvadorum?"

Ha'ark nodded. It had been Ha'ark's first campaign in the War of the False Pretender. The city had been struck by atomic weapons. There were places that were still hot, and his unit had been flung into the cauldron of battle. Most of the fighting had been underground, basement to basement, through the sewers, as here, vicious and unrelenting for forty-three days of poison gas, radioactive pockets, and fanatical resistance by the followers of the Pretender, who knew that capture equaled death.

"And you are saying this is as bad as Uvadorum?"

"Worse in some ways. The fighting is visceral, hatred we never knew. I wondered how our umens of horse riders would manage this. Would they break? I tell you, they are at that point now. The slightest reversal will set them running."

"As long as they believe in me they will never break," Ha'ark replied coolly, and he knew it was no idle boast. The madness of the cattle could be explained by their shamans in no other way than possession by demons. For across all the long centuries of the eternal ride, cattle had always submitted. There were riders and there were cattle ready to receive them. And then came the Yankees, the defeat of the Tugar and Merki Hordes, and finally his own arrival on this world as if in fulfillment of prophecy . . . the prophecy that there would be a time of demons and in that time a leader would be sent by the ancestors to reunite all the Hordes.

There were times of late when he could even wonder if indeed he was an instrument of the ancestors and this was not simply a coincidence to be taken advantage of for his own power and pleasure. For now he could see that if he did not win this war, if the Yankees and their Republic were allowed to survive, finally there would be a day of annihilation.

"We've broken ten umens in that damned city," Jurak pressed. "They're used up, exhausted. Warriors stare at you, dead-eyed. And disease, Ha'ark—hundreds have the spotted fever. They're finding corpses of the enemy buried in the rubble for days, already swollen, and are devouring them, part from hunger and part from rage. The next day they vomit, then roll over and die."

"We still have ten umens here in the line."

"I thought you said we needed them for the final assault."

Ha'ark nodded. "And that is why they will stay in reserve. We've identified two of their umens as the ones we overran. Elements of three more have fought as well. That leaves but two left. Once they're pulled in and identified, we know they are at the bottom of the barrel."

"What about the twenty umens strung out between here and our supply head at the sea? Can't we bring up just five, even three, of them?"

"They dropped off raiders on either flank all along the line of retreat."

"How many, half an umen? The line hasn't been touched, and supplies are moving."

"Barely," Ha'ark announced. "We only have twelve engines still running. We're getting three trains a day of supplies. I need five trains a day to properly equip this army and keep it fighting."

Ha'ark leaned back on his stool and stared at the flickering kerosene lamp suspended from the ceiling. A shell landed nearby, a clump of frozen earth shaking loose from the roof of the bunker and splattering on his map table.

Food wasn't the problem. They had tens of thousands of horses to provide meat, drink, and that could last till spring. It was the damn ammunition, and all the other things. He sensed it was getting difficult for the humans, with the port all but cut off except for ironclads, and his mortars could rain down shot on the dockside. They were undoubtedly digging deep into their reserves. They must break first, they had to, he could sense it.

But Ha'ark's forces were strung out two hundred leagues from the Great Sea. And from there dozens of galleys and his precious steamships were moving supplies across three hundred leagues of ocean all the way back to Xi'an. It was a rope stretched taut. One storm had taken more than twenty galleys and one of the steamships. Another loss like that would put him at the breaking point.

The few factories seized at Capua and in the countryside beyond Roum were useless, the machinery gone or smashed beyond repair. But the main concern was still the damn rail line, laid out on the frozen steppe, a hundred thousand cattle slaves laboring constantly to straighten track, repair the destroyed bridges, haul up the precious replacement rails stockpiled for over a year in preparation for this campaign. One thin ribbon, and again he wondered if arming his warriors with rifles and cannons had indeed been the wisest choice, for without such weapons there were no supply lines, the army feeding on wherever they were. If it wasn't for that he would abandon this siege now, ride on to Rus, leaving a devastated countryside, and then starve them out over the next spring and summer.

He knew he had to break them now, before the next moon feast, for the next one after that was the Feast of the Warming Moon, the first harbinger of the approaching thaw. With the thaw his supply system would break down and continuing a siege operation would be impossible.

"Five umens to be moved up from the rail line to be used in the next assault," he finally announced. "You select them, but do it wisely. I want airship patrols doubled along the flanks, the great forest to the north, the mountains to the south. Spot where there are centers of resistance and send raiding parties up to ferret them out. Take as many prisoners as possible, anything that can be eaten."

Jurak nodded in agreement.

"And our planned surprise?"

"I had hoped we'd take the sewer all the way up to the wall. If we had, we could spring it tomorrow. We're two blocks short. There's some small drain pipes, but far too small for one of our warriors to crawl through. I've ordered the digging of a passageway big enough. Once that's done we'll pack it with gunpowder."

Jurak nodded wearily. "I've reserved one entire train car load. We'll also pack in all our remaining oil."

"How long?"

"Five days at most."

"Make it four."

"Why?"

"Just a feeling, perhaps the hidden sight the shamans talk about. But something is wrong, I can sense it, and I want to strike quickly and finish this."

"Damn all to hell, what happened?" Hans roared, reining his mount in and looking down into the ravine. The ironclad was down on its side, flames licking out. Getting off his horse, he slid on the icy road, nearly losing his footing. Ketswana, who had arrived ahead of him, came up.

"It skidded and went over the side."

Hans could see that, and he turned to look at the engineers who had been guiding the column over the washed-out ravine that had been piled with timber and rocks to make a path for the ironclads.

He glared at them coldly, their captain saluting nervously.

"Sir, one of the logs snapped, the bedding gave way, and the machine fell."

"Damn it all, son, I can see that. I want to know why you didn't make this crossing stronger."

"Sir, we were told by you to have it ready in an hour, and we did the best we could."

Hans glared at him coldly. The boy was right, he had given him an hour, and now another of his precious machines was lost, the crew inside dead, burned alive.

"Get down here and douse that fire. Their flying machines could spot this smoke twenty miles away. And captain, next time when I say an hour, get it done right. Do you understand?"

"Yes sir." There was the slightest edge of bitterness in the captain's voice, but Hans let it pass.

Snapping off a salute, Hans remounted, motioning for Ketswana to mount and follow along.

His horse almost lost its footing as they pushed up the road and then struggled to edge around an ironclad that was pulling two wagons behind it. The machine labored, smoke billowing, and he thanked God the design had been changed to burning kerosene. If it had been coal they would have left columns of black soot that a blind pilot could see from thirty miles away.

The infantry, strung out in two lines to either side of the road, moved slowly, the men stepping carefully on the icy path. In a narrow clearing he passed an aid station that was filled to capacity with men down with frostbite, exhaustion, and broken wrists, arms, and legs from falling.

"It's taking a terrible toll," Ketswana said, finally catching up to Hans's side, sitting uncomfortably on his mount.

"We have to keep pushing. Chances are there are no flyers up today—too much wind. Have you spotted ours?"

Ketswana shook his head.

"Well, if Petracci isn't flying, they sure as hell aren't. It's less than ten miles to the quarry, according to that Tigranius. Our forward patrols should be reporting in. I want to make the quarry by nightfall."

Ketswana looked over at him and shook his head. "We've lost six machines so far, maybe three hundred or more men. You try and push them ten or more miles in this cold and you'll lose half of them before the day is out. They need time to rest, build shelters against the cold for the night."

"We push on. Hawthorne said we should be able to do the march to the quarry in two days from the end of the rail line. Well, it's three days now. I don't like being late."

"Hans, this damn road is nothing but ice. It's a miracle we got this far."

Hans fell silent as he was forced to rein in. The infantry was backed up, and cursing, he edged his way through the column. Another ironclad was stuck. Its front wheels had slid off the road and were dangling precariously over the side; the rear wheels were in reverse, spinning uselessly.

The engineer for the ironclad was standing atop the

turret, oblivious to his precarious situation, shouting orders as the wagons hauling kerosene were disconnected and dragged back by the troops. Heavy ropes were already secured to the aft end. An entire company of men grabbed hold of the ropes, and they started to pull.

Men went down in tangled heaps, slipping on the icy surface, cursing and yelling. Finally the ironclad started to budge, and with a roar of steam it lurched back up onto the road. The ropes were dropped, and Hans moved through the crowd and pressed on.

As they rounded a curve in the road the path finally leveled out. Turning to look back, he could see the long serpentine column struggling up through the forest, puffs of smoke marking the progress of the ironclads, one dark plume showing where the lost machine had fallen into the ravine. A wall of dark clouds was riding in on the wind, and even as he watched the reddish sun, low in the south, was obscured. In that instant it seemed as if the temperature had dropped another ten degrees and the air felt as if it was no longer dry, but laden with the first hint of yet another storm.

The road widened out along the summit. An ironclad was pulled to one side, the crew outside, emptying tins of fuel taken from the wagon they were towing, pouring the precious fluid into the fuel tank on the stern. Some infantry, pressed into service and none too pleased with the duty, were hauling buckets of water from a spring that bubbled even in the bitter cold and were pouring the contents into the water tanks mounted on either flank of the ironclad, trying to avoid getting wet in the process.

Colonel Timokin was atop the machine, hoisting up the buckets and pouring them into the open water tank, and at Hans's approach he snapped off a salute.

"Damn water's freezing in the outside tanks. We should have thought of that," he announced as he poured one more bucket in, then jumped off the machine.

"We lost one back at the washed-out ravine."

"Damn. Who?"

Hans looked over at Ketswana.

"The *St. Basil of Murom.*"

Timokin shook his head. "The crew?"

"Sorry, they're gone."

Timokin sighed. "Most of my men just haven't had the training. We figured on at least a couple of months, maybe until after spring thaw, before we'd be committed. They barely know how to drive these newer ironclads, let alone fight. My old veterans from the 1st Regiment are managing, but the newer lads, well, you can see what happened."

"How are the machines holding up?" Hans asked.

"Well, with *St. Basil* that's six down now. Number twenty-two, the *Spirit of Hispania,* cracked a piston head, and it's leaking steam like crazy."

"Do you have any spare piston heads?" Hans asked.

"I could send some men back to *St. Basil,* strip it of parts."

"Then do it."

"Hans, most of these machines went straight from the factory to the wharf for this mission. They haven't been broken in proper, and remember, this is a new design. All the machines will need to have the pistons repacked. Some of the pipe fittings are leaking, and they'll need to be resoldered. We got loose bearings on nearly half the driveshafts, and we're using more fuel than expected."

"So what are you telling me?" Hans said.

"A third of the machines won't be fit for the final move down into the flatlands."

Hans swore silently, while slapping his hands together to drive out the numbness.

"A third?"

"And that's for the start down the mountains. Remember, it's more dangerous going downslope than up. Going up, if something goes wrong you just stop. Going down, well, you keep on going until you either make it or run into something."

"Tell me, when Hawthorne first approached you with this mad scheme, what did you say?"

"I told him we could do it, sir."

Hans glared at him angrily.

"And now?"

Timokin hesitated for a moment. "Well, sir, I still think we can do it."

"Think or know?"

"Sir, what other alternative is there? I heard it was real bad at Roum. If we didn't try, then what?"

Hans nodded. "All right, son. It's supposed to be fairly level from here on out. Get every machine you can up to the quarry. You should be able to make fairly good time. Once there, sort out those you think are in the best shape, and we'll leave the rest behind. Hopefully the marines coming up behind will have a few more machines and maybe some spare parts and fuel."

"That was the plan, sir. The factory was supposed to skip assembling the next couple of ironclads. All the key parts we figured might break were to be crated up and shipped with us."

"Why the hell didn't you do that in the first place?"

"Sir, if we'd done that, that would be three or four less machines. I kind of figured we'd get as many as possible on the road, and when they started to break we'd salvage the good parts that were left and press on with the rest."

"I think there's some sort of logic there," Hans replied, "but frankly, son, I don't see it at the moment."

Timokin smiled and shrugged.

"Fine. Press on."

"Courier coming," Ketswana announced.

Hans saw the man coming around a bend in the road, riding hard. As he reined in, the rear of his horse went down, sliding, the mount nearly going completely over.

"What's the all-fired hurry?" Hans asked, finding that everything was annoying him today.

"Sir, the quarry. Colonel Vasily begs to report that it's occupied by the Bantag."

"What?"

"Just that, sir."

"Tell me."

"Sir, I was up with the head of the scouting column.

We had stopped for a break. We had pickets out, and then, sir, before we knew it, four Bantag riders trotted right into the middle of us. We all kind of stared at each other—I think they was as shocked as we were. We dropped them before they could get away."

"How far from the quarry?"

"Couple of miles. In fact, we could see part of the mountain where miners had cut it away."

"Did word get back to the Bantag?"

"No sir. We dismounted, moved up slowly through the woods. They were camped down in the quarry and in the village. Terrible sight, sir, parts of bodies. It looked like they just took it. Some folks were still alive. We could see them being driven like slaves, cutting wood."

The messenger's features were grim.

"Bastards—they killed a girl while we were watching. It was hard for the boys not to go right in."

"You did the right thing. How many?"

"We counted over five hundred horses, sir."

Damn.

"Where's Tigranius?"

"Up with the scouting party, sir."

Hans clumsily fumbled with the map case, finally tearing off his gloves to undo the latch. Dismounting, he pulled a map out, went over to Timokin's ironclad, and spread it against the ice-cold metal. Instantly his hand stuck to the side, and cursing, he pulled back, losing a bit of flesh from his palm.

"This map here. It shows the road into the quarry. The one leading down to the north goes through a narrow cut in the side of the mountain. Did you see that pass?"

"Yes sir. Kind of narrow, like a railroad cut."

"Good. Take my horse, ride back, order the mounted unit to concentrate, but to dismount and leave their horses back a good mile or two. Then try and flank around and secure that pass. With luck that scouting party that blundered into you won't be expected back much before dark. Tell Vasily to wait, and for God's sake don't get seen or drawn into a fight. Snow's coming on, and if we're lucky them bastards will think they're safe and keep indoors. I'll try and hit them just before dark and drive them into you. You understand that, son?"

"Yes sir."

"Repeat what I said."

The courier repeated Hans's order, and tossing over the reins to his horse, Hans sent him on his way.

As he watched the boy ride off, the first snowflake drifted down, followed within seconds by heavy wet flakes that danced on the breeze.

"Snow's going to make moving worse," Ketswana said.

"Hell, it might be heaven-sent."

"Want my horse? That nag the boy rode in is blown."

"No, my piles are killing me," Hans announced. "It's time to try something different," and he headed over to Timokin's ironclad.

Ignoring the stench, Ha'ark crouched low, squatting to peer down the length of the tunnel that had been carved out over the last four days.

He nodded his approval.

"You sure it's under the wall?"

"I think the only surveyors we could find on this damn world would be on the other side," Jurak replied. "The best we could do was run some warriors up to the wall with a string during the night. We lost twenty-three doing that, but we got a fairly accurate measure. If not directly under the wall it's within ten to fifteen paces either way. I've nearly doubled the amount of powder we first talked about just to make sure."

"Do they know?"

"I think so. We could hear them digging as well."

"How close?"

"We'll be safe till tomorrow morning. I've placed guards in with the charge just to be certain. They have orders to fire the short fuse if the Yankees break in."

"Fine. Make sure all umen commanders are alerted

to that. Once it gets dark I'll start moving the troops in for the assault."

Leaving Jurak, Ha'ark scrambled up the ladder and out into the covered trench which led to the mine's entrance. Moving back to the rear, his guards moving cautiously ahead and behind, he finally breathed a sigh of relief as they emerged into the ruins of a bathhouse. The sky overhead was clearing; the clouds scudding by were streaked with the brilliant red of sunset. The air seemed surprisingly warm. Warriors gathered in the bathhouse and lined up to receive their ration of dried bread and horseflesh were exclaiming about the weather, and many of them had loosened their heavy coats.

Dressed in the uniform of a common warrior so as not to draw attention, he passed them, only the more observant noticing the guards and wondering who deserved such an escort.

If this is an early thaw, how long do I have? he wondered. But if all goes as planned, thaw or not, it will be over in another day.

Glad for the burst of cold air, Hans went up to the open side hatch. Timokin edged past him and leaned out. Thick flakes of snow swirled into the machine, disappearing as they danced about the steaming boiler.

"Sergeant Major Schuder?"

"Here," and Hans poked his head out the hatch. It was Ketswana, heavy snow stuck in his woolly black hair, the shoulders of his greatcoat blanketed white.

"Think they're all down there. The storm's driven them inside."

"Think they're expecting us?"

"Hard to see. A couple of pickets down there. No, they didn't hear us. Wind's in our favor."

"The mounted unit?"

"I don't know. We have to hope they're covering the pass."

Hans nodded and shifted the chew in his mouth. To pass the long tedious hours of the ride he had taken a seat next to the boiler, chatting with the engineer, who was not at all pleased when he directed streams of tobacco juice against the side of the boiler.

The ride had been damn uncomfortable, every jolt of the road banging through the machine and up his spine. How anyone lived in these damn things was beyond him, but he had to admit it was better than riding a horse through the storm.

"How many machines we got?"

"There are five behind you, and the others are strung out back across ten miles."

"Infantry?"

"Just the boys riding on top. Not more than fifty."

Hans looked out the hatch. The sky was darkening. Wait for more machines to come up? No. They might get worried about the missing patrol, come up this way looking. Besides, if the boy's report was right, there were still civilians down there . . . and it was getting close to dinnertime.

"We move. Dismount the infantry and have them flank out to either side of the road. Tell them to be careful and be sure who they are shooting at. That mounted unit's on the other side of the town."

He looked back at Timokin.

"How you want to handle this?"

"Well sir, not knowing the village but guessing it's like the rest of them Roum towns, it'll maybe have a wall, a gate. Be laid out nice and square. We crash the gate, I'll go right up the middle, next two machines behind me turn right, other two left. With luck we trigger a panic, get them running."

"And if they have rockets, artillery?"

Timokin shrugged. "We'll see when we get there, I guess."

Hans liked the boy's spirit, and he nodded, looking back at Ketswana. "You get that?"

"Yes sir. You riding in with them?"

Hans smiled. "Might as well see what it's like. Now get the boys off. We start in two minutes."

Timokin slammed the hatch shut and bolted it.

"Sir, I have to ask you, just stay out of the way. If

one of my crew goes down, you replace him. If we get hit, there are two ways out—unbolt that door, or up through the turret. Got that?"

"Care for a chew, son?" Hans asked, offering a plug.

"Makes me sick, sir," and Hans laughed. "Sir, get behind the driver. You'll be able to see a little something from there."

Hans followed Timokin forward around the boiler. Directly ahead, the driver was back in his seat, gunner and assistant gunner to his left. A round was already chambered, and as the ironclad lurched forward the assistant gunner pulled the gunport shield aside. The two men then pulled on the tackle running the gun barrel out. Squatting down behind the driver, Hans felt claustrophobic with the narrow view, less than a foot square, that the driver had. The road ahead sloped down, canopied by fir trees covered with heavy snow. The scene was soft, the light diffused, quiet and peaceful, and there was a flash memory of boyhood, winter, going into the woods with his father to pick up the deadfall for firewood.

The road turned, sloped down to the left, and straightened out. The road was wider here, and he saw stone markers jutting out of the snow, the Roum ever efficient, curbing the side of the road even here at a remote quarry. A few low stone buildings were to one side, mausoleums, all of them ornately carved, miniature temples to departed ancestors.

The trees started to thin out, and there was an open field to the right, the grape arbors looking like humpbacked white giants. Something moved straight ahead, a lone Bantag, standing in the middle of the road, staring straight at them.

He turned, started to run.

"Full speed," Timokin roared from his position up in the turret.

The driver reached down, grabbing hold of the throttle, notching it forward. The ironclad lurched, and behind him Hans could hear the driveshaft turning over, speed increasing. The machine skidded on the road, sliding down the final slope, the driver frantically turning the steering wheel, the heavy iron studded wheels digging in.

They hit a bump, and Hans was knocked off his feet and slammed against the bulkhead.

There was a thump against the front armor, and two more an instant later. The driver reached forward, dropping his forward armor shield down so that his viewing area was reduced to a slit only two inches wide and nine inches across.

Hans caught a momentary glimpse of a gate, and the gun beside him recoiled with a cracking roar. The assistant gunner unscrewed the breech and pulled it open, the three-inch brass shell casing ejecting out, the stench of black powder filling the chamber, mixing with the smell of hot kerosene and oil.

The assistant gunner grabbed another cartridge off the holding rack lining the wall, slammed the shell in, and closed the breech. The two then ran the gun back out. Looking through the gunport, Hans saw the shattered gate ahead, another shell impacting on it, exploding.

They lurched forward, firing another round into the gate at near-point-blank range, the gunner screaming for a load of canister. The ironclad slammed into the gate, knocking Hans off his feet, flinging him up against the forward armor. Cursing, he rolled back, feeling like useless baggage as the assistant gunner screamed at him to get out of the way.

Hans came back up to his knees. They were inside the village. Bantag were swarming out of the buildings lining the street. A roaring staccato erupted above him. Looking up into the turret, he saw Timokin at the gatling gun wreathed in steam and gun smoke and roaring with delight. Looking back out the gunport, he saw Bantag writhing, crumpling in the snow, turning to run. The gun roared beside him, slamming back, canister shrieking down the street, picking up Bantag like broken dolls, tearing them apart.

The driver guided the ironclad straight down the street, laughing. The machine bumped, rode up, came down, rode up again, and Hans realized they were crushing bodies beneath them.

Rattling ignited along the sides of the machine, bits of paint and metal flecking off on the inside, pinging about. Swearing, Hans looked around, spotted the helmet he had taken off earlier, and put it back on, pulling down the goggles and the chain-mail face protection.

The gunner beside him started to say something, then seemed to leap backward, his face exploding from a bullet that had been fired straight through the open gunport.

The assistant gunner looked at his fallen comrade in stunned disbelief.

Hans crawled over, dragging the body aside.

"Load canister!" Hans shouted, kicking an ejected shell casing out of the way. The assistant leaped to work, sliding the cartridge in, slamming the breech shut. Together they pulled the tackle on either side, inched the gun forward so that the muzzle cleared the port. Hans knelt behind the barrel, sighting down it. Targets were everywhere, and he leaned to one side.

"Clear!"

He jerked the trigger lanyard. The gun kicked back, snagging on the recoil ropes, coming to a stop. The assistant was already at the breech, popping it open, then turning to pull down another cartridge.

Moving down the street, they swept it clear, and when they reached the opposite wall, Hans could see that the gate was open, Bantag streaming out, some of them mounted.

"Block the gate!" Timokin shouted.

"No! We trap them in the city, we have to dig them out house by house. Let 'em run—the pass is blocked."

The driver looked at him.

"Back away from the gate. Timokin, fire an occasional burst to keep them moving!"

In response, the gatling above Hans began to fire short three-second salvos, counterpointed by blasts of canister from his gun. The Bantag seemed to learn the rhythm and timed their rushes to get past the ironclad.

Suddenly a dark hand appeared in the gunport, holding something that hissed and sputtered. The grenade rolled into the ironclad, clattering on the floor.

Hans looked down, saw it rolling, saw just how short the fuse was. He started to go for it, but the assistant gunner went over him, pushing him aside, and then leaped on the grenade as if to sweep it up and throw it out the hatch. As if changing his mind at the last instant, he curled up, clutching the grenade tight against his body, and went down.

"No!" Hans screamed even as the dull concussive blast knocked him backward against the gun. The assistant gunner seemed to bounce into the air, and Hans felt something wet and warm splatter on his face.

Stunned, ears ringing, choking on the smoke, Hans crawled up to the gunner, who amazingly was still alive. He looked up at Hans, tried to whisper something, and then mercifully died.

"What the hell happened?" Timokin cried.

"Just keep shooting!" Hans shouted. "Where the hell is our infantry support?"

Timokin turned the turret about. "Coming up behind."

"Well, I wish to hell they'd get here. Driver, keep us moving."

Cursing, the driver engaged the driveshaft and they lurched forward again. Tracers snapped across the road ahead. One of the ironclads must be driving the rout from behind, Hans realized. A solid wall of Bantag came rushing past, half of them stumbling, falling. Unable to operate the gun alone, Hans loaded it just in case there was a rush straight at them, but at the sight of the ironclad on their flank the Bantag wailed with terror and redoubled their rush to escape.

Something emerged around the side of their ironclad, and with drawn revolver Hans prepared to fire, but it was a blue-clad infantryman, who went down on one knee to fire into the press, levered his breech open, reloaded, then moved forward. More infantry passed, and there was a banging on the side access hatch.

"Hans!"

Unbolting the side door, Hans gasped at the rush of cold air. Ketswana stood with rifle poised, grinning, his bayonet glistening red.

"Never seen the bastards run like this!" Ketswana shouted.

Hans stuck his head out, looking back down the street. Infantry were moving cautiously house to house, checking for any who had remained hidden inside. The entire street was carpeted with dead, dozens of bodies crushed and ground through the snow onto the hard paving stones.

"Timokin, I'm getting out. Follow them through the gate. The road leads toward the pass. Keep them running."

Bailing out of the machine, he ignored Ketswana's laughter over the helmet and goggles. Tearing them off, he looked around. The air was thick with the smell of powder and crushed Bantag.

A low wall was to his right, nothing more than a simple barrier to keep out an occasional bandit, made of upright logs. Climbing up a ladder, Hans looked out across the quarry. He could hear a roar of musketry ahead. Good, they were blocking the pass. The Bantag were screaming, and it was not their battle chants, it was panic, and Hans grinned. Only once before had he heard those screams of terror and panic—when the Tugars had broken at Suzdal and were being driven into the flooding river. After so many battles of facing them coming on in unrelenting waves, it was good to have this moment.

Gatling fire rattled beyond the gate, and he could catch occasional glimpses of tracers arcing across the quarry. Another ironclad chugged by behind him, turned, and went out the open gate to join the melee.

Turning, he looked back into the village, and he felt a wave of anger. In the tiny forum there was a smoldering fire. Piled up beside it was a pyramid of human skulls. The survivors had been freed and were pouring into the streets. Some were in shock, wandering aimlessly. A few had approached the ghastly pyramid and were shrieking in grief, while others were venting their rage on the Bantag wounded. Scattered rifle shots

echoed where the infantry were finishing off the last survivors, though some of his men were being turned away
from their task by outraged survivors who wanted to
draw out the death agonies of the prisoners. A dark
column of fire was boiling up from an ironclad, flames
pouring out the gunport and turret like a blowtorch. The
shells inside started to erupt, the ironclad shaking and
rocking from the explosions. Damn, another machine
down.

"Ketswana. Round up the survivors, see what you can
learn from them. And tell our men to dispatch the Bantag wounded quickly—I don't want us sinking to the
level of those hairy bastards."

"Can't blame them, though," Ketswana observed
darkly.

"We're human, Ketswana, not animals like them."

"All right, Hans."

The rifle fire out beyond the gate was dropping off.
The snow was still coming down hard, and darkness was
closing in. A lone rider came toward the gate, moving
slowly, holding a mounted infantry guidon aloft and waving it so that he wouldn't be mistaken for a Horde rider.
Reaching the gate, he spotted Hans and rode up, dismounting.

"Colonel Vasily, good job," Hans announced.

"Not good enough, I'm afraid."

"How's that?"

"We deployed on either side of the pass. As soon as
we heard the attack, I positioned a company right across
the road, shoulder to shoulder, and kept a dozen men
mounted behind them just in case there was a breakthrough."

Vasily breathed out noisily.

"They came on hard, at the run. Seemed to materialize out of nowhere, hundreds of them. We slaughtered
them in that pass, cut them to ribbons. But a few
broke through."

"Your mounted troopers—did they get them?"

"I can't promise it, sir. They ran down four of 'em,
but we're not sure if it was four, five, or six that broke

through. I got my men riding hard, but sir, I can't promise that no one got out. Some might've broke down the side of the mountain before the pass—we could hear something floundering around in the forest below us. I got men out there too."

Hans sighed. Damn. Too good to hope for. If only one gets back with a report of ironclads, that gives them time to move, to block us.

The surprise was blown. If he moved his force out in the middle of the steppe with ironclads already worn down and near to breaking, it'd be a slaughter.

Pull back or at least hold here?

No, dammit, no.

"You did the best you could. Throw a company as far down the road as you can, then report here. Officers meeting in one hour."

Vasily saluted and departed. Hans stepped down from the battlement and, spotting Ketswana, motioned him over.

"Good fight, Hans. Did we bag all of them?"

Hans shook his head and explained.

"So now what?"

"How long would it take to get the remaining ironclads up?"

"I don't know. Most of them, in another hour or two. I'd imagine, though, it'll be hard moving with night setting in."

Hans looked up. The snow was coming down, but there was a dull shimmer of light through the clouds to the south. One of the two moons was briefly visible, slipped behind the racing clouds, then appeared again.

"We have to move tonight," Hans said. "We have to assume the Bantag know we're coming. We can't waste any more time."

"Are you crazy, Hans? Most of the infantry won't be up till midnight."

"I know. They stay behind. Tomorrow, after they've rested, they can deploy down the pass, set up a blocking position. But as soon as we get the ironclads up, feed the crews. I'll give them four hours rest. Those ironclads that Timokin decides won't make the final run, their crews can service the machines that will. We transfer off the fuel and ammunition, load what infantry we can on the tops of the machines and in the wagons, and move at midnight."

"You're a madman, Hans."

"I know."

Chapter Eleven

"It's warmed considerably," Emil announced as Pat opened the door, yawning and rubbing his eyes.

"What time is it?"

"Four in the morning," Emil said as he handed over a steaming cup of tea and a plate with a slab of salt pork sandwiched between two pieces of hardtack. Pat gratefully accepted the meal, and sitting down on the edge of his cot, he sipped the tea.

"How is he?" Pat asked.

"I'm sending him back to Suzdal. Bullfinch is supposed to be in this morning. He'll go back on the monitor."

"Damn all," Pat sighed. "If word of that gets out, it'll break morale for certain."

"I'll make sure no one knows. He'll be mixed in with some serious cases I want to get out. I'll make sure he's hidden."

"Hidden. Andrew Lawrence Keane hidden. Never thought I'd see it."

"Physically he's turned the corner. Kathleen managed to get him up and walking in his room. But he's like a piece of gauze, transparent almost, as if he were a ghost."

"He is a ghost, Emil. If that's what Andrew's become, a frightened ghost, I for one wish the shell had killed him."

The crashing blow of Emil's hand across his face so shocked Pat that he dropped his mug of tea, which shattered on the floor. With a wild curse he rose to his feet, fists balled up, ready to strike.

"Go on, you goddam mick, go on, hit me!"

Pat stood balanced on the balls of his feet, arm half cocked back.

"My whole life," Pat hissed, "I've never let a man lay a hand on me and walk away from it."

Emil stood before him unflinching.

"If you weren't such a used-up old man . . ." His voice trailed off.

The words seemed to strike as hard as a fist. Emil turned away and started for the door.

Pat stood still, waiting. "Emil?" The one word escaped him, barely a whisper.

Emil turned and looked back, tears in his eyes.

"Emil, don't go."

"You said it, damn you, and you're right. I'm a used-up old man. Used up trying to put life back into you damn killers. And Andrew's used up, we're all used up. After all that, how dare you wish Andrew dead?"

"It's what he would have wanted, the old Andrew, to die clean, not this long lingering. You let him run from this battle, he'll never come back."

"There's nothing more I can do for him. Get him back to Suzdal. We've got a hospital for consumption patients, up at the edge of the Northern Forest. That's where I'm sending him. The air there's clean, not filled with the stench of death like this damn place. Besides, this city is lousy, typhoid's increasing, so is typhus, and I can't stop it, not with the water from the aqueducts cut off."

"And you'll kill him nevertheless," Pat snapped. "He'll hide up there, afraid of his own shadow, and never come back."

"Pat, I've seen this before. Give a boy a few months of rest away from the lines. Let him sleep in a clean bed, eat good food again, no sight of Bantag or Merki or any of them. Let his mind get whole again."

Pat violently shook his head. "First off, Andrew's not a boy, he's commander of the armies, by God. You remember what Hancock said at Gettysburg just before he got shot?"

Emil shook his head. "I wasn't interested in such heroics."

"Well, I was. I saw him that day. Him in his clean boiled shirt. The rebs pounding our lines just before Pickett came in. And there was Hancock riding slowly along the line as if out for an afternoon jaunt after a heavy dinner. One of the men begged him to get down, and Hancock laughed and said, 'There's times when a corps commander's life just doesn't count.' "

"And if I remember right, he got shot right after that."

"He braced the line, the men stood, we threw the rebs back, and Hancock did it, did it because he had the guts to show his men he wasn't afraid. Well, I'm telling you that at this moment, as far as this beleaguered army is concerned, the life of Andrew Keane no longer counts. More than once I saw Andrew do the same thing Hancock did at Gettysburg, riding down the line, letting the boys see he wasn't afraid, that victory was far more important than his staying alive. And now you're destroying him, helping to turn him into a coward."

Emil stiffened again, and Pat extended a hand in a calming gesture.

"You're concerned about saving Andrew, or at least saving what's left. I'm concerned about winning this damn war. And my gut feeling is, today is going to be a very bad day. You take Andrew out of this city and hide him or not, the boys will know. The rumor will shoot through this army like shit through a goose, and by sundown they'll be panicked, piled up on the docks begging to get out or going over the west wall.

"You know why Ha'ark hasn't hit us on the other side of the river? It's because he wants to keep the back door open for us when we panic. If the circle's drawn tight and there's nowhere to run, then a man fights like a cornered animal. But the boys know there isn't a Horde rider within five miles of that western road. They'll break and run, I tell you."

"He goes out. Pat, I'm trying to save what's left. Maybe six months, a year, from now, he'll be ready to command again."

"No. If he isn't ready to command today, then he'll

never be, and I'd rather the army had the legend of Andrew as he was than the pitiful remnant he now is."

"He's right, Emil."

Startled, Pat saw Kathleen standing in the door. She had lost weight, and the weeks in the basement with Andrew had robbed her face of its natural freckled Irish complexion, leaving her pale and drawn as if she had aged ten years.

She slowly walked into the room, the two men stepping back from each other.

"We could hear you out in the hallway. You don't want the men to hear this."

"I'm sorry," Pat replied.

She turned her attention on Emil. "Pat's right, not just for the army but for Andrew. We let him run today, it will be known by everyone, and he will never live that down. He thinks himself a coward. That will prove it to him, and he'll spend the rest of his life retreating from it."

"Damn all of you with your words, 'coward,' 'hero,' " Emil said. "Every man is both. Every man is frightened, and the only difference is that some just manage to hide it longer than others. Our dear Andrew went to the well once too often, Kathleen, can't you see that? Can't you see that doesn't make him anything less than what we know he is? That boy's been fighting for over ten years now, and not just in the line but commanding armies, terrified of a mistake that could cost an army, an entire nation.

"I'm sick to death of all you talking about heroes, cowards, when all I see is the wreckage of it."

"If we had no heroes," Pat sighed, "what kind of nation would we be?"

"He's paid his share of it. Just let the man be, can't you?"

"Well, I want him to go to that well again," Kathleen whispered, her voice choking. "Lord knows I love him more than my life, and no matter what he now is or will be I'll always love him. But this is for himself, not me. Because I know this, Emil. We could save his body today. I could take him to that hospital. The children could join us there, and I'd see that smile again when our little ones rush to his embrace."

She started to choke the words out. "They don't care if their father's a hero or coward. He's just their father. But he'll know, and he'll remember. And someday, Emil, I'll come home and find him dead, a gun in his hand, because he'll finally remember just who he was, and he won't be able to live with what is left. Emil, is that what you want to save him for?"

Emil seemed to sag as if shrinking up in defeat.

Before he could reply, the room swayed, followed seconds later by a deep rumbling thunder as if the world were being split apart.

"My God, they did it," Pat gasped.

Racing for the door, he stormed into the headquarters room. Plaster from the ceiling was raining down, the kerosene lamps overhead swaying violently. As he headed toward the stairway to the dome, an observer came staggering down, wide-eyed.

"The wall! They've blown the wall!"

Pat bounded up the steps. Coming out on to the platform he stopped, gape-mouthed.

Early dawn traced the eastern horizon and silhouetted the spreading mushroom cloud of smoke and debris still soaring up from the inner wall on the other side of the river. The cloud spread out, its interior lit by a hellish fire. Wreckage, bricks, blocks of stone, torn bodies, an entire artillery piece rained down, crashing into the river, trailed by burning fragments and sheets of fire.

"My God!"

Kathleen was by his side. The plume of debris continued to spread out, a hail of shattered bricks smashing across the docks on the west side of the river. He could hear glass shattering, the last few panes left in the city bursting from the shock wave and raining down on to the streets.

Grabbing hold of Kathleen, he shoved her back through the doorway, covering her with his body as the debris arched down over the palace.

Another sound now mingled with the thunder, the cries of hundreds of thousands shaken awake by the explosion, cries of terror, joined in another instant by the wild throaty cheering of the Horde, the braying of the nargas, and the staccato punch of hundreds of artillery pieces opening up, pouring a blanket of shells across the entire city.

The storm of debris passed, and Pat stepped back out onto the parapet, sweeping aside the fragments of stone from the sandbag wall. By the flash of the artillery shells he could see where a section of wall at least a hundred yards long had collapsed. From the wall halfway back to the dockyard, an area several blocks deep, buildings not yet destroyed in the siege had collapsed, stunned survivors staggering out of the wreckage. He thanked God he had had the foresight to pull his reserve regiments away from the wall, given the warnings about a mine, but never had he dreamed this would have so much power.

When he thought of mines he had remembered the Crater at Petersburg, having witnessed the blast. That, he later learned, had had five tons of powder in it. Given the power of this blast, there must have been thirty tons or more.

Storming up over the still-smoking debris and skirting the edge of the smoldering crater, advance units of the Bantag were already into the inner city. No return fire greeted them, and he pounded his fist against the sandbag, swearing at the sight of men breaking in panic, fleeing the still standing wall for a couple of hundred yards to either side.

Ha'ark had cut a hole in his defense big enough to push his entire army through and, at that moment, Pat saw no way to stop him.

Shaken awake by the explosion, Andrew looked around the darkened room in panic.

"Kathleen?"

Shadows flickered around him, and still there was the deep echoing thunder. He tried to pick up his glasses and realized that he was attempting to do so with his left hand, the hand, the arm, buried at Gettysburg.

For a moment he looked down numbly as if it were all a dream and the hand would materialize and do as he desired.

Gettysburg . . .

Johnnie. The boy looked asleep under that solitary elm. How do I tell Mother he's dead?

The tears came, seizing him, the grief all-consuming, and he was somehow standing removed from himself, watching his body shake. Each sob there was an agony of pain with the indrawn breath, a fitting penance perhaps.

A breath of agony for each of them. How many? How many did I lose, how many did I kill? That reb boy in the West Woods of Antietam was the first, point-blank in the face, the eyes wide with astonishment. Is he with Johnnie now? Young enough forever to perhaps be able to play, to laze along the riverbank of that far shore, two boys dead by me.

Oh, Johnnie, I never had time to cry for you. I couldn't weep over you as you slept beneath that tree. I never could find you later. They took me away to that place, that terrible place, where they cut into me, saying it would make me whole again.

Maybe you sleep now in that half circle of graves around the place that Lincoln spoke. More likely you're lost, your bones resting under that tree, forgotten. And I forgot you, I didn't keep the promise I made to see that you lived, that there would be a life for you, a return to Mama, a boy rushing home with nothing more than a skinned knee to be kissed rather than a bullet in the heart.

Maybe you're back in Maine. The lake, evening time, the warm breeze. The ghosts in the woods, they're my ghosts, my memories fled back home before all this. And he walked among them so that they were real. It seemed that everything else had now become the world of ghosts.

"Time, oh time, stop in thy flight . . ." The poem drifted, and he took wings upon it. Young again, that first love, walking hand in hand in the moonlight and the whisper of the breeze on Webber Pond . . . and he smiled.

"Andrew?"

He felt a light touch on his face, a handkerchief, stale scent, brushing the tears away. Though his eyes were opened, he could not see her at first, and there was a wondering if indeed he had crossed, had fled, and the soft gentle dream was real.

He felt something cold brushing against his ears and the cruel world came into sharp focus. Kathleen.

He stared at her, for a moment uncomprehending. And at that moment he wasn't sure if he loved her or hated her for being all that she was, tied to all that had become the ghosts.

"Andrew, look at me!"

The words were harsh, cold.

"Andrew, it's Kathleen. I need you to listen."

He turned his head toward her, and she was a ghost, distant, as if he were looking at her through the wrong end of a spyglass.

"Andrew, the Bantag have blown the inner wall. They're pouring through the breech. We're going to lose the harbor."

The harbor. What harbor? The words flowed in, but there was no registering for the longest moment. After all, they were ghosts. Finally there came some dim recognition. She wanted something from him yet again.

He gazed at her and felt as if the floor beneath had given way. A great black hole had opened and he was sliding into it, the sides of the hole made of glass, nothing to hold to even if he wanted to hold, which of course he didn't.

He took another breath, remembering that he had to will himself to breathe, and the pain stabbed through him.

"It hurts," he whispered. "I need something for it."

"No more morphine," she snapped. "That's finished. If it hurts you have to live with it."

He wanted to cry, but something in her face made

him stop. It was a look he could not bear, as if she were judging again. And he turned his head away.

"Did you hear me, Andrew? They're into the city."

"So?"

She let go of him, the drawing away of her hands as sharp as a blow.

He looked back, struggling to remember.

"If they're here, they're here. I can't do anything more."

"I have to go see to those worse hurt now than you," she said, and each word was a blow.

"Go then."

She reached into the pocket of her smock and drew out something, small, dark, and the sight of it made him want to recoil. It was a revolver. She placed it on the nightstand.

"If they break through, you'll want this," she said.

He gazed at the weapon, dark, sinister, the faint smell of oil. It seemed so familiar.

He looked back up at her in wonder. There was something else here, the gun was an offer of something else, he wasn't sure if she was even aware of it, and the thought sent a chill through him. Was it the offer of the dream, the atonement? Did she know that? And in a terrifying instant he knew that she did.

She reached back into her smock and pulled out something else, a small folded case. She looked down at it, her features seeming to go out of focus as she opened the case and gazed at it. Leaving the case open, she set it on the table by the gun.

Without another word, she turned and left the room, and as the door closed he thought he heard her sobbing.

He looked over at the table. The gun. He reached out for it, this time with his right hand. The polished handle was smooth, cold, like the skin of a snake. It was heavy. He lifted it up, feeling the balance, the sense of it striking some memory, and then his gaze fell on the case. Open, it revealed two daguerreotypes, one of a soldier sitting, a woman behind him, her hands resting on his shoulders, and something told him it was Kathleen and he from an eternity ago. The other image was hard to see through the mists . . . it was their children.

Stamping his feet, he looked down and saw the puddles of slush splashing, felt the cold wet soaking through his boots. A rolling salvo thundered to either side as forty guns moved up onto the top of the outer battlements during the night fired in unison, a thunderclap concussion, forty tongues of flame, smoke boiling out, seconds later the shells impacting on the facing of the inner wall. It wouldn't do much damage, unless a lucky hit detonated a shell atop the bastion, but that was not the purpose. The firepower was to demonstrate, to intimidate, to shatter what will was left.

Directly ahead a full umen, moving in column down the rubble-choked street, headed for the breach, which was still wreathed in dark coiling plumes of smoke and fire. Signal rockets rising up from the battlements to either side indicated where his warriors had widened the break to nearly twice the width of the hole blasted into the wall.

For the first time since the start of the war, prisoners were actually being taken. Remnants of one of the units cut off in the outer city had accepted the offer of surrender with the promise they would not be consumed. The line of men shuffled past, filthy, their stink wafting up to him. And yes, the promise would be kept, for now, for the sight of them could be of use later.

Ha'ark finally looked back down at the telegram a messenger had handed to him only moments before. He scanned the contents again. It was most likely nothing, one lone report, but it was enough to cause a stab of concern at the moment that promised to be victory.

The messenger still waited, and finally Ha'ark looked back at him.

"Signal the umen commander in that district. I want confirmation of this report. I can't send troops racing back and forth based on only this. Also an order to the flying machines posted in that area. The weather is good, so there are to be no excuses. Send them up to find out.

Tell the umen commander, as well, that if this report is confirmed, I expect the rail line to be held at all costs. Nothing must stop the supplies. I need those trainloads of ammunition tonight."

The warrior repeated the message, bowed, then raced back to his headquarters. Damn, if only this were a modern army. A radio, a damn radio, and I would know exactly what is going on. If there was a threat we could race the trains through or stop them outside the danger area and wait till it was cleared.

He pondered that thought for a moment. The damn things can't go any faster. Wait? But if I order them to wait tomorrow, we will be out of ammunition. Weeks of hoarding for this attack and half of it was expended in the first two hours. Order a slowdown? Never, not with the breakthrough accomplished.

His precious ironclads. After their first use in the city, when they had been destroyed in the narrow streets, they had been withdrawn, and they had lingered ever since in reserve at the rail depot. Part of his plan was to send them in for the killing blow, but he knew he'd lose half of them in the wreckage and confusion of the city, and for what? Victory was already assured. No, if there was a threat to the rear, he'd send them out there to match the Yankees, if indeed they were out there.

He waved for one of his staff officers.

"The ironclads in reserve—I want them on the next train out. That has priority over anything else. Send the train back up to the bridge on the Ebro River."

"Priority over everything else?"

What about the ammunition? The ironclads were already loaded on the rail cars, sitting on a siding, positioned thus in case of just such an emergency. Eight hours to get them back to the Ebro. If they waited for the three trains, it'd be after dark, useless if there was a threat. If the ammunition trains were delayed eight hours, they'd still be up by early tomorrow morning, and there was still enough in reserve to see the battle through till midday.

"Move the ironclads. Tell the ammunition trains to

keep coming forward, then sidetrack them for the ironclads. If the report is found to be false, then the ironclads can be sidetracked and the ammunition moved up
on schedule."

The staff officer nodded, sorting out the variables in
his head, and bowing low he ran toward the headquarters and conveyed the orders as he thought he remembered them.

Leaning against the open top hatch, Hans braced his
elbows on the cold metal and trained his field glasses on
the stone bridge spanning the Ebro. The few mounted
Bantag were fleeing eastward as the column of ten ironclads slid down the slope, and in less than a minute they
crossed the span without a single shot being fired. The
lead ironclad came to a stop, and a diminutive figure
rose up out of the hatch and waved.

Hans returned Timokin's gesture. Seconds later he
was moving forward again, following the old Roum road
which continued on to the northeast. According to the
map, there was a secondary road, unpaved, that turned
northward five miles ahead and then drove straight
north, intersecting the rail line ten miles farther on. The
ten ironclads crept up over the hill and disappeared, followed by a column of a hundred mounted infantry and
four horse-drawn wagons loaded with extra kerosene
and ammunition.

"Still think you should keep your force together?"
Ketswana asked, sitting astride a horse next to Hans's
ironclad, the *St. Mina.*

Hans shook his head.

"We've decided it. One column splits east, the other,
that's us, takes the west side of the river. If we both get
through, we turn on to the tracks, cutting fifteen, maybe
twenty miles of line, tear it up as we go until we meet
at the bridge, rejoin, and burn everything in between.
That way if they mobilize from either direction we have
time to react and pull back undisturbed, and maybe we
just might get lucky and bag an engine or two."

"Still don't like splitting. Hell, we have only eleven

machines left with us, and no telling how many by the time we get there. Rather have all our firepower together if they come up."

"And do what? Charge eleven gatling guns? We'll annihilate them," Hans chuckled.

"You've got two thousand rounds in that bucket of yours. Burn through that and then what?"

"Don't spoil my day," Hans replied, squinting and looking to the west. "I'm actually enjoying myself after that damned siege."

"I'd rather be back there. Had a nice hole, it was warm, I enjoyed sniping at the bastards. Out here we're naked."

"Well, I didn't ask you to come. You invited yourself."

"I'm supposed to be your bodyguard, remember."

"I don't need a bodyguard and never asked for one."

"That's the job the colonel gave me, and that's the job I took when you were running around like a damn fool back in Chin."

Hans looked at him, and his friend fell silent. The memory of fleeing Ha'ark was still too bitter. It was a little short of a year past and had not yet retreated, as most memories do, to the point where the pain is blunted and one can draw a smile at the shared hardship and the fantasy that there was adventure in it all.

Ketswana, as if having troubled himself as well with the recollection, nodded, and the two were silent for a moment.

Hans raised his field glasses, trained them on the horizon, and finally lowered them again.

"We're about to get company."

"Where?"

"A flyer," and he pointed.

The machine was moving quickly on the westerly breeze, and seconds later he spotted another one farther to the south, riding close to the slope of the mountains now a dozen miles away.

They were coming on straight toward him, and he knew they had been sent out to look. At least one Bantag must have escaped and spread the alarm. How many hours ahead of us? Maybe six hours' warning.

But if so, where was the resistance on the ground? The few guards on the stone bridge had obviously been surprised, and the bridge would have been a logical place to block them, keeping the attack on the west side of the river.

He's still not sure, Hans sensed. The warning is just going out and they're sending the flyers up to double-check. Good. But where are our damn flyers? He turned his glasses to the southwest, scanning the ridgeline. The weather had been good since midnight. Petracci should have at least flown up to the quarry, seen that it was occupied, and either landed or pushed on. But he was nowhere in sight.

Damn.

The flyer that was coming straight at him turned slightly in its path. Nose going up. Cautious bastard, making sure to stay out of gun range. The flyer passed a mile to the north and half a mile up, and even before it reached the river it turned and went into a shallow dive, racing north . . . toward the rail line.

"Let's move it!" Hans shouted, looking back at the other ironclads in his column and the mounted infantry behind. Clenching his fist, he jerked his arm up and down, then pointed forward.

The machine beneath him lurched and in a skidding turn swept around the flank of the hill and down toward the old Roum road running to the west and north.

He felt a thrill of excitement. It was like being back in the old cavalry again, out on the prairie, but this was a mechanical horse. Fine, never did like horses anyhow, always kicking you when your back was turned and dying just when you started getting attached.

Standing in the open turret, he looked back. The column was moving, all except for one machine with a burst of steam blowing out its stack. Damnation! The side hatch opened and the crew scrambled out, looking at the machine as if it had suddenly turned into a fire-breathing dragon that had mysteriously appeared before them.

Four mounted infantrymen pulled off from their column, leading extra mounts for the crew to ride back toward the mountains, while others dismounted, ready to strip out the gatling gun and ammunition and drain the fuel before setting the machine afire.

Ten ironclads left and twenty miles to go, Hans thought grimly, his cheery mood shattered.

The entire monitor seemed to recoil under Bullfinch's feet as the two massive ten-inch guns fired in salvo. The shells slammed into the warehouse on the other side of the river, less than a hundred yards away, and detonated. The entire structure collapsed, bringing down with it the dozens of Bantag snipers perched in the upper floors.

A shell slammed against the outside armor, a light-caliber round from a field gun on the east bank of the Tiber River, and harmlessly ricocheted off with a whine. It was like a mosquito trying to punch through the hide of an elephant.

"Keep up the fire," Bullfinch ordered, "and by God don't let them get on that bridge."

He started to the back hatch of the turret, which had been flung open. Looking at the gangplank run out to the dock, he took a deep breath. Bales of cotton had been rolled up on either side, and infantry men were behind it, firing across the river. A mortar round shrieked down, impacting in the icy water between the monitor and the dock, a geyser of spray splashing down on the deck.

Bullfinch stood in the hatchway and waved, and a colonel behind one of the bales held up a hand for him to wait. He turned to shout an order, and the rifle fire along the dock redoubled. From the smashed-out windows of one of the warehouses a fieldpiece barked, sending a spray of canister into the windows of the warehouses across the river.

The colonel held his arm up and jerked it.

Bullfinch leaped out of the hatch, scrambled across

the armored deck, gained the gangplank, and ran for the dock. A railing by his side exploded in splinters, and he heard another bullet hum past, tugging at his coat hem. Hitting the dock, he sprinted for the narrow opening between the bales, leaping over the body of one of the infantrymen who had been killed running the gang-plank out.

Dodging between the bales, he ducked down, gasping for breath.

"Hot out there, sir?"

Bullfinch nodded. "Damn, never expected to come up into this. What the hell happened?"

"The general's waiting for you, sir. He'll fill you in."

The colonel detailed off four infantrymen, pointed to an open door, and then called for another volley.

As the rifle fire erupted, Bullfinch was up, running hard for the door, outstripping his escorts, who were burdened with rifles and packs. Bursting through the splintered door, he lost his footing in the dark and slammed into a wall and fell.

The four escorts piled through behind him, picked him up, and dragged him out of the foyer and into a back room. They had barely stepped into the back room when a shell burst in the doorway behind them, a fragment slicing through the wall, bouncing off the ceiling, and coming to rest by Bullfinch's feet.

"Damn hot work."

The men said nothing as they helped him back to his feet. The mood of his four escorts was grim, and he wanted to comment on it, but looking into their eyes stilled his voice. They were gaunt, eyes sunken, the white circle insignia of 2nd Division, 1st Corps stained and blackened. The stench of them washed over him, and he saw that their uniforms were in rags. One of the men was wrapped in a dirty blanket held around his shoulders with a makeshift pin.

"Come on," he said, "let's go."

They went through the next door into a vast open space, the interior of the building, packed with troops. There was little order to them, just dozens of clusters of men sitting on the floor of the warehouse, leaning against the exterior walls, some of them asleep, others talking quietly among themselves, and he could sense their defeat. Officers wandered through the room, calling out unit numbers, trying to sort the rabble out.

Leaving the back of the building, they headed up a narrow street. Several of the buildings were on fire, and no one was making the slightest effort to put the flames out, except for a few emaciated civilians who were making a ludicrous attempt, scooping up snow and throwing it at the flames.

"No water," one of his escorts announced. "Aqueducts cut."

"What about a bucket brigade down to the . . ." And he fell silent; the river was now the front line.

Along the side streets that he passed he saw swarms of refugees huddled in alleyways, children crying, many of the adults in shock, trembling with fear at each new explosion.

A shout erupted ahead and a gun came around the corner, thin horses pulling, the ten-pounder bouncing and rattling as it raced past, followed by a lone caisson. No other pieces followed, and he watched it pass.

At last the rear of the Senate was in view. Bantag gunners across the river had made it the center of their attention, and barely a second passed without a shell impacting on the polished limestone walls which had been so lovingly restored after the damage sustained during the Cartha attack before the beginning of the Merki War. But that attack had been with a handful of old smoothbore cannons. Now the Senate was being systematically taken apart with high-powered rifles.

A continual rain of rubble was cascading down into the street behind the palace. Waiting for what he hoped was a pause, he sprinted for a doorway, jumping through just as another salvo exploded above him.

"Admiral Bullfinch?"

He nodded, panting hard.

"This way, sir."

Bullfinch looked back at his escort, who were in the

corridor. Opening his breast pocket, he pulled out a flask and tossed it to one of the men, and for the first time since coming to this damned city he saw a man smile.

"Stay alive, soldier."

"You too, sir."

As he weaved his way into the interior of the palace the roar of battle lessened, but the palatable sense of a disaster unfolding hung about him. The usual crisp sense of order at headquarters, evolved across three wars, seemed to be disintegrating.

Going down a flight of stairs, he heard shouting, and when he stepped into the headquarters room he was startled to see Pat and Marcus glaring at each other, standing but inches apart.

"I want my men out of there!" Marcus shouted. "Get them out while we still hold the bridge!"

Pat vehemently shook his head and slammed his fist down on the map board.

"They stay, dammit, they stay. He can't keep this sustained level of attack up. He just can't. He must be burning off ten thousand shells an hour, half a million rounds of small-arms ammunition an hour."

"And that fire is annihilating what's left of 11th and 12th Corps. I want them out of there."

"Dammit, Marcus, we still have a hold on the east side with them."

"I notice that all of the Rus troops are on this side of the river, though."

Pat's color drained, and wearily he shook his head.

"Do you really believe that? Do you really think I'd position units based on where they came from?"

"I don't know what to believe anymore," Marcus replied coldly. "All I know is that 9th Corps is gone, 11th and 12th are being annihilated, but your 1st, 3rd, 4th, and 6th all seem to be secured."

"And a third of the regiments in those corps are Roum, and ten of the regiments in the corps you call yours are Rus. Damn you, Marcus, retract what you're implying."

"I will not. I have to think about what will happen

next. Half my city is destroyed, my country is occupied, and I think you will pull out of here."

"How?"

Marcus pointed at Bullfinch.

"Isn't that what he's here for? To figure out how to evacuate?"

"No, sir, that's not why I'm here," Bullfinch snapped.

"They left the way open to you to the southwest. Pull out of here tonight, head down the coast, dig in, and get picked up."

"Are you offering a plan to me, Marcus?" Pat interjected before Bullfinch could point out that he couldn't marshal one-fifth the shipping needed to get what was left of four corps and their equipment out along with the thousands of wounded.

"If the plan fits, you take it," Marcus replied.

"And your plans?"

"I'm thinking of asking for terms."

"What? Are you mad?"

"No, I think it is you who are mad to continue this fight. Can't you see it's lost? Your precious thaw you always talked about has not come. This mad raid Hawthorne cooked up, well, the lad always did have more fighting spirit than brains. I always figured he'd get himself killed."

"Hans is leading it," Bullfinch interrupted.

Both turned and looked at him.

"That's right. Hawthorne's back in Suzdal. Hans is leading it."

"Why, for God's sake?" Pat asked.

"He was better suited to it, and I agreed. Vincent can barely walk, let alone go off on a raid like that. The men involved having fought with Hans, they know him, and he's got the cunning Vincent, God bless him, lacks."

"Damn all to hell," Pat sighed, sitting down as if already hearing that his old friend was dead.

"Well, he'll cut the rail for a day. So what?" Marcus said, shaking his head. "Then he gets killed, they bring their supplies up, and the attack continues."

"You actually think Ha'ark would honor whatever promise was offered?"

"He made an offer to Kal, didn't he? And I think that wily old peasant is half considering accepting. For all I know he has accepted."

"The president stands firm behind the war," Bullfinch replied, somewhat exaggerating the commitment he had heard when he had dropped Vincent off at the White House two and a half days ago.

There was fear that Marcus might actually do what he was now openly voicing, and if the Roum left the war and submitted to the Horde, that would mean that Suzdal would again stand alone, barely able to field an army a third smaller than the one that had faced the Merki.

"Months ago, Ha'ark said he would spare this city all but the old tribute of one in ten that existed in the old days before you Yankees came," Marcus said.

"Again the blame," Pat snapped. "You were damn eager to embrace the freedom we brought when we had already defeated the Tugars and there was no talk yet of Merki or Bantag."

"But tens of thousands of Roum citizens have died in this siege, tens of thousands more in the ranks, and only the gods know how many out in the countryside. One in ten was nothing in comparison."

"Because you and your nobles never had to pay the price," Pat snarled. "No, as you lords and grandees always have, you picked others to do the dying for you."

Marcus bristled.

"Anytime you want to settle this with arms, you know where to find me," Marcus growled.

Drawing a deep breath, Bullfinch stepped between the two. "Stop it, dammit!"

The two barely noticed the diminutive admiral until he thrust both arms out, pushing them back from each other.

"I have my monitor on the river, another one's coming up tomorrow, and one's already here. We anchor them by the bridges. That will keep them back—ten-inch guns packed with canister and shot. You can still hold this city."

"With what?" Marcus asked. "The harbor's cut, half our food stockpiles are burned, and ammunition's down to three days' supply. Just how do you propose to hold?"

"With guts," Pat replied, knowing he was playing his last card. "It's what Andrew ordered us to do."

Marcus sighed and shook his head. "Don't drag that poor man into it."

Never had Bullfinch heard Andrew referred to as "that poor man." Startled, he looked at Pat, who stood silent.

"Still, it was his orders."

Marcus finally lowered his head.

"All right, for the memory of his friendship and for that only. We give it a day, see what madness Hans can do. But if that fails, or if they get across the river at any point, I will surrender rather than witness a massacre."

"It will be a massacre anyhow if you do surrender."

"Maybe, but that's a maybe. Ha'ark wants a live domain, not a land of ghosts. But if they gain this side of the city, there are near to half a million people I must be responsible for, and they will be massacred for certain. I will take my chances with a surrender."

"If you do, I will take your offer of a duel," Pat replied bitterly.

"Anytime you wish." And without going through the ritual of exchanging salutes, Marcus stalked out of the room.

"Poor Andrew?" Bullfinch asked. "What the hell does he mean?"

Pat drew Bullfinch aside. "It doesn't look good. He's been alone down in his room all day. Kathleen ordered the guards to let no one in, not even me or Emil. They say they could hear him crying in there."

"Just what the hell is going on here?" Bullfinch asked. "Last time I was here you still held most of the city, and Andrew was hurt bad but mending. And I come back to this."

"Defeat," Pat whispered. "It looks like I've managed to lead us straight into a defeat."

Chapter Twelve

Turning toward the railroad track, Hans ordered the driver to stop and scrambled down from the side of the machine. The few pathetic Bantag who had attempted to offer resistance lay sprawled on the ground behind the gun emplacement. The seven machines still with him were strung out on the road, the closest coming on fast, while the mounted infantry were already fanning out.

Half a hundred Chin were huddled in a ditch on the far side of the track, looking up at him wide-eyed with terror.

He moved slowly, hands extended, trying to remember the words he had learned in the labor camp.

"Friend, Yankee."

One of them stood up and tentatively approached. Hans silently cursed himself for not remembering to bring along a few of the Chin refugees from his head-quarters company. Ketswana, who had mastered some of the language, came reining in, dismounted, and started to talk.

The Chin looked at Ketswana, then pointed at Schuder and said one word: "Hans?"

Hans quickly nodded, and the others in the ditch started to talk excitedly, crawling up out of the slush and mud. One of them pointed at himself, then back to Hans.

"He says he remembers you, Hans. He was moved from our camp before the breakout. His name is Jong See."

Hans looked at the emaciated slave, dressed in stink-ing rags, blackened feet poking out from torn strips of burlap. The man looked up at Hans expectantly. Hans stepped forward, making a show of grasping the Chin's hand.

"Tell him I remember," Hans said.

"Do you?" Ketswana asked, incredulous.

"Of course not, but the poor bastard needs to believe."

Ketswana started to talk, and the Chin dissolved into shuddering tears, flinging his arms around Hans, who towered over him. All the memory of it came back, the tens of thousands of faceless slaves left behind, the stench and squalor and unrelenting fear. He put his hands on the man's shoulders, patting him like a father soothing a child, struggling to control his own emotions.

He wanted to pull back, he had to, every second was precious, but he let the moment last a few seconds more. Finally the Chin released his hold and stepped back, saying something excitedly, pointing at the ironclad.

"He's asking if you are here to free them."

"Huh?" All focus had been on the mission, to get in, smash the bridge, tear up track, then get the hell out. He looked at the shivering slaves, many of them weeping, eyes fixed on his. How many did I leave behind knowing they would die because of my desire for freedom? he thought. I balmed my soul with the ideal of the Republic, I had to escape to save the Republic, but still, I condemned how many to death?

"Yes, we're here to free them," Hans announced.

"Hans? How? With what?" Ketswana asked.

Hans turned to his friend.

"These are our people, Ketswana. They're more ours than the Rus and Roum. They're our blood, for we were slaves with them."

"It's twenty-five miles back to the mountains. I thought we'd smash things up and get the hell back before tomorrow. The Bantag will be here in swarms."

"Ask him how many prisoners are here, between us and the bridge."

Ketswana asked, and there were excited answers.

"They say there are thousands at the bridge. They

only finished rebuilding it a couple of weeks ago. Rumor is they were to be moved up to feed the army. Before that they were used to haul supplies across the river."

"How many Bantag?"

"A regiment at the bridge."

A Bantag regiment of a thousand. Damn, they must know by now.

"Jong here rides with me."

Hans looked down at the track. It was a wretched affair, with unevenly spaced stringers. Here and there the ballast of the road laid by Rus and Roum was visible through the snow. Twisted rails, torn up and bent during the retreat, lay to either side. The new rails brought up by the Bantag were uneven, laid down haphazardly, the line weaving back and forth. It had taken years to train the Rus how to do the job professionally and with skill; the Bantag had used gangs of slaves and had been working in haste. Gazing at the track, Hans realized just how weak Ha'ark was in this area. He might have knowledge of the technology, but translating that into a skill mastered by thousands was another story. Looking over at the slaves, he saw even more clearly the major flaw: they were men who should have been trained, fed, and well maintained rather than simply used up.

One of the mounted infantrymen, an old railroad hand, rode slowly past Hans, shaking his head. "If they try to make more than fifteen miles an hour on this road, they'll wreck."

Hans nodded. Still, fifteen miles an hour was all they would need, if they could keep the road open.

He looked up at the mounted infantryman.

"Son, you worked on the railroad?"

"Yes sir. Helped you lay the first line from Suzdal up to the Ford before I got drafted into the army."

"You're section hand now. Dismount, pick two or three men from your unit who know railroads. Get those Chin over there working, start tearing up track, get a fire going, and turn them into Sherman's hairpins, wrap 'em around those telegraph poles."

Telegraph poles. He looked up at the line. "And for God's sake start by cutting that."

"And when the Bantag show up?" the infantryman asked, nodding to the Chin, obviously wondering what he would then do with fifty half-starved skeletons.

Hans held up his hand and walked up to the second ironclad in line, motioning for the machine's commander to dismount.

"Igor, isn't it?"

"Yes sir."

"Fine, Igor. We're heading east toward the bridge. You go west straight up this line. Ketswana, detail off twenty or so men to go with him."

Hans shaded his eyes and looked to the west. The open prairie undulated off to the horizon, the landscape a brilliant white, vineyards dotting the landscape, open meadows, orderly fields, all of it empty, the ruins of buildings sticking out of the ground like blackened, rotting teeth.

"Be careful. The sun's in your eyes. Don't get surprised by an artillery piece up close. Now, any Chin you find, point them back east to us. Try and pick a spot farther up where you can, if possible, ambush a train and smash the locomotive. Then get the hell out."

"To where, sir?"

Hans looked at the eager young ironclad commander. It was a simple calculation. If he could get five miles farther west before running into something, that bought an extra hour of time. If he could ambush a train, it would be worth a dozen ironclads, for chances were if there was one thing Ha'ark could not spare in this war it was locomotives. One ironclad would surely be worth it. A calculation that meant almost certain death for this man and his crew.

"Just try and get out. We'll pile up a stack of rails here, right on this battery position. If it's night, just follow the track to here, turn right, pick up the road, and it will take you straight back to the pass."

The ironclad commander nodded.

Hans shook the boy's hand. "Good luck, son."

"Sir, it sounds like I'll need it."

"I think you will. Signal a supply wagon over to you—they'll be along in a couple of minutes—and be sure you have enough fuel, and take some extra ammunition."

Not wanting to draw it out, Hans turned and walked back to his machine.

"I should go with him," Ketswana said.

"I need you to translate," Hans lied. There was simply no way he was going to send his friend to certain death. Hans climbed back up onto his machine, motioning for the terrified Jong to climb up and sit atop the turret behind him. Spotting the mounted infantryman handling the remaining Chin, he passed the order for a signal pile to be made and for them to start moving east, and to move quick if they heard gunfire behind them.

Looking back, Hans saw that the remaining machines had finally caught up, the momentary pause allowing them to pull a few more tins of kerosene from the wagons.

"When the wagons are emptied," Hans shouted, "pull in any Chin who are too weak to move."

Raising a clenched fist high, he jerked it up and down and pointed forward.

His driver tried to run the machine directly atop the rails, but it kept skidding and rattling, and after a couple of hundred yards he edged it off the track to run alongside the roadbed. With the shallow grade and the ballast underneath, the driver pushed his throttle forward, their speed picking up to what Hans estimated was a good six miles an hour.

The track ahead ran as straight as an arrow for several miles, dipping down into broad open valleys and up gentle slopes, then down again. At the top of the second low ridge a thin line of Bantag mounted warriors were deployed, dismounted. A light skirmish broke out between them and his own mounted troops riding to either flank. After several volleys and a loss of one of his own, they mounted and disappeared. Reaching the crest, he saw the Bantag riding ahead of him. A village of ugly shacks, made from the salvaged rubble of nearby farms, lined the track. Dozens of Chin lay in the snow, obviously slaughtered by their departing masters, but half a hundred more had scattered, staggering through the snow to either side of the line.

"Ketswana, detail a few more men. Round those people up, point 'em east, and get them smashing the rails."

The drive continued. As the Bantag fell back, their numbers increased. Obviously troops were being moved up from the bridge. On the next ridgeline ahead he could see a low earthen fort, the glint of rifle barrels catching the afternoon sun. Trying to steady himself, he raised his glasses. He could see the dark snouts of two fieldpieces projecting from the walls of the fort.

Hans looked back at the ironclad commanders behind him in column. He spread his arms wide, signaling they were to deploy from column into line, then pointed at the fort.

"Ketswana! Mounted infantry to the flanks, and stay behind us!"

A whispered cry fluttered overhead, a mortar round detonating to his left, catching a mounted infantryman.

"Jong, inside!"

Hans pulled himself out of the turret with just his legs dangling inside and pointed down.

Jong looked at him, terrified.

"Inside!" Hans snapped, and grabbing the man by the shoulders he half lifted him, and reluctantly the Chin went down into the bowels of the steam dragon. Hans followed him down, pulled the hatch shut, and locked it.

Sitting down behind the gatling, he opened the steam cock, raised the barrel, and waited. A puff of smoke ignited from the fort, and a geyser of dirt erupted a hundred yards ahead.

They were nervous—most likely hadn't seen action since the opening moves and had never faced ironclads.

He waited as the range closed through a thousand yards, eight hundred, six hundred. Turning the turret, he could see the other ironclads, deployed out as ordered. One of them fired a short burst of gatling fire at the fort, and the others joined in. Damn, not yet, save it.

The range closed to two hundred and fifty, extreme range if they had anti-ironclad bolts. The two guns continued to fire. He heard more gatling fire. Looking out the narrow view slit to his right, he saw that two of his flanking ironclads had angled off. A heavy skirmish line of Bantag were deploying out, mounted. Gatling bursts tore into the line, and within seconds it disintegrated. The two machines charged.

Watch it, he thought, they might be a lure into a rocket unit.

A thunderclap bang shook his machine, and he heard a high-pitched wail.

"All right down there?" Hans asked.

"Nothing, sir. It bounced—just scared the crap out of the Chin."

The gun below him recoiled, the gunner calling for shell.

Damn, every shot had to count. He watched as clumps of dirt erupted on the front of the battlement. They fired back, and again there was another clang . . . and still no breach.

"Take us to a hundred yards!" Hans shouted.

The ironclad lurched forward, and he held his breath. They fired again, and he heard the shot scream past his turret. Carefully aiming the gatling, he squeezed a short burst, the tracers arcing over the gun position. He tapped the barrel down slightly and squeezed again, a bit low and to the right. It was hard to aim while they were moving, and he waited.

The machine stopped. Another shot slammed into them, the blow knocking him half off his seat. Cursing, he grabbed hold of the gatling, aimed, and squeezed, the stream of fire slashing through the gunport, tearing into the crew. He released the trigger, cranked the turret, and lined up on the second gun, but it was already out of action.

"Forward!"

The ironclad crept up the snow-clad hill. Rifle fire pinged against the turret, one round ricocheting through the gatling's gunport, bouncing around past Hans like an angry bee, and landing on his neck, stinging him with its heat.

Cursing, he jerked his collar, looked back out, and saw several Bantag at the fieldpiece's gunport . . . a rocket crew. The gun below him recoiled, most of the canister slamming into the slope forward, but several balls sliced into the crew just as they were firing. The rocket soared up into the sky and disappeared.

His ironclad surged up, then slammed back down. They were inside the fort, dozens of Bantag running back and forth, obviously panicked, and his gatling fire tore into them, shredding bodies. They stormed for the rear sally port, piling up around it. If they were human he would have ceased fire out of pity, but he continued to fire, the ironclad crushing up over them and out onto the slope behind the fort.

The sight that greeted Hans filled him with awe. The valley of the Ebro River was below. Hundreds of Bantag swarmed down the slope, running in every direction. A small city, now nothing but burned-out ruins, was directly ahead. The train track went straight through it and onto a roughly made log bridge spanning the two-hundred-yard breadth of the river.

A dark swarming mass, looking like a hive of ants, undulated in the city, surging back and forth . . . the Chin laborers. He saw puffs of smoke around the periphery of the mob. The Bantag were slaughtering them. In the town he saw something else: three trains lined up, one behind the other.

"Forward, for God's sake, forward!" Hans screamed.

The ironclad started down the slope, far too slowly, and he reached down with his foot, kicking the back of the driver.

"Faster, full speed!"

"Sir, we'll skid out of control."

"They're murdering them, damn you! Full speed!"

The ironclad surged forward, and within seconds he could sense that the wheels were slipping, the machine sliding down the slope like a sled out of control.

He hung on, the driver screaming and cursing, as they

skied down the slope and smashed through a low stone wall. It was impossible to shoot the Bantag doing the slaughter; they were outside the stockade, firing blindly through the plank walls into the seething mob on the other side. So intent were they on murder they were not even aware of the death charging them from behind.

The ironclad slowed, the wheels grabbing, and the driver turned the machine until they were parallel to the wall. Hans pivoted his turret and poured in a long stream of fire, walking it up the length of the wall, dropping the guards. Finally realizing what was happening, they broke and started to flee. The driver smashed the ironclad straight into the stockade wall, which collapsed. Turning, he drove down the length of the barrier, tearing it to shreds.

Wild screams of madness, terror, ecstasy rose up. Turning his turret to the rear, Hans saw the Chin, hundreds of them, pouring out and in spite of their feeble condition staggering in pursuit of the fleeing guards. The Bantag who were wounded and trying to crawl away were swarmed, disappearing under a seething mass of bodies. Ahead, their way was finally blocked by the mob.

"The trains! We've got to get the trains!"

The ironclad turned, cutting straight through the slave compound, smashing down shacks, shelters made of bits of rags, Hans praying that those too weak to move would be dragged out of the way in time. Another stockade wall loomed ahead, and they drove through it and back up onto the tracks.

The damn trains were backing up, already on the bridge.

He fired his gatling at the locomotive, now several hundred yards away. Sparks splashed off its forward boiler plate.

The train farthest east was already climbing the slope on the opposite bank of the river, an artillery round detonating beside it.

"Gunner, fire on that damn thing!"

"Shell casing's jammed! I'm trying!"

"Goddamm it, they're getting away!"

Hans kicked the driver again, shouting for him to drive onto the bridge.

Obeying the order, the driver guided the ironclad onto the bridge, and Hans instantly regretted it as they edged out and he looked over the side. His stomach knotted at the sight of the swirling ice-choked river thirty feet below. The old road bridge to his right, blown in the retreat, had been repaired, the destroyed central span covered with logs. One of his ironclads was already on it, carefully moving forward, several dozen mounted Bantag fleeing before it, then going down in a burst of gatling fire.

But there were no side railings on the rail bridge, only the tracks, and he could feel the machine skidding, rocking back and forth, ready to slip off at any moment. He wanted to scream for the driver to stop but was afraid that the slightest diverting of his attention would send them over the side and into the river and straight to the bottom.

Terror he had not known since the days of his imprisonment overwhelmed him, and he closed his eyes, feeling every jolt, bump, and lurch.

The machine suddenly shifted, and he stifled a cry. They were on the other side and the driver was skidding to a halt, the ironclad still half on the track.

Straight ahead, the last train was cresting the hill, disappearing, wrapped in smoke. He didn't know whether to curse or weep with relief. He stared at the opposite ridge, bitter that the quarry had escaped, and then the entire horizon seemed to light up in a sheet of fire, debris soaring up from the other side of the ridge.

Timokin, dammit! He was on the track behind the retreating Bantag!

The explosion mushroomed out, and then, long seconds later, the engine that had been fleeing them reappeared, smoke belching from its stack.

"Gunner!"

"Clearing it!"

Hans watched the locomotive approaching, shells detonating to either side.

The train was less than two hundred yards away, gathering steam, coming on.

"Driver, maybe we should move?"

"We're hung up on the rail. Give me a minute."

"You don't have a minute."

Hans looked back at the locomotive. Well, at least they were blocking the bridge. He popped open the hatch above.

"Get out now," he shouted.

"Loading a bolt," came the reply from below.

He waited, holding his breath. The gun kicked back with a roar. A second later there was a flash, and the steel armor-piercing bolt sliced through the locomotive's boiler, spraying a wall of fire and burning coals back into the tender and on into the next car, which was loaded with five hundred rockets.

The fireball ignited, chain reaction sweeping into the next car, loaded with five hundred more rockets, then to the cars filled with artillery rounds, signal flares, millions of rounds of rifle ammunition, a car loaded with fifty barrels of kerosene and five barrels of benzene, and finally to the last two cars, packed with Bantag infantry.

The explosion stormed down the slope, debris tumbling, rockets spinning, artillery rounds, their fuses ignited, crashing down and bursting, rifle rounds exploding like five million firecrackers set off at once.

Hans slipped out of the turret and down into the hull, screaming for everyone to duck as the storm swept over them. It sounded as though a thousand bees, each one made of steel, were dashing themselves against the outside, joined by thumps, clangs, and explosives that sheared off interior bolt heads, which went bouncing back and forth inside the ironclad. One explosion seemed to lift the ironclad up and threatened to knock it over.

The storm passed, the torrent of noise subsiding to occasional pings, chatters, dull bangs, and then one more sharp explosion. Cautiously, Hans crawled up to the shield that the gunner had fortunately slammed down in front of his barrel. Lifting the one-inch iron plate, Hans looked out, then back at the gunner.

"Prettiest shot I ever saw," Hans exclaimed, and the gunner grinned like a boy who had personally set off the town's Fourth of July display prematurely as a prank.

Hans stood up and saw Jong, curled up in front of the boiler.

"Poor beggar," the engineer announced, patting Jong, who was rocking back and forth and keening softly.

Hans unlatched the side door and leaned on it. It gave back slowly, the engineer adding his weight so that it finally creaked open. Hans stepped out. A driveshaft still attached to a locomotive wheel leaned against the side of his machine.

The ironclad was half buried under the burning debris, and Hans shouted for the engineer to try to back up.

Stepping away, Hans climbed over a smoldering box-car door. There were still explosions out in the fields. A shell behind him sprayed him with mud, but he ignored the danger.

The sight was beyond his imagining, a joy to behold. Where the train had stood less than a minute before there were now only blackened ruins. The snow to either side in a vast circle a hundred yards across had instantly been transformed to water and mud. The column of smoke from the explosion was still climbing, spreading out, fragments of debris pattering down.

There was another sound now, and it caused his heart to swell, the joyful cry of thousands who had lived long enough to see their tormentors vanquished. Looking back across the river, he could see the Chin surging down to the riverbank, oblivious to the danger, cheering, waving. A chant rose up, and he struggled to blink back the tears.

"Yankee . . . Yankee . . . Yankee . . ."

An ironclad was coming down the ridge, skirting the inferno. The turret popped open, and Timokin stood up, waving triumphantly. The chanting roared to a crescendo, and Hans looked back, realizing that he was an actor upon the stage and for that brief instant the boyish dreams of glory had again become real. Unable to contain himself, he waved, and then bowed.

"By Perm, Kesus, and Saint Malady!" Timokin roared, climbing out of the turret as his steaming iron-clad skidded to a halt. "Have you ever seen anything like it?"

Hans grinned. "Honestly, son . . . no."

"Thought they were getting away. We got the train in sight as we crossed the tracks and he was backing up with two more trains in front of him. Well, they slammed on their brakes and went ahead again. The bastards poured on the steam and raced ahead of us. We chased them but figured they were gone. Well, we come moving up here and then suddenly they're coming backward, straight at us."

Timokin was talking so excitedly that he had to pause for breath.

"Bagged the first one myself. The two stop, start going forward, and then boom . . . boom!" As he spoke he waved his arms over his head.

"Ammunition trains," Hans replied, finally getting himself back under control.

His own ironclad, having extracted itself from the track and the burning rubble, backed around, coming up beside Timokin's machine. Both crews were out, slapping each other on the back, talking excitedly, and Hans let them go for the moment. Even Jong was out, gazing in wonder at the wreckage and then back at his liberators. Hans looked back at Timokin.

"How many machines left?"

"Six. Four more broke down, lost one at an artillery position while we were chasing the train. I'm sorry, our blood was up and we were coming on hard, didn't want to stop."

"It happens, son."

Timokin looked past Hans to the bridge.

"It'll be a bastard to burn that. Green lumber. We could soak it with a hundred gallons of kerosene and it will still wink out."

"There must be tools. We get the Chin working on it, chop it down if need be."

Timokin shaded his eyes and looked to the west.

"If you want to get out by dark, we'd better start moving, Hans."

"We're not getting out at dark."

"What?"

Hans motioned toward the still-cheering prisoners. "What about them?"

Timokin lowered his head. "Didn't think of that."

"Honestly, neither did I till I saw them. It's twenty-five miles back to the pass. You should see those people. We try to march them at night, they'll all be dead in the snow by morning."

"Hans, they might be dead anyhow when the Bantag finally pull themselves together and close in on us."

Hans shook his head.

"Not right away. I see this. We broke their line, destroyed enough ammunition for a week's worth of fighting. We'll tear up fifteen miles of track or more and destroy the bridges. But they need their slaves, Timokin. There must be six, maybe eight to ten thousand of them back there. We take away the slaves, how are they going to rebuild all this? It'll cut his line for days, maybe weeks. We save these people, and by doing that we kill Ha'ark's army."

"They'll be on us maybe tonight."

"We'll see. I'm going back over. We've got to get some organization. First off, let's give them a feed."

"Of what?" Timokin asked nervously.

"See all those horses?" And he pointed at the hundreds of riderless mounts spreading out into the open fields. "Get my mounted infantry to round them up. Get some food in the Chin, smash up everything we can here, then start moving them out. I'll send a courier back up to our infantry in the pass to come down to meet us."

"Infantry unsupported in the open?"

"See any alternative?"

The cheering washed over them again, and Hans looked at Timokin, who finally smiled.

"Guess this is what we're fighting for."

"You're damn straight it is."

Ha'ark stood silent, watching the city of Roum in flames. Memories of the past stirred, the burning cities of the old world, the flash glow in the night sky of an atomic blast burning yet another million in a single flash, their cities, his cities, all of it merging into one unrelenting slaughter.

But this is different, he thought. Another race bent upon our destruction, and I am the Redeemer sent to destroy them.

At his order the guns had fallen silent. Ammunition was all but depleted, but it could be replenished tomorrow and the assault continued.

He looked down at the messenger holding the white flag.

"Be sure to wave it over your head, and let them see you clearly. Deliver the message and wait for the reply."

"Yes, my Qar Qarth."

The messenger disappeared into the dark, and Ha'ark grinned. It would make them pause, it would play upon their weaknesses.

"My Qarth."

It was Jurak, and from his manner Ha'ark sensed something was wrong.

"What is it?"

"There's a problem."

"Go on."

"You know the telegraph line is down near the bridge over the Ebro."

"Yes."

"Our flyer just reported. They spotted two columns of ironclads moving to either side of the bridge. The position was stormed."

"Damn."

"Ha'ark, the flyer reported three trains blew up. From the sound of it, they were ammunition trains."

"By all the Ancestors," Ha'ark roared. Kicking the

slushy ground, he turned away, aware that his assembled staff of umen commanders were watching him.

"They were told to wait till our own ironclads had cleared the way."

"Somehow the order was mistaken. They're gone, Ha'ark."

"Move another umen up. I want that line repaired no later than tomorrow."

"Move them with what? There were only two trains on this side of the break, the one now moving the armor, the second departing with rocket crews and the remaining armor. There's no way to signal those on the other side of the break to coordinate."

Ha'ark lowered his head. Three trainloads of ammunition. His army needed more than five million small-arms rounds a day to sustain the siege, and ten thousand artillery and mortar rounds. In the one moon since this battle had started he had consumed nearly a full year's worth of production, a rate he had never anticipated, and it had stretched his supply system to the limit. And now because of a damn raid everything was in jeopardy.

"Signal as far as you can up the line. Strip every mounted unit and send them in. I want this break contained, those who did it annihilated, and supplies moved up within three days."

Jurak looked at him. "What about here?"

"They'll break tomorrow if they do not surrender tonight, I'm certain of that. We open with a bombardment at dawn and push the assault. They will break tomorrow. But as for those who raided us, they are to be annihilated, and make sure it is done right!"

"Here are the terms," Pat announced, looking down at the note from Ha'ark written in clumsy Cyrillic script. "Cease-fire. All Rus troops to abandon the city within two days and be granted free passage out by sea. Roum to surrender to the Horde."

Pat looked around at his staff, his corps officers, and Marcus, who stood in the corner of the room with arms folded.

"Tell him to go to hell," Schneid barked, rising from his stretcher, obviously in agony with his broken ribs. "Damn all to hell, I'll take a gun and go up on the line myself."

"Very commendable, Rick," Marcus said, "but I don't think it will make a difference."

Schneid glared at him, and Marcus extended his hand in a consoling gesture. "You're a good soldier, Rick, but you're used up. All of us are used up."

"I'm not," growled General Matthews, commander of the 6th Corps, and the other Rus corps commanders nodded their agreement, even Barker, whose 4th Corps had all but been destroyed in the breakthrough.

Pat looked over at the commanders of the 9th, 11th, and 12th Corps, the Roum units. One of them was of the old 35th Maine, the other two Roum patricians. Bamberg, commander of the ill-fated 9th, nodded in agreement with Matthews, but the patricians were silent, their gazes fixed on Marcus.

There was a long awkward silence, and Pat thought of the dispatch in his breast pocket handed to him by Bullfinch, who sat in the corner of the room, saying nothing. The letter was from Kal, stating that if Roum made a move to a separate peace, it was Pat's responsibility to get the Rus units out of the city as quickly as possible. If he dared to make that news public, Marcus would see it as proof of double dealing on the part of Rus and most certainly go for a separate peace.

"The rest of the note?" Marcus said. "I think there was more in it."

"Nothing important."

"Read it," Marcus snapped.

Pat took a deep breath. "It states that the president of Rus is considering terms as well. If Rus agrees to a cease-fire and Roum does not do so, Roum will be annihilated."

"There," Marcus replied, as if this were indeed proof.

"It's a damned lie," Pat snapped. "This army fights to the end. Rus will never surrender."

"I wonder."

"Marcus, he is playing us against each other. If he splits us apart, we will all die. He must be desperate to try this. We've got to hang on just a little longer. The temperature today, it got above freezing for the first time in weeks. It could be the start of an early thaw."

"I've been hearing that for months, Pat—another day, another week, and things will turn around. Well, here we are, half my city destroyed, the Bantag encamped on the Tiber six hundred paces from this very building. You must see it from my side. If we continue to fight, we will lose anyhow, and every one of my people will be put to the sword."

He lowered his head. "Pat, harsh words were said between us this morning. I am willing to ascribe them to the heat of battle."

Pat nodded. "Thank you, and I apologize."

It was hard for him to choke the words out. Marcus was dead wrong, but he had to play every chance he could.

"This dream of the Republic, it was glorious while it lasted, but we are all dying because of it. I think if we surrender now, some of us will survive, then perhaps ten, twenty years from now we will gather our strength and win."

"Gentlemen."

Emil wearily stood up, and all the room fell silent out of respect for the old doctor.

"I'm a doctor. My job is to save lives. That's all I ever wanted to do. Too much stupidity in my business, and I wanted to change some of it, and the Eternal God has given me the pleasure of seeing that. Since coming here I've seen much change, and I've seen tens of thousands of boys dying in my hospital to bring those changes about. If you agree to Ha'ark's terms, Marcus, it will be for naught. All those boys, Rus and Roum, who died at Hispania, Rocky Hill, here, they will have died for nothing, and their shadows will curse you all for betraying them."

"They're dead," Marcus whispered. "That cannot be

changed. I'm not willing to put more into the grave beside them to honor their restless spirits."

"You will put all of us into the grave, or more likely the feasting pits of the Hordes. Once they've split us, once they have occupied and disarmed us, they will most surely turn on us and kill us all. Do you honestly think they will leave anyone alive who can remember how to accomplish what we did? They rule this world through terror, a terror so complete that all submitted, never realizing their own strength if only they would unite and fight back. Marcus, what you are contemplating is a death sentence for this entire planet. Once they have killed all of us, they will have to murder every last Chin, because the Chin know of us. Then after the Chin the Nippon, and whatever nations of people exist beyond them, and so on all the way about this world."

"Marcus, you said one more day," Pat quickly interjected. "You promised that this morning. For the love of God, give us one more day. Maybe Hans has broken through."

"That was a madman's scheme."

"Give it one more day."

Marcus lowered his head, then finally nodded. "One more day and that is it."

The meeting broke up, the commanders heading back to their units. Pat followed Emil out of the room and down the corridor to the doctor's room and closed the door behind them.

"He'll break tomorrow," Emil said. "I can see it. Marcus is a good man at heart. Remember, he joined us when it was to his advantage to stay out of the war we all knew was coming with the Merki. He just can't stand the strain of seeing his beloved city smashed to pieces. To him Roum is this city, and he wants something of it to survive."

"They'll all die."

"We might all die anyhow, from the looks of things. Do you honestly think you can hold them back tomorrow? I understand Ha'ark's shifting more troops to the west side north of the city."

Pat nodded. "Five umens. They'll attack at dawn, that's for certain. We'll pile 'em up, but I don't have any reserves left. The regiments holding the outer perimeter are from the 1st and 6th—I hate to say it, but I don't trust holding it with Roum units anymore. We'll lose the outer wall, we just don't have the strength, and then he'll throw everything he has in from the eastern side, try and take the bridges. And remember, the river above the harbor is frozen solid. They'll come right across in waves."

"Can't you smash the ice up?"

"Trying, now that it's dark, but they'll still get over it."

"So what do you propose to do, Pat?"

"Die fighting. Always figured that would be how I'd go. It's what Andrew would have expected."

At the mention of the ghostly presence in the room below them, Emil shifted uncomfortably.

"Any change?"

"No. He hasn't stepped foot out of the room all day."

"Kathleen?"

"She's down in the main hospital now helping with the wounded."

"It must be killing her doing that to him."

Emil sighed. "Poor lass. Maybe more courage than all of us together. I wouldn't have the heart to do to him what she has. I'd've held him and told him it would be all right. Damn, he's like a son to me he is," and as he spoke the words he struggled to hold the tears back. "Always feared I'd see this happen to him. Could see him getting used up, digging deeper and deeper into his strength, but it was like a body with cancer—it finally starts devouring the very thing that keeps it alive until there is collapse and death."

"Maybe you should stop it," Pat said, feeling a growing sense of alarm. "Emil, I was wrong when I said what I did. I'd rather see him live. You can go down there and stop it, take the damn gun, get him on Bullfinch's ship and get him the hell out of this goddam hellhole."

Emil shook his head.

"She is the next of kin. I have to observe her wishes."

"To hell with her wishes."

"Pat, I have to follow Andrew's wishes as well. Twice, once at Gettysburg and again when he was on the floor of that train, just before I put him under, he told me that if it meant he'd be a cripple to let him die instead. He's a cripple—I saved his body, but this time I didn't save his mind, Pat. The Andrew I knew would want me to leave him alone until he decided for himself what was to be done."

Pacing the riverbank, Hans watched the bridge burn. It had taken hours to finally get it going, after tearing down most of the prisoner hovels to provide enough fuel to get the green lumber of the trestle ignited. What precious kerosene was left had to be saved for the iron-clads. The moonlight had disappeared shortly before midnight, and the sky was overcast again, but this time the air was warm. After the weeks of unrelenting cold it actually felt intolerably hot. He felt something wet splash on his face . . . a raindrop.

Damn. At this point rain would be worse than snow. The poor bastards would be soaked to the skin. Throughout the evening the Chin had been evacuated across to the east bank of the river. Huge bonfires blazed, the smell of roasting horsemeat heavy on the air. They had no thought of tomorrow; all they knew was that tonight they were warm and their bellies filled to bursting. Dozens had died during the feast, gorging, trying to soak in a month of sustenance in one meal, which had become their last. He didn't feel any sense of loss in that—there was almost a melancholic joy to it. At least the poor bastards had died warm and full rather than screaming out their last breath under a Bantag's butcher knife. He remembered many a night as a slave when he would have traded his so-called life at dawn for a meal and a warm place to sleep that night.

And come dawn, what then? He had sent half his ironclads under Timokin back south to try to secure and hold the lower bridge over the Ebro. If the Bantag did not come up tonight, they'd march a couple of hours before dawn. Maybe the strongest could reach the pass, but he doubted if that would be even half of them. And dozens, maybe hundreds, would die.

But the Bantag would come up, that was a given, and placing the bet that Ha'ark would move troops and equipment from around Roum, he had decided to withdraw to the east bank. The river would provide some sort of shield, at least down to the lower bridge. And they will come up and they will block us, he thought. What was coming from behind he didn't know. Timokin, like him, had sent a lone ironclad eastward up the track with a company of mounted infantry to round up escaped Chin and to tear up track. For all he knew there could be a full mounted umen moving up from behind, maybe half a dozen of them. If so, he thought, we'll be pinned on this side of the river, the enemy holding the other side, and we'll be annihilated.

If it was only mounted or infantry, the ironclads could fight through, but that was wistful dreaming. Ha'ark had ironclads and he would bring them here. But as he watched his comrades, for as slaves they were his comrades, singing their incomprehensible songs, those with a little strength up and dancing, silhouetted by the soaring flames, all of them happy for at least one brief evening to breathe air that was free, he felt no remorse. They would die tomorrow, but they would die as free men, perhaps a precious Bantag rifle in their hand, more likely a club, a rock, but they would die fighting, and that was enough. There was no better company on this godforsaken world, Hans thought, than to die among men who would die in order to be free.

Chapter Thirteen

"All right, let's take them up."

Jack Petracci broke from his ground crew and started to where his Eagle was parked.

"Jack."

Controlling his anger, Jack stopped, waiting for Feyodor, his copilot, to catch up.

"Jack, I still think this is madness. It's raining, visibility is terrible. Just what the hell do you expect to accomplish?"

"We know nothing of what is going on up there. Just some damn vague report from one courier that they broke through. Now the infantry is leaving the safety of the pass to go out looking for Hans. Those boys need to know if the Bantag are closing in. I suspect Hans is blind as well."

"Jack, you call this an aerosteamer field?" Feyodor pointed to the narrow stretch of open ground running along the edge of the quarry. "Hell, Jack, we have a crosswind, there's mountains straight ahead, and besides, you can't see fifty yards."

Jack said nothing. There was no sense in admitting he was scared to death again. He was supposed to have been up with Hans as soon as he seized the quarry. The last storm had kept them grounded. Fog on the coast had kept him on the ground till midday yesterday, and he would be damned if he stayed down again. What was worse, though, was that one of the Hornets was gone. It had suddenly burst into flames ten miles short of the quarry and disappeared. A wing had simply folded up and the aerosteamer had spiraled down, taking its pilot with it. Something had shaken loose, but the realization did nothing to solve the problem now. In the dim morning light he looked over at his one remaining Hornet pilot. The boy was game enough, and that was always the problem—they were so damn eager they didn't think of the odds, while he was all too aware just how short a time the boy would most likely wear his sky-blue uniform before going down to his death.

He heard the sound of propellers turning over, and, ghostlike, his aerosteamer came into view. Wings were extended, gas bags topped off, top gunner and bottom gunner standing by the ladder. Grinning, they saluted.

Jack barely returned the salute as he broke away and did one final walk-around. Behind his ship the diminutive Hornet was ready as well, the pilot imitating him, walking around, checking the pins that held the wings to the frame, the guywires and the control surfaces.

Finishing his own preflight, he looked back at Bugarin, the Hornet pilot, who waved that everything was ready.

Jack climbed up the ladder into the forward cockpit, Feyodor slipping in beside him. He felt the machine settle slightly as his top gunner climbed up the outside of the machine and into his cramped position, and finally the bottom gunner scrambled into the rear position.

Jack checked the speaking tubes connecting to the other two, scanned the dials showing the engine temperatures and fuel, and took the control wheel, turning it back and forth while Feyodor checked the lever for the elevator. He looked out the window, and his ground crew sergeant held his hand up and saluted, indicating that all control surfaces appeared to be working. The rest of the ground crew, which had hiked all the way up here with the advancing column, hauling the mixing tank, jars of sulfuric acid, zinc for the making of hydrogen, and extra fuel and ammunition, stood to one side, watching expectantly.

The sergeant pointed straight ahead. Jack spared one final look at the flag fluttering to one side. The breeze was coming out of the southwest, maybe ten miles an hour, and he would be taking off heading south. This was going to be tough—the breeze might very well push them right over the edge and into the quarry.

"Well, here goes."

Feyodor made the sign of the cross as Jack took the fuel knobs and turned them open, then opened up the steam cocks for all four engines.

The propellers, which had been lazily turning over, picked up speed, shifting to a blur. The aerosteamer edged forward, hesitated for an instant as the wheels dug into the slushy snow, then started forward again. All they needed was ten miles an hour of ground speed and there should be positive lift when combined with the headwind. He watched the wind speed gauge as it inched up to fifteen and finally to twenty. Feyodor, hand on the elevator lever, pulled back. Nothing happened. He held his breath, wondering just how much room they had ahead. He could feel the aerosteamer crabbing, pushed to his left by the wind. Looking out the window, he felt his heart stop at the sight of the edge of the quarry wall, which dropped straight down into the mists. The portside wheel went over the edge, and the machine started to drop over. Jack turned the wheel to starboard, trying to hold the wing up.

"Warning flag!" Feyodor shouted.

From the corner of his eye he saw the red banner, a Bantag regimental standard which had been stuck in the ground a hundred yards from the edge of the open field. A wall of snow-clad pine trees was just ahead.

"Hang on!" Jack shouted, and he pushed the wheel to port, the wing dropping over into the quarry. His mind raced. They had tested the machine at Suzdal. This was higher—maybe the theory about higher air being thinner was true. The starboard wing lifted. Reaching out with his right hand, he put it over Feyodor's death-like grip on the elevator and pushed it forward. The nose of the aerosteamer went over the edge and pointed down into the quarry. He felt their speed picking up, the controls becoming firmer. As he held the machine in a tight banking turn to the left, the compass mounted at eye level spun through east to northeast to north. He pulled back hard on the elevator and continued the turn. In the shadows he sensed the bulk of the mountain wall looming on his right, the side of the quarry curving along with him as he turned. He steadied out pointing to the southwest, straight into the wind, elevator still held back, the machine clawing for every inch of space.

"Wall!" Feyodor shouted.

Jack ignored him. He heard shouting from outside. Sparing a quick glance straight ahead, he saw the ground crew, still at his point of takeoff, scattering as he skimmed up out of the quarry. The Hornet was still on the ground, pilot looking up at him wide-eyed as he skimmed over the machine, clearing it with barely a dozen feet to spare.

Gaining another twenty feet, he gradually edged the portside wing over again, turning to an easterly heading.

"The village," Feyodor announced, pointing down to his right.

Eyes glued straight ahead, he scanned the forest ahead and then saw the road climbing up through the pass. He had more speed now, and he edged the elevator back, threading his way through the cut. Clouds hung low, cloaking the treetops. The ground dropped away underneath and then instantly disappeared when he climbed too high. He edged back down, wingtips barely clearing the trees on either side of the gorge. Heavy raindrops started to splatter on the forward windscreen, distorting the view, and he wondered if there was some device they could make to wipe the water off.

The road below rose and fell in gentle undulations, and finally he released his deathlike grip on Feyodor's hand.

"Remind me never to fly with you again," Feyodor announced.

"Anytime you want to quit is fine with me."

"Sir?"

It was his bottom gunner, Julius Crassus, a nephew of Marcus, on the speaker tube.

"You all right back there?" Jack asked.

"Sir, is every takeoff that exciting?" the boy asked, his Rus barely understandable.

Feyodor grabbed the tube. "With this insane bastard flying it gets even better at times."

"I was just wondering, sir," the boy replied, his voice shaking.

The miles down to the pass slipped by. With the tailwind Jack estimated they were making at least forty miles an hour.

"Sir, I see Bugarin—he's behind us," Julius announced excitedly.

Jack grinned. The pilot had less than eight hours in the air, half of them on the flight from the coast up to the quarry. It was a miracle he'd gotten off.

"Pass ahead," Feyodor announced.

Jack nodded, saying nothing. The ground ahead sloped up through a notch in the hills, and the notch was completely obscured by clouds.

"Here goes," he whispered. Nosing down slightly, he swept down to treetop level, skimming along the road, then edged back up as the road started to climb. He looked at the compass, fixing it.

"Let's hope these damn Roum build their roads straight."

"We do," came an angry reply from the rear.

Jack ignored him, eye on the compass, putting on more elevator. A shadow raced past to his left, and he flinched as a tree, clad in snow, raced past, a shudder running through the machine as the portside wing brushed against it.

"Barely see the road," Feyodor announced. "Still see it, still see it."

He continued the chant, Jack holding the controls. According to the chart the road went straight through the pass, then turned to the right and followed the side of the slope down into the open prairie below. If he turned too late he'd fly straight into the opposite slope; too soon and again there would be a crash. He was threading a needle through the fog.

He waited a few more seconds.

"Road's turned east!" Feyodor shouted.

Jack pulled the wheel to the right. The starboard wing dipped, the aerosteamer turning. Gently he edged the elevator down, and then in a startling instant they were out of the clouds.

Directly below, a long column of wagons was moving, led by three ironclads that had been salvaged from the path of the march up to the quarry and put back into running condition. The road turned again to the left, and he followed it. The rain had abated somewhat on the lee side of the mountains, only a light drizzle streaking the windscreen, and there, to his absolute delight, was a long serpentine column of blue . . . 3rd Division, 8th Corps, on the march, spilling out of the pass and onto the open plain, thousands of faces upturned, men waving, cheering, as he passed. To his right he could see the road curving down to the valley of the Ebro, and in the distance he could even see the span of a bridge crossing the river. Far beyond in the distance a dark smoky smudge filled the horizon. That had to be the railroad crossing—Hans must be burning the bridge. All the drama of the campaign was laid out before him, visible in a single glance, and he grinned.

There were times, he realized, when in spite of the terror, being a pilot of an aerosteamer was godlike in its power and joy. Up here, out of the mud, the stink and squalor war still held a certain grandeur, and he now soared over the center of the stage.

He waged his wings in salute, tempted to circle around for another pass.

"Jack, off to the northwest," Feyodor announced.

Jack looked to where his friend was pointing. On the horizon he could see smoke, dozens of small columns of smoke, and his heart sank. Ha'ark's ironclads were coming.

Wiping the rain from his eyes, Pat raised his field glasses, training them on the outer wall on the west side of the city. The banners lining it for more than a hundred yards, from the edge of the Tiber up to the base of a four-gun battery position, were red, the standards of half a dozen Bantag regiments. A curtain of rain swept across his vision, then lifted, and he saw a solid block formation of a thousand cresting the battlement, swooping down the inside wall. Blasts of canister from the four-gun battery cut down a hundred or more, but still they surged on. In the warren of streets it was impossible to see what was happening. Fortunately the rain helped to keep the fires down, but he could well imagine the panic that was breaking out. Half a million refugees had been crammed into the west half of a city that before the war had housed, in its entirety, not more than a hundred thousand. If the outer suburbs on the west side fell, all those people would be shoved into the tiny enclave of the old city. There simply would not be enough room for them all.

He had positioned his troops long before dawn, knowing that once the blow struck it would be impossible to maneuver, to bring up reinforcements or pull men back. Down in the headquarters room the telegraphs were chattering, desperate pleas for more men, for ammunition, for permission to withdraw. There was nothing he could do now, the battle was out of his control, and all he could hope was that the veterans of his army, after years of combat experience, could stem the attack on their own.

The bombardment, which had erupted the hour before dawn, continued unabated. But as he listened, the ears of an old artilleryman caught on to something. The fire was more measured. A battery would fire, wait for several minutes, then fire again. The mass of guns was such that the explosions were continuous, but the barrage lacked the savage fury of the first breakthrough assault or of the weeks of vicious fighting on the eastern side and was definitely slower than yesterday's barrage when they stormed over the inner wall on the east bank.

Ha'ark's rate of fire was slowing down. Why?

There was a moment when almost no shells were exploding in the old city, then a renewal, as if they had rushed to fill a silence.

Clapping his hands together, he raced back down the steps into the headquarters room. Staff looked up anxiously. Pat turned to the row of telegraphers and shouted for their attention.

"I want a message up to all units. Message is as follows," and the men grabbed scratch pads, pencils raised. "Report immediately. On bodies of Bantag dead, how many rounds of ammunition are they carrying?"

The message went out, and Pat paced back and forth nervously. Finally after long minutes of delay the first report came in from 2nd Division, 6th Corps. "Count on four dead, one with thirty rounds, other two around twenty, one with eight."

Another report came in, this one of nine dead counted, with an average of twelve rounds, and other reports confirmed the numbers. Not one of them had a standard issue of sixty or more rounds.

"They're running out," Pat shouted, looking back at his staff. "Not one had more than thirty rounds on him. By God, you don't assault a city with thirty rounds in your cartridge box. You carry a hundred at least for a fight like this. They're running out."

"But we're running out of city to hold," and Pat saw Marcus standing in the doorway. "Even with ten rounds per warrior, Pat, everyone in this city will be slaughtered by nightfall."

"Keep them moving," Hans shouted, the three words a litany he had repeated endlessly since dawn.

Sitting atop his ironclad, he watched the ragged procession dragging past him in the rain, and he felt as if he were watching some scene of the ancient world caught in an etching in a Bible. The long column of Chin refugees stretched off into the mist in either direction, spilling over the road, staggering through the mud and slush, rags pulled tightly over emaciated bodies, shivering in the cold rain. Clumps of huddled rags lay alongside the road, those who could no longer keep up, and yet again he had to close his eyes, yet again he had to wrestle with the bitter realization that he could not save all of them and had to settle for but some of them. But that did not ease the pain of watching comrades clutching each other, one sinking to the ground, waving a feeble hand, with a dying breath urging his friend, or father, or wife, or son or daughter, to go on.

Even in this hell the Chin did not forget their humanity. Food was shared, the few precious spaces on wagons or horses given to those who needed them the most, and Hans had witnessed more than one case of someone surrendering that spot to save another, thereby condemning himself to this death march to safety.

Ketswana reined in beside Hans's ironclad and paused to watch the column.

"Brings back too many memories," Ketswana said.

"How far back are we?"

"Still strung out several miles behind us. A few stragglers back by the city. We tried to round them up, get them going, but it's hard work, Hans. I think we were wrong on our earlier estimate—there must be at least ten thousand Chin moving with us."

"This is how the Bantag managed it, not just the factories but here. They must have had a hundred thousand or more along the rail line to ensure the supplies moved. Well, this will cut a hole fifty miles across. It'll choke the bastard."

"Flyer, one of ours," Ketswana announced, pointing to the west.

The aerosteamer was coming in low, dipping down slightly as it crossed over the valley of the Ebro a half mile to the south. The flyer arced up, skimming just beneath the low-hanging clouds, circled south, and disappeared. Hans knew the flyer was looking, and several minutes later it emerged back out of the mists to the south.

Hans pulled his shot-torn guidon out of its mount behind the turret, held it up, and started to wave it back and forth. The flyer came straight toward him, skimming over his head so low he could clearly see Jack in the pilot's seat looking down. The flyer turned and came back around at a right angle to its first approach. A red streamer fell from the cockpit and slapped into the snow less than fifty feet away.

The Chin, initially terrified at the sight of the machine, quickly came to realize that it was on their side and in spite of their exhaustion cheered wildly. One of them brought the streamer and the attached message cylinder up to Hans. He took a deep breath before opening it. In this situation no news was good news.

He quickly scanned the message, Ketswana watching him anxiously.

"Our infantry out of the pass, with three ironclads. Thirty Bantag ironclads, four miles to west," Hans read, "closing at full speed. Supported by umen or more mounted. Will check east."

Hans lowered the message and looked across the river. As if wishing to confirm the note, a dispersed column of mounted Bantag came into view, reining in their mounts. Word spread through the swarm of refugees, and shouts erupted, a few even staggering out of the column and trying to run off to the east even though they were still protected by the river.

Petracci continued east and disappeared, and Hans shouted down below for his driver to keep moving.

"We'll see what happens down at the bridge," Hans announced. "Let's hope Timokin can hold. Then we have to hang on."

"For what? The infantry?"

Hans smiled and said nothing, slipping halfway back into the turret. As the ironclad eased back on the road, the engineer gave several blasts on his whistle, warning the Chin to clear the way, and they edged forward. When they slipped down into a narrow hollow he saw several hundred Chin sprawled under a grove of trees, shivering around a smoky fire.

"Keep moving! Bantag coming!"

They struggled up, but more than one remained prone, unable to continue. The toll was heavy going up the next hill; scores of exhausted stragglers were sprawled to either side of the road, and Hans forced himself to look straight ahead, to not let their eyes meet.

He looked up, startled, as Petracci winged over low, skimming the trees lining the road. He banked up and swept back again, crossing, dropping another streamer. Hans motioned to it, and several Chin staggered through the mushy snow, recovered the streamer, came up to the side of the ironclad, and tossed it up.

"Hans. Two regiments of Bantag advancing on road behind you, already out of city. Light screen of skirmishers five miles to your east. What are your orders?"

Hans shouted down for his driver to stop. Damn all. He crawled up out of the turret, unclipped his guidon, and slipped down to the ground. He walked clear of the ironclad and out beyond the trees lining the road.

What to do? he thought. Timokin with six ironclads will be down by the bridge where the second column is coming in. I have six left, and they're needed there. Can't wait to delay the attack from behind.

He waited, watching as Jack circled around, coming in low. Raising the guidon, he waved it, then pointed it straight back up the road they had been retreating down all morning. As Jack soared past, wingtip racing over Hans's head, Jack leaned out of the cockpit, pointing up the road, and Hans saluted.

The aerosteamer, staying low, continued on. Seconds later a second airship, the Hornet, swept past on the other side of the road and disappeared into the mist.

It would be interesting to watch, Hans thought, but his battle was ahead. Climbing back into his machine, he shouted again for the column to keep moving. The Bantag were closing in; he had to calculate how to deploy, how to shepherd his flock and keep the wolves at bay. Cresting the hill, he uttered a curse: yet another ironclad was by the side of the road, steam pouring out of the open hatch, the crew standing dejectedly behind it. The gatling gun had already been stripped out, along with the cases of ammunition and the breechblock for the cannon.

His driver slowed as Hans, shaking his head, shouted for the men to climb atop his machine. Now I'm down to five, he thought glumly.

*   *   *

Streaking low, Jack hugged the ground, dipping down, rising back up. The column of refugees was thinning out. The dark litter of bodies to either side of the road was heartbreaking, some of them still crawling, desperate to escape. Approaching the next rise he saw a small knot of stragglers running. The Bantag must be ahead.

"Julius, remember, short bursts and only at thick clusters. Same for you, Feyodor. Oleg, keep an eye topside for their flyers. Hang on!"

He pushed the throttles all the way up, climbing the hill, the road directly beneath him. Clearing the crest, they saw the Bantag straight ahead, a long column crowding the road and advancing at a canter, outriders to either side in the fields, chasing down the few pathetic Chin who had risen up in a final desperate bid for life and staggered off. Slaughtered bodies hung from saddles, and the sight filled Jack with a bitter rage.

Feyodor, roaring a curse, grasped the trigger of his gatling. A stream of fire erupted, the cockpit filling with steam and the smell of powder as five hundred rounds a minute snapped out, slashing straight into the head of the column, the first burst dropping the standard-bearer.

He continued straight up the road, the surprise so complete that in the first seconds not a single shot was returned. Bantag by the dozens tumbled from the saddle, horses rearing in agony, pitching over, tangling with each other and crushing their riders. Through the speaking tube he could hear Julius shouting, the chatter of his gatling erupting as the aerosteamer passed over the head of the column less than thirty feet below.

Jack reveled in the screams of the Bantag echoing up in spite of the roar of the engines as he raced down the length of the road at nearly sixty miles an hour, guns blazing fore and aft. The column, several miles in length and laid out straight as an arrow, finally started to split apart. Horde riders turning their mounts, plunging off the road, desperate to escape. A knot of riders trapped on a narrow bridge twenty yards in length had no place to go, and some of the Bantag leaped off their mounts to crash through the ice below and drown in the turbulent stream.

Finally he could see Bantag dismounting on either side of the road, raising their rifles. A bullet cracked through the forward windscreen, the glass shattering, spraying him with splintered shards. More rifle fire erupted.

"Pulling up!" Jack shouted, and he yanked the elevator full back. Turning the wheel to the right, he broke into a spiraling climb. Another bullet came up through the floor, and he felt a tug on his boot but no pain.

Climbing through five hundred, then six hundred feet, he eased the elevator forward as airspeed dropped below thirty miles an hour. He had yet to experiment much with the machine but, when it dropped down below twenty, he knew it would begin to shake and the nose would drop. Used to the older aerosteamers, which relied exclusively on hydrogen for their lift, he nevertheless sensed that losing airspeed would cause his machine to go into a fatal fall.

He heard the topside gun fire, sweeping the road, as he continued to climb away and turned to run parallel to the enemy a quarter mile to their starboard side.

"Everyone all right?"

"Great here!" Julius cried. "Killed hundreds of them!"

"Oleg?"

"Wished I could've shot more."

"See any damage?"

"Looks like a few bullet holes punched through topside."

"Get the patches on. I'll hold steady for a couple of minutes."

There was a pause before the boy replied that he was going out. Jack looked over at Feyodor. The patches had been another of Chuck's ideas—a sticky glue patch of canvas with a small handle on one side. All one had to do was slap it over a bullet hole and the leak was temporarily sealed. The only problem was that it meant someone had to crawl atop the airbags to do it.

Jack eased back on the throttles and felt the weight

shifting as Oleg crawled along the top of the ship. Rising up in his seat, Jack looked out to his right. They had dropped maybe two or three hundred feet, and the column was a tangled confusion. But already, up at the front of the formation, the Bantag were reorganizing, this time spreading out from the road, pressing forward, urging their mounts on through the snow. The rain was all but finished, and far off on the horizon he could see the smudges of smoke of Hans's ironclads, while to the west he could see the Bantag ironclads closing in as well.

Jack waited, and just as he drew parallel to the head of the column he heard Oleg hooking back into his speaking tube.

"Got five holes covered. Saw a few more down on the sides, though."

"Well, hang on, we're going to pick up a few more! Julius, where's our escort?"

"Still behind us, sir."

Jack wagged his wing, wanting to signal the Hornet to stay up and away. No sense in getting the smaller aerosteamer chewed up by ground fire, especially when the Bantag flyers would show up sooner or later.

Jack pushed the starboard wing down, edged the elevator forward, and went into a shallow dive, cutting across the head of the column but this time leveling off at six hundred feet. Feyodor let loose with short burst, columns of wet snow spraying up. Knots of riders broke apart, scattering. Riders dismounted again, raising rifles, firing back. As they passed over the road, Feyodor let loose with long bursts of fire, Julius joining in, streaks of fire stitching up the road, knocking down any who had thought they could stay on the open path. Farther back, the enemy formation, though out of range, broke off the road and spread out into a vast wave. Jack jerked the aerosteamer back up higher, turning south again as if leaving the scene of battle.

"He's going down!"

As he turned, Jack looked back and saw the Hornet, one wing collapsed, spinning in a tight circle, spiraling down, slamming into the snow and bursting into flames.

Diminutive figures on the ground danced about in obvious ecstasy.

"Julius, what happened?"

"He was diving, started to pull out, and I saw the wing snap up."

"Goddam," he whispered and then said nothing, the death of their escort damping the joy of only seconds before. Surely a rifle ball wouldn't cause a wing to fold up. The Hornet was a deathtrap if a wing simply folded up like that. The Hornets would have to be grounded.

He flew on for several miles, deciding to feign leaving. The converging lines of action were spread out before him. Down by the bridge he could see a flash of light, a gun firing, a line of toylike ironclads deployed on a hill to the west of the river, the Bantag they were firing on, a long line of mounted warriors deploying out into open formation and dismounting. Directly ahead and below there was a mass of movement, reminding him of an ant heap that had been stirred up. Thousands upon thousands were on the road and to either side, struggling toward the bridge, the head of the column already pouring over and scrambling down along the riverbank in a desperate search for shelter.

If they were stopped at the bridge, the enemy from the rear would circle in for the slaughter. He had to keep them at bay.

"How's ammunition?"

"Half gone here," Feyodor replied.

"One case left," came the reply from the rear, and Jack struggled not to curse the boy for being too enthusiastic in his firing.

"Well, hang on. We're going back in."

He nosed over, dropping down, and once sure he was well clear of observers from the column to the rear he pushed the wheel hard over, skidding through a turn and lining back up on the road, and started back in for another pass.

The road raced by underneath. The Chin were moving faster, the sound of gunfire behind them urging the mob onward. Dropping down into a valley, he started back up, and then saw advanced riders of the Horde halfway down the slope, scattering, firing their guns, obviously deployed as a warning. Cresting up over the ridge, he saw a wall of them, some still struggling to dismount, but at least several dozen deployed across the road and to either side with rifles raised. Feyodor sprayed a burst at them, and a score or more dropped, but the return fire was heavier now. All down the length of the road they were deploying. Cursing, Jack pulled back hard, then, changing his mind, he nosed over, diving into a shallow ravine that curved down toward the river, Julius and Oleg firing nonstop as they retreated.

"Damn close," Feyodor announced. "Good move, dropping like that."

"Flyers!"

It was Oleg, his voice pitched high with excitement.

"Where?"

"South! Two of them!"

Jack looked to his left and up, and dropping out of the clouds he saw the two Bantag machines racing down.

"Hans, how the hell are we going to manage this?" Ketswana roared, trying to be heard above the terrified shouting of the Chin and the shriek of shells raining into the mob from the other side of the river.

The Chin surged back and forth in an agony of terror and frustration. With the appearance of the Bantag on the far side, the movement over the bridge had stopped, and all was confusion. On the other side of the river, Timokin had his six remaining ironclads deployed on a low hill, firing on a long dark wall of dismounted Bantag swarming out across the open fields beyond. The Bantag ironclads were coming down the same road he had advanced up the day before, and already the lead unit had stopped, guns raised high to toss shells across the river into the swarm of refugees, while the rest of the ironclads came up and started to deploy.

"We need every machine over there," Hans shouted. "The guns in the supply wagons—pass them out to any

Chin who thinks he can use one. Have the mines been set on this bridge by Timokin?"

"Two hundred pounds of powder under the center span."

"Fine. Once we get the rest of the ironclads across, open the bridge and push these people across, then get them down onto the slope by the river on the other shore. That should offer a little protection. If you can get everyone across, then blow it, but not before. Let's hope Jack can keep that rear column delayed a bit longer."

"Not with the fight he's got now."

Hans looked up and saw the two Bantag airships that had passed over the bridge only minutes before heading north, and then caught a glimpse of Jack's aerosteamer, low in the river valley, rising up to meet them.

"Ketswana, just get them across. But no one gets left behind, understand me."

"Great orders, Hans," but then he smiled, understanding.

"That's all I got left."

Ketswana snapped off a formal salute, called his comrades around him, and urged his mount through the mob of Chin, shouting for their attention.

Hans's driver, with long blasts on his steam whistle, edged his machine up to the approach to the bridge, the remaining five machines following. The mounted infantry, standing nervously with bayonets poised to keep the mob back from blocking the bridge while the ironclads crossed, parted at the last second to let them through.

Crossing the bridge, Hans directed his unit of five up the slope to fall in on Timokin's right to anchor the line down toward the river.

In the damp rain-soaked air the smoke from Timokin's gunfire wreathed the hill in a heavy yellow-gray fog. Cresting the hill and coming to a stop, Hans stood up in the turret, raising his field glasses.

The valley below was aswarm with Bantag, thousands of them dismounted, advancing in open formation, while units still mounted moved to the left, swinging out to envelop the other flank and the road down which salvation, if it was to come, would arrive. He could see knots of Bantag advancing, carrying heavy pipes, the damn rocket launchers, while up on the opposite slope wagons bearing mortars were being unloaded.

The opposing ironclads, deployed into a line thirty across, lurched forward and started down the slope, coming straight at them. Hans looked over at Timokin, who was up like him in the turret. Climbing out, in spite of the spatter of rifle fire, Timokin came up to the side of Hans's machine.

"Glad to see you here, sir," Timokin shouted, his voice all but drowned out as their gunners continued to fire shells at the advancing enemy line of dismounted infantry.

"We're getting pressed from behind. Two regiments or more of mounted."

"Kind of figured that."

"Don't look good here either."

"Saw that as well."

Hans looked back at the road leading up to the pass. He could still order Timokin to take all the ironclads and make a run for the pass. It would be sound doctrine. They could link up with the infantry, hold the high ground, and smash up any attack. If the Bantag ironclads beat them here and the infantry division was still out in the open, it would be a massacre when the Bantag turned on them.

He looked back at the thousands on the other side of the bridge who were now streaming across and moving down into the shelter of the riverbank.

A mortar round hissed overhead, plunging down into the field, halfway back to the riverbank. Damn, if they started shelling the Chin down there, he thought grimly, there'll be no way to protect them.

More rounds soared overhead, aiming high. One detonated on the ice in the river, a second bracketed the bridge on the other side. Panic broke on the bridge, the Chin swarming ahead, the press of the mob forcing some over the side railings.

"We've got to drive those damn mortars back," Timokin shouted. "Otherwise it'll be a slaughter."

"It'll be a slaughter if we move," Hans replied, pulling a plug out from his haversack and offering a bite. To his delight, Timokin nodded, bit a piece off the plug, and handed the plug back to Hans, who shoved the rest in his mouth. Timokin grimaced but gamely worked his jaw.

The Bantag dismounted infantry, still fanning out, began to press in, with the range down to less than six hundred yards, the ironclads behind them now a thousand yards out.

"Better button up," Hans announced. "You know this fighting better than me—you decide what to do, son."

Timokin grinned as Hans saluted, and with a groan he climbed back up onto his turret and slipped inside, slamming the lid shut. He swung his gatling forward and waited.

A rifle ball pinged against the turret, and then another. Hans waited, finger resting lightly on the trigger.

The Bantag seemed to be taking their time now, moving deliberately, infantry advancing cautiously, ironclads coming on at a slow walk while the bombardment of mortar shells streaked overhead and down along the riverbank and bridge. The infantry moved to within two hundred yards, spread out in long open order, standing up, dashing forward, going back down. Timokin held fire, and discipline in the other ironclads held as well. Ammunition was low; every shot would have to count. Finally there was a short burst aimed at a rocket unit, which was cut apart and went down. Bursts erupted along the line of ironclads, the gunners aiming for the rocket units. Knots of Bantag rushed forward at the double, one large group disappearing behind a stone wall a hundred yards ahead. Dark heads would bob up, aim a shot, there'd be another ping on the ironclad, and they'd disappear.

The enemy ironclads were now less than three hundred yards out and stopped. Fire erupted all along the line, shells and solid bolt screaming in. Hans was slammed forward as a shell detonated on the forward armor, sparks flying up past his view port. A blanket of smoke spread out, drifting across the field, and still the Bantag continued to fire, geysers of dirty snow and slush springing up, thunderclap bursts echoing outside.

Visibility dropped, disappeared. A shadowy figure moved up ahead, a Bantag emerging out of the gloom, rushing straight at him. He fired a burst, cutting him down.

Change of tactics, he realized. The weather played to it, kept the smoke low to the ground, making it impossible to see, and now they'd send the infantry up first.

Another burst of fire, a flash of light streaking past his view port, startling him. A damn rocket now.

He heard three long bursts of a stream whistle, followed by two more. Timokin signaling a retreat. Not what he'd do in the confusion, but the boy was in command.

"Driver full steam astern! Gunner load bolt!"

The ironclad lurched, wheels spinning on the slushy ground, then started backward. Dropping off the ridge, they retreated through clouds of smoke drifting down from the ridge, pulling back a hundred yards. There was a long single burst of a whistle, the signal to stop.

Coming over the crest of the hill they had just vacated came a long charging line of Bantag, phantomlike, standing out starkly between the slushy gray of the ridge and the dark skies above.

Hans held down the trigger, sweeping the crest, remembering to aim low, walk his shots up, and then sweep his fire across the crest of the hill. The charge broke, falling back.

The whistle sounded again, and Hans grinned. The boy was playing the game right.

"Driver, full steam ahead!"

"I wish he'd make up his damn mind."

The ironclad, wheels spinning, labored back up the slope, and Hans held his breath.

"Gunner, driver target right!" Hans roared.

A Bantag ironclad loomed out of the smoke on the

crest less than fifty yards away. The ironclad beneath him shifted, turning, his gunner shouting for his assistant to help traverse the piece.

The Bantag fired first. A rasping thunder lashed against the side of Hans's turret, a bolt head snapping off and tearing into his shoulder. The gunner below fired several seconds later. A snap of light erupted just above the enemy's gunport, followed an instant later by a burst of steam and fire.

"That's a kill!" Hans screamed. Another round cracked into their forward shield, nearly slamming the ironclad to a halt. He saw a Bantag ironclad to his left, barely visible in the gloom, and while shouting to the gunner and driver pivoted his turret, aimed for the gunport, and fired. Tracers pinged and flashed on the forward armor and then slashed straight into the open port. He held fire on it for a couple of seconds until the driver, pivoting their own ironclad, threw his aim off.

The gunner below fired again, at what Hans couldn't see.

A swarm of Bantag came racing past, one of them pausing to aim his rifle straight at Hans's view port. The Bantag fired, the bullet slipping inside the turret, banging into the hatch overhead, slamming a dent into Hans's helmet.

He dropped the Bantag infantry. The ironclad he had been shooting at was almost abreast of them, starting to turn for a broadside shot. Hans shouted a warning, and the two ironclads, chugging along not ten yards apart, slowly circled like two dinosaurs looking for an opening. Slush and mud spraying up behind them. Hans turned his own turret, firing long bursts, but there was no openings along the side armor for his rounds to pierce.

He lost focus on everything else for a moment, mesmerized by the battle which had narrowed to his view port until two Bantag raced straight through the middle of the circle. He fired, killing both. The faster speed of his own ironclad finally paid off as they cut in behind their opponent. The gun below recoiled, driving a bolt clean through the rear armor of the Bantag ironclad, bursting the boiler.

Disoriented, Hans wasn't even sure which direction they were facing. A rocket bolt skidded across their front armor, ricocheting off and streaking straight up past the turret.

The driver straightened the machine out and, apparently not sure where to go either, simply drove straight into the clouds of smoke.

"He's going down!" Julius shouted.

Grinning, Jack slapped Feyodor on the back as his copilot looked up from the narrow confines of the gatling position below Jack's feet.

Jack looked out at his portside wing. It seemed to be holding on, though the fabric just inside the number three engine and wire struts flapped in the wind from the hole the Bantag machine had punched. The second machine now turned directly ahead, lining up for a straight-in run.

There was no time to play around, and Jack aimed straight at it. The Bantag gunner fired. Jack held his breath . . . nothing. Feyodor opened up again, tracers pouring into the nose of the enemy airship. Flames erupted, the bag split open, wings collapsing in, and the machine spiraled down, trailing smoke and fire until it crashed into the frozen river.

"Two kills!" Feyodor shouted. "Damn good!"

Too damn good, Jack thought. Advantage of the moment, and the secret of our new machine is gone. Next time, if there is a next time, then what?

He circled around tightly, looking back south. The battle was chaos, smoke drifting in heavy clouds, ironclads exploding, burned-out hulks wrapped in flames. The only way he could tell the difference between the machines was that the Bantag coal boilers poured out thick black smoke while the Republic's kerosene burned cleaner. But when a Republic machine was hit it burned fiercely from the kerosene, a terrible trade-off for increased speed and power.

He tried to count what was left, and his heart sank. The Bantag still outnumbered the Republic, and the umen of warriors were now beginning to circle around the edge of the ironclad battle, moving down to the river.

He looked back to the east, and his stomach knotted. The diversion to fight the enemy aerosteamers had given the advancing column time to regroup and forge ahead at the gallop. They were less than a mile from the bridge, and thousands were still struggling to get across.

"We're going back in," Jack said.

"With what?" Feyodor cried. "I'm damn near out."

"Then fake it. We've got to slow them down."

Ketswana struggled to maintain control of his mounted infantry. He could not blame them for being on the edge of panic. The Chin, screaming to get across the bridge, were terrified, with the battle ahead clearly in view through occasional gaps in the smoke, the advancing enemy behind lining the slope less than a mile away and coming on fast.

He rode along the line of men ringing the back of the circle pressed around the bridge.

"We've got to hold!" he kept shouting. "We've got to hold!"

A forward line of Bantag skirmishers continued to press down the slope, closing to eight hundred yards, staying mounted.

A stone wall snaking off at a right angle was the only protection for his line, and he shouted for the men to advance to it and dismount. There was a moment of reluctance until he rode forward, followed by his Zulu warriors of the headquarters company. At the sight of their discipline the rest followed, dismounting in groups of five, one man holding the traces of the horses while the other four went up the wall, knelt down, and cocked their Sharps rifles, resting them on the ice-covered stones.

"Let 'em get close!" Ketswana shouted. "Make every shot count!"

He looked back at the mob, the circle receding to the bridge, dozens of bodies of those who had collapsed in the crush littering the compacted snow.

A rifle ball fluttered overhead. The mounted line was firing, plunging shot into the crowd, unable to miss. The shots redoubled the surge to get across.

Bastards! The range was still four hundred yards.

"All right, measured fire, make it count!"

Men took careful aim, squeezed off a round, reloaded, and aimed again. Shots began to tell, mounted warriors dropping. They hesitated, then dismounted, starting forward. The line gathered in strength as more and yet more mounted Bantag came down the slope, pressing forward. On the road a heavy column started forward at a canter, then broke into a gallop.

Good, let 'em come.

"Break that charge!" But he didn't need to give the order, as rifle barrels swung in a converging arc, aimed at the road. Rifle fire snapped, rippled, built in fury. Bantag dropped from the saddle, those coming up from behind jerking their mounts off the road, dodging around and through the trees, crashing down into the slush. The charge broke down at a hundred yards, the column of warriors reining in behind the confusion, dismounting, racing through the trees, stopping to fire, advancing.

Rocky splinters kicked up near Ketswana made him duck down. Crouching, he looked back over the wall. The charge had diverted their attention long enough to enable the Bantag farther out in the field to race forward, a line of them stopping behind a stone wall less than two hundred yards out, where they opened fire. Off to his right he could see mounted warriors coming around, preparing to flank.

It was getting hot. Men were starting to go down, and shots were hitting the line of horses, the animals plunging screaming in pain, the troopers holding the traces, struggling to hang on.

He looked back at the bridge. The swarm was thinning. Maybe another two minutes, he thought, but if he was going to get out, it had to be now. The ring was closing in too tight.

Out on the road some of the Bantag were less than fifty yards away, creeping through the trees. A knot of them suddenly stood up and with wild cries charged. The Chin at the back of the mob who were armed with Bantag rifles raised their cumbersome weapons, firing wildly. His own troops poured a volley in, dropping half the charge down, and then the Bantag were into the Chin, slashing and hacking.

A few of the Chin, using the bayonets on their rifles, fought back, killing some of their tormentors. Ketswana looked back to his line, sensing the rising panic as the enemy closed in on the right flank and to the front.

Ketswana detailed off a dozen troopers to go back, then focused his attention forward as yet another column of the enemy came up the road, riding hard, then dismounted just short of where the last charge had been broken and started forward in a heavy column. This one was going to break him.

"Bugler, sound retreat!"

Ketswana raced to his own mount and swung up into the saddle, his company forming around him.

At the sound of the bugle, men raced from the wall, discipline still holding enough so that they stopped to push wounded comrades up to their saddles. NCOs and officers waited, firing as they withdrew to the line of horses. Ketswana swung his mount around, slapping his rifle back into its scabbard and drawing a revolver.

The last of the Chin were across the bridge, the few survivors of the men he had sent back on foot, weapons raised, firing straight down the road.

The first troop galloped past, racing for the bridge, thundering onto it, and the Bantag on the road came to their feet, standard raised, and started forward with a wild blood-curdling scream.

Ketswana reined around, roaring for his company to stand, to buy time, to die.

The Bantag came straight at them and then, miraculously, stopped, looking back over their shoulders, then scattering to either side of the road. A staccato roar erupted straight overhead.

Petracci, flying at treetop level, came straight down the road from behind the attacking line. Bullets stitched up the road, tearing the attack apart, while fire from the top of the aerosteamer laced across the field, plunging into the mounted column maneuvering to roll into Ketswana from his flank and rear.

"Move it! Move it!"

He reined his mount back around, edging toward the bridge, waiting as the last of his mounted infantry galloped across, praying that some Bantag did not drop a horse at mid-bridge and tangle up their retreat. The aerosteamer soared overhead, turning straight over the bridge, as if to draw fire, top gun still firing.

The last of the mounted infantry passed, and screaming for his men to move, he started onto the bridge, spurring his mount. Hooves struck sparks as they crossed the span.

Reaching the opposite shore, he reined in sharply. Two men stood with sputtering torches.

"All over now! Blow her to hell!"

A torch brushed against the quick fuse. Flame raced along the side of the bridge, and an instant later a flash ignited under the center stone arch. Fire gushed out from either side, the bridge bucking. For a heart-stopping instant he thought it was going to hold, and then the keystone gave way, the central arch collapsing down to the river fifty feet below.

The Bantag, recovering from the shock of Jack's attack, surged to the other side, screaming in rage. But less than a hundred yards separated the two sides, and leveling their rifles, they fired.

Ketswana's horse bucked and plunged, a ball slamming into its neck. Cursing, he reined it back under control and pushed down the road.

Directly ahead, Chin by the thousands huddled in the snow, gazing in awe at the battle raging along the crest. From out of the smoke, ragged bands of Bantag were emerging and now coming down the hill, heading straight toward them.

Ketswana looked back across the river. On the opposite shore Bantag were starting to spread out, running along the riverbank, preparing to pour a slaughtering fire into the thousands of refugees less than a hundred yards away.

They were caught.

"Now what the hell do we do?" one of his men cried.

"Nothing left to do except charge," Ketswana roared.

"With what?"

He raised his hand and pointed.

"With them. If they want freedom, they'd better learn to fight for it. Now get them up! We've stopped running."

Blinded, choking from the smoke, Hans lifted his goggles and wiped his tear-streaked eyes.

He saw an ironclad pass in front, one of theirs, and it was flying Timokin's shot-torn standard.

"Follow Timokin!" Hans shouted. "Maybe he knows what he's doing."

Swinging in to the flank of Timokin's machine, they plunged through the gloom. He could hear the gurgling groans of the driver, shot by a Bantag who had poked a rifle through the view port. Fortunately none of the bastards had grenades or we'd all be dead, Hans thought, cursing silently as the assistant gunner, now in the driver's seat, pushed his throttle forward again.

Suddenly they were in the clear, but where the hell were they?

He saw puffs of smoke up on the ridge ahead. The mortar teams, maybe four hundred yards away. Timokin ignored them, turning, and Hans's new driver followed. Back on the opposite ridge everything was blanketed in smoke. Dozens of fires were burning. A massive explosion erupted atop the ridge, the shells inside an ironclad cooking off.

He spotted five enemy ironclads moving in loose formation, emerging out of the cauldron. He could see other shadows, was not sure who they were.

Timokin started forward again, aiming straight at them. Hans saw a knot of Bantag infantry, squeezed. Half a dozen shots streamed out and then nothing. The ammunition was gone.

Slipping out of the turret, he dropped down into the body of the ironclad.

"Out of ammunition above," he shouted.

"Two bolts left here," the gunner replied. Hans looked over at the driver, lying in the narrow pathway back to the engineer's compartment. The man was dead.

Hans crouched down into the assistant gunner's position and waited.

The five enemy ironclads halted, gunports opened. Fire slashed out, Hans flinching as one of the bolts struck their forward shield, denting the metal overhead, the hammer blow ringing through the machine.

"Hundred and fifty yards!" the driver screamed as he pulled the throttle back, bringing them to a halt. The gunner, directly behind his piece, sighted, then scrambled to one side, lanyard pulled taut.

"Stand clear!"

A second later the gun recoiled. Not even bothering to see if the bolt had struck, Hans reached back and took off the rack the last shell with a red band painted around the casing, indicating it was an anti-ironclad bolt. He slammed it into the open breech, and the gunner closed the breech and turned the interruption screw tight. Together they worked the tackle, traversing the piece while the gunner shouted for the driver to edge the ironclad slightly to port.

"Halt. Sir, drop the line."

The gunner swung back behind his piece, sighted, touching the elevation screw.

"Stand clear!"

The gun recoiled again, followed in almost the same instant by another bolt hitting the turret above. Steam erupted overhead, the line hooked to the gatling gun severed, snaking back and forth, the breech of the gatling slamming down through the hatch to the turret, followed by a rain of shell casings.

The driver screamed for the engineer to shut the line down, and Hans looked up through the mist, thanking God he had run out of ammunition.

"Still two left," the gunner groaned.

Hans leaned over the hot gun to look out the port. Three of the enemy machines were burning, but two were still coming on, followed by two more that were emerging out of the smoke farther up the hill.

He saw Bantag infantry moving back down the slope, running, and his heart sank.

Timokin fired again, and another ironclad exploded, but still they came on.

The Bantag infantry continued to advance, and then it started to be apparent that something was strange about their movements. They were running, but looking back over their shoulders. A darkness seemed to gather in the shadows, and then it resolved, a black wall of men, staggering, lurching forward, some running, others barely able to walk, thousands of them coming down the slope, mounted infantry mingled in among them.

The Chin were charging!

The ragged line of Bantag infantry turned at last to fight, and though each warrior might slay five, six, a dozen in his final moments, still they were swarmed under. Knots of Chin swirled around the ironclad farthest from Hans. What they could do was beyond his comprehension. They beat upon it with bare fists. Dozens climbed atop the machine, and finally several of them slid down the front armor, grabbing hold of the view port, blinding the driver. A body fell away, and another replaced it. Several mounted infantry came up, joining the mob, leaped up onto the front of the machine, poked pistols inside, and fired. One of the machines turned, skidded, and came to a stop. Seconds later a second machine was swarmed under, reminding Hans of ants dragging down an animal a thousand times their strength.

Mortar rounds detonated in the press, catching Bantag as well as men.

"Driver, we've still got canister. Get the mortars."

The ironclad beneath him turned. Clawing up the slope, he waited till they were less than two hundred yards away, the first burst tearing a wagon and the firing crew apart.

They pressed forward, and the mortar crews started to throw their weapons up into the limber wagons, racing to pull back. The few supporting infantry joined in the rout. Clearing the crest, they fired one more burst at a crew that had tried to hang on too long, wiping out the entire section.

Suddenly he felt very alone. It was impossible to see anything through the gunport other than the narrow view ahead.

Looking up at the turret, he grabbed the shattered breech of the gatling, again burning his hands as he tore it free, letting it drop down. Climbing up, he gratefully took a gulp of cool air pouring in through the shattered view port. The inside of the turret was a shambles of torn metal.

Reaching up, he popped the hatch. It barely gave; the plates were bent. Leaning his shoulder against it, he pushed harder until it popped back, and cautiously he stuck his head out.

On either side the ridge was all but empty. Down in the valley directly ahead, the Bantag mortar teams and their infantry were still pulling back.

He heard a rattle of musketry to his left, and fumbling for the field glasses still dangling from his neck, he lifted them up. Yellow-gray smoke rolled across the field, and there were flashes of fire beyond it. Bantag were coming back out of the smoke, moving quickly, one of them spinning around, dropping. A unit of mounted Bantag forming into line charged into the smoke. A thunder of rifle fire erupted, and less than a minute later the broken charge came back out, chased by a roaring staccato . . . the sound of a gatling. A lone ironclad emerged, gun still winking.

The relief force had arrived and was driving the Bantag back.

Hans sighed, leaning back against his machine, oblivious to the random shots still cutting the air around him. He suddenly realized he was cold, very cold, soaked in sweat, the cold air seeping in through his soaked wool uniform.

He started to shiver, and fumbling in his haversack, he pulled out a flask of vodka and took a long pull. A bugle sounded, the clarion call was picked up by others, and from out of the smoke a long line of infantry emerged, rifles at the ready, moving at the double time across the field, up over a stone wall, surging around a villa, driving the Bantag before them. Spaced along the line were three ironclads, gatlings sweeping the field ahead.

He heard shouting, crying, and looking back toward where the ironclad battle had been fought, he saw Chin by the thousands, up, waving their arms, staggering toward the line. Ketswana slowly came up the hill and dismounted by Hans's side.

"You should have seen that charge," Ketswana announced. "Madness. We must have lost a thousand, two thousand, but by God they saw a chance to fight, to get even, and by God they did charge. We've captured four ironclads."

Hans nodded, flinching as one of the machines exploded in a fireball, half lifting into the air and crashing down on its side.

"Any idea how many of ours are left?" he asked.

"I think four, counting you and Timokin."

"We started yesterday morning with twenty-two. Hell of a price. Let's hope it's worth it."

His attention was diverted as Petracci, who had been circling high above the fighting, swept down low over them, wagging his wings and dropping another streamer, which Ketswana retrieved. Hans opened the message.

"Suggest you get moving. More Bantag coming down from the railroad, at least half an umen. Should I go to Suzdal and report?"

Jack banked back around, and Hans fetched his guidon and waved it, then pointed it due west. Jack wagged his wings again, nosed up, and started to climb toward the clouds.

"Strange war, Ketswana. Never dreamed I'd live long enough to see anything like this."

"You're wounded, Hans."

He looked down dumbly at the blood soaking through his sleeve, and for the first time the pain registered. It was bad, but there had been worse.

"We'd better get them moving," Hans said. "Still a long day's march back to the pass. See if you can round up some survivors from the other ironclads, get them to take over the captured Bantag machines. We've got some mortars here as well we can take. Let's move quickly—they'll reorganize soon enough."

"Proud to have served with you today, Hans. This is what we are supposed to be fighting for," and he pointed back to the Chin. "It's not to defend what we've got, it's to free those who deserve to be free."

"Tell that to the Senate," Hans sighed. "Now get moving."

Just as he started to climb back up, he heard loud cursing from inside and a rush of steam poured up into the turret. His crew came bailing out the side hatch, coughing and gasping, the engineer and assistant driver arguing.

Both looked at Hans.

"I tell you he pushed it too hard," the engineer shouted. "I kept telling you people to slow down. Now the piston head's cracked wide open."

Hans sighed. Sadly he looked at the precious ironclad that had carried him over the mountain, into battle, and safely back out. The old warhorse was finished. Hardly a fleck of white paint was left. The flame-scorched sides were dented from hundreds of rifle balls, a dozen or more artillery shells and bolts, and the rain of debris from the exploding ammunition train.

"See if you can get in, crack a fuel line, and burn her," he said wearily.

The crew looked at the machine, stricken as if he had ordered the death of a beloved pet.

"Give me a couple of hours, I can pull the piston," the engineer said. "Replace it from one of the wrecks."

Hans pointed back to the northwest.

"They'll be back before then, son. Burn her."

Not bothering to wait for a reply, he slowly trudged through the slush and back down the valley to where Timokin's machine was at a stop, crew out, walking around their machine, inspecting the damage. Timokin looked up and smiled.

"So now you know what it's like, sir. Join us on our next outing?"

Hans shook his head. "Just give me a hand up inside, and wake me when we get back to our base."

Climbing through the side hatch, he curled up in a corner by the boiler. It was warm and comforting, and within seconds Hans Schuder was fast asleep.

Chapter Fourteen

He was at the lake again, early dawn, mists rising, the wonderful time of day when one awoke early to the smell of hot coffee, and eggs and bacon frying. Then slip the boat out, the water so still that the fading stars were mirrored, so that it looked as if one could dive down and by so doing soar into the heavens.

The only distortion to the water was the expanding ripples of trout surfacing, feeding on the morning hatches. One just had to cast a line, let the fly touch the surface, and silent, rising from the deep, they would come.

He stood looking out over the lake, knowing they were behind him, watching, waiting. He was afraid to turn, but something beyond his control compelled him to. It was them, dark, silent, all the memories, and all the dreams cut short and now frozen forever. Like phantom battalions they were arrayed. So simple now to drift into the past, to join Johnnie, all the others, and then to stay here forever.

"Johnnie?"

His brother smiled. He was a boy again, delighted that his big brother took notice, and he stepped forward, the shy grin.

"Andrew, why are you here?"

"I don't know, Johnnie."

"I think you do."

Andrew sat down on soft grass, cool dew chilling his hands, both hands. He looked down, noticing that. Curious to have it back again, as if it was never gone.

Johnnie sat beside him, plucking a stem of grass, chewing on it.

"You always liked it here, didn't you?"

Andrew nodded, gazing off across the lake. Boyhood memories, the summer cottage, the old man and the boys coming here to fish. And then the other memories, a lovely summer of studying for his exams here, alone, writing, studying. The last place of peace, the spring before volunteering, coming here to think, to be alone. Always dreamed of coming back here . . . but I am here.

"Is this where you came, Johnnie?"

His brother smiled.

"It's a long way away for you. Yes, I come here now, we can do that, visit where we loved."

He giggled, nodding toward the meadow behind the cabin.

"The only kiss I ever had was out there. It was so wonderful. The night before I left to join you in the army, I came here to say good-bye to her, and she promised to wait."

"Did she?"

He sighed and shook his head. "No, but then she is alive and I am not."

Andrew looked back again at his brother. He was dead, is dead.

"I'm sorry, John. I never should have let you join the regiment."

"I wanted to, Andrew. It was my duty."

"You were only seventeen."

"A lot of the boys back there were younger." As he spoke he nodded toward the woods, where wisps of smoke drifted in the shadows.

"Andrew, why are you here?"

"I don't know."

"Do you want to stay?"

Andrew looked back at the lake again. So peaceful. All of it so peaceful. And my children? They seemed to call from somewhere else, as if they were of the shadow world now and this was real.

"I'm dead, Andrew," Johnnie whispered, and his voice was distant, as if receding into the void.

"I'm sorry. Oh God, I'm sorry."

John smiled, hand slipping out, touching his left hand.

"Don't be. Not for me, for any of us. It is a thing of shadow and mystery, and our lives were written on burnished steel, our hearts touched with fire. And if it had to be that way, then I am glad I was part of it."

"But your life?"

"A flicker, a shadow of a moment. I would have wanted it to be different. To have a wife as you do, children. But it is not your fault, and Andrew, you have to decide."

"I know. But I'm afraid to."

"I don't think so."

Andrew smiled. Johnnie always believed in him, never knew about the fear, for Andrew was the older brother, always there to protect, to understand, to defend. Yet I let him die, let so many die, and now he wants me to go back to it.

He wanted to cry, but strangely he found he couldn't, not now.

"You already decided before you came here in your dream one last time. You wanted to see Maine one more time, to forget for a little while, to heal, to be whole within your soul again. But I think the dream has ended, Andrew. I think it's time to leave."

Andrew smiled.

"Now you sound like the older brother."

"I'm dead, Andrew. I'll forever be seventeen to you. But yes, I'm older now, older than you in so many ways."

"I'll always love you, Johnnie."

"Love the dead, Andrew, and love the living, but the living you can still serve."

"My children." He whispered the words softly.

A breeze stirred. He looked up. "Johnnie?"

He was gone, the mist, the souls of so many, drifting past, and he felt so many touch him, a parting, a reunion.

"Goodbye, Johnnie."

He looked back at the lake one last time. The breeze had stirred the water, all of it so soft, lovely, as if he had indeed crossed over the river and for a brief moment had rested under the shade of the trees. He felt the hand touch him, his left hand, and then slip away.

"Johnnie." Even as he awoke he whispered the name. His eyes were damp with tears.

He looked down at his left hand. No, of course not, that was gone forever, or at least for now. In his right hand was still clutched the daguerreotype of his children, and as he gazed at them, holding the image close so that he could see it clearly, he sighed.

He heard voices in the corridor, arguing. Slowly he sat up. There was a strange terrible aching, a desire, a craving. What was it? Yes, the morphine. Morphius, Goddess of Sleep, of Death. Was that the place I was? The mere thought of the bliss, the pain disappearing, the drifting.

The pain. God, yes, the pain was there. Terrible, twisting through him. His hand started to shake, and a thirst.

No, dammit, no, not anymore.

He put his feet on the icy cold flagstones, tentatively stood up. He was naked, and looking down at himself he was frightened. What have I become? Skeletal. Bandages around the ribs, yes, the wound, and the memory flashes, that final second, hearing the shell and knowing that this indeed was the one that would sear and cut and tear.

He closed his eyes at the flash of light, the falling away and the pain, never such pain, and the panic, drowning, unable to breathe.

He drew a breath in, tentatively, waiting for the agony. Pain, but bearable now.

The voices outside were louder. One of them was Emil, the other Kathleen. What was it?

And then there was some memory. Of her standing by the bed. Startled, he looked at the table. A gun, cocked, rested by the guttering candle.

God, she gave me that. There was a flash of anger,

and with it the realization. And as he looked at the door he felt a terrible fear, a desire to curl up, to hide forever.

And the anger came again, but now it was directed to something else . . . himself. He reached over to a robe draped over the end of the bed and struggled to slip his right arm in, then the stump, and drew the robe about his emaciated body. Going to the door, he reached down and touched the handle.

If I open it, all will come rushing back in. And then he looked back at the night table . . . the daguerreotype catching the light of the candle. He opened the latch.

Startled, they both looked up.

"What the hell is going on?" he asked, his voice barely a whisper.

Kathleen gazed at him. There was a look in her eyes, almost of fear. She stared at him, unable to move.

"Andrew?"

And though it was a struggle, such a long infinite step, he smiled.

As her arms slipped around him, he felt as if he would dissolve again, that the tears would flow, but he fought against it. Looking over her shoulder, he saw Emil gazing at him, eyes bright, and then the smile came again, this time for real.

"I asked what was going on," he said.

"There's a problem, Andrew," Emil said.

"Emil, not now, for God's sake," and she started to guide him back into the room.

"No. I need to hear it."

She looked up at him, and he could sense the fear in her. Fear of what she had done, what he might say.

"You were right, Kathleen."

She lowered her head. "I know." But even as she spoke he could feel her starting to shake in his arms.

The memory of it all was forming, and he was ashamed. Ashamed of what he had forced her to do, of the terrible struggle that still boiled inside him. He wanted to scream at Emil to leave, to not drag him back so quickly. But the doctor was already in the room, waiting.

"Go ahead, Emil."

"Marcus has informed Pat that he will surrender the city."

"Why? My God, Emil, they haven't even breached the outer wall."

Emil sighed, looking now at Kathleen, and she finally nodded her head.

"Go on, Emil. You'd better tell him."

Pat sat disbelieving, unable to continue the argument any longer. Though he was tempted to arrest Marcus, or better yet shoot him, he knew he could never do that. To do so would trigger not just a surrender but a civil war in the ranks of the army. They were played out to the end, and he saw nothing left to do.

It was obvious, though, that something was wrong with the Bantag army. Their rate of fire had dropped significantly since dawn and was falling off even more in the early afternoon. They were nevertheless pushing in on the inner wall and at one point had even gained a temporary foothold before being driven off.

And he could not blame the Roum soldiers for melting away from their units. In the panic consuming the city they now believed the battle lost and sought their families if for no other reason than to die with them.

Pat looked back up at Marcus.

"I never thought I'd say something like this," Pat sighed. "I'm begging you, Marcus. I know the battle's turning. I've been a soldier far too long not to know it. Hans broke their line, they're out of supplies. We hold on till sunset, we have them."

"We fight till sunset and they'll be into the inner city. And once they're in, there'll be no acceptance of terms. They will murder everyone. I must think of my people now, Pat. You fought a good fight, but it's over. I have to save what is left."

"I can't accept this. Andrew would never accept this."

Marcus shook his head. "But Andrew is no longer in command."

"I might disagree with that, Marcus." The voice came from the far side of the room.

Pat stood up, mouth open as if he were seeing a ghost. And for a moment he thought Andrew had indeed passed over and his shade had come to him to bid a final farewell. His uniform hung limply from his shoulders. His features were pale, white, like the face of a consumptive. The only thing that was still recognizable was the eyes, the pale blue eyes that at times could look so absent, distant, but in an instant could flash with the fire of battle, and the fire was there.

All in the room fell silent, everyone freezing in place. Weary, dejected staff officers gazed upon him, then came to their feet. No one spoke, no one moved, as he slowly, painfully walked into the room. His gaze fell upon the map table, studying the lines tracing the Bantag advance, the wooden blocks marking where units were positioned, all the blocks now crowded into the inner city or cut off, surrounded, out in the suburbs.

He studied the map for several minutes, everyone silent, and then finally looked back up at Pat.

Pat could see the strain, the struggle, his one hand resting on the table in order to brace himself, to keep standing.

"What is the report on their ammunition?"

"We're finding bodies without a single round on them now, no more than six to eight rounds usually. Artillery fire has almost stopped as well."

Andrew nodded and then looked back at Marcus.

"What is this about surrender?"

"Andrew, a lot has happened since you were wounded."

"I know. We've fought a campaign. We retreated five hundred miles, we stretched him out to the breaking point. Fabian tactics, we call it, named after a Roman general of our ancient world."

He paused for a moment, as if each word was paid for with pain.

"We stretched him out, and now the line's broken as I knew it would be. We've won."

"You call what is going on out there a victory?" Marcus asked, struggling to control his frustration.

"I've fought enough wars to know a victory, Marcus. He's exhausted. We hold the rest of the day, we counterattack at sunset, and they'll run."

"If they don't, we all die."

"Then we die," Andrew snapped, and now there was a whisper of strength in his voice. "Because, Marcus, if you surrender we will all die anyway."

Marcus was silent. Andrew looked around the dimly lit room. Too many people here for what needed to be said.

"I want to see the fighting," Andrew said. "Marcus, Pat, follow me."

He walked slowly, deliberately. His hand shot out to the narrow wall of the staircase as if to brace himself as he cautiously took the steps one at a time.

When they reached the observation platform, Pat moved around Andrew, guiding him over to a sandbagged niche. The startled observers gaped at Andrew, then came to attention, grins lighting their features as they saluted.

Andrew smiled, half raising his hand, then Pat shooed them away.

Andrew stood silent for a moment, breathing deeply. In spite of the drifting smoke, the wet damp smell of battle, the air smelled good to him, the scent restoring something, reminding him of what he was. A bullet smacked into the pockmarked dome behind them, and he flinched at the sound of it.

"It'll take some getting used to again," he said self-consciously.

Pat gazed at him, still not quite believing.

"Jack Petracci flew over an hour ago and dropped a message that they had cut the line for nearly fifteen miles. Blew some trains and rescued at least seven thousand Chin slaves. Andrew, it'll be days, maybe a week or more, before they can bring up more supplies. And listen to the battle, Andrew—the rate of fire is dropping. They're running out of ammunition even now!"

Andrew turned his head. It was hard to tell, for the roar of battle was all-encompassing. There was nothing to compare it to in terms of what it must have been like a week, two weeks ago. But whether their rate of fire was dropping or not, he knew that Pat had to be right, and if their supplies were cut it was over.

He looked back at Marcus.

"We fight."

"And if I refuse?"

Andrew stared at him.

"Refuse as what?"

"Vice president, leader of the people of Roum."

"You mean vice president of the Republic of which Roum is but one state."

Marcus said nothing, staring at him.

"Marcus. Between you and me. If you give the order to surrender, I'll have you arrested."

"I doubt that."

Andrew smiled. "What is said between us, Marcus, I pray is never repeated. I have admired you since I first laid eyes upon you. I believed you to be the embodiment of all that was good of the ancient Roman Republic. I still believe that. But, my friend, we are winning this fight, and if you try to surrender I will overthrow the government if need be in order to save it."

"You who designed it? Then what will you be, Andrew?"

"A traitor, Marcus, plain and simple. But I can see the ghosts of a hundred thousand boys, Marcus. Boys who died to create this Republic and save it. I must answer to them too, and they will want us to fight. So I will overthrow the government in order to save it, to save every person on this world, for that is what this fight is for. The Republic is everyone, not just us, but all those still waiting to be free.

"And as for me? Well, I'll take the responsibility for it. And once we've won, I'll resign my commission, reinstate you and Kal, and then, if you feel like it, you can shoot me for treason."

"You're joking."

"I've never been more serious in my life, Marcus."

Marcus looked back out over the city in flames, the thunder of battle, the screams of terror, the braying of the Bantag nargas, all of it washing over him. Finally he lowered his head.

"We fight till sundown."

"We fight to the death," Andrew replied sharply.

Marcus nodded, unable to speak.

"Marcus?"

"What is it?"

"Help me to make this victory. You sacrificed Roum. The Rus sacrificed Suzdal. I need you now. Will you take my hand?"

Marcus looked at Andrew as he extended a hand and came toward him.

The old Roum general hesitated, then finally smiled.

"You Yankees. You are madmen."

"And that is why we win."

Grinning, Pat burst away, racing down the stairs and back into the headquarters.

"We fight!" he roared. "By God, we fight. I want every one of you out of here, out to anyone you can find. Full loads of ammunition to be moved up. The reserve units on the eastern sector, make sure they get full cartridge boxes first. I want fire suppressed along the docks and ammunition on those monitors offloaded. Then I want everyone to open up and pour it on non-stop. Every rocket we have, to be fired simultaneously to signal the counterattack. And pass the word. Andrew Lawrence Keane is back in command!"

The rocket barrage, volley after volley, lifted up from the center of the old city, soaring up almost as high as the lowering clouds, then came streaking back down, detonating among the flaming ruins of the suburbs on the western side of the city.

The concussive roar of explosions washed over him, hundreds of explosions, flashes of light, smoke rising, boiling into the sky. Along the battlement walls, fieldpieces and heavy siege guns redoubled their fire, spraying canister, shell, and solid shot into the confusion.

Ha'ark stood silent, field glasses raised, trying to pierce the gloom, to see, to grasp what was happening. He could hear bugles, high clarion tones, chilling, the call echoing and reechoing above the roar of battle. It was their signal for the charge.

Smoke—there was too much smoke. All he could judge now was the sound, and the volume of it was increasing with every passing second. Volleys of rifle fire erupted now, sweeping the dim outline of the inner wall. They had to be firing blindly. But whether they hit anything or not wasn't the intent, it was a display of power, and he waited tensely.

The smoke parted for a brief instant, caught by a gust of wind coming up off the sea, and it was as if a curtain were pulling back. The gates of the inner wall were open, columns pouring out, blue-clad, moving fast, and they were cheering. No, it was a chant, a single word, over and over . . .

"Keane . . . Keane . . . Keane . . ."

On the battlement wall he saw a standard go up. A blue banner, the wind catching it, unfurling, and he looked to the standard behind him that was flapping in the breeze. The standard was the same.

Keane? Was he alive after all?

The cheer rose. Ha'ark looked at his staff. They were gazing at him in wonder. He had said Keane was dead.

"Ha'ark, there, by the standard," Jurak said, pointing.

Ha'ark raised his field glasses. Someone stood on the battlement, one arm raised, surrounded by others, all of them cheering, waving their hats, shouting their defiance. He studied him and then lowered his head. Yes, it was Keane.

The roar of rifle fire was spreading out, a distinctive higher pitch. They were charging, and there was no fire in return.

Ha'ark lowered his glasses, turning angrily to a battery commander who stood by his silent guns.

"I want fire on that bastion!" he shouted. "We can still turn this back!"

"With what, Ha'ark?" Jurak sneered. "All ammunition is expended."

Down in the streets below he could see shadows moving back, first just one or two, then dozens, then finally a river of black-clad forms. They were not pulling back in formation, they were running!

To add to the confusion, an airship came in low out of the smoke, aimed straight at him. Diving down against the battlement wall, he tensed. Rapid gunfire erupted, bullets streaking past, slamming into the battery, cutting down the battery commander, most of his staff. It roared overhead, turning up, then disappearing.

Ha'ark stood up, ignoring the screams of the wounded. He could sense the rising terror, the eyes upon him.

"Keane is . . . he must be a demon, an undead," Ha'ark announced. He knew his words were a guarantee of terror, but it was that or accept the blame for what was happening now.

Those who wished to believe him nodded. For after all, he was the Redeemer, and the Redeemer had to be right in all things.

Ha'ark sighed, lowering his head. But one more trainload of ammunition and we could have broken through, he thought. Surely they are expending their last gasp here. But one more day and we would have had them. Keane must know we are out, that our supplies are gone, otherwise he would not waste so much powder in a display of power. But one damn train and we could outlast them and tomorrow walk into a city unarmed and slaughter them all. Even two umens armed with bows and lances could do it, but they are all elsewhere. My own dependence on guns, on rails, powder, shot, and iron, which was to bring victory, now spells defeat.

"Against such power we cannot stand. Order the retreat."

"To where, my Qar Qarth?" Jurak replied coldly.

Ha'ark turned, staring at his lieutenant. The contempt

in Jurak's eyes was evident. Behind him others of the staff were staring as well.

"Out of here!" Ha'ark roared. "We must save this army while we still can."

"Yes, we must save this army," Jurak replied coldly. No one moved for a moment, until finally Jurak turned, nodding to the staff officers, who finally broke away and disappeared into the confusion.

"What is wrong with you?" Ha'ark asked.

"Do you actually expect this army to follow you after what happened here today?"

"What do you mean?" He felt a shiver of coldness, as if a light inside were blowing out, the last of his power waning away, when only hours before he had been so close to final victory.

"Exactly that, Ha'ark. We'll be lucky if we're both alive tonight. After this those barbarians we lead will tear us apart."

"I am the Redeemer," Ha'ark replied sharply. "They wouldn't dare."

He looked craftily at Jurak. If there was blame it was here. Jurak should have kept better control of the flow of supplies. Jurak would be the offering. He started to turn away, reaching into his belt to pull out a Yankee-made revolver. He heard a click and looked back over his shoulder. Jurak had a revolver out, cocked, and pointed straight at his head.

"I am the Redeemer!"

"You were the Redeemer." And Jurak squeezed the trigger.

Taking the captured standard of Keane, Jurak looked at it for a moment. Slamming the staff down, he planted the flag on the battlement by Ha'ark's body, then walked down from the battlement. To his surprise the staff were waiting, and he felt a moment of fear but hid it. Show fear and it's over.

"Ha'ark?" one of them asked.

"He's staying here."

Grins slowly broke out. For a long moment Jurak

stared at them, and then one finally went down on his knees, followed by the others.

"I am not a Redeemer," Jurak announced, "but I can still lead you to victory. Now let us leave this accursed place."

Lowering his head, Andrew stepped down from the battlement, struggling for control, control over a body racked with pain, over his fear, which threatened to take hold again with the whisper of every bullet streaking overhead, the detonation of each shell.

Pat looked at him, wide-eyed, like a child on Christmas morning. In the street below, the column of troops heading for the gate and to the fight beyond looked up at him. They were the veterans, the hard-fighting survivors of the old 1st Corps, their ranks pitifully thin, uniforms torn, ragged, mud-streaked ponchos rain-soaked, reflecting the light of the fires.

The men looked up at him, hats off, raised in salute. He stood silent, unable to speak, the men cheering, chanting his name.

They looked ghostlike in the gloom. Faceless battalions of the living, so many of them soon to be dead, yet they cheered him. For a moment they all looked the same, all were Johnnie, all of them the shadows lurking in the woods. And then the vision passed. No, they were the living, fighting for the living now. The citizens of Roum, clogging the sides of the street, watched the procession pass, and a cheer rippled through the crowd, rising, sweeping up the streets, into the packed alleyways, houses, across the city. It was a cry of the living . . . of the delivered.

Andrew looked over at Pat and smiled.

"Your victory, Andrew. You did it."

Andrew shook his head.

"Our victory, Pat. A victory for all of us."

Chapter Fifteen

Stepping off the gangplank, Sergeant Major Hans Schuder came to attention and saluted the commander of the Armies of the Republic. He could barely contain himself as he looked appraisingly at Andrew, who came forward, hand extended.

The two stopped shyly, only inches from each other, aware that their staffs were watching. Hans broke the tension, putting his arms around Andrew, hugging him. Andrew winced, and Hans let go.

"Sorry."

"Still a bit sore, Hans."

Hans stepped back a foot, gazing into Andrew's eyes.

"Still not over it, are you, son?"

"Don't know if I'll ever be."

Hans looked at his staff, waving them off. Ketswana, grinning, shoved the eager boys along. They fell in with Andrew's staff and wandered off along the dockside, looking about gape-mouthed at the destruction from the battle.

Hans motioned Andrew over to a sandbagged barricade, and the two sat down. The day was warm, the first hint of spring. Looking about, he was amazed at the devastation. The entire east bank of the river was a shambles of broken buildings, flame-scorched walls, windows looking like empty eye sockets of a blackened skeleton. There was the cloying smell of wet burned wood, rubble, filth, and bodies yet to be discovered.

Work crews were all about them, clearing rubble, pushing mounds of ice off the street and into the river, which was flowing again but choked with litter. Bobbing in the filthy dark water he saw the swollen bodies of Bantag drifting down to the sea.

A steamer just arrived from Suzdal was tied off below the monitor that had brought Hans in, and a gang of soldiers were off-loading barrels of salt pork, dried fruit, and vegetables, crates of canned milk for the hospitals and the children. The next ship down was laden with coal, and beyond that was another ship carrying ammunition and a dozen land ironclads.

Banners atop each of the ships flapped in the warm breeze. Written on the flags in Cyrillic and Latin: "From the grateful people of Rus to the gallant city of Roum." Hans smiled. The banners had been Gate's idea, enthusiastically endorsed by Vincent. Lying on the battlement was a copy of *Gates's Illustrated,* the headline proclaiming, ROUM STANDS. Beneath it a woodcut of a heroic Andrew, sword in hand, standing on the battlement, Marcus and Pat behind him.

Andrew saw Hans gazing at the paper and shook his head. "It wasn't quite like that."

"I know. Still scared, aren't you?"

Andrew looked off, his gaze distant. "Terrified."

"And ashamed?"

Andrew nodded.

"I know. At night. When I'm alone. I'm back there. Back in the prison. And they're waiting for me. The Bantag, knives drawn, leering, waiting. And all those poor damned souls who look to me for strength. Even my wife, the child. I want them to just go away, to let me hide."

Andrew said nothing.

"When you go through what we've been forced to do, Andrew, it will always be like that. The price is too high. We wonder, why us? There is no answer other than the fact that we are here and someone must do it."

"I wonder, why me? You know I wanted to die, to escape."

"I know. But what stopped you? I heard a bit about what happened."

Embarrassed, Andrew lowered his head, remembering

Kathleen as she put the gun by the side of the bed, then walked out.

"I could say all this," Andrew replied, nodding to the city, to the men going past, to the knot of children who stood shyly by the side of an upended wagon half buried in rubble. A sergeant came up to them, gently shooing them away, but stopping first to fish into his haversack and pull out a handful of hardtack and a piece of salt pork.

"His day's rations," Hans said admiringly as the soldier realized they were watching him. The sergeant shrugged, embarrassed that his gesture had been observed. He saluted, Hans and Andrew returning the salute, then quickly returned to his men, yelling at them to get back to work.

"It all became personal in the end. It wasn't the abstraction of the Republic, this city, even my men. It was my children that pushed me back. The thought that I could not betray them, that for their sake I had to live, to keep on fighting."

"I heard someone say that when you have children, suddenly all children become your own. I learned that with Tamira and our baby. Haven't seen them now for five months."

Andrew clumsily reached into his pocket and pulled out a bound packet of letters, a tintype wrapped in them.

"From your wife," Andrew said. "They came here yesterday."

"I didn't know she could write."

"Vincent's wife took them down."

Hans opened the packet, gazing at the notes, then the tintype. He smiled proudly. The two sat together in comfortable silence while Hans read the notes. Finally, pulling out a handkerchief, he blew his nose noisily and sighed.

"Is it true about Ha'ark?" Hans asked, obviously wishing to change the subject for a moment while he regained his composure.

"Not sure. We just have some rumors from a few Chin slaves who've escaped into our lines."

Hans nodded. "Funny, I had this sense he was gone. If so, that might mean one of his companions is in charge now, and the way this war is being fought will change once again."

The blast of a steam whistle echoed on the river. Yet another boat was slowly coming up against the flood of the river, this one maneuvering to tie off on the other side of the river, Gates's banner fluttering brightly. Piled on the decks were crates of ammunition and two more ironclads.

A thumping whine rolled over them, and looking up, Hans saw an aerosteamer coming in low over the river. It was Petracci's airship. One of the wings was frayed, an engine out. It was obvious he had seen action this morning.

"That boy, Andrew. Wish you could have seen him fight. The way of war is changing beyond anything we imagined. Without those new machines they would have crushed us on both sides of the Ebro. Petracci stopped an entire column cold for a half hour or more, gave us enough time to get out."

"What's this about you leading an ironclad charge?"

Hans smiled. "Rather like the machines. Never did care much for horses the way you do."

"Still, you shouldn't been up there like that."

"But that's where we have to be, Andrew. This new war, we could get trapped by it. Sit in our bunker, listen to the telegraph, lose sight of how we fight, what it is we fight for. I would not have missed the moment when I saw those Chin attack for anything. And Andrew, they are who we must fight for now. There are millions of them still enslaved. We owe them that. This Republic is nothing but a fraud if it's not willing to lay itself on the line for them."

"The price of this one was terrible, Hans. 1st Corps is a ghost, 9th Corps all but annihilated. We lost more than we did at Hispania. And Ha'ark's army is holding at Capua."

"I heard we got at least an umen trapped, though, between Hispania and Kev."

Andrew nodded. "We took the other end of the rail line this morning at Hispania. Telegraph is still down, but Vincent's pushing an armored train up the line, work crews following behind it, along with mounted infantry deploying out from here. They'll most likely slip around us, but if the damage isn't too bad the rail between here and Roum will be up by spring."

"And then we start again. Too bad we couldn't have pushed the bastard harder. I think we'd have driven him all the way back to Junction City, maybe even right off the Great Sea."

Andrew shook his head. "We're both exhausted. We're barely bringing in enough food to feed the city right now. The troops need to rest, refit, resupply. It'll be spring before we're ready to move again."

"And that gives him time as well."

"This new war you keep talking about. It's no longer one battle and someone wins and we go home. It's a war now of exhaustion. Who can make the most guns, the most shells, the newest weapons, and then bring them to where the fight must be fought. How much longer will this go on, Hans?"

"A year. Five years. Until we destroy their factories, push them completely off balance, then free the Chin and all those who labor for them."

"It may be for years, and it may be forever," Andrew sighed, remembering the tragic refrain from an old song.

Hans nodded.

"There's still a bit of nip in the air, Andrew." The two looked up to see Kathleen approaching.

Hans was up on his feet and smiling as she came up and hugged him.

"Andrew showed me the tintype. The baby is thriving."

Hans grinned, nodding his head proudly.

Kathleen looked down at Andrew shyly, then extended her hand.

Andrew slowly stood up, and Hans watched the two closely. There was still something of a distance there. Andrew was not yet sure of himself. She came closer, leaning over slightly, resting her head lightly on his shoulder. For a moment Andrew did nothing, then his hand came up and drew her in.

It would take time, Hans thought, but all things can indeed heal, if only the Lord will give us the time.

"Come on, you two. Pat's howling that he wants a drink with you. Says he needs one, and Emil has given his official approval to the venture. Then our commander in chief here needs a little rest."

The three started off, Kathleen gently wrapping her arm around Andrew's waist.

"I'm proud of you, son," Hans Schuder whispered softly so that no one would hear, and he followed the couple up the hill to where their friends waited.

ABOUT THE AUTHOR

William R. Forstchen lives near Asheville, North Carolina, and teaches history at Montreat College. He completed his Ph.D. in American history at Purdue University, with specializations in military history, the history of technology, and the American Civil War. His interests, besides anything related to the Civil War, include scuba diving, metal detecting, and politics.

SHADOWRUN

Dragon Heart Saga

☐ **#1 STRANGER SOULS**

0-451-45610-6/$5.99

☐ **#2 CLOCKWORK ASYLUM**

0-451-45620-3/$5.99

☐ **#3 BEYOND THE PALE**

0-451-45674-2/$5.99

Prices slightly higher in Canada

Payable in U.S. funds only. No cash/COD accepted. Postage & handling: U.S./CAN. $2.75 for one book, $1.00 for each additional, not to exceed $6.75; Int'l $5.00 for one book, $1.00 each additional. We accept Visa, Amex, MC ($10.00 min.), checks ($15.00 fee for returned checks) and money orders. Call 800-788-6262 or 201-933-9292, fax 201-896-8569; refer to ad # SHDW1

Penguin Putnam Inc.	Bill my: ☐ Visa ☐ MasterCard ☐ Amex _____ (expires)
P.O. Box 12289, Dept. B	Card#_____
Newark, NJ 07101-5289	
Please allow 4-6 weeks for delivery.	Signature_____
Foreign and Canadian delivery 6-8 weeks.	

Bill to:

Name_____

Address_____City_____

State/ZIP_____

Daytime Phone #_____

Ship to:

Name_____	Book Total $_____
Address_____	Applicable Sales Tax $_____
City_____	Postage & Handling $_____
State/ZIP_____	Total Amount Due $_____

This offer subject to change without notice.